Praise for Barbara Dawson Smith and her novels

The Wedding Night

"A great story! Barbara Dawson Smith is a wonderful story-teller and shows her talent especially well in this tale . . . fast-paced . . . a great book."

—*Affaire de Coeur*

"The story is loaded with lots of good dialogue and sexual tension."

—*Rendezvous*

"This book had me staying up late to finish it. This touching story of love and betrayal will go on the shelf to be read again."

—*Old Book Barn Gazette*

"A continuation of the Kenyon family series, but make no mistake, it's quite good all by itself. *The Wedding Night* is a cute and sexy read . . . lots and lots of intrigue and surprises are involved."

—romancereaderatheart.com

More . . .

Tempt Me Twice

"A fabulous hero who has finally met his match—the tension sizzles."

—Christina Dodd

"Don't miss an extraordinary author, and one of the best romances of the year!"

—Doubleday Book Club on *Tempt Me Twice*

"A delectable, fast-paced tale with charming characters . . . great dialogue and heart-melting love scenes make this a book you don't want to miss."

—*The Oakland Press*

"Another keeper from Barbara Dawson Smith . . . a wonderful mix of mystery, humor, and romance."

—*Heartland Critiques*

"Capturing both the era and the essence of suspense, Ms. Smith draws readers into her web and spins a tale that holds their attention and wins their praise."

—*Romantic Times Magazine*

"With Barbara Dawson Smith's deserved reputation for strong novels, Regency romantic suspense fans will not need a second temptation to read her latest tale . . . the story line is exciting, loaded with intrigue, and never slows down for a breather as the plot spins to a fabulous climax. Smith goes to the bestseller lists as usual."

—*Reviewer's Bookwatch*

St. Martin's Paperbacks Titles
by Barbara Dawson Smith

The Wedding Night

One Wild Night

With All My Heart

Tempt Me Twice

Romancing the Rogue

Seduced by a Scoundrel

Too Wicked to Love

Once Upon a Scandal

Never a Lady

A Glimpse of Heaven

The
Duchess
Diaries

~

Barbara Dawson Smith

St. Martin's Paperbacks

THE DUCHESS DIARIES

Copyright © 2005 by Barbara Dawson Smith.

ISBN: 0-312-93238-3
EAN: 9780312-93238-1

Printed in the United States of America

St. Martin's Paperbacks edition / November 2005

St. Martin's Paperbacks are published by St. Martin's Press, 175 Fifth Avenue, New York, NY 10010.

10 9 8 7 6 5 4 3 2 1

The
Duchess
Diaries

Prologue

Running for his life was something he did well.

A swarm of guards at his heels, Grant Chandler sprinted through the twisting corridors of the sultan's palace. The shouts of his pursuers echoed off the pale stucco walls. Oil-burning braziers cast a flickering light over the carved archways and marble pillars. The shadows of midnight cloaked the cavernous rooms to either side.

By Grant's calculation, he was halfway to freedom. He had only to stay ahead of his sword-wielding entourage until he reached the rear of the palace. Despite this one complication, his mission had succeeded with military precision. He had no intention of being caught now.

He had spent nearly a year in Constantinople, studying the Turkish tongue until he could speak like a native. A fortnight ago, he had traveled here to Smyrna by caravan. His blousy trousers and embroidered vest had enabled him to blend in with the locals. His swarthy complexion was enhanced by a liberal application of walnut juice. Like his pursuers, he sported a thick black moustache and a flat turban. Unlike the men behind him, however, he had no scimitar to protect himself, and he'd already used the single shot in his pistol to incapacitate one of the guards.

The challenge exhilarated Grant. So did the weight of the pouch tucked inside his shirt.

He had it at last. He had stolen the Devil's Eye.

A ruby of rare depth and clarity, the Devil's Eye was the stuff of legends. Nearly two thousand years ago, Cleopatra had presented the gem to Marc Antony. After the fall of Rome, the ruby had vanished for a long stretch of time, turning up hundreds of years later in the possession of Sultan Hadji, a Turkish despot with money to burn.

Grant suffered no qualms over stealing the precious stone. The sultan had gained his immense wealth through the opium trade, and any man who profited from the ruination of others was fair game for theft.

A tall brass urn loomed against the shadowy wall. Seizing the vessel, Grant sent it rolling straight at his pursuers. Two men went down, screaming and cursing, white robes flying and swords clattering. The other three guards scattered as they dodged the missile.

Taking advantage of the confusion, Grant veered down yet another dim-lit corridor. He'd spent the past fortnight studying the plans of the palace, plans obtained by means of a hefty bribe. Greased palms had a remarkable way of opening locked doors.

A guttural shout announced that he'd been spotted again. He spared a glance over his shoulder into the gloom. Only two guards followed now. Quite likely, one of the others had gone for reinforcements.

Despite his predicament, Grant found himself grinning as he ducked into an enormous, deserted chamber. Moonlight glinted on the throne at the far end of the room. A thick Persian carpet muffled his swift footfalls. Heading toward a door in the opposite wall, he kept his eyes peeled for trouble.

Moments ago, he'd been caught in the sultan's chambers by the wheezing old bastard himself. Apparently the women in the harem hadn't held the tyrant's attention tonight. But Grant had known the risk of discovery. In truth, he relished danger as much as he needed air to breathe.

For as far back as he could remember, he'd been the one to take the chances, the one to race his horse at breakneck speed, the one to pit himself in a fight against a master pugilist, the one to leap off a cliff on a dare. His family had never understood his need to take risks.

Grant couldn't explain it, either. All he knew was that without excitement, life wasn't worth living.

Accordingly, he paused in the doorway of an antechamber and waited until the two remaining guards were almost upon him. Then he slammed the door shut and shoved a chair beneath the handle. The air resounded with their futile pounding and muffled cries.

Grant sped through a series of smaller rooms and corridors. He reached a lavishly carved door overlooking the gardens and ran out into the night. A fountain played musically, and a gentle breeze carried the sweet aroma of jasmine. The moon shed a silvery glow over the stone benches, the lush beds of exotic flowers. The innocuous setting could fool a man into thinking he was safe.

But Grant knew better.

His dagger held ready, he kept close to the gloom of the trees that lined the stone wall. The precaution paid off.

Several sentries ran out of the dark, sprawling palace. Their superior barked an order in Turkish, and the men fanned out on a systematic search of the gardens.

Grant studied the layout. His path to the gate was blocked. It would be prudent to hide in a murky corner, to wait for his pursuers to leave. Instead, he sprinted toward the back wall.

A shout sounded the alarm.

But he was already shinnying up the gnarled branches of an olive tree. As he vaulted over the high stone wall, the crack of a gunshot split the air.

A jolt to his upper arm threw him off balance. Grant managed to land on his feet in the graveled alley, though he staggered before righting himself.

He raced for the horse waiting in the shadows. A slash of his knife cut the tether. Leaping into the saddle, he kicked his booted heels, and the fiery Arab steed set off at a gallop.

Only then did he notice the pain. His shoulder burned as if branded by a hot poker. Warm blood trickled down his arm, wetting his sleeve.

He'd been shot.

Gritting his teeth, Grant guided his mount through the narrow, twisting streets that led to the harbor. There, a *buggalow* awaited him, a native boat that would transport him up the coast to Constantinople, where he'd catch a merchant ship to Italy. With the sale of the Devil's Eye, his fortune would be secured.

Anticipation spread a balm over his throbbing wound. It didn't matter anymore that his father had thrown him out of the house at age sixteen or that his brother, now the Earl of Litton, had disowned him as well. Grant had no desire to go slinking like a chastened child back into the family fold.

But he did want the freedom that only money could buy. He wanted to pay off his debts; he wanted to hold up his head among the privileged gentlemen he counted as his friends.

He wanted the lady of his choice.

His stomach twisted with cold resolve. He had fallen prey to a pretty face once. He wouldn't do so again.

No, he had another plan in mind. Once he collected his money, he knew exactly where he would go.

Back to London. Back to Sophie. This time, she wouldn't push him away after one night of passion. This time, he would enjoy his fill of her.

And when he was done, then he would prove her a murderess.

3 October 1701

My Life lies in utter Ruin. When Papa summoned me to his chambers this Morn, I hoped—I prayed!—'twas to give me the glad Tidings that he would bless the courtship of my dearest William. But Papa's announcement struck me near senseless. He proclaimed to have made a brilliant match for me. I am betrothed to the Duke of Mulford. Sold to the highest bidder!

Many a lady would rejoice at the notion of becoming a Duchess. But I was stricken with horror. How could I wed a stranger when I love another? Alas, neither tears nor beseeching softened Papa's stern countenance. The deed is done, the papers signed.

O, William! All our fondest dreams are lost. Lost!

—the diaries of Annabelle Chatham Ramsey, 3rd Duchess of Mulford

1

London, April 1816

As Sophie Huntington Ramsey, the eighth duchess of Mulford, stalked down the long, chilly corridor at Mulford House, a blaze of anger lent fire to her footsteps. Her heels rang on the floor of checkered marble. Her fingers clenched the edges of the black merino shawl that draped her shoulders. Seldom did she abandon the restraint that had guided her life for nearly ten years. But by heavens, she would allow no one to meddle with her son's future.

She had just come from the nursery, and her throat clenched at the memory of Lucien's fearful hazel eyes, the small hands gripping hers, the quaver in his voice as he'd asked when he would be sent away. Though his lower lip had trembled, he had put up a brave face, for he had tried to be the man of the house ever since Robert's death the previous summer. But no child of nine should be forced to leave home. Especially not a boy who still grieved for his father.

Blast Helena! She had gone too far this time. Much too far.

Reaching the end of the passageway, Sophie flung open a door half-hidden in the gilt and white paneling. She descended a narrow stone staircase that led to the basement. The distant clattering of breakfast dishes came from the scullery. The air held the mingled scents of starch from the laundry and baking bread from the kitchen.

On this lower level, out of sight of the sumptuous receiving rooms abovestairs, the servants toiled at the myriad tasks necessary to the smooth running of the ducal household. A duchess had no place down here, Robert had insisted. He had appointed his elder sister Helena to supervise the housekeeping, and Sophie had complied with his decree, partly because she had other interests to keep her busy and partly because she had owed so very much to Robert.

A dim corridor lit by oil lamps stretched out in both directions. At the far end, a pair of gossiping maids spied her and stared, then scuttled back into the steamy laundry room. At the same instant, Phelps stepped out of another doorway across the corridor.

As gaunt and tall as a lamppost, the butler paced toward her with measured steps. His white gloves and sober black frock coat appeared as meticulous as ever. Sophie had never seen him with so much as a single gray hair out of place. Phelps was a bachelor, in service to the dukes of Mulford for nearly half a century, and he bore the weight of his position with haughty dignity—a dignity in contrast to her own state of high turmoil.

Phelps bowed. His cold gray eyes seemed to pinpoint her agitation at once. "Your Grace. May I be of assistance?"

"I'm seeking Lady Helena. Have you seen her?"

"She is presently consulting with Mrs. Jenks on the weekly menus. Shall I ask her to join you in the library?"

"No, thank you. I'll fetch her myself."

"With all due respect," he went on, "you would be more comfortable upstairs—"

"And *I* said I would attend to the matter myself."

On that cold statement, Sophie proceeded past the steward's room and the pantry. Insolent man! She drew a deep, calming breath. She mustn't let trivialities distract her. Giving vent to passionate emotion only brought disaster, a lesson she had learned at the tender age of eighteen.

For Lucien's sake, she must keep an unruffled façade in dealing with her sister-in-law, too. Lucien needed her so much. Sophie had coached her son on his studies, taken him on long walks to the park, gently encouraged him to emerge from his cocoon of grief over Robert's death.

But if Helena had her way, all that would change.

Nothing would change, Sophie vowed. Because this time she intended to put a stop to Helena's maneuvering.

Stepping through an open doorway at the end of the corridor, she entered a small, cozy parlor with dark, striped wallpaper and embroidered pillows arranged on the chaise. An orange tabby cat slept near the hearth, where a coal fire burned on the grate. Across the room, her sister-in-law sat at a desk. She dipped her quill pen into the inkpot, then marked a change to the menu lying on the blotter.

The plump, middle-aged housekeeper stood at attention beside her. Mrs. Jenks spied Sophie and bobbed a swift curtsy. "Your Grace. This is a most unexpected honor!"

Lady Helena glanced over, then replaced the pen in the inkstand. A striking woman in her middle thirties, she looked slim and elegant in black crepe, with a dainty spinster's cap perched on her upswept blond curls. In profile, she appeared to be the epitome of perfection—until she turned her face toward Sophie.

A disfiguring birthmark the color of port wine covered her left cheek, disappearing into the fichu of black lace around her throat. Although Sophie scarcely noticed the blemish anymore, Helena seemed always conscious of it, wearing high necklines and a discreet application of concealing powder. Over the years, a number of gentlemen had been willing to accept the flaw for a chance to wed the sister of a duke. But Helena had summarily refused their courtship, preferring spinsterhood to an arranged marriage.

"Ah, Sophie," she said without rising from her chair. "Have you come to review the week's menus?"

"No. I should like a word with you, though."

"As you wish. I shall be finished here shortly."

Sophie clenched her teeth. Nearly ten years her senior, Helena had a habit of treating Sophie like a child. "I would speak with you *now*," she said pleasantly. "Mrs. Jenks, would you mind leaving us for a few moments?"

The housekeeper scurried out, closing the door.

Helena tilted her head inquiringly. Her blue eyes intent, she held the pen poised over the paper. "What is it? Have you found the missing journal?"

For the past year, Sophie had been engaged in compiling the family history. While poking through boxes of bric-a-brac in the attic, she had come across a diary written by the third duchess, Lady Annabelle, who had been a reluctant bride. But the pages had run out at a critical moment and Sophie had been searching for a second volume ever since.

"This is about Lucien. He told me what you said to him. That he is to go away to boarding school come autumn."

Helena calmly made a notation on the menu. "It's for his own good," she said. "The boy should be prepared for the inevitable."

Sophie stalked to the desk, itching to snatch the pen out of her sister-in-law's fingers. But she matched Helena's coolness. "It is *not* inevitable," she stated. "I forbid it. Lucien is far too young to be sent away from home."

"The dukes of Mulford have always attended a private boarding school at the age of nine. It will prepare him for the rigors of Eton. You wouldn't break a family tradition, would you?"

"It can be postponed until a time that *I* deem appropriate."

Helena placed the pen on the blotter and cast her an unexpectedly sympathetic look. "My dear, please understand that I have his best interests at heart. Lucien has been distraught over Robert's death—as we all have been. It would do him well to escape this house and the constant reminder of his loss."

"It will do him ill to be separated from those he loves."

Rising to her feet, Helena took Sophie's hand in a gentle grip. "Pray, hear me out. Lucien has been overly attached to you of late. It cannot be wise to encourage such dependence in a boy, especially one who must someday wield the power of his elevated position. Without a father's guidance, his maturation must be fostered by other means."

Nothing could have been more calculated to strike at Sophie's heart. *Was* she overprotective? But she couldn't shrug off the sight of Lucien's fearful face. Drawing back her hands, she said firmly, "Any decisions about Lucien's schooling will be made by me. He shall remain here at

Mulford House at least until the following school year. Is that clear?"

Helena thinned her lips. "I would not gainsay the word of his mother, of course. However, I feel it my duty to mention that Elliot is in agreement with me on the matter."

Sophie tensed from that blow. So, Helena had enlisted the support of Robert's cousin and Lucien's temporary guardian. "Elliot is too absorbed in his Roman ruins to care about Lucien's schooling. He would agree simply to keep you from bothering him about it."

"I prefer to think he's looking out for Lucien's future."

Clearly, there was no reasoning with Helena. "I shall speak to Elliot, then," Sophie said coldly. "If you'll excuse me."

Fuming, she took her leave and marched back upstairs. Elliot! The man blew in and out of Lucien's life like a fickle wind, showering him with expensive gifts one day and then vanishing for weeks on end. He spent the majority of his time excavating the ruins of an ancient villa in Surrey. She would have to postpone talking to him until the next time he came to town.

Unfortunately, patience had never been her best trait.

Sophie stalked through a gilt-framed doorway and into the library. The dim light of a gray afternoon drizzled through the tall windows and shone dully on the floor-to-ceiling shelves of books that had been collected for centuries by the dukes of Mulford. The musty aroma of leather bindings scented the air, along with the tang of smoke from the fire.

Despite the comfortable surroundings, Sophie could find no peace. She felt restive and angry and frustrated as she paced back and forth by a long oak table. Elliot favored shards of pottery over the company of a fatherless boy. A more indifferent guardian could not be found—except for Lucien's other guardian. His permanent guardian.

Grant Chandler.

Her heart lurched, and that involuntary reaction fed the furor of her emotions. The knave made Elliot look like an attentive saint. Oh, why had Robert not seen fit to warn her that he'd put Lucien's care in the hands of that disreputable rogue? The man who had once broken Sophie's heart.

She could remember vividly the sense of horror and betrayal she'd felt after Robert's will had been read. She had wasted no time in writing to Grant, absolving him of all duty toward her son. She had sent the letter in care of his favorite aunt, requesting that it be forwarded to him, wherever he might be. There had been no reply from Grant, nor had Sophie really expected one.

Men! A woman could seldom rely upon them, and yet they directed the workings of the world. Why should two ne'er-do-wells be appointed guardians of a boy instead of his own mother? *She* should be in charge of her son. She, and no other!

The dam around her emotions broke, releasing a flood of fury. She seized a crystal goblet from the sideboard and pitched it at the hearth.

The glass shattered against the marble with a satisfying crash. Shards rained over the gold and blue patterned carpet.

Sophie stood unmoving. Not since she'd been an unmarried girl had she lost her temper. She had believed the wild hellion in her long tamed. A shaky sigh eddied from her. If truth be told, she felt better for the impetuous release of emotion.

But only for a moment.

Someone rose from the overstuffed wing chair that faced the fireplace. A man who turned to regard her with amused brown eyes. A man whose tall physique and handsome features were a jolt from the past.

Now, his presence struck Sophie like a tidal wave. It was as if she had conjured him by the intensity of her thoughts.

She spoke his name through dry lips. *"Grant?"*

"Sophie," he said with a nod of ironic enjoyment. He glanced meaningfully at the broken glass. "It seems nothing has changed. You still have the very devil of a temper."

10 October 1701

> *I am done weeping. Tho' my heart breaks, I must be a dutiful daughter. Thusly, I met my future husband in the Grand Saloon this day. I shall hereby record a Truthful Accounting of my Betrothed:*
>
> *His name: Francis George Phineas Ramsey, third Duke of Mulford, Earl of Pickering, Viscount Whittington (I am to call him Mulford).*
>
> *His age: one-and-forty (nearly ancient).*
>
> *His visage: powdered periwig, hawk nose, cold brown eyes (he studied me in a most discomfiting manner).*
>
> *His character: proud (he is a Duke, after all), vain ('tis rumored he owns more than fifty pairs of buckled shoes), reserved (he spoke no more than a dozen words to me).*
>
> *O, I dare not recall the warm blue eyes of my Darling William . . .*
>
> —*the diaries of Annabelle Chatham Ramsey, 3rd Duchess of Mulford*

2

Sophie struggled to regain her equilibrium. Her heart thumping, she groped for the back of a chair. The wood bit into her palm, proof that she was awake, that Grant was no figment of her imagination. *Dear God.* The memory of their final quarrel came rushing back, bringing with it the sting of all the hurtful words they'd flung at each other.

Nonsense. Grant Chandler meant nothing to her. She had banished him from her heart when she'd banished him from her life. No longer was she the impetuous girl who had fallen head over heels in love with a rogue.

She regarded him now with studied dispassion. He was as handsome as ever, yet different somehow. A hard angularity defined his features, and the brownness of his skin bespoke exposure to the sun. He was no dandy despite the fine tailoring of his dark blue coat and fashionable buckskins. She knew him to be a man who would stop at nothing to get what he wanted, a man who scorned the rules of civilized behavior.

Where had he spent the last ten years? She didn't care and she wouldn't ask.

Grant watched her, too. His gaze swept her on a slow evaluation, starting at the top of her reddish-brown curls and proceeding downward over the modest black mourning gown, lingering on her bosom longer than was proper. The fluttering of her pulse disconcerted Sophie. But it could only be an echo of the past. Her desire for him had burned to cinders long ago.

Still, she felt mortified that he'd witnessed her lapse of temper. "It's you who haven't changed," she said with outward calm. "You still have the effrontery to walk into people's homes without an invitation."

"The footman let me in."

"Then you should be waiting in the Grand Saloon, rather than wandering through my house."

He flashed her that charming half-smile, the one she had worked so diligently to forget. "The man went off to find you and didn't return," he said. "I was looking for paper to leave you a note. That's when I found this."

For the first time, Sophie noticed the slim, leather-bound volume he clasped in his hand. "Annabelle's diary!"

"It was on the desk over there," he said, nodding at the dainty escritoire that Sophie had installed here after Robert's death.

"The diary was *in* the desk," she said, stepping forward to take it from him. Their fingers brushed, and the fleeting contact flashed like sparks over her skin. Fighting resentment, she clutched the book to her bosom. "You had no right to search through my things. Nor to read something so private. What if it had been *my* diary?"

"Your penmanship is different. Besides, I wouldn't have read much farther. The style is rather mawkish for my tastes."

"*Mawkish?* Annabelle was a real person with true and honest feelings. Like many young girls, she learned the folly of dallying with a scoundrel."

"Ah. A pity you didn't read it before you met me, then."

Sophie compressed her lips to hold back a retort. He was baiting her. But she mustn't be drawn into a quarrel about their long-buried past.

Why was she trying to explain, anyway? Annabelle's story was precious to her in a way that Grant could never fathom. "The diary is a valuable piece of the Mulford family history," Sophie said with forced calm. "The pages are quite fragile. They shouldn't be handled without necessity."

"Do pardon me, Your Grace. I truly meant no harm."

His voice was smooth, polite, revealing nothing of his thoughts. How unlike the carefree rake she had known. His intent stare made her uncomfortable, so she resorted to chilly hauteur. "Apology accepted."

Sophie walked to the desk and replaced the diary in the top drawer. She was irked at him for invading her private domain, and at herself for allowing him to perturb her. She needed a moment to collect herself.

When she turned around, she found Grant standing right in front of her. He had moved with the stealthy silence of a wolf. He stood so close she caught a whiff of his spicy scent, a scent that evoked an involuntary response deep within her.

"I'm curious," he said. "You didn't know I was here when you threw that glass. So what has your dander up today?"

"Your question is impertinent, sir. I shan't dignify it with an answer."

"How very proper you've become. We were friends once. We shared everything with each other."

His husky tone held a wealth of meaning. Long ago, in the heady whirl of her first season, she had watched Grant race his curricle against a host of young bucks and win. His wild recklessness had drawn her like a lodestone. He had dueled with as much gusto as he romanced the ladies.

The only child of indulgent parents, Sophie had grown up spoiled, yet sheltered in the country. She had loved the freedom and excitement that London offered. From the moment she'd seen Grant, she'd wanted him. He had taught her the thrill of breaking the rigid rules of society . . .

But all that had ended with marriage and the birth of her son. Nothing mattered more to Sophie than to be a good mother to Lucien. Grant could never understand that.

"Things change," she said. "I'm not the naïve girl I used to be."

"So I see." He glanced at her lips, further unnerving her. "You're a woman now. A very beautiful woman."

The air suddenly seemed charged with energy. It had been a long time since Sophie had been the focus of such concentrated interest. The heat of it scorched her . . . with anger. Had he no shame, to turn his sensual charm on a woman in mourning? The widow of an old friend?

Or was he simply treating her as he treated all women?

With jerky movements, she picked up a small bin and went to the hearth, where she knelt to collect the shards of glass. "I'm rather busy today," she said over her shoulder. "Perhaps you should tell me why you've come here."

It had to be that letter. The one in which she'd urged him to give up the guardianship. Would he too interfere with her raising of Lucien?

Surely not. Grant Chandler abhorred responsibility. He despised anything that interfered with his freewheeling ways. He was a wild stallion who would never be put to pasture.

He crouched down beside her, picked up a fragment of crystal, and tossed it into the bin, where it landed with a clatter. "I heard the news about Robert," he said, helping her clean up the shattered glass. "I wanted to offer you my condolences."

"Thank you. That's very kind." It was the same polite cliché she had spoken to every mourner at the funeral.

"I mean it, Sophie. I'm sorry for any pain you've suffered."

The sympathy in Grant's deep voice was too polished to be real. She had every reason to mistrust him, and yet a part of her wanted to burrow against him and seek comfort in his arms.

Foolish. Never again would she be as foolishly naïve as Annabelle.

"I appreciate your concern," she said stiffly.

Ignoring him, she hunted diligently for all the slivers that glinted in the hearth rug. Sometimes, Lucien played here with his tin soldiers. She would take no risk of him suffering an injury because of her carelessness.

"Tell me," Grant said. "How did Robert die? What happened?"

The still-raw wound throbbed to life inside her. She turned her gaze to Grant and saw him leaning on one knee, watching her. She wanted to snap out a refusal, but something in his grave expression hinted at his sincerity.

He and Robert had been friends, brought together by circumstance. The two had grown up on neighboring estates in Sussex and had played together as children. Otherwise, there would have been no reason for quiet, bookish Robert to have associated with a notorious womanizer like Grant.

Nevertheless, Sophie had always felt a certain guilt that she had come between the two men. She reluctantly acknowledged the fact that he deserved an explanation.

She sat back on her heels and fixed her attention on the fire, watching the dancing flames. "Robert fell ill last summer," she murmured. "The doctors diagnosed a digestive disorder from eating tainted food. They tried everything, tonics, purgatives, bleeding, but . . . he steadily worsened. Within a fortnight, he was dead." Her words trailed off as she relived the sleepless nights spent at his bedside, the helplessness of not knowing how to ease his pain, the panicked grief of watching him slip away . . .

"Tainted food?" Grant asked. "Was anyone else in the house ill?"

"No, Robert's illness was caused by a prune tart that only he ate. It was his favorite, you see."

"What did your chef have to say?"

"Monsieur Ferrand denied any wrongdoing, of course. But . . . he had to be let go. I couldn't bear to have him continue to cook for us."

The silence in the library weighed on her. This had been Robert's favorite room, and after his death, she had derived a certain comfort from spending time in his domain. But not today. Today, Sophie felt a disturbing awareness of Grant Chandler, as if his very presence had upset the balance of peace and tranquility.

She shifted her gaze to him, and for a moment, she had the impression that his eyes glittered with icy malevolence. But when she blinked, his chiseled face showed only a neutral expression.

His hand cupping her elbow, he helped Sophie to her feet. "You're distraught," he said, guiding her to a chaise and seating her beside him. "I'll ring for tea."

"No, I'm perfectly fine." Sophie had no wish to prolong his visit by providing refreshment. She sat rigidly upright, keeping a circumspect space between them. "I presume you've received my letter—about Lucien."

He nodded. "It took some time to catch up to me. I'd been traveling for a while, you see."

"Traveling where?" It was politeness, and certainly not curiosity, that prompted her question.

"Turkey. Constantinople, to be precise."

"Good heavens. What were you doing there?"

"Sightseeing. Studying the language. Mingling with the natives."

His bland gaze hid all manner of secrets. He'd likely been drinking and gambling. Perhaps he'd kept a harem of adoring women, too.

Let him. She had no interest whatsoever in his peccadilloes.

"I'm sure you're a busy man," she said in a tone of frosty politeness. "We should settle the matter of my son so that you can be on your way."

He shifted into a more comfortable position, draping his arm across the back of the chaise. "Indeed, we should."

"I can only suppose you came here out of a sense of obligation," she said. "However, as my letter stated, you're absolved of any and all responsibility toward my son. Robert's cousin, Elliot, also has been appointed guardian, so there's no need for you to trouble yourself. I trust you brought the agreement I enclosed with the letter?"

"No, I did not."

Sophie couldn't rest until the issue was legal and binding. "If you've misplaced it, I'll contact my solicitor. It should be a simple matter to draw up another deed."

Grant shook his head. "I shan't sign it, Sophie."

An inkling of alarm gripped her. "You must, else you'll have to be involved in any decisions about Lucien's future. It's a tremendous obligation and hardly suited to a man of your . . . pursuits."

"I'll manage. Since Robert wanted me to act as guardian to his son, I intend to do just that. I've already leased a house in Berkeley Square."

Her heart gave an appalled thump. He would live three blocks from here? Did he intend to come here every *day*? "Don't be ridiculous. You're completely unsuitable."

"So is Elliot Ramsey. I imagine he's still digging up old ruins somewhere. He's completely unreliable as a guardian."

Sophie privately agreed, but Elliot was the lesser of two evils. "Elliot is Lucien's cousin," she said. "He's known my son since birth. *You've* never even met Lucien."

"Then send for him. We can rectify that at once."

Too distraught to sit still, Sophie shot to her feet and paced away from him. She felt as if she were sinking deeper and deeper into a bog of complications. Dear God, how had this situation become so tangled? She didn't want Grant anywhere near her son. Why was he being so obstinate?

Why, indeed?

She whirled to face him. "For shame! If this is some sort of revenge on me, then don't do so at the expense of an innocent child."

A subtle hardening of his features gave proof of his animosity toward her. "Is that your opinion of me, then?"

"Yes! You despise children. You've told me so yourself."

"Your memory serves better than mine, then."

"You *did* say it. During one of our quarrels." She stood near the hearth, but the heat of the fire failed to penetrate the chill inside her. At the time, his careless words had crushed her romantic dreams. That had been the moment when she'd realized the hopelessness of their affair. He loved his freedom more than he could ever love her. "I will not allow you near my son. You're a poor influence."

Grant rose from the chaise and sauntered toward her, taking up a stance at the opposite end of the mantelpiece, so that they faced each other across the hearth rug. Sophie desperately cast about for a way to convince him. She hated feeling helpless, but the law was on his side. Until he signed away his rights, he could override her orders. He could demand to see Lucien, and she would have no way to stop him . . .

Unexpectedly, he reached out and touched her cheek in a stirring caress. "Sophie, I mean you no harm. Please believe that. I wish only to—"

The patter of footsteps interrupted him. In confusion, Sophie looked to the door and caught a sharp breath.

Lucien trotted into the library, his small, usually serious face alight with rare excitement. A lock of reddish-brown hair had tumbled on his forehead, and he looked infinitely precious in his dark brown coat and breeches. He waved a tiny figurine in his hand.

"Mummy, look! Look what I found!"

Then he spied Grant. He stopped in his tracks and stared, goggle-eyed, clearly wary of this stranger.

Sophie rushed forward in an instinctive effort to shield him from Grant. Her fingers trembled as she reached down to smooth Lucien's rumpled hair. "I see you've recovered the general. Was he hiding in the cupboard, then?"

Lucien gave a slow nod, though he peeked around her at Grant. "B-behind the boxes, j-just as you said." In a whisper, he added, "W-who is *he*?"

Sophie's heart clutched. Lucien stuttered only when faced with an unfamiliar situation or person. It was one of the reasons she wanted to keep him home. Away at boarding school, he would be teased mercilessly about the speech impediment.

Her palms felt cold, damp. Although impulse urged her to hustle her son out of the library, she knew the futility of that. It was too late to hide. Grant had already walked up to them.

"My visitor is . . . an old friend," she said, her throat dry. "His name is Mr. Chandler. Grant, this is my son, Lucien, the Duke of Mulford."

Grant held out his hand. "It's a pleasure to meet you, Mr. Duke."

The boy hesitated, then solemnly shook Grant's hand. "I—I'm not a *mister*. You're supposed to s-say *your grace*."

"Lucien," Sophie chided, directing a little shake of her head at him. "You mustn't correct your elders."

"It's my mistake," Grant said with an easy grin. "Your Grace, I confess I'm interested in the general. May I see him?"

Lucien slowly uncurled his fingers and surrendered the tin soldier. He watched Grant closely as if expecting him to take off running with the booty at any moment.

Grant sat down on a chair. Propping his elbows on his knees, he turned the piece over in his hands, examining it in the gray light from a nearby window. "Ah, yes. I thought I recognized this. It comes from a set that belonged to your father."

"You—you knew Papa?" Lucien asked wonderingly.

"I did, indeed. We met when he was just your age. You see, I grew up in Sussex, too, not three miles from your father's house."

"T-truly?" Lucien stepped closer, his eyes brightening with interest. "But—but why did you never come to call on him, then?"

"Mr. Chandler has been out of England," Sophie cut

in. "He returned only recently. And I'm afraid he can't stay and chat." She aimed a fierce frown at Grant, but he paid her no heed.

"Actually, I'm not in any hurry." Grant handed the figurine back to Lucien. "Do you have the rest of the army? It was quite an enormous one, as I recall."

"Oh, yes. Papa kept them just for me. Mummy and I hold battles sometimes." He lowered his chin in dejection. "When she isn't giving me lessons, that is. And Miss Oliver is always too busy with duties."

Grant leaned closer to him in a confiding manner. "I'll tell you something. Ladies don't care much for warfare. Not the way we men do. Perhaps sometime you and I could have a battle. A good long one."

"I shall be the Duke of Wellington," Lucien said promptly. "I'll lead the English to victory."

Grant laughed. "I'll play Napoleon, then. But mind, you'll have to work hard to defeat me."

Gripped by a feverish tension, Sophie realized that Lucien had ceased stuttering. But she couldn't rejoice in the swift rapport between him and Grant. It only made her feel more trapped in a vise of dread. At any moment Grant would surely notice what she could see so clearly . . .

Dear God. The shock of seeing the two of them together pierced her heart like an arrow. They had the same high cheekbones and facial structure, though Lucien's was softened by youth. The resemblance ended there, she reassured herself. Lucien had hazel eyes and her reddish-brown hair. In character, he and Grant were as far apart as night and day.

Yet her throat felt choked with the fear of having her secret exposed. The secret that only she and Robert had known. The secret that she would guard fiercely to the grave. The secret that Grant must never guess.

He must never, ever know that Lucien was *his* son.

14 October 1701

Today I was fitted for my trousseau by the finest mantua-maker in London. Five assistants swarmed 'round me with bolts of satin, silk, damask, and brocade. Mama is determined that I be dressed in Grand Fashion as befitting the wife of a Duke. Accordingly, each gown must be adorned with lace and ribbons and frills. When I protested, Mama scolded me for scorning the Kind Generosity of my Father.

By Mulford's decree, the Wedding shall take place on the first day of January. There is much to do 'twixt now and then, yet I find myself gazing out the window and wishing I might flee to my dearest William.

—*the diaries of Annabelle Chatham Ramsey, 3rd Duchess of Mulford*

3

The first phase of his plan had gone well. Nevertheless, Grant felt tense and dissatisfied as he walked into the club on St. James's Street later that afternoon.

A balding majordomo in ivy-green livery with gold buttons stood guard inside the door. He afforded Grant a snooty perusal as if prepared to send an interloper packing. Then his stern expression eased into a broad smile. "Why, Mr. Chandler! How good it is to see you here again."

Grant briefly returned the smile. "Thank you, Pennington. Is there the usual gathering in the card chamber?"

"Yes, indeed."

Grant headed past the front parlor, a large, comfortable room where several gentlemen sat reading their newspapers and smoking their cheroots. But he had only a peripheral awareness of his rich surroundings. His mind dwelled on Sophie.

After leaving Mulford House, he'd been too restless to return home. He needed a diversion to temper the impact of seeing her again.

She was everything he remembered . . . and more. Even in drab black mourning, she radiated an earthy sensuality. Maturity had added lushness to her curves, enhancing the feminine allure of full breasts, slender waist, flaring hips. He had been sorely tempted to kiss her, especially when she had regarded him with cool disdain. He wanted those expressive green eyes to heat with desire for him. He wanted to strip away her pretenses, to make her abandon the haughty airs of a duchess. They would have an affair, and he would scourge himself of this obsession for Sophie once and for all.

But he must never forget his true purpose. To find proof that Robert had been murdered. And Sophie was his prime suspect . . .

Up ahead, a man entered the corridor from the dining chamber. He epitomized the distinguished aristocrat with his neatly combed brown hair winged with gray, a folded newspaper tucked beneath the arm of his sober blue coat, his carriage straight and proud. He turned his head to speak to someone inside the room, and the sight of that haughty profile with its Roman nose and high brow froze Grant in place.

For one powerful stroke of his heart, he thought he was gazing at his father, risen from the grave. But the old brute was long dead. It was only Randolph, Grant's elder brother, now the Earl of Litton.

Grant considered ducking into a nearby chamber. Bloody hell. Was he so craven?

He strode grimly forward. At the same moment, Randolph finished his conversation and came down the passageway. His steps faltered and his gaze met Grant's. The two men stood in the dim-lit corridor and stared at each other. Like the previous Earl of Litton, Randolph had steel-blue eyes sharp enough to cut a diamond.

Unlike the previous earl, however, Randolph at least knew how to be gracious. Smiling, he strode forward and extended his hand. "Well, this is a surprise, Grant! I was beginning to wonder if you'd ever return to England."

Grant shook his brother's hand, although he found Randolph's warm welcome highly suspect. The favored elder son, Randolph had always been full of self-importance, a fact that had caused many a childhood battle. Usually, Grant had been the one to throw the first punch, egged on by his brother's sneering taunts. "Litton. You're looking well."

"Marriage will do that to a man," Randolph said heartily. "I trust you received my letter? I wed Ingleham's daughter last year. Jane is expecting our first in a few months."

"Congratulations. A rich heiress, a duke's daughter, and a good breeder. With any luck, I won't be your heir much longer. What more could you want?"

A hint of annoyance banished his brother's smile. "Have a care how you speak of my countess. Jane will want to meet you. I'll have her send you an invitation for dinner later this week—"

"Don't bother. I'm occupied with other matters at the moment."

"Then visit us this summer at Kendall Park," Randolph persisted. "You can meet your new niece or nephew."

The last time Grant had been to Kendall Park had been for his father's funeral when he had been twenty years old. When he'd left his childhood home at sixteen, he'd vowed never to return. He had gone back that one time only because his aunt Phoebe had asked it of him. "Rural life has never suited me," he said. "I prefer the pleasures of the city."

"You'd do well to marry and settle down." A cold, disapproving look made Randolph look exactly like his sire. "But no doubt, you're too busy gambling."

"Speaking of which, I've a game to join. If you'll excuse me."

Grant brushed past his brother and strode down the corridor. A host of unwelcome emotions glutted his chest, the chief of which was anger. Damn! He didn't need a family. He needed a good stiff drink and a game of cards.

As he entered the rear chamber, he had the uncanny sensation of stepping straight into the past, a more familiar, comfortable past. The same crimson draperies hung from the tall windows, the same groups of gentlemen huddled at the tables, the same pall of smoke hung in the air. Yes, this was where he belonged. He wouldn't waste another thought on his brother.

"Chandler! I say, is it really you?"

One of the gamesters rose from his chair and hurried toward him. A portly man of middling height, he had an overfed belly that strained at the buttons of his sky-blue waistcoat. A vague familiarity about that jowly face struck a chord in Grant. Then he dredged up a name, coupled with the realization that his old crony had packed on a significant amount of weight.

Breaking into a grin, he pumped the man's hand. "Hockridge," he said.

"The one and only," Viscount Hockridge said, clapping Grant on the shoulder. "You're a sight for sore eyes. Where the devil have you been?"

"Italy," Grant said succinctly. It was a partial truth, for he had made Rome his base. In the shadow of the ancient temple of the Pantheon, he had planned his heists, selecting his targets carefully so that he never robbed an honest man. But the dishonest ones were fair game.

"Do join us," Hockridge invited, drawing Grant over to a table. "We could use a fourth in our game. You remember Kilminster and Updike, don't you?"

"The fellows who once set set fire to Sally Chasen's bawdy house so they could watch the whores run naked into the street? Certainly."

Guffaws of laughter erupted from the other two men. "That was us all right," Kilminster said. "Jolly good show, indeed."

"Although the gents were none too pleased to be caught with their breeches down," Updike added with a nasty chuckle.

The Earl of Kilminster had a rangy form and chalky features as rough as if they'd been hewn with an ax. By contrast, Jeremy Updike looked as if he'd been sculpted by a master. He had artfully curled black hair and the mien of a fallen angel, although the weathering of time had added lines of dissipation to the chiseled marble of his face.

"Tell us about those Italian wenches," Kilminster said, lechery shining in his pale blue eyes. "I hear they'll spread their legs at the crook of a man's finger."

"*I* hear they like orgies," Updike added. "What a feast it would be to initiate all those vestal virgins." He and Kilminster and Hockridge leaned forward, as avid as three boys peeping into a lady's window.

"You'd have to regress to ancient Rome, then," Grant said, chuckling more at them than with them. "I'm afraid the old temples hold only tourists now."

As Hockridge dealt the cards for a game of vingt-et-un, Grant satisfied their curiosity with a tale about a lusty Italian countess and her succession of lovers. He had no wish to speak of his own exploits; in truth, there had been little time to spare for women. But the other men freely boasted of their conquests over the past decade.

It was just like old times.

Or was it?

Grant concentrated to keep his mind from wandering back to the encounter with his brother. The cards weren't favoring him, and he found himself reluctant to place reckless wagers as he had in the past. Back then, in the space of a few years, he'd frittered away a generous legacy from his maternal grandmother. The experience had soured him on gambling.

The sale of the Devil's Eye to an agent of the Russian tsar had provided Grant with a tidy nest egg. He had invested the proceeds from that and other heists. With his holdings in shipping and other enterprises, he was a wealthy man now. He could afford to squander a portion of his gold.

Yet somehow, he couldn't shake his distaste. He'd worked too damned hard to go floundering in River Tick again.

After a time, he took his leave amid a chorus of protests. "There's a carriage race on Friday," Hockridge said. "Surely you'll join us."

"I'll see," Grant said noncommittally. They couldn't know that he had more important things on his mind than idle pursuits. Nothing mattered but solving the mystery of Robert's death.

As he rode home on his bay gelding, he breathed deeply to clear the smoke from his lungs. The evening was misty and cold, smelling of refuse and rain. It was the perfect night for brooding in front of a warm hearth.

The appeal of that scenario shook Grant. Damnation, he wasn't an old man in his dotage. A codger who preferred his creature comforts to carousing into the wee hours.

He only needed to think. To plan his next move with Sophie. To decide how best to pursue his seduction of her. Once he'd accomplished his goals, he'd be eager to return to his old life.

In the mews, he dismounted and tossed the reins to a waiting groom. He tramped through the small garden, his boot heels crunching on the graveled path. Out of the blue, the back of his neck prickled.

He had the uncanny feeling that someone was watching him.

With instant icy alertness, Grant paused in the shadow of an oak tree. He surveyed the grounds in a slow sweep. Ghostly streamers of fog drifted over the dark mounds of shrubbery. The pale shape of a granite bench stood beneath a mulberry tree. A damp, earthy odor permeated the air.

He took a stealthy walk around the perimeter of the area until he'd satisfied himself that no one lurked in the bushes. Gradually, the sense of being observed faded. If any would-be thief had been watching through a gap in the wall, he had moved on to a safer target.

He turned back to his leased town house. The tall edifice was built of gray stone and set at the end of a row of identical residences. A single candle winked in an upstairs window. His bedchamber.

He would bring Sophie here very soon.

Despite the damp chill in the air, his blood surged hotly. Her pretense of propriety masked a spirit that could never be tamed, as she'd proven by shattering that glass. But those sultry green eyes also hid the mind of a murderess.

Mulling over that grim fact, he entered the house, locking the door behind him. His footsteps echoed in the gloomy corridor. Besides his valet and the groom, there were only two other servants, an elderly couple who filled the roles of housekeeper and butler. At this hour, they likely would be in the servants' hall in the basement, eating their dinner. Grant might have been the only person in the house.

For an instant, he felt as cold and empty as the formal chambers along the corridor. Then he shook off the sentiment. Visiting Mulford House had left him with a sense of loss, that was all. It had been a visceral reminder that Robert was gone forever.

Although they'd had vastly different natures, one serious and the other daring, he and Robert had been inseparable in childhood, linked by the geographic placement of their homes and a penchant for mock warfare. They had drifted apart during adolescence as their interests had shifted to adult matters. Yet they had remained friends, paying the occasional visit or meeting for dinner at the club. At least, that is, until Sophie had burst into their lives.

Cunning, ambitious, vivacious Sophie Huntington.

She had taken society by storm and collected dozens of suitors, including himself—and Robert. With her sparkling eyes and enticing smile, she had been an outrageous flirt. Grant had fallen deeply in lust, gripped by a more powerful craving than he'd ever before felt. In his hotheaded determination to claim Sophie for himself, he had done the unthinkable. He had taken her chastity in a wild night of passion.

In the aftermath, they'd quarreled bitterly, especially when his tarnished honor had prompted him to make a reckless offer of marriage. She'd coldly informed him that she could never wed a disowned younger son with no prospects. She wanted what he could never give her—a title, wealth, and a secure position in the top tier of society.

Within the fortnight, she'd betrothed herself to Robert. Crazed with fury, Grant had thrown a punch at his friend, knocking him down and bloodying his nose. It had been that galling incident, as much as the shocking agony of losing her, that had sent him into self-imposed exile.

Grant realized he was standing in the darkened foyer with his fingers clenched around the carved mahogany newel post. Forcing himself to relax, he went into the study and poured himself a generous dose of brandy. He stood in the gloom and drank deeply. The fiery liquid slid down his throat with a revitalizing sharpness.

By Sophie's account, Robert had died a painful, lingering death. She had looked so pale and vulnerable that Grant had wanted to hold her close. But he knew Sophie was capable of subterfuge. Indeed, she was a brilliant actress who could make a man believe all of her honeycoated lies.

Had she grown weary of living with staid, bookish Robert? Had she plotted his death for months, or had it been an act of impulse to poison him? Had she sat at his bedside and gloated as her husband gasped his last breath? The probability of that filled Grant with a sickening rage.

God, he despised her!

He also desired her.

A dark, damning heat coiled like a serpent in his gut. It should disgust him that he could crave the widow of an old friend. It should repel him that she very likely had murdered her husband. Yet when he looked at Sophie, he could think only of hot, passionate bedsport.

For too long, thoughts of her had obsessed him. No matter where he went in the world, no matter how often he endangered himself, no matter how many other women he met, he had never succeeded in forgetting Sophie.

So he would have his fill of her at last. She wouldn't be able to shut him out of her life this time. His role as Lucien's guardian gave him the perfect excuse to visit Mulford House as often as he liked.

The thought of Robert's son caused a stirring of disquiet in Grant. Lucien was an unanticipated hitch in an otherwise perfect plan.

Solemn and earnest, the boy resembled his father in temperament and his mother in appearance. He had looked so woebegone and defenseless while speaking of his papa that Grant had felt an involuntary twist of pity. His own upbringing had been different, yet he knew what it was like to feel starved for paternal affection.

How would Lucien react to seeing his mother branded a murderess and sent to prison? Grant had no wish to cause the boy any more pain. It was clear that Lucien adored his mother and that she doted on him.

Given her probable role in the death of Lucien's father, Sophie was a surprisingly protective mother. She had hovered over Lucien, her expressive face revealing a nervous anxiety. Clearly she had been waiting for a chance to whisk him away. At the first opportunity, she had sent the boy back up to the nursery on the pretext of studying his lessons.

I will not allow you near my son. You're a poor influence.

Her condemnation rankled Grant. Did she truly believe he would corrupt a *child*? Yes, her opinion of him had sunk that low. He had no doubt she'd consulted an army of lawyers in an effort to overturn the guardianship.

Why *had* Robert commited the care of his only son to him—a man who knew nothing of being a father? There was only one logical explanation. Clearly, Robert had turned to a trusted old friend to guard his son because he had suspected his wife of poisoning him.

The brandy suddenly tasted sour, and Grant put down

his glass. He mustn't underestimate Sophie; she was an intelligent, ingenious woman. It would take considerable charm and finesse to gain her confidence and wrest a confession from her. In the meantime, he intended to ask discreet questions and construct a clearer picture of Robert's final days.

Grant headed for the staircase. He wanted to read Robert's letter again, as he had a dozen times already, hoping to find some clue that he'd missed. On his deathbed, Robert had scribbled the disjointed message—

A muffled shriek shattered the silence of the house.

Yanked from his reverie, Grant stopped in the middle of the foyer. The scream had been distinctly female. It had come not from the formal rooms on the first story, but higher. From one of the bedchambers.

His bedchamber?

Spurred by alarm, he took the stairs at a run.

O, bliss! O, Joy! I have seen William! It happened at the Opera whilst I sat in the Ducal box with Mulford and my parents. During the Interval, Mulford went to pay his Addresses to an acquaintance. 'Twas then that a footman entered the box and delivered a secret note into my hands.

My heart leapt to see 'twas from my Darling William. Until that moment, I had no notion of his presence, for he lacks the coin to attend such Frivolities. At once, I scanned the noble gathering and spied his handsome visage in the topmost balcony, where he lifted his hand in greeting.

I pressed his note to my lips most fervently to show my receipt of his missive. He has begged me to meet him on the morrow, and tho' I risk incurring the wrath of my Parents, I must contrive a way . . .

—*the diaries of Annabelle Chatham Ramsey, 3ʳᵈ Duchess of Mulford*

"I understand you had a visitor earlier today," Helena said.

In the dining chamber, she aimed a pointed stare at Sophie. They were seated opposite each other at one end of the long table, in their habitual places flanking Robert's empty chair. Sophie had kept the conversation on household matters, determined not to spoil the meal with the news of Grant's reappearance. She should have known that Helena never missed anything that happened under this roof.

Taking a sip of wine from her goblet, Sophie coolly

met her sister-in-law's gaze. "Yes, Grant Chandler has returned from abroad. He came to pay his respects . . . and
to meet Lucien."

"Surely he isn't taking this guardianship seriously,"
Helena said, her blue eyes wide against her fair skin with
its port-wine stain on the left cheek. "Did he not receive
the deed about renouncing his rights?"

"He did, but he won't sign it. Believe me, I'm not any
happier about the situation than you are." *Furious* might
be a more apt description of her feelings, Sophie reflected. Add to that, *worried, frustrated, alarmed.*

After Grant's departure, she had spent the remainder
of the day pacing the library, trying to determine a way
out of the dilemma. She had taken out her copy of
Robert's will and studied the dry legal language, even
though a team of solicitors had already advised her there
were no loopholes.

Grant Chandler was Lucien's primary guardian. His
decisions took precedence over Elliot's.

And hers.

"What else did he say?" Helena asked, daintily slicing
the roast beef on her plate. "How long will he remain in
London?"

"He didn't specify. But he's leased a house only a few
blocks from here, in Berkeley Square."

Helena set down her fork and knife with an uncharacteristic clatter. "Good God! That means he intends to
stay."

"Apparently so."

The news deepened Helena's scowl. "I'm appalled,"
she said bitterly. "I don't understand why my brother con-
ferred such a responsibility on a ne'er-do-well—a man
who is not even a member of our family."

Sophie knew why. She pretended an interest in her
food, swirling the tines of her fork in a mound of peas,

although the knot in her stomach had banished all appetite. Helena didn't know the truth—and she would never know—that Robert knew the child wasn't his and yet had wholeheartedly accepted Grant's son as his own. "They were good friends once. I suppose that would explain it."

"That hardly constitutes a reason to place Lucien's care in the hands of a scoundrel. Grant Chandler was always a bad seed, even as a child."

Sophie had always been scrupulously careful never to show an interest in him. But now curiosity overwhelmed her. "You knew Mr. Chandler, too, didn't you? Aren't you a few years older than him?"

"Three years, so I certainly do remember that scapegrace." Helena patted her lips with her napkin as if a trifle embarrassed to admit to her advanced age of thirty-seven. "He was forever leading Robert into trouble, sneaking out of church service or playing tricks on the neighbors. Once, they went up to the roof and dropped eggs on the guests who were leaving a party. Another time, they built a raft and nearly drowned themselves in the lake."

Sophie didn't doubt that Grant had instigated their exploits; he'd always had the more inventive mind. How well she could imagine Robert as a quiet, reserved boy who hero-worshipped his dashing, adventuresome neighbor. "Why was Robert not forbidden the association, then?"

"Papa had a genial, forgiving nature. It was his opinion that boys will be boys. But *I* was appalled. Grant Chandler was a disgrace to the neighborhood. Why, by the time he was sixteen, his own father cast him out of the family fold. There were rumors . . ."

Sophie had to force herself not to lean forward on the edge of her seat. Grant had always refused to speak of his family. "Rumors?"

Helena hesitated another moment, then rang the tiny
silver bell that sat on the table. The musical sound summoned a pair of footmen from the next room. They
cleared away the dishes and brought a steaming pot of
tea, which was a habit with the ladies in lieu of dessert.

As she poured, Sophie curbed her impatience. She
handed a delicate porcelain cup to her sister-in-law. "Please,
Helena, you mustn't stop there," she said in a light tone.
"It isn't fair to pique my curiosity so grievously. I wish to
learn every detail about my son's guardian."

"I should think you'd already know the story. Mr.
Chandler was a particular interest of yours at one time,
was he not?"

Sophie willed steadiness into her hand. Helena's tone
implied not suspicion, but scorn for any woman who
could favor a rogue over the Duke of Mulford. She met
Helena's gaze with unflinching directness. "Yes, he was
one of my beaus. But he never told me why he was es-
tranged from his father."

"Well, then, I suppose you ought to hear it," Helena
said as she added a dollop of cream to her tea. She
glanced over her shoulder as if to make certain the footmen had left the chamber. "It's been said that he doesn't
share his father's noble blood."

Sophie's cold fingers absorbed the heat of her cup.
Dear God. Grant was a bastard? No, not a bastard, for
he'd been born a legitimate son. "His mother—?"

"Lady Litton was a notorious flirt. Apparently she had
a fling with one of the footmen and was caught in the act
by the earl himself."

"Oh, dear heavens," Sophie said faintly.

"She died giving birth." Helena's single upraised eyebrow conveyed her opinion that it was a righteous fate.
"To his credit, the earl never renounced her son. But there
was never any affection between them, either. One cannot

blame the earl. After all, Grant inherited his mother's brazen nature."

But Sophie did blame the earl. Every child was born innocent of the wrongdoings of his parents. Robert had opened his heart to Lucien, overlooking the circumstances of his conception. Grant's father had had the choice to do likewise. Would Grant have grown up a more settled, responsible man if he'd felt secure in his father's love?

Sophie shut her mind to any undue softening. The answer didn't signify. "A tragic tale," she mused aloud. "But all that matters is that he stays away from Lucien."

"I quite agree," Helena said firmly. "It is our duty to protect young Mulford. I shall tell Phelps to bar Mr. Chandler from this house."

"No," Sophie countermanded. "Grant would take that as a challenge to cause trouble. And don't forget, he has the law on his side."

"We must do *something*. I won't have him luring my nephew into a life of dissipation."

Sophie wanted to scoff at the absurdity of that—until she realized she'd accused Grant of the very same thing. "It won't happen," she said. "Grant is hardly a man to sit through hours of arithmetic and reading and geography. If we allow him to visit a time or two, he'll grow weary of Lucien's routine. At that point, I'll present him with the document again."

"Ah," Helena said, her eyes brightening over the rim of her cup. "I see your point. Very clever, Sophie."

But as they finished their tea, Sophie didn't feel clever. In mind and body, she felt fraught with stress. Certainly Grant would leave at some point; his easily jaded nature would demand it. But when? For how long would she have to be civil to the man?

For as long as she must.

Even though the heat in his eyes stirred a flame in her, even though that one passionate night still burned in her memory, Sophie resolutely shut the damper on her reckless past. She was a sensible woman now. She had dedicated herself to being a good mother to Lucien. Her son needed her love and attention to soften the blow of losing his father.

Grant is his father.

Her stomach lurched. But Sophie refused to feel even a particle of guilt for concealing the truth from him.

Robert had been Lucien's true father. Robert had soothed Lucien's tears and taken him on excursions to the park. Robert had listened to Lucien recite his lessons by day and read stories to him each night.

Grant lacked the steady nature required of a parent. Even as a naïve debutante, she had seen that flaw in him and realized that he could never change. For all his grandiose promises to Lucien, he had no interest in childish pursuits. She would fight tooth and nail to keep him from trifling with Lucien's affections.

And hers.

Grant reached the second floor in the space of a few seconds. The corridor lay empty in either direction, lit by glass sconces set in the walls at regular intervals. He wondered at the source of the scream. It could only be the housekeeper. Had she injured herself?

Mrs. Howell burst out of the open doorway of his bedchamber. Her white cap lay askew on her iron-gray hair. Clearly in a dither, the housekeeper ran toward him, clutching her hands to her plump cheeks.

Grant met her halfway down the passage. By reflex, he took hold of her shoulders. She gasped out, "Sir! Oh, sir! Praise God in heaven . . . ye're here!"

"Calm yourself," he ordered. "Tell me what's wrong."

She drew a shaky breath and glanced back fearfully over her shoulder. "I—I was just gone into your chamber to light the fire . . . not knowin' if ye'd be home soon. 'Tis when I spied the clutter . . ."

"Clutter?"

She nodded vigorously. "Aye, sir, yer things be strewn everywhere. But that's not the worst. I—I saw . . ."

An intruder? Damnation, there *had* been someone skulking in the garden! Probably an accomplice.

Grant pulled her around the corner to safety. In a harsh whisper, he demanded, "What is it? Answer me!"

"'Tis yer Mr. Wren, sir. Lying there . . . all bloody and still . . ." She broke off, weeping, pressing her hands to her mouth.

Good God. His manservant had been attacked during the robbery.

"Send for a doctor," Grant snapped. "At once."

"Aye, sir." Mrs. Howell fled toward the servants' staircase at the end of the passage.

Despite Grant's belief that the thief had left the house, he kept watch as he hurried into the bedchamber. The flame of a single candle fluttered in the window, showing a scene of jumbled disorder. Drawers had been pulled out and left open, the contents littering the carpet. The sheets and coverlet hung half off the four-poster bed. Books had been swept from the shelves by the unlit hearth. Even the landscape paintings had been torn from the walls.

Grant absorbed it all in one sweep of a glance. Then he spied the crumpled form of a man lying in the doorway of the dressing room.

Seizing the candle, Grant took a quick look inside that chamber to make certain no one hid there. He'd be of no help to Wren if he himself were assaulted.

Then again, it might already be too late to help.

Grant clenched his teeth against the rush of a powerful

fear. Wren had been with him since Grant had been a headstrong youth bent on risking his life at every turn. The past decade of adventuring had made them close comrades. Indeed, the crusty old valet had been more of a father to him than the almighty Earl of Litton.

Crouching down, Grant held up the candle to examine the man. Wren lay on his side, his small, scrawny form clad in one of the blue coats he'd worn ever since a woman in the distant past had complimented him on how the color matched his eyes. Those eyes were closed now as if he were asleep. Blood trickled over his stubbled cheek, dark against the waxen hue of his skin. More blood pooled beneath his balding head. It appeared he'd been struck savagely from behind.

Muttering a curse and a prayer, Grant sought a pulse in Wren's neck. He could feel nothing at first . . . then he detected the welcome throb of life, faint and reedy.

Relief spread through Grant, though the feeling was edged with anxiety. Wren might be a tough old bird who'd survived other close scrapes, but a sharp blow to the head could kill a man.

Grant seized one of his own clean white shirts from a tumbled heap on the floor. Using it to blot the blood, he took a closer look at the wound. The ugly gash had bled quite a lot.

Wren groaned and shifted slightly. One of his gnarled hands curled into a fist. His eyes cracking open, he muttered something and flailed out in a feeble swing.

Grant easily deflected the blow. "Easy there, old man," he said. "I'm only trying to help you."

Those stubby lashes lifted as Wren squinted up at Grant. He blinked as if struggling to focus. "There be two o' ye, guv'nor. An' one's plenty enough for the world."

A faint humor stirred in the midst of Grant's concern.

If the valet could jest, maybe he wasn't lying at death's door. "You're seeing double because you've been hit in the head. Do you remember what happened?"

Frowning, Wren gingerly touched the injury. "I . . . I was bringin' yer laundry upstairs after supper. I heard somebody in the dressin' room. I thought 'twas ye, returned from her ladyship's house." He glowered up at Grant. "Did the duchess throw ye out on yer ear, like I warned ye?"

"Never mind her," Grant said tightly. "Did you see your attacker?"

"Nay. Don't remember nothin' more."

"So the chamber hadn't been ransacked when you came in."

"Ransacked?" The old man made a move as if to sit up, then grunted in pain and slumped back down. "Buggerin' thieves, was they?"

"For God's sake, lie still. I'm going to move you to the bed while we wait for the doctor."

Wren protested feebly as Grant did so. "I can't be usin' the master's bed. It ain't fittin' ."

"You'll do as you're told."

The old man was a featherweight who would have made a good jockey if he'd been so inclined. A keen awareness of his frailty worried Grant. He made a pad of another shirt and gently tucked it beneath the valet's head.

"Them shirts are brand-new," Wren continued to grumble. "Don't ye be ruinin' yer fine linens on my account."

"I'll purchase more. Now, don't move or you'll start bleeding again."

When he was convinced the old man was settled comfortably in the four-poster bed, Grant lit a branch of candles. He knelt down before the hearth and ignited the kindling, and soon, a fire wafted warmth into the chilly air. Only then did he take a look around to determine if anything was missing. If so, it could be nothing of consequence.

He, of all men, knew better than to leave valuables unguarded for any prowler with sticky fingers. He had deposited the bulk of his uninvested wealth in the bank and kept only enough for weekly expenses locked in his desk in the downstairs library. He didn't wear jeweled stickpins or rings as other gentlemen did, and he always kept his silver pocketwatch with him.

The intruder had been hiding in the garden, no doubt having done his handiwork while the servants were at dinner. Grant had sensed a presence out there, and now he berated himself for not searching more thoroughly.

From his perch in the bed, Wren scornfully regarded the clutter. "Common thief. No manners atall. He could take a few lessons from ye."

Grant made a noncommittal sound as he picked up several books from the floor. Why would a petty burglar empty these shelves? It was hardly a typical place to hide jewels or money. Had the man been angry that he'd found nothing of value?

Possibly. Yet something nagged at the edge of his consciousness. Perhaps it was the savage nature of the vandalism, as if the perpetrator had harbored a personal vendetta against Grant . . .

The sound of voices and footsteps in the corridor heralded the arrival of the doctor and the housekeeper. On seeing the valet lying awake, Mrs. Howell exclaimed, "Oh, praise heavens, ye're alive, Mr. Wren!"

"I'm right as rain," he muttered. "I certainly don't need a sawbones!"

"Then 'tis well my name is MacPherson," quipped the stout, middle-aged physician. In the efficient manner of one accustomed to dealing with peevish patients,

MacPherson examined Wren, dressed the injury, and administered a sleeping draught. He also prescribed bed rest for the coming week, and when Wren objected, Grant threatened to tie him to the bedposts if he didn't behave.

As the physician left, Grant followed him into the corridor. After discussing Wren's care for a few moments, Grant decided to use the opportunity to further another goal. "Tell me, did you by chance treat the Duke of Mulford last year? He was a good friend of mine."

"I, sir, administer to a duke?" Chuckling, MacPherson shook his head. "That would be the Regent's physician, Dr. Atherton."

Resolving to pay a visit to that man very soon, Grant went back into the chamber. To his relief, Wren had dozed off, and Grant took the branch of candles into the dressing room. A suspicion preyed on his mind.

He found his clothing strewn in all four corners, his shaving equipment scattered over the carpet. The china pitcher teetered on the edge of the washstand. Not surprisingly, his traveling valise had been pulled out of the wardrobe and lay atop a snowdrift of cravats on the floor.

He crouched down to examine the satchel. The leather had been sliced open at the bottom, exposing the small, empty compartment concealed in the base, which Grant often had used to transport stolen jewels.

But there was another hiding place, too.

He felt along the inside of the valise for a tiny hook hidden in the lining. Opening it, he retrieved a folded sheet of paper.

The letter was still safe.

The candlelight illuminated Robert's penmanship, shaky from his illness. The message was brief, as if written in haste.

*I fear I've been poisoned by someone dear to
me . . . I know not who else to trust but you,
old friend . . . come quickly . . .*

The letter had reached him in Constantinople in the
same packet with two others, one from Robert's solicitor
announcing the duke's death and naming Grant as Lucien's guardian. The other had been from Sophie, a terse,
formal request that he relinquish all responsibility toward
her son.

Clearly, Robert had written his note in secret, then had
sent it to Grant's Aunt Phoebe, the only member of his
family who had remained his staunch supporter. She had
forwarded the letter to him, but with the delays in foreign
mail, it had been months too late for Grant to help
Robert.

Grief and rage choked him anew. That earthshaking
letter had been his first and last correspondence from
Robert in nearly ten years. Grant had surmised Sophie's guilt at once. Certainly there were other possible
suspects—Robert's cantankerous sister, Helena, and his
cousin Elliot, to name two.

But one telling fact had decided Grant. If Robert had
believed in his wife's innocence, wouldn't he have confided his fears to *her*?

Today, Sophie had played the tragic widow. She had
managed to look forlorn, even desolate with grief, while
describing Robert's death from eating tainted food. She
had mentioned nothing at all of poison.

Grant hardened his jaw. Was it mere coincidence that
only hours after his visit to her, his house had been bur-
glarized? Hell, no!

What if, before his death, Robert had confessed to her
that he'd written to Grant of his suspicions?

Given that scenario, Grant's sudden reappearance

would have caused Sophie to panic. She would fear exposure of her crime. No duchess would willingly exchange her gilded life for a cold prison cell.

But she had one hope of escaping the hangman's noose. To find the damning letter and destroy it.

22 October 1701

> *I would never have made good my Escape this day without the aid of Dear Mary, most loyal of servants. The very moment Mama left for the shops, Mary smuggled me down the servants' staircase to Freedom.*
>
> *'Twas but a short walk to the rendezvous in Hyde Park, where William waited most Anxiously. Words cannot describe the Joy of our Reunion. We made haste down a little traveled pathway into the trees. I feared not for my Virtue, for William does love and respect me to the very depths of his Soul. We spent a delightful afternoon in close company and made plans to meet again.*
>
> *Yet my Heart weeps, for I know our days are numbered. William has no title to tempt my Father, and I am bound to marry Mulford.*

> *—the diaries of Annabelle Chatham Ramsey, 3rd Duchess of Mulford*

5

"Do you really think the missing diary could be hidden way up there?" Caroline asked.

Perched atop the ladder in the library, Sophie glanced down at her dearest friend and neighbor, who sat comfortably ensconced in a chair, sipping a glass of sherry. Caroline, the Countess of Belgrove, had dazzling blue eyes that enlivened her otherwise plain features. Threads of silver in her brown hair betrayed the fact that she was more than two decades older than Sophie, with two grown sons and another away at Eton. Despite the age difference, however, they had formed a fast friendship shortly after Sophie had moved into the ducal mansion next door to Caroline's town house.

"I don't know where else to look," Sophie said, returning to her task of moving the books aside so that she could peer behind them. "I scoured the country manor when we were there at Christmas. I've gone over every inch of Mulford House, too, except for this library." Given the many tall rows of shelves, she estimated the search would take her the better part of the week.

"Where did you say you found the first diary? It seems logical to look there."

"It was in the attic, in a trunk of old clothing. But I've already combed every box and chest up there." Given the abrupt end to the first diary, Sophie felt certain that another volume existed. It would have covered the beginning of Annabelle's marriage to the third duke, a period of her life that held particular interest for Sophie.

Like Sophie, Annabelle too had been duped by a rogue. But Sophie burned to know if there had been other similarities, as well. More precisely, Annabelle's first son had been born not quite nine months after the wedding. Had her child been sired by the third duke—or by her true love, William?

And if so, had William ever learned the truth?

Sophie dared not voice those questions aloud. Not even Caroline knew the truth about Lucien. No one had known but Sophie and Robert.

Caroline thoughtfully tapped her glass. "Perhaps the diary was lost—or destroyed on purpose. Annabelle wouldn't be the first person to see the value in hiding an indiscretion."

Ever since Sophie had told her about Grant's return the previous day, Caroline had been eyeing her speculatively. Parrying that keen stare, Sophie wiped her dusty fingers on her white apron. "Then Annabelle would have destroyed the first volume as well," she said. "After all, she writes in great detail about stealing away to meet William."

"Hmm. That *is* a salient point. I wonder if she couldn't bear to part with the memory of her first love." Caroline paused a moment, then added in a significant tone, "Speaking of which, I've been thinking about your Mr. Chandler."

Sophie stiffened. "He isn't *mine*. He's Lucien's guardian and a nuisance I don't need."

Caroline went on blithely, "I've been thinking about a solution to your dilemma. Pray don't be offended, but . . ."

"But?"

"But perhaps you should have an affair with him."

Aghast, Sophie almost tumbled off the ladder. She clutched at the topmost bookshelf and sent a startled glance downward. "God in heaven, Caro! Have you gone completely *mad*? He's a scoundrel. He was the bane of society when I was a debutante."

"Indeed, he was quite beyond the pale, from what little *I* knew of him. Precisely the sort of handsome, dashing knave who attracts flocks of female admirers." Eyes twinkling, Caroline took a sip of sherry. "If memory serves, he ignored them all and paid particular attention to *you*."

Not even to Caroline had Sophie ever admitted how close she and Grant had once been. But if Sophie denied any attraction to him whatsoever, Caroline would shrewdly assume the worst. "He *did* have a certain charm for a girl fresh out of the country," Sophie admitted. "But that was a long time ago, before I'd acquired any good sense. I certainly don't want such a man anywhere near my son."

"Precisely. An affair would offer the perfect distraction. Tell your Mr. Chandler that you cannot risk your son discovering the two of you together. Therefore, you can meet him only away from this house. Then poof, all your problems are solved."

A flush suffused Sophie's body as she imagined making such a scandalous proposal to Grant. He would draw her into his arms and kiss her passionately, touch her all over—"My problems would multiply into a complete disaster," she said, shoving an old atlas aside with enough force to raise a nose-tickling puff of dust. "To suggest an affair is outrageous and wicked, and I'm appalled you would even voice it to me. Especially now, when I'm still in mourning."

Caroline rose from her chair and strolled over to the ladder, where she looked up at Sophie. Concern etched the soft set of her lips. "My dear, I realize you're still grieving," she said in a gentle tone. "But it isn't wicked to seek a bit of happiness for yourself. You've been starved so long for a man's attentions. We both know that Robert—"

"Don't say it," Sophie broke in. "Please." The notion of discussing the intimate details of her marriage horrified her. At one time, in desperate need of guidance, she had discreetly sought Caroline's advice on how to please her husband in the bedchamber. But Robert was gone now, and she would feel disloyal reiterating his deficiencies.

"Forgive me," Caroline said rather sheepishly. "Belgrove always tells me that I dish out advice in dollops too big to swallow. But if you'll hear me out, I might have another idea for resolving the situation with Mr. Chandler."

"If it's anything like the last one . . ."

Smiling, Caroline shook her head. "No, certainly not, although it does have to do with his rakehell reputation." Her expression turning thoughtful, she strolled back and forth at the foot of the ladder, her aqua gown rustling. "Do you suppose you could recall specific examples of his unsuitability?"

"Certainly. But . . . what do you have in mind?"

"I'm thinking that if you can prove him an irredeemable blackguard, you might convince the courts to rescind his guardianship."

Holding on to a rung of the ladder, Sophie caught her breath. "Do you really think it possible that a judge might overrule Robert's will?"

"Considering that Lucien is a duke, there's a chance, albeit a slim one. You can but try. And there is no time like the present to start your campaign." Caroline seated herself at the escritoire and took up a pen and a sheet of stationery. "Come now, search your memory for all of Mr. Chandler's misdeeds, and I shall take notes."

The worst of his misdeeds had been seducing a young lady, a fact that Sophie refrained from mentioning. Besides, in her heart she knew that she couldn't heap the blame entirely on him. She had been foolishly, madly in love with him. . . .

Casting that memory aside, she thought back to less salacious incidents. "Where shall I begin? How about the time he rode his horse into Lord Harrington's ballroom? He'd laid a wager that his mare could dance the quadrille as well as any debutante."

"Yes, I remember the uproar," Caroline said with an amused shake of her head. "Unfortunately, the prank was spoiled when *you* were judged to be the better dancer."

Sophie blushed at the memory of her unruly behavior. Heady with the pleasures of her first Season, she had ignored the disapproval of society matrons and stuffy gentlemen. She had quite nearly put herself beyond the pale. Choosing another example at random, she said, "There was also the time he swam naked in the Serpentine. It was a cold spring night, but he never could resist a dare."

Caroline's pen ceased scratching over the paper. She stared up at Sophie on the ladder. "Truly? Were *you* present?"

"No!" Sophie hastened to clarify. "I only heard his friends laughing about it the next day."

"Who were these friends?"

"Viscount Hockridge, Lord Kilminster, and Jeremy Updike."

"Hardly credible witnesses," Caroline said with a grimace. "They are three peas in a pod—a rotten pod, at that."

"Quite." Sophie leaned down to examine a lower shelf. She had never felt comfortable with Grant's cronies, partly because they gambled too much and partly because they had eyed her with rather lewd interest. "I doubt I could depend upon them to testify against Mr. Chandler, anyway."

"Testify against me?"

For the second time that morning, Sophie almost fell off the ladder. Her horrified gaze fixed on Grant in the doorway. He stood with his arms crossed and one broad shoulder propped against the frame. A charcoal-gray coat and crisp white stock enhanced his stark male beauty, and pale gray riding breeches delineated his long, powerful legs. He scanned her in a slow, insulting perusal.

A mortifying heat suffused Sophie, making her heart race and her knees wobble. Both she and Caroline had had their backs to the door. How long had he been standing there?

Surely not long enough to have overheard their plan.

Donning a mantle of icy decorum, she said, "Good morning, Mr. Chandler. I see you're wandering about the house again, uninvited."

"Apparently that's the least of my sins." He pushed away from the door and strolled into the library with his confident swagger, as if he owned the world. "By the by, it was late winter when I swam the Serpentine. There was still snow on the ground."

He *had* heard, the scoundrel.

"That only proves the weakness of your character," Sophie snapped.

"Or the strength of my constitution."

"I was referring to your eavesdropping, Mr. Chandler."

She descended the ladder, a difficult maneuver given her long skirts and her awareness of his scrutiny. It took all of her concentration to avoid trodding on her hem and taking an ignominious fall. Upon reaching the bottom, she resisted the urge to tidy her hair and straighten her clothing. She didn't bother to remove the long white apron that protected her gown of black crepe.

Caroline rose from the desk and came to her side. In a loud whisper, she said, "I see what you mean about his charm."

"Charm?" Sophie murmured, also projecting her voice so that he could hear. "He's anything *but* charming."

Grant looked amused by the biting commentary. He laid waste to it by bowing to Caroline and gallantly kissing her hand. "I'm afraid you have the better of me," he said. "You know my name, but I don't know yours."

Sophie grudgingly performed the introductions. "Caroline, this is the *Honorable* Grant Chandler. Mr. Chandler, the Countess of Belgrove."

Grant released her hand. "A pleasure, Lady Belgrove. Is your husband still a reckoning force in the House of Lords?"

"Not since the Whigs lost power, I'm afraid. But he still practices his speeches on me." Caroline gave Grant a look of interest. "I confess I'm surprised you'd remember James. Have you an interest in politics?"

"Only insofar as it enables me to wager on the outcome of elections."

"You're incorrigible, Mr. Chandler." With mock sternness, she shook her forefinger at him. "It makes me wonder if I ought to stay and chaperone the two of you."

Pricked by dismay, Sophie exclaimed, "You needn't leave, Caro. Truly." To underscore the words, she scowled a plea at her friend, who blithely ignored her.

"I'm afraid I must. I've just remembered an errand I promised to run for Philip." With a smile at Grant, Caroline added, "He's my youngest. He's away at Eton and he begged me to send him a particular set of quill pens that can only be purchased at the stationer's on Regent Street."

It was a sham excuse, but etiquette prevented Sophie from saying so aloud. Caroline would have denied it, anyway. She seemed doggedly determined to leave Sophie alone with Grant.

Caroline wanted them to have an affair. A wild, passionate, intimate romance. The forbidden thought ignited a fire of longing inside Sophie. It sensitized her skin and made her breasts ache. And it made her dread being alone with Grant.

"You needn't accompany me to the door," Caroline went on breezily. "I'll see myself out." She collected her reticule from the table and sashayed out of the library, closing the door behind her.

Sophie tamed the reckless pounding of her heart. It wouldn't do for Grant to guess her immoral thoughts or to see the flush of desire in her face. He would only press his advantage.

To her relief, he wasn't even looking at her. He strolled to the desk and picked up the paper listing his misdeeds. "Only two incidents. I'm offended. Is this *all* you can remember?"

Sophie marched to his side and snatched the sheet out of his fingers. "Hardly. I'd only begun when you interrupted us."

"Perhaps I could help. There was that time you lured me into the linen closet at Lord Duncombe's party. There were people coming down the corridor, and you didn't want anyone to know we'd gone upstairs together."

The memory sprang free from the locked vault of her past. Grant holding her in the close confines of the darkened closet. His hands roving over her gown. His lips tracing a downward path along her throat and down to her breasts . . . "I didn't *lure* you," she felt compelled to clarify. "I went upstairs to the ladies' retiring chamber. *You* followed *me*."

"Perhaps the truth lies somewhere in between." His gaze flitted to her mouth, making her think of passionate kisses. "But I don't suppose you'd want that episode on your list, anyway. Even if it would prove the wretched state of my moral code."

"You're right. I'd be ashamed for anyone to learn of my girlish follies." She folded the paper and then marched past him. Bending down, she tucked the unfinished list into a cubbyhole of the desk. Over her shoulder, she said, "But I won't have to strain my mind to find many other occasions that involve only you and your indiscreet approach to life."

"Ah, Sophie," he said, his voice lowering to a caressing tone. "You once loved my indiscretions."

To her shock, she felt the whisper of his breath on the nape of her neck, the touch of his hands at the back of her waist. Her wayward body responded instantly. A treacherous heat bathed her insides, spreading warmth throughout her limbs. Unable to draw a breath, she was keenly aware of his male strength, the long legs planted firmly behind her, the hands that could stroke a woman to ecstasy. No other man had ever affected her so completely. Not even her husband.

The disloyal thought was like a dash of cold water. Regaining her strength, Sophie spun around to face Grant. That was a mistake, for it brought her breasts flush against the muscled contour of his chest. With every breath, she inhaled his spicy scent, an allure that evoked the memory of putting her lips to his bare skin.

She leaned back, bracing her palms on the desk behind her. "I'll thank you not to touch me."

"No thanks needed. I was merely untying your apron for you."

He shifted his hands to her shoulders and started to remove the long white overgarment. The action brought a searing reminder of him undressing her that night long ago . . .

Furious at him and at herself, Sophie forcefully shoved him away. "Stop it at once! I won't suffer your insolence, Grant. I'll summon the footman and have you thrown out of this house."

Grant stepped back and regarded her. His dark eyes held an icy hardness that vanished so swiftly she wondered if she'd imagined it. With an air of insouciance, he sauntered to a chair by the hearth and sat down, stretching out his legs and crossing them at the ankles. "All right, then. We'll exchange social niceties. What did you do after I left yesterday?"

The question set her off-kilter, as did the sight of him ensconced in Robert's favorite chair. "I worked here in the library."

"Worked?" Skepticism rang in his voice. "Have you fallen on hard times, Your Grace? Are you reduced to doing the dusting yourself?"

"Don't be absurd." She resented the way he regarded her, as a pretty ornament with no purpose in life but to wallow in luxury. Never mind that she had led him to believe just that by lying to him about her reasons for marrying Robert. Removing the apron, she carefully folded it on the long oak library table. "If you must know, I'm compiling a history of the Ramsey family. As a memorial to Robert . . . and a legacy for my son."

Sophie rationalized away a familiar jolt of guilt. Although Lucien was no blood relation, he was a Ramsey to the core. Robert himself had said so on numerous occasions . . .

"So you didn't leave the house?" Grant asked.

The trace of tension in his voice caught her attention. "No. Why do you ask?"

He shrugged. "I find myself curious about your life, duchess. Were you alone yesterday?"

"Yes, except for spending time with Lucien and then eating a late dinner with Helena." Having the distinct feeling that he was dissimulating for his own obscure reasons, Sophie decided to change the subject. "There is no point to this interrogation. If you've come to visit my son, he's at his lessons. You're welcome to go up to the schoolroom and observe him if you like. Otherwise . . ."

A gentleman would heed the hint. A gentleman also would never sit while the lady remained standing. But then, Grant had never conformed to the standards of polite society.

He shifted in the chair as if settling in for a long conversation. "So Helena still lives here, does she? Has she never married?"

"No, she has not." As Sophie had expected, he showed no interest in Lucien. She should be glad of that, yet a restless anger threatened to manifest itself. She walked to the globe that stood on a pedestal and pressed her hand to its smooth, cool roundness. In a tone of heavy sarcasm, she said, "Is there anything else you wish to know before you leave me to my work?"

"Yes." Perversely, he seemed to take her words as an invitation. His narrowed eyes studied her with disconcerting directness. "For one, I'm wondering about your marriage. Were you and Robert happy together?"

Sophie's hand slipped from the globe, sending it spinning madly. Did Grant know—? Impossible. With her fingertips, she stopped the globe's wild orbit. "Extremely, gloriously so," she embellished. "Beyond that, I've no wish to share confidences with you."

His mouth crooked in a wry smile. "Let me assure you, I mean no offense," he said smoothly. "I was wrong not to mend the rift with Robert. And now I've only you, Sophie, to find out how he spent the past decade."

The eloquent appeal stirred her suspicions. She couldn't help but conclude that Grant was trying to coax her into letting down her guard. To restore the intimacy of camaraderie to their relationship.

Or perhaps he really *was* interested in hearing about Robert.

Guilt niggled at Sophie. She had never been able to shed a sense of responsibility for breaking up their childhood friendship, and the need to assuage that burden convinced her to relent. Whether she approved of Grant or not, he had a right to ask about the final years of Robert's life. She had an equal right to tell him only a selective version of the truth.

Wearing her dignity like a protective cloak, Sophie walked to the circle of chairs by the hearth and sat down opposite Grant. She folded her hands in her lap and met his unnerving gaze. "As you wish, then," she said coolly. "I'll start at the beginning, from the point at which you'd left town. Robert and I preferred to have a quiet wedding,

so we married by special license. We spent our honeymoon at his estate in Sussex."

"Is that when he found out you were no virgin?"

The blunt words were sharp enough to cut. And his
vulgar question revealed more than simple interest in
Robert's life. Was Grant goading her for some purpose of
his own?

An angry reprimand sprang to her lips. But she was determined to maintain her calm. "No, I'd told him about us
beforehand. I couldn't have started out a marriage based
on a lie, so I was completely honest with Robert. He
knew everything."

Even that she was pregnant with his friend's child.

Shortly after her lovemaking with Grant, she had
awakened one morning to an unsettled stomach and the
awareness that her monthly courses were a few days late.
Frightened and desperate, she had gone straight to
Robert. He had been her friend and confidant, the only
one of her suitors whom she trusted completely. True to
form, he had neither chastised her nor recoiled in horror.
He simply arranged for a discreet examination by a
physician who confirmed the likelihood of the diagnosis.

Afterward, she had wept on Robert's shoulder, unable
to think beyond the terror of her predicament. An unwed
lady who found herself in a delicate condition was
shunned forever by society, and Sophie had dreaded bur-
dening her aging parents with this shocking proof of her
recklessness. She couldn't go to Grant for help, either. Although he had offered to marry her, his proposal had been
made so grudgingly that it was torment to remember . . .

*Lying in bed with Grant, the wild yearnings of her body
sated at last, she reveled in their closeness. His warmth
and his scent enveloped her in a dreamlike cocoon. Her*

drifting thoughts clung to the wondrous excitement they had shared. She thrilled to the feel of him inside of her, and it seemed they were one spirit, one body, one entity, never to be separated.

"Grant . . . oh, Grant, I love you." The impassioned words rose straight from her heart, and it was the second time that evening she had voiced them. The first time, she and Grant had been fully clothed and in the midst of feverishly caressing each other, and it had been her confession that had driven him mad with passion.

But now, he lifted his head to stare at her. She could see the awareness come over him in the tightening of his jaw and the starkness of his eyes. "My God, Sophie. What have I done?"

His look frightened her. She touched his smooth-shaven cheek, willing him to feel the same strength of union that she felt. "We've found love. We'll never be parted again."

As if she hadn't spoken, he drew away from her and sat up, running his fingers through his tousled black hair. "Damnation! I can't afford a wife, but I'll have to marry you now . . ."

Sophie realized she was gazing down at her lap. Her fingers were clenched around the folds of her skirt, wrinkling the black crepe. Forcing herself to relax, she looked up at Grant.

He was staring at her with that peculiar intensity of his, and for an instant she could almost believe that he had read her thoughts, that he too remembered the appalling agony of their quarrel. But that was absurd. His had been a shallow pain, centered on his selfish need to preserve his freewheeling bachelor ways. Love had been the farthest thing from his mind.

Yes, Grant would have married her, but he would have

grown to despise her for trapping him into wedlock. She had chosen instead to accept Robert's offer, for it had been tendered with true affection.

She drew a shaky breath. "Robert and I were very happy together. He was a devoted, settled man, exactly the husband I needed. And I found that we shared many of the same interests."

With a pang of nostalgia, she remembered the long walks they had taken, the way he had coddled her. They had remained on the estate for the duration of her pregnancy, and thankfully, Lucien had been tardy in putting in his appearance, just barely enough to waylay any gossip. With the birth, Robert had been as ecstatic as any father holding his firstborn son . . .

Grant gave a low, harsh laugh. "You needn't pretend with me, Sophie. You and Robert were as different as oil and water. You loved the thrill of danger the same way I did. You still do."

"No," she said sharply. "I examined my heart and realized that I couldn't tolerate my own rash behavior. I wanted a family and a happy marriage as my parents had shared. I found that with Robert."

"You also found a title, wealth, and a position at the top of society."

Sophie stiffened. She had uttered that lie to Grant at a time when she had been desperate to resist the temptation of his forced offer. "Are you *trying* to find fault with my marriage?" she said with frosty disdain. "If so, you're being impossibly rude and I see no point in continuing."

Grant arched a dark eyebrow. "Pardon me," he said in a milder tone. "So you and Robert settled down to a quiet domestic life. You bore his heir and the three of you lived happily. Until Robert fell ill last summer."

"Yes, and he was an excellent father, I must add. Lucien misses him dreadfully." To her chagrin, she felt the sting of tears. But she wouldn't weep in front of Grant; he would only accuse her of playacting for sympathy. That thought firmed her backbone. It was time she directed the conversation to a subject that had been weighing on her mind. "Speaking of Lucien, I would like to settle his future. In particular, his schooling."

Grant shot her a distracted frown. "He has a governess, does he not?"

Sophie nodded. "Miss Oliver is an excellent instructress, and he also has tutors in mathematics and Latin."

"Is he an indifferent student, then?"

"Quite the contrary, he's very bright and a hard worker." She paused, considering how best to convince Grant. For certain, she would leave Helena and Elliot out of the matter. "It's a family tradition to send the boys to boarding school at his age. However, Lucien has had enough upheaval in his life for now. I'd like to keep him at home for an additional year"—she forced out the last, galling phrase—"with your permission."

Grant's thoughts were hidden within the darkness of his eyes. He lounged in his chair, watching her with the cool deliberation of a king regarding an irksome peasant. Sophie clenched her teeth to keep from snapping at him to answer. It was better to remain silent than to antagonize him. In all matters involving Lucien, she needed Grant's cooperation, for he had the power to override her wishes.

Abruptly, he rose from his chair and walked to her. He held out his hand. "I'd like to observe your son in the schoolroom. Will you take me there?"

28 October 1701

I fear Mulford suspects my faithlessness. 'Twas due to my own folly in sending a note to William, begging him for a secret Rendezvous at a Ball given by Lady Hearthstone. With penitence and hope at war in my Heart, I passed the time until the appointed hour by dancing with many partners, including two sets with the Esteemed Mulford.

As on other occasions, he spoke little to me, and in due course, went off to another chamber to play cards with the gentlemen. Whilst my parents were otherwise engaged, I slipped outside and found my True Love. O, the Kisses he did rain upon my person! Alas, our happiness was doomed, for as we were locked in love's embrace, Mulford came outside in search of me.

——the diaries of Annabelle Chatham Ramsey, 3rd Duchess of Mulford

6

To Grant's satisfaction, Sophie hesitated only a moment before placing her hand on his sleeve. She rose gracefully, a nymph with pale skin and coppery brown hair. The black mourning gown embraced her beautiful breasts and skimmed the slender curves of waist and hips. But he was no fool to trust that aura of demure submissiveness. When she glanced up at him, a spark of rebellion glinted in those expressive green eyes. Sophie would accept his polite gesture, but only for one reason.

She wanted to maneuver him.

Well, he wanted something in return.

She started to step away, but he tucked her fingers into

the crook of his arm. At once, he experienced the rush of primitive desire. The softness of her skin brought to mind warm, velvety, hidden places. Places he intended to explore in the very near future.

But had those dainty hands administered poison?

As they strolled out of the library and into the corridor, Sophie gave him a sidelong, assessing look. "We've spoken only of me. What have *you* been doing these past ten years?"

Prowling through palaces. Stealing rare jewels. Running from armed guards. "Traveling."

"You've been to Constantinople—and many other exotic places, I'm sure. But since I've been frank with you, perhaps you'll do me the same honor."

Had she been frank with him? He doubted it. Lowering his voice to a caressing murmur, he said, "If you must know, I've been to Italy, Germany, Russia, and a host of countries in between. Sometime, we'll sit down together and I'll tell you all about my adventures."

"That isn't what I meant." Their footsteps echoed in the vast corridor lined with portraits of long-dead Ramsey ancestors. She regarded him with guileless eyes. "Your father cut you off without a penny. I'm curious as to how you could afford to live abroad."

His gut twisted. But he had sworn long ago never to waste another thought on the Earl of Litton. "Gambling," he lied. "A few years ago, I won the pot in a high-stakes game in Rome."

"I see." Her eyes were cool, faintly haughty. He knew what she was thinking, that he very likely had gone back to the tables and lost every last pence.

Though it was stupidly prideful, he said, "I put my stake in a number of shipping ventures, and the investments have paid off handsomely. I'm a wealthy man now."

Her eyes widened slightly, then unexpectedly she

laughed. "Invested your ill-gotten gains? Really, Grant. I don't know whether to congratulate you or chastise you."

Why don't you kiss me? Grant held back the question; the time was not yet right. But he was enchanted by the mirth on her face. Sophie had a smile like no other woman, a smile that animated her beauty and sparkled in her eyes, a smile that expressed a reckless exuberance for life. A smile that he hadn't seen since he'd taken her innocence and then shocked himself by offering to marry her.

She had thrown the offer in his face.

As if suddenly ashamed of her nakedness, Sophie drew the bedsheets up to her chin. Her eyes were a cool, clear green, devoid of the passion she'd displayed only moments ago. "You're right, this was a mistake," she said in a sharp tone. "I can't marry you, Grant. I thought you knew that. The man I wed will have money and a title. He won't be a wretch who's a pariah in his own family . . ."

The memory still stung, far more than it ought. He would possess Sophie again, and this time she wouldn't push him away afterward. He would give her no opportunity to do so. He would wear down her defenses and enslave her with endless pleasure. Then, when he had her breathless and vulnerable, he would coax a confession from her.

But for now, Sophie was as skittish as a mare in heat. It would require skilled handling to prevent her from fleeing the inevitable mating.

As they reached the entrance hall, he took her hand, lightly stroking the tender skin of her palm. Always before, she had melted at that subtle caress. This time, however, Sophie tensed and attempted a retreat. He held on to her, determined to find her vulnerabilities. All of them.

Bending his head closer, he murmured, "Enough about me. Tell me about Lucien."

Sophie's heart jolted with a fear that had nothing to do with his relentless stroking of her hand. Alarm choked her throat. She had wondered at the closed expression, his momentary lapse into silence. Dear God, had Grant guessed the truth? Did he suspect that Lucien was his son?

In the next breath, she realized the absurdity of her fright. His dark eyes burned, not with anger, but with male hunger. His gaze rested on her lips as if he craved her kiss. And her willful body responded with a deep-seated throb of desire.

She turned toward the graceful arc of the grand staircase. This time, when she tugged at his hold, he released her, allowing her to lift the hem of her long skirts as she ascended the steps. Her palm still tingled from his touch, but she concentrated on making casual conversation. "You've already met my son," she said carefully. "What else do you wish to know about him?"

Grant mounted the stairs with her. "What are his interests aside from tin soldiers? Does he dislike being confined to the classroom as much as I once did? Does he ever slide down the banister for fun?"

Sophie's entire mind focused on that last question. Her stomach clenched as she glanced downward at the dizzying expanse of marble floor in the foyer. "He most certainly does not!"

"A pity." Grant rubbed his hand along the curving oak balustrade. "As I recall, this one gives an excellent ride."

Her steps faltered as she noticed the gleam in his eyes. What if Grant used his powers of guardianship to influence her son? The thought made her feel ill. "You're not to encourage Lucien to take such a dangerous risk," she said urgently. "I want your promise on that."

"I've no intention of harming a child. But he is a boy—"

"A very small, quiet boy. He's not as rambunctious as you undoubtedly once were. Now give me your promise."

Grant frowned, then shrugged. "If it pleases you, I won't send him careening down the banister."

"Thank you." Sophie breathed a little easier. She would watch Grant to make certain he kept his word. Besides, he would soon realize how humdrum the duties of a guardian were, and then he wouldn't be troubling her any longer. "Now, as to your other questions, Lucien enjoys walks in the park and sailing his toy boat on the pond. And he loves learning. But I'll let you see that for yourself."

Upon arriving at the third-floor landing, she swept ahead of Grant, leading the way to the schoolroom midway down the corridor. The door stood open, and she could hear the faint sound of Miss Oliver's modulated tones.

Aware of Grant close at her heels, Sophie paused in the doorway. Lucien sat at a table with his back to the door, his small form bent over a book. The governess sat beside him, pointing out an illustration in the volume. She was a pleasant woman in her forties, large-boned and sturdy, and given to wearing high-necked gowns of serviceable gray.

Sunlight bathed the spacious, oblong chamber with its maps on the walls and the low shelves filled with textbooks. The comfortable scents of chalk and pencil shavings and beeswax usually gave Sophie a sense of well-being, but not today. Today she was altogether too conscious of Grant.

She rapped lightly on the doorframe, and Miss Oliver rose quickly and curtsied. Smiling, the governess adjusted the gold-rimmed spectacles perched on her nose. "Your Grace. Lucien and I wondered if you would come by today."

When she cast an inquiring look at Grant, Sophie said, "Miss Oliver, this is Lucien's guardian, Mr. Chandler."

As Grant exchanged greetings with the governess, Lucien fairly bounced on his chair, his face wreathed in a smile. "You came back, Mr. Chandler! You really did!"

Grant's expression eased into a grin, and he ruffled the boy's hair. "I said I would."

"Uncle Elliot always promises, but *he* hardly ever comes to visit."

"Lucien," Sophie corrected gently, "you shouldn't criticize your uncle."

"The boy has every right to speak the truth," Grant countered. He bent down to address her son. "I'd say Uncle Elliot is a ninny for making promises he doesn't keep. And a dunderhead, too."

"A ninny," Lucien repeated with relish. "A silly, dunderhead ninny!"

"Right you are."

Watching their male camaraderie, Sophie felt torn between the undisciplined urge to laugh and the need to teach her son manners. "Name-calling is not allowed in this house," she said sternly. "Miss Oliver, pray continue with your lesson. If you don't mind, we shall observe for a little while."

"Certainly, Your Grace. We were just finishing a history lecture about King Henry the Fifth."

Sophie directed Grant to a small table nearby. She seated herself on one of a pair of half-size chairs for children. He grimaced at the one opposite her, then perched on the edge of the table instead, so close that his leg brushed hers.

As Miss Oliver resumed the lesson, Sophie sat rigidly upright on her seat in stark contrast to his relaxed pose. Only half-listening, she tried to fathom her roiling emotions. She didn't want Lucien to form a bond with Grant. She didn't want Grant gainsaying her instructions, either. And she certainly didn't want to sit so near to him. His masculine scent intoxicated her; his overbearing presence dominated her awareness. He disturbed her in an elemental way, disrupting the quiet pleasure of observing her son.

His son.

A pang struck her heart. She couldn't stop a series of morbid questions from pushing into her mind. What if she had gone to Grant instead of Robert all those years ago? Would Grant have welcomed the prospect of becoming a father? Or would he have viewed her pregnancy as yet another trap to end his carefree ways?

Her palms felt damp and cold. No, Grant was *not* a family man. He would *not* have wanted the responsibility. And she must never speculate otherwise, for it was disloyal to Robert's memory.

Miss Oliver cleared her throat. "Lucien, perhaps you would tell your guests what you've learned today."

Lucien looked far from willing. Ducking his chin, he stood up slowly. He fidgeted with the buttons on his fine blue coat, then used the toe of one shoe to scratch his ankle as he slid an imploring glance first at Grant and then at Sophie.

She bit her lip to keep from interfering. She and Miss Oliver had agreed that Lucien needed to become more comfortable with recitations, for the skill would be required of him when he went away to school. She gave him an encouraging smile. "I know you are very good at memorizing," she prodded gently. "What do you know of King Henry the Fifth?"

"B-born 1387, d-died 1422, b-buried at Westminster Abbey." He glanced at Miss Oliver, who nodded at him to go on. "Er . . . he wanted to conquer the French, and he defeated them at A—A—"

"Agincourt," Grant said. He rose to his feet and strolled around the schoolroom. "It was an enormous battle and the English were outnumbered. But under Henry's brilliant leadership, the English archers and knights managed to crush the French."

Lucien perked up. "Knights?"

"In shining armor with great blades of steel." Grant took up a long wooden pointer and brandished it like a sword. "It was the Middle Ages, at the height of chivalry. Our English knights were the bravest, finest fighters the world had ever seen. They rode into battle on great destriers—"

"Des—what is that?"

"A destrier is a large warhorse bred for its strength. You see, all that armor on a knight weighed quite a lot—in fact, even the horses wore armor."

"My book said nothing about that," Lucien said doubtfully.

"It's the truth. You see, if a knight lost his mount, he wouldn't be able to gallop straight at the enemy and kill them with his lance." In Grant's nimble hand, the pointer became a lance thrusting out at an invisible foe.

Clearly fascinated, Lucien ventured a few steps toward him. "I should like to know everything about knights. Please, sir, will you tell me?"

"Better yet, we could visit the Tower and see the armor and weaponry on display." Grant cast an enigmatic look at Sophie. "However, your mother may have an opinion on the matter."

Lucien darted to her, practically bowling her over in his excitement. "May we, Mummy? Please?"

Sophie found herself caught in a dilemma. Her pragmatic side told her that Lucien needed a dependable daily routine in his life. He needed to keep regular study habits, so that when the time came for him to go away to school he would be able to apply himself diligently. Yet she also could understand his enthusiasm for knights; she herself had been entertained by Grant's descriptions. More than that, however, Lucien's enthusiasm decided her.

"Well," she said briskly, "if you promise to work especially hard on your studies with Miss Oliver, I see no reason why we shouldn't have an outing."

"I'll study day and night," Lucien vowed fervently. He tugged on Sophie's arm. "Come, might we go right now?"

Amused, she shook her head. "Tomorrow will be soon enough, for we'll want to get an early start. But we mustn't expect Mr. Chandler to accompany us. He's no doubt a busy man." *Who couldn't possibly enjoy spending a full day in the company of a young child.*

She conveyed that silent message to Grant, frowning at him in a meaningful way. He stood with one foot propped on a stool, looking every inch the gentleman rogue in his charcoal-gray coat, skintight breeches, and polished black Hessians. He met her challenging stare with a rakish quirk of his lips, as if he enjoyed tormenting her.

"I wouldn't miss it for the world."

Grant detested pomposity. It was especially unpalatable in a physican whose fancy office exhibited all the gruesome implements of his trade.

Glass-fronted display cases housed tools worthy of a torturer from the Inquisition: knives and saws, forceps and scalpels, suture needles and cautery irons. Another wall held shelves of herbs and potions, enough to rival a chemist's shop. In one corner, a human skeleton stared sightlessly from empty eyesockets.

Dr. Felix Atherton bristled with self-importance as he seated himself behind an expansive mahogany desk. He was a large man of well-fed proportions, his face florid beneath an old-fashioned powdered wig. With an air of impatience, he consulted his gold timepiece. "I'm afraid I can give you only a few minutes of my time, Mr. Chandler. I'm scheduled to call at Carleton House within the hour, and the Regent dislikes being kept waiting."

Unimpressed and too restless to sit, Grant paced to a grisly display of human organs embalmed in jars. "I've just returned from an extended trip abroad. I was a friend of the Duke of Mulford's, and I'm inquiring about the circumstances of his death. You were his physician, were you not?"

"I was, indeed. However, it would be most improper for me to divulge private information about a case. You would do better to speak to his family."

Grant aimed a lordly stare at the physician. "As guardian to the present duke, I must demand that you answer my questions."

Atherton's nostrils flared with indignation. But apparently he saw the value of complicity, for he said tightly, "Go on, then."

"What were his symptoms? And what was your diagnosis?"

"His Grace was struck by an attack of colic and biliousness, exhibited by vomiting and diarrhea, and complicated by a rapid heartbeat. Since the illness came upon him shortly after dinner one evening, 'twas my belief he had ingested a spoilt foodstuff, possibly a prune tart which no one else in the household had consumed."

"What was your treatment?"

"A tincture of pennyroyal to encourage the expelling of bile, and of course, a rigorous course of phlebotomy— bloodletting—to purge the tainted humors from his system."

Grant's stomach clenched. Gad, he hated to think of

Robert suffering. "And when that didn't work, what did you do? Did you call in another physician?"

"I consulted with my colleagues at the Royal College of Physicians, as I always do in the more difficult cases. They were in full agreement with my course of treatment."

"Even though Mulford continued to worsen?"

"Unfortunately," Atherton said in a condescending tone, "medical science cannot cure all illnesses. The fate of every patient ultimately lies in the hands of God."

Or in the hands of a murderer. *Sophie.* Forcing a bland expression, Grant said, "Tell me, Doctor. Did it ever occur to you that Mulford might have been deliberately poisoned?"

Atherton recoiled, his face aghast. "Are you suggesting . . . murder? That is preposterous!"

"Mulford himself put the idea in my mind. He wrote to me on his deathbed, expressing precisely that fear."

The physician stared in abject disbelief. "What? I've heard nothing of it! Who did he name?"

"No one in particular. The letter was rather disjointed."

"Ah!" Atherton said with a nod of comprehension. "His Grace was delirious toward the end. No doubt it was an illusion brought on by his reduced mental capabilities."

"Was it? The symptoms of arsenic poisoning bear a close similarity to the colic you described."

"Bah. He would have died at once, then, instead of lingering for a fortnight. And I can assure you, His Grace consumed no more prune tarts—indeed, he could barely swallow a bit of beef broth."

Grant wanted to seize the man by his stiff white collar and shake him out of his rigid skepticism. A physician of his training should have been alert for poison. After receiving that letter, Grant had studied poisons. Odorless and nearly tasteless, arsenic seldom could be detected in food. For centuries it had been the poison of choice, dating all the way back to ancient Rome. "Additional doses of arsenic could have been added to the broth," Grant said. "Or to his medication. Surely you can at least admit to the possibility."

"To do so would be an insult to his loved ones. Should I accuse Her Grace, who tended him faithfully, without sleep or a care for her own health? Or perhaps his sister, his cousin, his servants?" Atherton decisively shook his head. "I saw nothing but anxiety and distress in all of them."

Grant could imagine Sophie playing the distraught wife. This morning, looking beautiful and innocent in her black mourning gown, she had claimed to have been gloriously happy with Robert. But Grant had seen for himself her chameleon skills. On the night he'd taken her virginity, she had declared her undying love for him, then had turned right around and thrown his marriage proposal in his face.

She was more than capable of deception.

He gritted his teeth to hold in his anger. "A killer would hardly show glee, thereby announcing his—or her—guilt."

"Enough, Mr. Chandler." His face cold, Atherton rose from his chair to point his finger at Grant. "You are making a grave accusation against a member of a highly respected noble family, and I will not be a party to your vile speculations. If necessary, I shall testify to that fact in a court of law."

Frustrated, Grant forced himself to bow politely. "Rest assured, Doctor. I've no plans at present to call you to the witness stand."

Striding out the door, he felt as if he'd run into a brick wall. So much for his hope that the doctor would shed light on the case.

But Grant had plenty of other witnesses to interview:

Helena, Elliot, the chef, the other servants. And he would pursue Sophie with relentless charm. She wanted him already; there was no mistaking the quickening of her breath and the longing in her eyes whenever he drew near her. Once she trusted him again, she would succumb to his seduction—and she would confess to her crime.

Then he would make her pay.

29 October 1701 (continued)

When Mulford stepped into the gardens, William released me from his embrace and made to draw his sword. Only my whispered plea kept him from spilling Mulford's blood. Brushing one last sweet kiss o'er my lips, my True Love bade me farewell. Then he melted into the shadows of the stone wall.

I confess, my heart pounded mightily with fear as I set forth to meet my Betrothed on the pathway. Mulford demanded to know why I had left my chaperon. I scarce recall the lies that spilled from my tongue, my wish to admire the moon, to escape the crush of the ballroom. He listened in frosty silence, his manner so aggrieved that I knew the Shame of my conduct.

I hereby record my Vow to resist the lure of Temptation. Tho' my heart breaks, I shall not meet William again. I shall not!

—*the diaries of Annabelle Chatham Ramsey, 3rd Duchess of Mulford*

7

The next morning, Sophie awakened with a lightness of spirit that she hadn't felt in a very long time. She wanted to attribute the thrill inside her to the gorgeous spring sunshine and the expectation of an outing with Lucien. Yet deep down, she knew that part of her giddy anticipation sprang from the prospect of spending the day in Grant's company.

He was all charm and courtesy when he came for them in his sporty yellow curricle. Lucien perched between them on the high seat, chattering nonstop, asking Grant numerous questions about the equipage, the passing sites, and the Royal Armory at the Tower, all of which Grant answered with remarkable patience. With a pang, she realized Lucien had been too long in the company of only herself, Helena, and Miss Oliver. Her son was starved for male companionship. Perhaps—as Caroline had pointed out—Sophie was, too.

A special warmth glowed inside her whenever she looked at Grant. The breeze ruffled his black hair and the sunlight caressed his strong features, reminding her of earlier times, when he had taken her on wild jaunts out of the city, driving too fast and making her laugh with exhilaration. His devil-may-care approach to life had drawn out the sense of adventure in her, tempting her beyond the border of propriety.

Sophie certainly didn't want her son to model his behavior after such a rascal. Yet even though she knew the danger of allowing Lucien to elevate Grant to the status of a hero, she convinced herself that a few hours would do no real harm. For now, she would set aside her misgivings and enjoy the day.

After a cold and gloomy winter, the sun shone brightly and the birds twittered in the trees. They left the carriage with a groom and joined the throng of tourists outside the fortress to purchase entry tickets and a small guidebook. Lucien gazed around with goggle-eyed excitement, clinging to Sophie's hand as they passed through the huge stone gatehouse where red-clad Yeoman warders stood at attention.

As the three of them strolled the Tower Green on their way to the Royal Armory, the air smelled damp and fresh, untainted despite their proximity to the river. Sophie scanned her guidebook and read bits aloud for Lucien's benefit, deeming it wise to skip over the more gruesome aspects of the castle's history. Grant, however, had no such compunction.

"Look over there," he said, pointing at a stone slab in the midst of an innocuous patch of new grass. "That's the block where the executioner swung his axe."

Lucien stopped in his tracks. In a hushed tone, he said, "Do you mean people were *beheaded* . . . right *here*?"

Grant nodded. "The Tower serves as a prison, mostly for traitors to the crown—including those who have unlawfully claimed the throne. Several kings lost their lives here during the War of the Roses. And over the years, even a few women."

"Who, Mummy?" Lucien demanded. "What does your book say?"

"Anne Boleyn, wife to King Henry the Eighth," Sophie said, checking the pamphlet. "And Lady Jane Grey. Dear heaven, she was only seventeen."

His eyes bright with interest, Lucien tugged on her arm. "Please, may I go and look?"

Sophie nodded uncertainly, and as Lucien bounded ahead, she followed more slowly with Grant. "I don't know if I like for him to be so excited over people being put to death," she said. "It's all rather grisly, isn't it?"

"Most boys are fascinated by the macabre. As he grows older, he'll turn his mind to other interests."

"But what if he suffers nightmares?"

"Is he prone to waking at night?" Grant countered.

Watching Lucien cautiously circle the block, as if imagining an execution, she shook her head. "No, he's always been a very sound sleeper."

"Then you needn't worry. After we tour the armory, he's far more likely to dream of knights riding into battle on white steeds."

Grant's reassurance eased her mind—until Sophie realized that they had been discussing Lucien as a husband and wife might talk over a problem involving their son. *Their son.* That undeniable truth formed a knot in her breast. Lucien *was* their son, although Grant would never know it. She would permit no regrets to weigh on her conscience. Long ago, she had made the only sensible choice in securing her child's future. Grant hadn't wanted a wife or a family; he had made that clear in no uncertain terms.

Today, however, contrary to her expectations, he seemed to enjoy Lucien's company. Yet she knew better than to pin any real significance to that fact. It wasn't in Grant's nature to take his responsibilities seriously. Lucien was no more than a temporary diversion. Grant sought amusement in new experiences, but when the novelty wore off, he moved on to something else. She had witnessed that flaw too many times to believe otherwise.

Lucien came skipping back, and Sophie was relieved to see that he appeared unaffected by his examination of the executioner's block. He bade them hurry to the Royal Armory, and they proceeded there at once.

After the warm sunshine, the stone building was cold and dank. As she stepped over the threshold and into the first display chamber, Grant politely held her arm. Awareness of him tingled over her skin, causing her to shiver. She said quickly, "It's chilly in these old castles."

"It is, indeed," he murmured.

In a seemingly casual gesture, he slid his hand down the back of her pelisse, his palm coming to rest at the base of her spine. The light pressure felt unbearably intimate. Warmth spread through her hidden places, and she felt a deep pulsebeat of desire.

Perhaps you should have an affair with him.

Caroline's suggestion of the previous day held a shocking allure. Ever since, Sophie had unable to purge it from her thoughts. Her friend didn't know that Sophie had already been introduced to the intense pleasure of Grant's lovemaking, that for years, she had successfully repressed the memory. But with his return had come a flood of images and feelings.

The caress of his hands and mouth on her flesh. The weight of his body covering hers. The indescribable joy of becoming one with him.

Dismayed by her weakness, she glanced up at Grant. He was undoubtedly trying to beguile her—or was that merely her fevered mind at work? He wasn't even looking at her, and the Grant she remembered would have been teasing, charming, attentive. He had been a master of repartee, his witty commentary stimulating her in both body and mind. But now she sensed a self-restraint in him that had not been present all those years ago. An iron wall of reserve hid his thoughts from her.

Yet as they toured the armory, he took her hand to draw her over to a display of swords, touched her shoulder to show her an old musket, held her elbow to guide her into the next chamber. More than once, she caught him eyeing her speculatively. It was as if he were watching and waiting . . .

Thankfully, Lucien was oblivious to the undercurrents. He was too enthralled by the displays of medieval weaponry and instruments of torture. In one long chamber, effigies of the kings of England were mounted on horses, each monarch clad in full armor as if heading into battle. Grant entertained the boy with tales of knightly valor, while Sophie added snippets of history, using the opportunity to bring the past to life for Lucien.

Afterward, they purchased hot meat pies from a vendor, which they ate while strolling the battlements. "The king would hold tournaments right here inside the castle walls," Grant told Lucien, "and the knights would joust to see who was the very best of them all. It was considered great luck to carry a token from your lady."

"A token?" Lucien said. "What's that?"

"A handkerchief or a sash of some sort." Before Sophie realized his intention, Grant plucked the dainty black fichu from inside her pelisse. He tied the scrap of lace around his upper arm, using his teeth to tighten the knot. Then he struck a courtly pose with his hands on his hips and the lacy token fluttering from his arm.

Lucien convulsed with laughter. "You look like a silly ninny."

"A silly dunderhead ninny, I imagine."

"Look, Mummy, I'm a knight. I'm off to win the tournament." Lucien scampered away down the battlement.

A lump rose in Sophie's throat, and she glanced at Grant. "It's good to see him play like any other small boy," she said in a husky tone. "Since Robert's death, he's been so quiet and forlorn."

"He's been grieving. In time, he'll recover."

There was something dark and calculating in his gaze, something that made her heart leap. "Thank you for suggesting this outing," she said. "I hadn't realized how much Lucien and I both needed it."

"It's been my pleasure."

The air seemed to shimmer with something hotter than sunshine. Grant untied her fichu from his arm and draped it around her neck again, his fingers brushing her bare skin as if by accident. She didn't know whether to be relieved or disappointed when again he ignored the opportunity to entice her. Instead, he turned away and called to Lucien to finish their tour.

They spent the afternoon viewing the crown jewels and then visiting the Lion Tower. The Menagerie was housed in an ancient stone building that smelled of animal droppings, but Lucien didn't appear to notice the rundown conditions. He exclaimed over the exotic animals, among them several lions, a grizzly bear, and an old tigress.

When they finally left the Tower, the purple shadows of dusk lay over the city. Lucien was beginning to drag his feet and roused himself only when Grant insisted on purchasing souvenirs from one of the street sellers, a miniature figurine of a knight for Lucien, and a posy of violets for Sophie. Within moments of setting out for home, Lucien leaned his head against Sophie's arm and fell fast asleep, clutching the tin knight to his chest.

She curved her arm around his small form. A wave of love washed through her, and she lightly kissed the top of his tousled hair, relishing his boyish scent of fresh air and dust. Whenever she held him of late, he seemed to have grown larger and sturdier than the last time. Aware that he wouldn't be snuggling against her for much longer, she treasured the moment.

Grant skillfully navigated the narrow streets. He glanced at her from time to time, his eyes shadowed, unreadable. He said nothing to enlighten her to his thoughts, and Sophie wisely held her silence, too. Conversation would only nurture a closeness with him, and she was no longer certain she could resist his masculine allure.

And she must resist, not just for her own sake, but for Lucien's as well. An affair would only give Grant a reason to prolong his interest in them. Already she feared that her son would be sorely disappointed when his erstwhile guardian went on his merry way.

At last the elegant mansion across from Green Park loomed through the darkness. Although the night had grown chilly, Sophie felt reluctant to go inside and end their outing. A groom held the horses as Grant leaped down from the high seat. He reached up to take Lucien from her. Cradling the sleeping boy in one strong arm, he lent a hand to Sophie.

Torches flickered on either side of the entryway, the brass fittings gleaming. A footman in blue livery opened the door for them. As they stepped into the entrance hall, she felt a curious sense of their being a family, the three of them, warm and close and happy.

"Poor fellow," Grant mused, gazing down at Lucien. "He's worn out."

"Yes, he is," she said softly.

A silver candelabrum rested on a table near the door, and its glow bathed father and son. A fringe of dark lashes edged Lucien's closed eyes, and his features had the soft innocence of youth. Yet she could see in his face the same strong bone structure as Grant's.

No. Robert was Lucien's father, Sophie firmly reminded herself. To let herself think otherwise could lead only to pain and distress.

As she shifted her attention away, she noticed Helena standing at the top of the grand staircase. Her sister-in-law stood as if transfixed, her hands pressed to her face with its birthmark stain. She looked as shocked as if she'd seen a ghost.

Sophie's heart jerked in painful strokes. *Dear God.* Had Helena noticed the likeness between Grant and Lucien? Surely the resemblance was subtle, evident only to someone who sought it . . .

All at once, Helena flowed down the steps in a mad rush. "Oh, my stars! What's happened? Is Lucien ill?"

Realizing the source of Helena's concern, Sophie breathed easier. Helena saw only Lucien lying limp as a rag doll in Grant's arms. "He's perfectly fine," she said in a hushed tone, lifting her gloved fingers to stroke the softness of her son's hair. "He fell asleep on the way home, that's all."

Helena stopped at the base of the stairs and sagged against the newel post, gripping it as if she needed its support in the aftermath of fright. "I—I thought . . . after what happened to Robert . . ."

"Forgive me for frightening you," Grant said smoothly. "It seems I haven't lost my knack for that."

Helena's lips formed a shaky smile. She stood up straight, primly clasping her hands together. "Indeed so. I've never recovered from the time you and my brother put a skull in my bed on All Hallows' Eve."

Grant chuckled. "We'll have to reminisce another time," he said. "If you don't mind, I'll take the boy upstairs to his bed."

Helena moved aside, watching as he strode past her and mounted the stairs. Before Sophie could follow, Helena caught her arm. In the candlelight, her blue eyes were eloquent with suspicion. "Why are you so late?" she whispered. "I've been very anxious this past hour."

"You needn't have worried. Lucien was fascinated by the exhibits, so we lingered a bit longer than I'd intended."

"Humph. I cannot help but wonder if that's the only reason." Helena frowned at Sophie's hand.

Sophie looked down to see that she was still holding the nosegay of violets that Grant had purchased for her. She had forgotten all about it—and the foolish thrill she'd felt when he'd presented the bouquet to her.

In the face of Helena's disapproving stare, however, she felt a surge of irritation. Even if her year of mourning wouldn't be up for several months, it was no one else's concern if she chose to accept flowers from a man.

She handed the bouquet to Helena. "If you would be so kind, have the footman place these in water for me. The silver vase in the breakfast room."

Without giving her sister-in-law a chance to complain, Sophie hastened up the staircase. She removed her kid gloves and tossed them onto a chair on the landing. Ascending the next flight of steps, she untied her bonnet, left it on the newel post, and tidied her hair. She had something to ask Grant, and she needed to look her best.

At the third floor, she caught up to him and led the way to the nursery, located in the same suite of rooms as the schoolroom.

Miss Oliver was sitting in the rocking chair by the hearth, her nimble fingers working a pair of knitting needles. She rose at once, clucking over her charge as Grant laid him down in the bed. Lucien grumbled, but didn't open his eyes, the toy knight still locked in his fist.

"I'll see that he readies himself for bed, Your Grace," Miss Oliver said comfortingly. "He'll be a bit cross to be awakened, but he's a good-natured child."

Sophie leaned down to press a gentle kiss to her son's brow. He was her dearest purpose in life, and she fervently thanked God every day for the miracle of his existence. She allowed herself to remember that Lucien had been conceived in love . . . or at least love had been in *her* heart. On that bittersweet thought, she turned to find Grant watching them.

Or more precisely, watching *her*. A smoldering quality heated his dark eyes. A thrill shimmered through her, but Sophie shunned the reaction. Did he think that with Lucien out of the way, he was free to wage his campaign of seduction?

She wouldn't give him the opportunity.

As they left the nursery and walked out into the empty corridor, she said politely, "Now that you've spent some time with Lucien, will you consider my petition?"

"Petition?" Grant shot her a distracted frown. "Oh, his schooling."

Sophie inclined her head in a regal nod. "As I said, my son hasn't had enough of a chance to recover from the loss of his father. I don't believe he'll be ready to go away to boarding school come autumn."

"Or perhaps it's his mother who isn't ready," Grant observed.

The hint of levity in his tone pierced Sophie's composure. "I beg your pardon?" she said icily. "I've always done what's best for my son. I've never let my own wishes sway me—"

"Sheathe your claws," Grant said, his amusement more obvious now. Taking hold of her hands, he brought them to his mouth, kissing each in turn. "I shouldn't tease you. You can be quite fearsome when it comes to your son."

The stirring warmth of his touch threatened to beguile her, so she withdrew her hands. She detested having to curry his favor, but for Lucien's sake, she modulated her tone. "Does that mean you'll approve my request?"

"Yes, keep him here if you like." Before Sophie could feel more than a moment's relief, Grant reached out to caress her cheek. "There, now, have I soothed your temper? You needn't look around for something to throw at me."

"I don't have a temper. Not anymore." It was a lie, and they both knew it, but Sophie held her head high. She would play the duchess if it would discourage him from pursuing her.

"More's the pity," he murmured. "I've always admired the fire in you."

"That is precisely why you and I never suited. You brought out the worst in me."

Turning, Sophie headed down the dim-lit corridor with its plush carpet and muted gold wallpaper. She should have known he wouldn't give up so easily. His arms surrounded her from behind, enfolding her against the solid male strength of his body. Grant smelled of wind and wildness, and his heat seared her like a living flame, warming every fiber of her body. Heaven help her, it felt so good to be held by a man. By *this* man . . .

If she'd had the slightest doubt about his intentions, she knew the truth with a dizzying certainty. Grant played a game of seduction. All day, he had been maneuvering her to this moment.

"Sophie," he murmured. "We *did* suit. Remarkably, amazingly well."

Determined to hide her inner turmoil, she held herself stiff and rigid. Struggling would only bring her in closer contact with his body. She must show him that she was impervious to his touch. "I was young and stupid."

"You were beautiful and bright—and chafing at the bit to experience life." His lips touched the nape of her neck. "I wanted you from the instant I spied you, watching from the front of the crowd while I raced my curricle."

With crystal-like clarity, Sophie remembered that moment. It had been prior to the start of the Season, her mother having brought her to London in late winter to purchase an extensive wardrobe in preparation for her debut. Although Sophie wasn't supposed to mingle with the *ton* yet, she had been returning from the dressmaker's in the company of a maid when she had spied the throng of gentlemen and ladies gathered in Hyde Park.

Curiosity getting the better of her, she bade the driver to stop. She intended to look only from a distance, but the excitement of the race lured her closer, and she found herself cheering the forerunner, a yellow curricle driven by a dashing buck. She heard his name bandied about by the ladies. *"Oh, that devilish Grant Chandler. I hear he's a stallion in the bedchamber."* *"Mmm, he can enjoy my favors for free."* In her naïveté, she hadn't realized until later that they were not ladies at all but members of the *demi-monde,* that class of fallen women who entertained wealthy noblemen in exchange for money and jewels.

But at the time Sophie had been too fascinated by the object of their admiration to consider any impropriety. In a daze of wonder, she had watched his long-legged elegance in leaping down from the carriage, his rakish smile as he'd accepted congratulations and slaps on the back from the other gentlemen. He had come straight toward her then, and led her away from the others. He had gazed into her eyes . . . and she had fallen in love. Her mistake was believing he'd loved her, too.

Now, wrapped in his close embrace, she was irked to find herself *still* wanting to believe it. "Whatever we had is gone. There is no point to dredging up the mistakes of the past."

"Was it a mistake?" he asked, his breath warm against her ear. "We found a rare passion together. It's never been so extraordinary for me, not before or since."

Sophie veered between an entirely inappropriate pleasure at his declaration and another, newer emotion. It couldn't be jealousy. What did she care about his other women? He could make love to half the female population of the world, and it wouldn't matter to her. In her haughtiest tone, she said, "This conversation has gone beyond all propriety. Release me at once."

Instead, Grant turned her in his arms. She found herself caught between the wall of the corridor and his broad chest, trapped by the stimulating pressure of his body. Tilting up her chin, he looked deeply into her eyes. "Tell me you've forgotten what we shared, Sophie," he said roughly. "Just tell me that sincerely and I'll go."

She looked straight at him and lied. "I've forgotten. I've completely put it out of my mind."

His eyes flashed with desire and frustration and something darker, something dangerous. "Then allow me to remind you, duchess."

His mouth swooped down to ply hers with a practiced skill that could only have been inspired by the devil himself. When she tried to turn her head aside, his hands held her in place while his tongue coaxed its way inside to wreak the magic she remembered so well. But oh, sweet heaven, memory paled beneath the reality of his kiss. Sophie's breasts ached and her legs weakened, and she would have collapsed if not for his firm support. In a futile attempt to keep him at a distance, she put her hands between them, pressing her fingers to his smooth coat. But he seemed only to take that as a challenge. Caressing her with his mouth, his hands, his body, he continued his relentless assault on her senses.

She both craved and despised his expertise, for even through the daze of desire, she recognized the calculated nature of his seduction. His manner was controlled and ruthless, as if he were holding his own passion in check. He wasn't even breathing hard. He wanted to enrapture her to prove his point, and blast him, she would not relent unless he did, too.

Somehow, that resolution took on greater importance than resisting him. Spurred by recklessness, she molded herself to his hard form, wreathing her arms around his neck and running her hands through his hair. The strands were as thick and silken as she remembered, and she traced his ears with light fingertips in the way that he had once professed to love. Dimly aware that she was playing with fire, she undulated her hips, determined to ensure his arousal despite the layers of clothing between them.

Sophie savored the moment that passion laid waste to his control. He groaned deep in his chest and his hands tightened on her shoulders. His caresses took on a fervid quality; his kiss grew ravenous, demanding. But her triumph was short-lived, lost to the madness that coursed through her own veins. She felt intoxicated by his taste, invigorated by his scent, and she absorbed him as if she had been parched in body and soul.

He wrested open the buttons of her pelisse and slipped his hand inside her bodice. His fingers strained to reach the aching tip of one breast, and when he succeeded, she moaned as the glorious sensation seared into the deepest part of herself. The place that wept for his touch.

Through a mindless cloud of desire, she heard him mutter her name. "Sophie . . . tell me . . . where is your bedchamber?"

Opening weighted eyelids, Sophie realized he was drawing her toward the staircase, his arm snug around her waist to keep her from falling. The shock of his intention slapped her with a cold rush of reality. She wrested herself from his arms, groped for the wall to steady herself. "No, Grant. *No.*"

Frustration twisting his mouth, he reached for her. "You desire me, Sophie, every bit as much as I desire you. There's nothing stopping us from taking our pleasure of each other."

"There's my son to consider." They stood only a short distance from Lucien's quarters. If he had walked out into the corridor and seen them locked in a passionate embrace . . . if *anyone* had seen them . . . The horrifying thought gave strength to her voice. "I won't have an affair. Especially not *here.*"

Grant pulled her close, his fingers stroking the sensitive skin of her throat. "Then we'll go to my house. We'll be completely alone there, free to indulge ourselves."

The proposal had a dark, depraved appeal that threatened her wisdom. She could once again experience the powerful, combustive joy of mating. She could bask in the pleasure of knowing that a man desired her. In desperation, Sophie voiced her deepest fear. "I can't be so irresponsible, Grant. Don't you see? You might get me with child." *Again.*

That gave him pause. A muscle tightened in his jaw. "There are methods of prevention," he said. "Surely you know that, since you haven't spoiled your figure but once."

His harsh insult cut into Sophie. He believed her to be shallow and vain, allowing her husband only one child. How little he knew of her—and Robert. With cold resolve, she stepped away. "The subject is closed. I must ask you to leave. At once."

Grant regarded her a moment, as if gauging her mood. Then he afforded her a cool nod. "As you wish, duchess. But know this—it isn't over between us." Turning, he headed down the stairs.

As his footsteps faded away, Sophie stood in the silent corridor and rubbed her arms. She felt cold and bereft, and she resented him for that. She had been perfectly content to live without a man, but Grant had reawakened the passion in her, the impossible yearning for a love she had turned her back on long ago.

It isn't over between us.

Yes, it was over, it had to be over. She had believed herself cured of her affliction for him—or at least mature enough to control her reckless impulses. But tonight had proven how easily she could fall from grace again. She had been ready to abandon all pride and decency for a few fleeting moments of ecstasy.

Dear God, his kiss . . . his wonderful, stirring, passionate kiss . . .

It was difficult to forget Grant when his taste and scent and touch still haunted her. How was it that he could wield such power over her? How could he make her forget that the loss of her reputation would heap scandal upon her son?

Lucien. Sophie focused her mind on him. For Lucien's sake, she must fight temptation. And she couldn't help wondering how wise she had been to antagonize her son's guardian.

'Tis Guy Fawkes Night, when the glorious defeat of Infamy is celebrated throughout all of England. There was a bonfire in our Square, and I was permitted to attend the festivities in the company of my Faithful Mary. O, what a wondrous delight! Bells pealed all over London, and cannon boomed in the distance. Old Colonel Dickenson marched the stuffed effigy of Fawkes 'round the street, leading a parade of cheering citizens, both noble and servant alike. Amid a roar of hurrahs, I found myself encircled by a man's arms.

'Twas William! He drew me into the shadows, where we kissed with all the ardor of Forbidden Love. In my weakened state, I promised to meet him at his rooms on the morrow.

O, what am I to do? Shall I break my vow to remain true to Mulford? Or break the heart of my dearest William?

—the diaries of Annabelle Chatham Ramsey, 3rd Duchess of Mulford

8

The following afternoon, disgruntled and frustrated after a fruitless day of investigation, Grant stopped his mount before an elegant town house on Park Lane. The weather had turned as nasty as his mood, and a cold downpour threatened to soak him to the skin. He tossed his dripping hat and greatcoat to the footman by the front door, then stomped into the parlor to announce himself.

Aunt Phoebe sat on a chaise like a queen, her beringed fingers wielding a quill as she penned a letter at her lapdesk. She resembled old Queen Bess, with heavy-lidded brown eyes, pale skin, and a haughty nose beneath iron-gray hair. In manner too she had a decisive, commanding quality that set her apart from lesser beings. Unlike the Virgin Queen, however, his aunt had buried three titled husbands, declaring after the last one that she would live alone lest she deplete the aristocracy of yet another of its ranks.

Spying him, Lady Phoebe showed no visible surprise, as if he'd been gone for a few days instead of nearly a decade. She placed her pen in its holder and then fixed him with a regal glare. "I see you've finally deigned to visit me. Randolph said he saw you at his club."

Grant tensed at the mention of his brother. But he didn't intend to quarrel with his aunt. He needed to use her network of informants. "So I've been found out," he said lightly, giving her a charming smile. "Can you ever forgive me?"

"Humph. Considering that you are my heir, it would have been prudent of you to call upon me at once. But then, you're seldom prudent."

She extended her age-spotted hand for him to kiss. Instead, Grant leaned down to give her a peck on her powdered cheek. Her flowery scent evoked fond memories of holidays spent in her company. She had been his refuge whenever he'd been banished from home by her brother, the almighty Earl of Litton. "Dear Aunt Phoebe, I've missed you dreadfully. May I say, you're as lovely as ever."

"Flatterer," she accused, though a small smile lifted the corners of her prim mouth. She set her lapdesk on a table, then patted the cushion beside her. "Sit down now and let me have a look at you without having to crane my neck."

"First, I need a brandy. Will you join me?"

Her eyes gleamed. "Need you ask?"

Grant went across the hall and into her library, returning with a decanter and two glasses. He filled both almost to the brim and handed one to his aunt. She took a hearty swallow, then sighed with hedonistic pleasure.

"Excellent," she said, holding her glass up to admire its amber depths. "I've missed our little chats, for I don't care to imbibe alone. I shan't turn into an old tabby adding brandy to her tea and calling it French cream."

Sitting down beside her, Grant laughed, his ill humor easing. "Then enjoy it, for I've quite a lot to tell you."

One thin brow arched, she eyed him craftily. "My sources tell me that you've been back for a fortnight. You've leased Lord Tallyrood's former town house. You're dressed in the high stare of fashion. And given that you detest debt, I would presume that means you've come into some money."

He tasted his brandy to cover his uneasiness. His aunt must never know of his thievery. As tolerant as she was, she would be devastated. "You'd do well not to ask."

"And why shouldn't I ask? After jaunting through the Continent for so many years, you should entertain me with all sorts of adventuresome tales." With an air of injury, she held up her hand. "But it shall be as you wish, provided you'll answer me this: what has kept you so busy here in London?"

He leaned back, relaxing for the first time since leaving Sophie the previous night. "I suspect you know I've been appointed guardian of young Mulford."

"Ah, yes." Aunt Phoebe drew out the words in a tone ripe with interest. "And that means you've renewed your acquaintance with the duchess."

Grant kept his expression carefully bland. On the subject of Sophie, he would offer no confidences and brook no interference. "Yes, I have. In truth, I need your advice on a rather delicate matter concerning her."

"What is it, my boy? You haven't already gotten her in the family way, have you?"

"Hell, no." He spoke sharply, denying the fantasy that had plagued him since the previous night. *You might get me with child.* He hadn't been able to rid himself of the image of Sophie pregnant with his baby. The notion should horrify him. Instead, he felt a primitive craving to brand her with the ultimate proof of possession. Dangerous, foolish thought . . .

"A pity," his aunt said with uncharacteristic wistfulness. "I'd always hoped you two would find each other again, that you would marry this time."

Ill humor took hold of him again. "Good God, Aunt. Are you still harping on that?"

"I don't *harp*. And you must admit, you did show a marked partiality for her, more than for any other woman."

"That was before she married my friend. It was a long time ago." His voice clipped, Grant rose to his feet and roamed around the parlor with its Chinese wallpaper and lacquered black cabinets. "Besides, I haven't the slightest interest in leg-shackling myself to her or anyone else. I value my freedom far too much."

Watching him pace, Aunt Phoebe sipped pensively at her brandy. "I suppose 'tis only to be expected. Your parents showed you a paltry example of marital accord. 'Tis little wonder you don't trust yourself to fall in love. Or even to admit to the possibility."

Love. That soft emotion belonged to poets and starry-eyed youths. It had nothing whatsoever to do with the lust he felt for Sophie. She obsessed him, distracted him, tempted him to forget his purpose. Only yesterday, he'd been reminded of how easily she could destroy his control. If he wasn't careful, she'd have him believing any lie that spilled from her beautiful lips.

Noting his aunt's astute brown eyes, he plucked a red rose from a porcelain vase on a table. With an exaggerated bow, he presented it to her. "*You're* the only woman I'll ever love. You and no other."

Aunt Phoebe shook her head in exasperation as she accepted the token. "You're very skilled at charming women, Grant. But I await the day when a woman will tie *you* in knots."

Sophie had already done that ten years ago. It wouldn't happen again. Impatient with the topic, he changed it. "We've strayed from the matter of importance I mentioned. Do you remember forwarding a letter to me from Mulford shortly before he died?"

"Yes. And a week later, one from Sophie, too, directly after his death." Aunt Phoebe paused. "I've wondered if he wished to reconcile with you. The need to make reparations often comes on one's deathbed."

Grant walked to the hearth and rested his arm on the mantelpiece. He took a long swallow of brandy. Regrets served no purpose. Better he should use his energies to avenge Robert's death. "Mulford had a different purpose. In his letter, he said he'd been poisoned."

"By tainted food, I heard. It's fortunate no one else in the household took ill."

"I meant, *deliberately* poisoned."

Aunt Phoebe's hand froze in the act of lifting the glass to her lips. She uttered a strangled gasp, searching his face as if to seek proof that he was jesting. "*What?* Mulford, *murdered*? I don't believe it."

"It's true. A few days ago, I interviewed Dr. Atherton, and he agreed that the symptoms of Mulford's digestive disorder bore a marked similarity to those of arsenic poisoning. Unfortunately, Atherton is too pretentious to admit he made a mistake."

"But . . . my dear boy . . . are you quite *sure*? Perhaps the duke himself was mistaken. He was very ill, perhaps delirious when he wrote to you."

"The letter had a strong ring of truth to it. Mulford was truly afraid."

Aunt Phoebe slowly shook her head. "Why would anyone do such a thing? And *who*?"

Strangely loath to put his suspicion into words, Grant said heavily, "Mulford said it was someone very dear to him. I believe the culprit is none other than the duchess herself."

His aunt stared a moment. Then she set down her glass with a sharp clink. "Sophie . . . a murderess? Absurd!"

"It isn't absurd at all. She married Mulford for his title and his money. She told me so herself. If she'd tired of him—"

"Bah. The world is filled with wives who are tired of their husbands." His aunt rose from the chaise, a tall, well-proportioned woman despite her advanced age. In a mode of abject disbelief, she paced the parlor as if searching for facts to disprove his statement. "I saw Sophie from time to time at society functions, and she seemed content with Mulford. At his funeral, she was distraught . . . she *wept*. That hardly fits the image of a murderess."

Grant steeled himself against a surge of dark emotion. "She's a brilliant actress, then. She's played the grieving widow as a means of covering up her crime."

His aunt looked unconvinced. "Did you not consider his sister, Helena? Or his cousin—what's that scrawny fellow's name? The one who always has dirt beneath his fingernails."

"Elliot," Grant supplied. Irked that his aunt seemed so anxious to discredit his theory, he struggled to keep his voice even. "And yes, I did think of them. But I found it telling that Sophie said nothing whatsoever to me of poisoning. Mulford surely would have told her of his suspicions—unless he believed *her* to be the guilty party."

"Or perhaps he was protecting her. Mulford was one of those men who views his wife as a porcelain doll to be coddled and insulated."

Grant couldn't picture Sophie permitting such conduct. It gave another enlightening glimpse into the marriage, adding a hint of clarity to his foggy understanding of her motive. If she'd despised Mulford's treatment of her . . . "Perhaps this will convince you. I believe Sophie somehow found out about the letter he posted to me. The day I went to visit her, she seemed none too pleased about my return—"

"Naturally," Aunt Phoebe said with a snort. "You spurned her ten years ago, and now she's forced to accept you as guardian to her son. That's enough to turn the most mild-mannered woman into a shrew."

He clenched his teeth. If only his aunt knew, *Sophie* had spurned *him*. She had scorned a black sheep with no prospects. "Kindly allow me to finish," he said tightly. "That very evening, someone broke into my house, struck my manservant, and ransacked my chambers."

Aunt Phoebe clutched at the back of a chair. "You cannot think that Sophie—"

"I can, indeed. She would want to destroy any proof of the poisoning."

"Was the letter stolen?"

"No, I'd hidden it well. There was nothing whatsoever missing."

"I see." As if the strength had drained from her legs, his aunt sat down again, sipping her brandy with considerably less gusto than before. "I can scarce imagine Sophie striking a man—though I suppose she would have hired a minion to do so. And yet . . ."

"And yet it's too far-fetched to be a coincidence. She murdered Robert, and I intend to prove it."

Giving his aunt a moment to absorb the truth, Grant strode to the window and stared into the pouring rain. A dull gray curtain shrouded the street with its row of stately homes. The deluge had forced most people indoors. Only a postman, bundled against the storm, splashed through the puddles on his late afternoon rounds.

Grant wondered if Sophie too might be gazing into the rain at this very moment. Was she remembering the heat of their kiss? Was she afraid that if she let him get too close, he might guess the truth? Several times over the past few days, he'd caught her looking at him with a hint of guilty desperation. Sophie was hiding an explosive secret, he was sure of it.

"Do you intend to go to Bow Street with your suspicions?" his aunt asked.

He turned from the window to face her. "No. I'll handle the matter myself, as quietly as possible. For one, there's the young duke to consider. I've no wish to see him harmed in any way."

The problem of Lucien troubled Grant. Robert's son was a bright, inquisitive, happy child, and Grant hadn't expected to enjoy viewing the world through his eyes. Nor had he expected to feel any misgivings over proving Lucien's mother guilty of murder. But he remembered how Sophie had held the sleeping boy on the way home. Her tenderness disturbed Grant more than he cared to admit. Despite her other sins, Sophie did love her son.

That was the one fact Grant still couldn't reconcile with his theory—that Sophie would have deprived her son of his father. That she would murder Robert simply because she had tired of him. She had to have had a more powerful inducement . . .

"You must find proof before you make any accusations," his aunt said musingly. "Have you interviewed anyone besides the physician?"

Grant told her about spending his day searching for the chef who had prepared the allegedly tainted prune tart. Shortly after the incident, Sophie had discharged the man without a reference, and although Grant had queried the kitchen staff at several great houses, Monsieur Ferrand seemed to have vanished from sight.

"Hmm," his aunt said. "It's doubtful any noble household would employ a man who had caused the death of a duke. However, one of the lesser gentry may have been willing to overlook that fact for the chance to have a chef of his caliber. If you like, I can make discreet inquiries."

"I was hoping you'd offer. Ferrand might be able to tell me if Sophie was in the kitchen that day while he was preparing dinner."

Chilly air seeped from the window, enhancing the coldness inside Grant. The monotonous patter of raindrops echoed his morbid mood. He forced himself to picture Sophie stealing into the kitchen with a cache of rat poison, perhaps concealed in her handkerchief. She might have gone there on a pretext, and when Ferrand's back was turned, she'd sprinkled the poison on the dessert prepared for her husband . . .

"But why?" Grant mused aloud, frustration gripping him. "Why did she do it?"

"I wonder . . . if perhaps I might know."

His gaze shot to Aunt Phoebe, who sat frowning at her hands in her lap. In an untypical show of anxiety, she absently turned one of her gold rings around and around on her finger. She appeared lost in deep reflection, as if she were weighing the sides of an important issue.

"What is it?" Grant prodded.

His aunt lifted her troubled gaze to him. "There was a

vague rumor I heard about Mulford a few years ago, unsubstantiated, you understand. I had put it out of my mind until now."

Her grave tone gave Grant a prickle of foreboding. "Go on."

"I heard that Mulford . . ." She paused as if searching for the right words. Very slowly, she went on, "That Mulford sometimes sought his pleasure not in the marriage bed . . . but with other men."

Sophie was heading for the stairs on her way to the library when Helena emerged from her chambers. She hadn't seen her sister-in-law since the previous evening, although perhaps that wasn't so odd. Aside from a brief sojourn in the schoolroom, Sophie had spent most of the day in the library. She had been diligently searching for Annabelle's diary in an attempt to push Grant from her thoughts.

She had not been successful in either task.

All day, the glowing memory of his kiss had warred with her better judgment. It had warmed the dreary cold of a rainy day. It had lent color and brightness to her surroundings. It had made her long to shed the drab black of mourning for the sunny hues of springtime: greens and yellows and pinks.

She could only imagine how Helena would react to *that*. Like any true lady, Robert's sister had been raised with a strict code of proper behavior. In fact, Sophie was somewhat surprised that she'd been spared another lecture about yesterday's excursion to the Tower. But now she braced herself for the inevitable confrontation by adopting the cool, unruffled air of a duchess.

"Good afternoon, Helena. This house must be entirely too large because I haven't seen you all day."

Amazingly, the older woman smiled. Her blue eyes

alight, she held up a stack of folded and sealed correspondence. "I've been busy in my chamber today, writing letters and invitations."

"Invitations?"

Nodding, Helena slipped her arm through Sophie's. "Come, walk downstairs with me so that I may set these out for the late afternoon post."

As they headed toward the grand staircase, Sophie puzzled at Helena's friendly manner. Why wasn't she scolding Sophie about Grant? "I don't understand. We haven't entertained since—"

"Since before my brother's death." A shadow passed over Helena's face, and she glanced away for a moment. When she looked back at Sophie, her lips formed a determined smile. "But I hardly think Robert would have wanted us to become hermits, do you? A dinner party next week will be perfectly appropriate."

Sophie couldn't stop a flash of annoyance. Hadn't Helena thought to ask her opinion? Or at the very least, to approve the guest list? "Who, may I ask, are *we* inviting?"

Her sister-in-law's smile faded into a somewhat sheepish expression. "Forgive me, I've been so caught up in my plans that I haven't fully explained. Next Thursday is Elliot's birthday. The dinner party is in *his* honor. I took the liberty of inviting a few members of the *ton*."

Elliot. Why did Sophie have the sudden suspicion that Helena was up to no good? "We've never celebrated Elliot's birthday before."

"This is a special occasion. He shall be turning forty, and that milestone is ample reason for festivity, don't you think?"

"Yes, but how do you intend to entice him here? He prefers his Roman ruins to social events—or anything else in London."

Helena sent her a look of sly amusement. "It's quite

simple. I've told him we're considering lending the Chichester artifacts to the Montagu House Museum."

Stunned, Sophie came to a halt at the top of the stairs. The previous year, a farmer's plow on one of Robert's estates had disturbed an ancient Roman gravesite containing many valuable objects, among them a gold disk, a jeweled brooch, and a number of gold and silver coins. Elliot had coveted the antiquities at once, but Robert had declared his intention of donating them to the museum. The cousins had squabbled, Robert had died before acting on his plan, and the artifacts were now stored in a bank vault.

"You're luring Elliot here under false pretenses," Sophie protested as they started down the long, curving staircase. "He'll realize that as soon as he arrives."

Helena raised an eyebrow. "Nevertheless, it's guaranteed to bring him to our doorstep in time for the dinner party, wouldn't you say?"

"Yes," Sophie conceded. "It's quite clever—diabolically so. But what's to stop him from turning straight around and departing?"

"Leave him to me. I intend for him to stay at least for a few days."

The cause of her secretive manner jolted Sophie. "If this has to do with Lucien's schooling, you needn't curry Elliot's favor. Mr. Chandler has already approved my request to let Lucien remain at home for another year."

Helena cast a faintly jaundiced look at her. "Has he, now? You certainly wasted no time in charming the man."

Sophie coolly met her gaze. "I have no interest in charming anyone. Only in doing what is best for my son."

"Then I shall leave his education to you. In the meantime, *my* interest lies in these invitations." Reaching the bottom of the stairs, Helena glided to a side table near the door. She placed the letters on a silver tray for the postman, giving the topmost one a loving caress as if it were a newborn baby.

Sophie waited by the newel post, resisting the urge to tap the toe of her slipper on the marble floor. She found it difficult to believe Helena would give up so easily in the matter of Lucien. Watching her sister-in-law return, Sophie said, "There's something you're not telling me."

Helena's mouth curved in an arch smile. "Dear Sophie, you're entirely too astute," she said. "I do indeed have a plan. You see, I've invited a number of unmarried ladies to the party. It's past time I found Elliot a wife."

The rain had stopped when Grant finally left his aunt and rode for home. With the fall of darkness, fog crept like a specter through the neighborhood, wrapping clammy fingers around trees and fences. The hollow clopping of hooves echoed off the grand houses. From time to time, the hazy yellow orb of a street lamp appeared through the mist like a watchful eye.

Grant paid little heed to the dismal scene. He was too caught up in his turbulent thoughts. Aunt Phoebe had persuaded him to stay for dinner—as she also had persuaded him not to go tearing off in a wild fury to confront Sophie. He had been in a devil of a temper, and although he had curbed his violent reaction, his aunt's disclosure continued to roil beneath the surface of his rigid control.

Mulford sometimes sought his pleasure not in the marriage bed . . . but with other men.

The words had hit Grant as hard as a kick to the stomach. He had been incredulous and scoffing, furious and contentious. He still felt at war with himself, his mind caught in a struggle to reconcile two opposing images of his friend. Quiet, proud, well-mannered Robert, a sodomist? Impossible!

Grant swore under his breath. Bloody hell, he would have known. *He would have known!*

But his aunt had reminded him of a number of facts. He and Robert had formed their fast friendship in childhood. By the time they were of an age to notice the fairer sex, they had already gone their separate ways, Robert to Eton and Grant to Harrow. In adulthood, they'd met only for an occasional dinner to reminisce over old times. Every argument Grant had brought up, his aunt had countered with a plausible explanation.

"Dammit, he courted women—he married one."

"So he hid the truth from the world. Can you blame him? Sodomy is punishable by death."

"He fathered a son."

"Such men often do have children. A wife and family are the perfect cover for their propensity."

"He never once made any advance toward me."

His aunt had laughed. *"You, Grant, are quite blatantly interested only in women. He'd have to have been blind not to realize that."*

"I won't put credence in gossip."

"Nor did I, when first I heard it. But keep your mind open to the possibility, for it may have a bearing on this case."

Grant scowled into the misty darkness. The revelation had a bearing, all right. It gave Sophie a motive for murder.

He could imagine her horror at discovering the truth about her husband. If the news had shocked Grant, it must have been far worse for her. She probably hadn't even been aware that such a penchant existed.

At least *he* had known. In his school days, he had heard whispers about other boys doing forbidden acts in secret. As an adult, he knew of men who made furtive visits to certain brothels that catered to their whims with no questions asked. Grant had shrugged off their behavior, though he didn't understand it. He couldn't fathom how any man could *not* desire women.

Especially Robert.

Robert had been married to *Sophie*.

Beautiful, fiery, sensual Sophie who loved coupling. But Robert had used her to mask his vice. Had she discovered his secret, then poisoned him in revenge? Another possibility sickened Grant. Or had she been a party to the ruse from the start? Maybe she'd made a devil's bargain: in exchange for the title of duchess, she would allow Robert his peccadilloes. Then in the end, she'd tired of the charade.

Whatever the case, Grant wanted to throw back his head and howl.

His horse shied at the side street adjoining his town house. Realizing the bay gelding must have sensed his volatile mood, he eased his grip on the reins. In the next instant, he spied movement in the black depths of the mews.

Someone lurked there. A furtive, distinctly human figure. A thief?

The ransacked chambers. Wren laid flat by a blow to the head. Robert's damning letter.

In a flash, Grant redirected his fury. Forsaking the finesse of a master thief, he kicked his heels and charged straight at his quarry. If it was Sophie, by God he'd give her no chance to flee. In one fluid movement, he leaped off his mount and caught a fistful of baggy coat.

The intruder twisted. An arm slashed upward. The faint glimmer of a blade caught Grant's attention.

Loath to harm Sophie, he resisted the instinct to lash out with a hard chop to the wrist. Instead, he feinted to the side and grabbed for the coat sleeve, intending to pry the knife away.

He realized his mistake at once. A whiff of musky sweat and the strength of a muscular arm revealed his foe to be a man. But that moment of hesitation had cost Grant the advantage.

The man landed a swift undercut to the jaw and simultaneously spun around, wrenching himself free. The jarring blow clashed Grant's teeth together. He staggered backward, landing against the wall of the garden. Using the brick as leverage, he thrust himself back into the fight.

Too late. A blur of movement in the darkness, his opponent darted to Grant's horse and vaulted into the saddle. The gelding danced sideways, but the ruffian controlled the animal with the skill of an experienced rider.

Infuriated, Grant lunged. "Stop, damn you!"

His outstretched hand reached for the reins. The very moment his fingertips brushed the mane, the man swung the gelding around and galloped off into the night.

Grant ran in pursuit, then stopped in the side street, realizing the futility of giving chase. The fog had already swallowed his prey and the clatter of hooves had faded. He cursed and raged over his own stupidity. Only a week ago, the gelding had cost him a pretty penny at Tattersall's. But he could always purchase another mount.

He might never have another chance, though, to prove Sophie had hired that ruffian.

All my hopes of meeting William were laid to waste by a Horrid Event. Mulford's Aunt Edith has come to Town. She arrived upon my Father's doorstep in a sedan chair conveyed by four stout footmen.

She is a fearsome lady, all sharp nose and haughty manners. I wobbled upon making my curtsy, and she scowled as if I had proved myself unworthy of being a Duchess. 'Twas a dismal beginning to a most vexing afternoon. She found cause to criticize all my bride clothes, even the lace on my shifts, and has quite unstrung my poor Mother. Worse, she is to move into my house and protect my Virtue until the Wedding. O, I knew Mulford suspected me of wrongdoing!

—*the diaries of Annabelle Chatham Ramsey, 3rd Duchess of Mulford*

9

Beset by covetous longing, Sophie fingered the bolt of plum silk in the linen-draper's warehouse off Regent Street. The soft fabric had a beautiful sheen in the light of the oil lamps, and after she'd spent nearly ten months in dull black crepe even this subdued color called to her heart. Yet she glanced doubtfully at her companion. "Surely you can't be serious about this one, Caro. I haven't yet completed my first year of mourning."

Caroline smiled, her lustrous blue eyes framed by the stylish yellow bonnet that matched her muslin gown. "You've already worn black for longer than Robert would have wished. He preferred you in rich colors, did he not?"

Sophie couldn't deny it. Unlike other husbands, Robert had enjoyed accompanying her to the dressmaker's. He'd had exquisite taste and a keen eye for beauty, and she felt guilty to recall the times she'd resented being dressed like his personal fashion doll. "I cannot thwart convention," she said resolutely, stepping away from the plum silk to examine a bolt of black taffeta. "Robert would have agreed with *that*."

"Nonsense. He would have said the plum is sober enough. And he would have pointed out how lovely it would look with your fair skin."

"He was a stickler for propriety, too. He always said a duke and duchess must set the standard of decorum."

Taking hold of Sophie's arm, Caroline gently steered her back to the plum silk. "But remember, dear, you're to be hostess at Elliot's birthday dinner. Deep mourning would cast a pall over the festivities."

Gazing down at the luxurious fabric, Sophie felt the tug of temptation. How wonderfully feminine she would feel wearing it . . . how she could enjoy seeing the appreciative glint in Grant's eyes. "People will talk. They'll say that I'm not showing the proper respect."

"Come now, were you not the daring Sophie Huntington? The nonpareil who never spared a thought for scandal?"

Caroline was right, that reckless girl *did* still live inside her. Sophie had faced that truth on the night Grant had kissed her. In the two days since then, she'd been aware of a fervid beating inside her like the wings of a wild bird constrained by the bars of a cage. After ten years of proper behavior, why shouldn't she embrace this one small rebellion? Was she truly so afraid of a little gossip?

Laughing, she shook her head. "Caroline, *you* should

be the Member of Parliament instead of James. You are entirely too persuasive. I must surrender the debate."

Her friend's smile widened, lending a sparkle to her otherwise plain features. "Excellent. We shall order a good many gowns, and they will all be ready by next week, when I return from visiting the dowager in Wimbledon."

She beckoned to a clerk who had been waiting for them to make a decision. At Caroline's behest, Sophie found herself approving a dozen other purchases as well, including a bolt of charcoal-gray silk, another of dark marine-blue muslin, and yards of white Brussels lace to lessen the severity of her black gowns. They had everything sent next door to Sophie's dressmaker, then spent a few leisurely hours at that establishment sipping tea and examining books of the latest fashions.

Sophie enjoyed the outing almost as much as she'd enjoyed the one with Grant and Lucien. She had nearly forgotten the relaxing pleasure of shopping with a friend. By the time they arrived back home and she left Caroline at the town house next door, the hour was nearly four o'clock. Sophie felt a trifle abashed to realize that she hadn't seen her son since the early morning. The moment she'd freshened up, she would go to the schoolroom for a long visit with him.

Greeting Phelps in the entrance hall, she handed him her pelisse. "How is the duke today? Did Miss Oliver take him for a walk in the park?"

Tall and gaunt, the old butler looked more dour than ever. "No, Your Grace. I fear she did not."

Sophie paused in the act of peeling off her kid gloves. The governess believed in keeping a precise schedule. "But the weather is fair. She knows how I feel about Lucien needing his exercise. It isn't healthy for him to stay in the schoolroom all day."

"His Grace has not been in the schoolroom since this morning."

"I beg your pardon?"

"He had a visitor shortly after Your Grace's departure. Or rather I should say, Your Grace had a visitor." Phelps narrowed his gray eyes in a blatant show of displeasure. "A Mr. Chandler."

Grant. Her heart cavorted in a madcap dance. Was he upstairs at this very moment? Had he waited all day just to see her? *"It's not over between us."* His warning had thrilled her far more than it ought. Foolish, impossible thought, for she dared not succumb to his seduction . . .

Disciplining her unruly thoughts, Sophie deemed it wise to give the butler a subtle reminder of Grant's status. "He's my son's guardian. He probably came to check on Lucien's schoolwork."

"Hardly." Phelps compressed his thin lips. "Mr. Chandler gave Miss Oliver the afternoon off. He and His Grace played with tin soldiers for half the day."

Bless Grant for remembering his promise. Lucien must have been delighted to have male companionship. She wouldn't let herself fret over his growing attachment to Grant. Rather, she wanted nothing more than to run up the stairs with undignified haste.

"That will be all," she told the butler. "You needn't inform Mr. Chandler of my return. I'll see to it myself."

But as she started toward the grand staircase, Phelps spoke again, sour disgruntlement in his raspy voice. "I'm afraid that is impossible. Mr. Chandler is no longer here. He and the duke left nearly two hours ago."

Sophie spun back around. "What do you mean, *left*? Where have they gone?"

"To Hyde Park. I heard Mr. Chandler say something to His Grace about a carriage race."

The news struck her with the force of an ice storm. Her

blossoming anticipation withered under the cold breath of alarm. Horrifying images thrust into her mind. *A throng of carriages thundering down a dirt track. The drivers jockeying for position, the wheels bumping and jolting. Grant in their midst with Lucien at his side . . .*

Choked by fear, she snatched her black pelisse out of the butler's white-gloved hands. "You should have said so at once," she snapped. "Make haste and order my coach brought back round."

"Yes, Your Grace. At once." Looking almost pleased by her wrath, Phelps hastened to do her bidding.

Sophie wasted no thought on the impertinence of the old retainer. With trembling hands, she clutched the pelisse to her bosom. She paced the cavernous entry hall while reciting to herself a litany of reassurances. The grooms would not have unhitched the horses in so short a time. She would be on her way in a matter of minutes. It was only a short distance to the park. She would stop Grant from endangering her son . . .

Fraught with panic, she wrenched open the front door and hurried out onto the porch. A bank of heavy gray clouds blotted out the lowering sun, and a damp, chilly breeze penetrated the thin black muslin of her gown. Dear God, *would* she reach the park in time? At this very moment, Lucien could be frightened out of his wits. Worse, he could be lying on the ground beside the shattered curricle . . .

Teeth chattering more from dread than cold, Sophie went to the edge of the porch. A number of vehicles thronged the cobbled street, but she couldn't see the stately black box of the Mulford coach. Drat that Phelps! Had he not conveyed to the driver the need for extreme haste?

On the off chance that the coach might be coming from the other direction, she glanced behind her. And uttered a strangled gasp.

Grant's sleek yellow curricle came down the street, its large wheels rolling smoothly on the cobblestones. On the high perch, Lucien sat between Grant's legs. Grant had his arms around the boy, guiding his hands on the reins.

The tight band eased around her heart. Sophie leaned against the massive white pillar as the curricle drew to a stop at the curbstone. Somehow, she found the strength to make her way down the steps, all the while studying her son for any sign of injury. He appeared blessedly whole, his cheeks pink and his hazel eyes bright beneath a thatch of windswept coppery-brown hair.

"Mummy, Mummy," Lucien called out excitedly. "I drove all the way home from the park. Did you see me coming down the street?"

Sophie forced a shaky smile. "I did, indeed. You managed the horses very well." She extended a hand to her son. In the aftermath of fear, she could think only of holding him close. "Come down now. It's nearly time for your dinner."

His face fell. He tilted his head back to give Grant a beseeching look. "Please, sir, mightn't I drive around the square just once?"

"Another time," Grant said, his tone indulgent as he glanced at Sophie. "For now, you'd best obey your mother."

Grumbling a little, Lucien clambered down at once. Sophie crouched down and caught him into her arms. He felt small and sturdy and infinitely precious, his hair soft against her cheek. But even as part of her reveled in her son's safety, another part reeled with resentment.

Instead of obeying her request, Lucien had turned to Grant for permission. As if Grant's decisions took precedence over hers. She was galled by how swiftly Grant had become the object of Lucien's hero worship. Dear heaven, had she been wrong to allow her son any contact with him?

The bitter truth intruded. She had no right to forbid the connection. As Lucien's guardian, Grant possessed all the rights.

While his groom held the horses, Grant leaped down from the high perch to stand behind Lucien. Her gaze flashed over his tall form, up the polished black knee-boots and tight buckskins, past the fine blue riding coat and stark white cravat, to his devilishly handsome face. From his superior height, he watched her with cool brown eyes. It was as if he were challenging her to question his authority to take Lucien wherever and whenever he liked.

Fury poured into the void of her emotions. Blast him for charming her son! And for usurping her status in Lucien's eyes.

Lucien wriggled free. "Please, Mummy. I'm not a baby anymore."

With affable male camaraderie, Grant ruffled the boy's hair. "A fellow is never too old for a hug from his mother."

His statement only made Sophie feel patronized. But she couldn't retort, not with Lucien present. She must curb her anger until the appropriate time.

The Ramsey coach lumbered up behind the curricle, and Sophie informed the baffled coachman that she had changed her mind about going out again. She could see by Grant's frown that he'd comprehended her intention to go in search of them. Excellent. Let him realize that she would not sit back and allow him to imperil her son.

He placed his hand on Lucien's back. "Come along, scamp, into the house. You've had enough fun for one day."

At her son's side, Sophie mounted the marble steps to the porch and made an effort to keep her voice light. "What did you do at the park, darling? Phelps said there was to be a race of some sort." Over Lucien's head, she shot Grant an irate stare.

Lucien looked distinctly uncomfortable. "Er . . . I mustn't say . . . that is . . ." He slid a glance up at Grant.

"It's all right," Grant said easily. "I'll tell your mother all about it in a moment. Sophie?"

All urbane politeness, he held open the door for her to precede him into the house. Lucien started forward, then stopped in imitation of his mentor. Under other circumstances, Sophie would have delighted in her son's show of manners. But she was too irked at Grant. Clearly, he had warned Lucien to say nothing of the carriage race.

She marched inside to find Phelps returning from his errand to the stables. The butler scowled from her to Lucien. "Your Grace."

"Is Miss Oliver back in the nursery?" Sophie asked him.

"She is downstairs in the kitchen. Shall I send her—"

"No." To Lucien, Sophie added in a milder tone, "You may go down to the kitchen and see if Cook has any fresh scones."

Lucien's eyes lit up. He threw his arms around her and gave her a peck on the cheek. "Thank you, Mummy." Then he dashed down the corridor toward the back of the house.

Her throat tight, she wondered if he'd hugged her spontaneously . . . or because Grant had given him permission to embrace his mother.

No. She wouldn't question her son's displays of affection. Nor would she allow an interloper to revoke her rights as a parent. She'd been wrong to ignore her goal of convincing Grant to sign the papers that would nullify his guardianship. In the meanwhile, it was time she set certain boundaries in regard to her son.

She swung to Grant. "We'll speak in the library. Follow me."

"With pleasure."

Grant sincerely meant those words. As Sophie led the way down the long marble passageway, he watched with a keen appreciation of the view. Her hips swayed beneath the slim-fitting black dress, giving him a glimpse of womanly curves and a hint of long slender legs. He remembered how those legs had felt wrapped around him in bed . . .

He cudgeled his thoughts back to the present. Sophie was in high dudgeon. When he and Lucien had driven up, the anxiety on her face had spoken volumes. Belatedly, he considered the shock it must have been for her to return home to discover her son missing.

She might be a murderess, but she did love her son.

But dammit, couldn't she trust him to take care of the boy?

Grant hadn't intended to visit Lucien, much less spend the day with him. He had come to Mulford House to confront Sophie about Robert's secret life. Much to his frustration, however, she'd left on a shopping trip, so he'd been forced to cool his heels by playing tin soldiers with Lucien. Grant had found himself enjoying the boy's delight as they fought the battle of Waterloo from start to finish. Yet by the time Napoleon had been banished to his island prison in the cupboard, Sophie still hadn't returned. Impatient and restless, Grant had decided to take Lucien for a drive. He hadn't spared more than a thought for how Sophie might react.

As she ushered him into the library and shut the door, he caught a glimpse of her resolute expression. Her delicate features wore the look of the haughty duchess—upraised chin, compressed lips, narrowed eyes. No doubt, she was spoiling for a fight.

So was he. However, his quarrel with Sophie had nothing to do with her son. And he didn't wish to hinder his purpose of seduction. So he'd allow her to vent her wrath. If the moment called for it, maybe he'd even grovel a bit. Women always liked that.

She proceeded to the grouping of chairs by the fireplace, then turned to face him. Since she remained standing, he did likewise, resting his arm on the mantelpiece and assuming a contrite expression. "Sophie, I'm sorry for worrying you. That was never my intention."

Her fingers gripped at her sides, she stood perfectly still, as if it took all of her self-control to keep from flying at him in a rage. "Very charmingly put. However, I'm not so easily appeased anymore. It's time you understood certain facts. First of all, you will not continue to disrupt my son's schedule."

"He's only a child," Grant felt compelled to point out. "It won't hurt him to skip a few lessons."

"He's already had one outing this week, and I won't have you spoiling him. You were wrong to give Miss Oliver the afternoon off—"

"I didn't. I told her she could do as she pleased until you returned, since I would be keeping an eye on Lucien."

"Keeping an eye on him," Sophie repeated in a scathing tone. "Is that what you call taking him out of the house without my permission? Allowing him to participate in a carriage race? Then encouraging him to *lie* to me?"

Grant deemed it wise not to remind her that as Lucien's guardian, he had the right to take the boy anywhere he pleased. "We *watched* a race," he clarified. "We did not participate. As for lying, I merely told him it would be expedient to keep silent and allow me to explain."

"So now you're teaching my son your wretched moral code. I won't allow it, Grant. I've taught Lucien that keeping secrets is the same as telling a lie."

She glanced down at the coal fire on the hearth, Grant

noted coldly, as if meditating on her own hypocrisy. A faint blush stained her cheeks, further proof of her guilt in holding her son to a higher standard than her own.

Anger burned in his gut. For years, Sophie had abetted Robert in hiding his predilection. Very likely, she'd also concealed her part in his murder. More recently, she'd hired a thug to ransack Grant's chambers—the same bastard who'd stolen his horse.

Provoked, he went to her and tilted up her chin with his forefinger and thumb. He caught a whiff of her scent, something light and mysterious, alluringly feminine. With effort, he conquered the urge to kiss her, to turn all that glorious fury into passion. "Are you truly so virtuous, Sophie? I can't help wondering what secrets *you* keep."

Her wide green eyes betrayed an inner turmoil—but only for a moment. Blinking, she stepped back, once again the aloof duchess. "I know all your tactics, Grant. I won't be distracted from what needs to be said. Whether you raced your curricle or not, you exposed my son to danger. Had there been an accident, a carriage that veered into the bystanders . . ."

The touch of horror in her voice reached past his anger. He placed his hands on her shoulders and rubbed soothingly. "I brought him home, safe and sound. I assure you, he was never in the slightest peril."

She thrust Grant's hands away. "And what of the people who frequent these races? Men like Lord Kilminster and Jeremy Updike. And very likely women of the *demi-monde*. Do you really think them appropriate companions for a young boy?"

The censure in her voice discomfited Grant. Unaccustomed to watching out for children, he hadn't lent a thought to the suitability of the occasion. He swallowed

his pride and admitted, "You're right. It was poor judgment on my part to take Lucien there."

"And it won't happen again," Sophie stated. "Henceforth, you will abide by the procedures I set out for you."

"Procedures?"

"Yes, if you'd be so kind as to listen closely." She
ticked off the items on her fingers. "First, you will not take
Lucien from this house without my permission. Second,
you will visit only at times that I deem appropriate—"

"Wouldn't you rather just throw something at me?"
Grant cut in.

"I beg your pardon?"

Annoyed by her freezing manner, he plucked a small
porcelain vase from a nearby table and wrapped her fingers around it. "Since you won't accept my apology, perhaps you'll feel better if you release all that temper."

Her hands tightened around the vase. Sophie glared
fiercely as if debating whether or not to break it over his
head. He was almost disappointed when she carefully replaced the vase on the table.

Closing her eyes a moment, she drew a deep breath.
When she looked at him again, the prim duchess was
gone and in her place was a woman with deeply troubled
eyes. "I *will* accept your apology. But please try to understand why I'm so distraught. It isn't simply a fit of temper. The truth is, I'm frightened—for Lucien's sake."

The eloquence in her voice jolted him. Did she know
he was investigating her for murder? Did she worry about
what would happen to her son if she went to prison? "Explain yourself."

"I'm afraid because of the way he admires you." She
stepped forward, put her hand on his coat in supplication.
"Oh, Grant, you're the only man in his life right now, so
he's looking to you for guidance."

Her words took him aback. "I'm aware that I made a mistake, Sophie. I thought I made that clear."

"It's more than what happened today." She paused, her gaze searching his for something he didn't quite understand. "I know you have little interest in family matters. So if you're planning to walk away from Lucien, then please do so now, before he becomes even more attached to you. He's already lost his father, and it will hurt him dreadfully to lose you, too."

Unwillingly, he pictured Lucien's trusting face. He himself knew the pain of having an indifferent father. Avoiding that quagmire of emotion, Grant resorted to charm. He took her hand and gallantly kissed the back. "I won't forsake him," he said. "I promise you that."

Sophie only shook her head, clearly unmoved by his declaration. "Promises mean little, Grant. It's what you *do* that counts. Lucien needs to know that he can depend on you—or you shouldn't be visiting him at all. You ought to sign the papers relinquishing his guardianship."

Glib reassurances sprang to his mind. But he knew Sophie wasn't looking for platitudes. With the fierceness of a mother lion, she loved her son. She had thrown out a challenge to Grant, one he couldn't gloss over with effusive words. Could he commit himself to the care of a small boy? He must, though the notion daunted him. Worse, it was mortifying to realize he had viewed the guardianship merely as a means to spend time with Sophie, to seduce her and then wrest a confession from her. But what would happen to Lucien when his mother went to prison for murder?

Therein lay the fatal flaw in his plan for revenge. Lucien would be immeasurably hurt. Lucien, who had accepted him with the innocent trust of youth. Lucien, whose face lit up when Grant walked into the room.

Lucien, whose father had been murdered.

Grant hardened his resolve. He had vowed to bring the killer to justice. He couldn't let himself falter now.

Keeping that in mind, he took Sophie's arm and guided her toward the chaise. "Signing away my rights isn't a decision to be made lightly," he said. "I'll have to give the matter a good deal of thought. Sit down and we'll talk."

Sophie regarded him warily, though she took the enticement and sat beside him. "It shouldn't be a difficult decision," she said. "Supervising a child's upbringing can hardly be of interest to you."

"However, it's a role that Robert wished for me to fulfill. I can't easily disregard his last request. He was my good friend and—"

The door to the library burst open, interrupting Grant's opportunity to maneuver her into revealing her husband's secret vice. Irked, he turned to see a man stomp into the chamber.

He looked like a common laborer in a loose brown coat over baggy breeches. Dirt smudged his dingy white shirt. His stringy brown hair, thinning on top, straggled down to his shoulders. He had the dark, scaly skin of a lizard, chapped and rough from spending too much time outdoors.

Recognizing Robert's cousin, Grant groaned under his breath. He had waited all day to speak to Sophie alone, and here came another delay.

Her eyes wide, she gazed at the visitor in obvious dismay. "Elliot! Whatever are you doing here?"

I am in prison, and Mulford's Aunt Edith is my Warden. Here is a True Accounting of how I spent this day:

Nine of the clock. Broke my fast with the Warden. Received a Lecture on the rules of precedence.

Ten 'til noon. Helped Mama finish writing invitations for the Grand Wedding. Received a Lecture from the Warden on proper penmanship.

Noon 'til one. Practiced my curtsy for my presentation at Court. Received a Lecture on how to Address His Majesty the King.

One of the clock. Nuncheon with Mama and the Warden. Received a Lecture on the illuminaries of the Mulford family tree.

Two 'til four. Confined to my chambers whilst the Warden takes her nap. O woe, I am trapped in a gilded cage. Am I never again to be free?

—the diaries of Annabelle Chatham Ramsey, 3rd Duchess of Mulford

10

Feeling somewhat disoriented, Sophie rose to her feet. She had been intent on the conversation with Grant, and it took considerable skill to mask her disappointment. At last she'd had the chance to talk to him about revoking his guardianship, but now she would have to put off the matter.

Although he hadn't visited in several weeks, Elliot didn't bother with a greeting. "You know perfectly well why I've come," he snapped. He fumbled in his pocket, pulled out a bit of string, a shard of pottery, then a square of paper, which he waved in her face. "It's all right here in

Helena's letter. You're giving away the Chichester artifacts. I won't allow it. By God, I won't!"

Dismayed, Sophie remembered Helena's ruse to lure
Elliot here for the dinner party next Thursday. Apparently
he had been too angry to wait.

Wondering where her sister-in-law was, she glanced at
the empty doorway. "I'm not giving them away. You
know very well I haven't the right to do so. Have you spoken to Helena about this?"

"The footman went to find her." Elliot rattled the letter
again. "But this must be your doing. You must have gone
to the trustees at the bank and convinced them—"

"We'll discuss the matter in private," Sophie said
firmly. She had no wish to embroil herself in yet another
lie, especially not while Grant sat watching. Already, he
looked extremely curious. "First, I must bid farewell to
my other guest."

On cue, Grant rose from the chaise. He politely extended his hand to Robert's cousin. "Elliot. It's been a
long time."

Startled, Elliot swung around as if just now realizing
they weren't alone. He stared uncomprehendingly; then
his expression lightened and he shook hands. "I say,
you're the fellow who lived near Robert a long time ago.
Chandler, isn't it?"

"One and the same. I'm also Lucien's guardian, so you
may set your mind at ease about his care."

"Lucien?" Elliot frowned in befuddlement as if he'd
forgotten his own nephew. "Ah, yes, the boy. Capital of
you! It's a trial getting away from the site once a month.
I'm excavating a Roman villa in Surrey, and those
wretched workers—"

"Mr. Chandler can hear all about it another time," Sophie said icily. She resented the reminder that Elliot con-

sidered his precious ruins more important than her son. "He was just about to leave."

"In a moment," Grant said. "Your project sounds fascinating, Elliot. And what, pray tell, are the Chichester artifacts?"

"A trove of Roman treasures that were found on one of my cousin's estates last year." A rapacious gleam in his eyes, Elliot walked around the library, gesturing wildly. "Some of the finest examples of Roman curios ever discovered in Britain. A gold disk embossed with goddesses—Fortuna, Venus, Minerva. A jeweled fibula that once fastened a Roman's cloak. Coins depicting the Emperor Caligula." A glower creasing his sun-browned face, he swung toward Sophie. "But Robert refused to give any of the antiquities to me. He wanted to donate them to a museum, knowing full well that *I'm* planning to open my villa to the public someday—"

"Elliot," Sophie broke in, enunciating every syllable, "that is quite enough. This is a family matter, and Mr. Chandler has no part in it."

Without giving Grant a chance to disagree, she took hold of his arm and steered him to the door of the library. The close contact made it difficult to ignore the power of his attraction. Beneath the sleeve of his coat, his muscles were hard and thick. With every breath, she inhaled his faint spicy aroma, a scent that sparked the memory of lying naked in bed with him. Even now, when she should be thinking of other matters, her body ached for his.

Perhaps you should have an affair with him.

Despite all her best efforts to banish it, Caroline's advice had taken up residence in Sophie's mind. She knew that part of her frustration at Elliot's arrival stemmed from the dashed hope that Grant might kiss her again.

Blast her foolishness! Had she not learned her lesson about playing with fire?

At the doorway, he took her hand and idly stroked it. "I need to speak with you further," he murmured. "Shall I wait?"

The prospect tempted her. She wanted to hear what he had to say—and to say a few things to him herself. But Sophie suspected Elliot would stay on the topic of the Chichester artifacts all evening, so she shook her head. "Tomorrow will do. We'll settle the matter of the guardianship."

He merely smiled, pressing her hand before releasing it. "We'll talk about it—among other things."

As he strode down the corridor and vanished, Sophie puzzled over his evasiveness. His smile had not reached his eyes. Once again, she was reminded that he had a hidden purpose, and it could only be a single-minded determination to seduce her.

Helena came hurrying down the passageway from the direction opposite to the one Grant had taken. She peered over Sophie's shoulder at Elliot, who was angrily poking through the row of books on a shelf and muttering to himself. "I never imagined he'd come so swiftly," Helena said in an undertone. "I mailed the letter only yesterday. Do stand by me while I smooth his ruffled feathers."

Her lips forming a determined smile, Helena glided into the library, with Sophie reluctantly following. She disliked abetting one of her sister-in-law's schemes. Especially now, when she would rather be alone to mull over the problem with Grant.

"I can't help wondering what secrets you keep."

What had he meant by that? If he suspected that Lucien was his son, surely he'd have come straight out and said so. He'd had ample opportunity. Unless . . .

Her stomach clenched. He couldn't know about Robert . . . could he?

Impossible. She and her husband had always been careful to show a warm, loving façade to the world. And Robert had been extremely discreet in his liaisons. No one, not even Helena, had ever suspected the truth.

There had to be another explanation. A simpler one. Grant only meant to prod her into admitting that she still desired him. It was clear that he resented her for spurning him long ago. To pacify his pride, he intended to coax her into another slip from virtue.

A deep-seated quiver eddied through her. For once, just once, she longed to abandon the role of duchess and be that reckless girl again—to be like Annabelle, running off to meet her lover. Sophie sighed. If only Grant knew, she'd never truly desired any man but him.

The hour was late when Sophie finally escaped to her suite of rooms. Dinner had been interminable, with Elliot rattling on about the artifacts and Helena attempting to wrest a promise from him to remain in London for a while. But Elliot was adamant; he would return to his Roman villa in the morning. So Helena had concocted another lie about having scheduled a meeting with the directors of the Montagu House Museum on the afternoon of the party. Since it was the only way to lure Elliot back for the birthday festivities, Sophie had supported the fib.

As she stepped into her bedchamber, she expected to feel a sense of relief at finally being alone. She wanted nothing more than to shed the confinement of corset and shoes and gown, to don her nightdress and burrow into bed to ponder her next move with Grant.

Instead, an uneasy feeling prickled over her skin.

Shadows cloaked the cavernous room with its fancy scrollwork and gilt and white furnishings. A candle in a glass chimney burned on the table beside the bed with its hangings of pale blue satin. Painted cherubs cavorted on the gloomy, vaulted ceiling. It took only a moment for Sophie to realize what was wrong.

Despite the fire that burned on the hearth, the chamber was far too drafty and cold. Much to her surprise, one of the glass doors to the balcony stood ajar, and the curtains undulated in the chilly night breeze.

She hastened there at once to close the door. It had not been open when she'd changed for dinner, which meant her maid must have returned to air out the room for some reason. But the explanation made no sense, for Polly was too meticulous to have forgotten to complete her task. Perhaps the latch hadn't been secured and a gust of wind had blown the door open. Yes, that was far more likely.

Shivering, Sophie tested the handle to make sure it wouldn't spring open during the night. She would add a few more coals to the fire to help warm the room. As she turned to do so, a lightning bolt of fright hit her.

A man sat in the shadowed corner. From the corner of her eye, she saw him sprawled in a chair, his long legs propped on a hassock.

A scream gathered in her throat. Then his form took on a recognizable shape. "Grant!"

He set aside the book he'd been reading. He appeared as comfortably situated as a husband awaiting his wife. His cravat lay on the table beside him, and the open collar of his shirt revealed a tantalizing glimpse of his bare throat. Like an apparition from her most private fantasies, he regarded her with one dark eyebrow rakishly crooked. "Well," he drawled, "you took long enough to finish your dinner."

Sophie raised a hand to her thumping heart, aware that

its swift pace had altered from fright to fervor. His presence made the enormous chamber seem small and unbearably intimate. How had he gained entry—

The opened door, of course.

Disbelief giving way to anger, she stepped toward him. "You climbed the drainpipe to my balcony."

"Actually, the rose trellis." He inspected his palms. "I suffered a few thorns along the way, but all's well that ends well."

Two nights ago, he hadn't known the location of her bedchamber. Evidently, he had done some snooping. "All's *not* well," Sophie snapped. "Nor will it end well if you don't leave here at once."

He stood up and sauntered toward her. "I mean you no harm," he said in his most charming voice. "I only wish to speak to you in private, where no one will disturb us."

He disturbed her. In a most primitive, alluring manner. But it would be extremely unwise to admit that aloud.

He stopped a foot away from her, his eyes dark and mysterious in the dim light. His faint, masculine scent beckoned to her. She wanted to step into his arms, to tuck her face in the crook of his neck, to taste his skin. She wanted him to sweep her up and carry her to the bed . . .

To hide her lusty thoughts, Sophie donned a sheath of icy disdain. "Your efforts are for naught. I will speak to you on the morrow."

"Tomorrow, you'll be busy with Elliot or Helena or Lucien. And I've no intention of being interrupted again." Arrogantly taking charge, he cupped her elbow and compelled her to a blue-striped chaise by the white marble chimneypiece. "You'll want to sit down when you hear what I have to say."

Curiosity got the better of her. If his purpose had anything to do with the guardianship papers, she ought to listen.

Cautiously, Sophie perched on the chaise. When he moved to sit beside her, she pointed at the chair opposite her, the one he'd occupied for heaven only knew how long. "Over there," she said. "Else I'll summon the footman."

His look mocked her threat. Clearly, he knew as well as she how easily he could stop her from reaching the bell rope in the dressing room. But with the hint of a smile, he conceded. "As you wish, duchess."

Instead of taking the chair, however, he pulled over the round hassock and sat directly in front of her, so close she had to turn her legs slightly to avoid touching him. Unfortunately, looking straight at Grant was hardly an improvement over sitting beside him. The softness of the firelight on his strong-boned face and the casual state of his garb made Sophie feel as if they were lovers. His black hair was tousled as if he'd just risen from bed, and his masculine aura lured her as it had on that long-ago night when she had gone with him to his town house. The night Lucien had been conceived . . .

Sophie focused her thoughts on her son. "I hope this means you've decided to sign the guardianship papers," she said. "We'll need witnesses. I can arrange for a meeting at the office of my solicitor."

"You mistake me," Grant said smoothly. "I wanted to speak to you about something else entirely. It concerns Robert."

The directness of his eyes paralyzed her. *He knew*.

But he couldn't know. No one had known but herself and Robert and one other person . . . nay, two. Four people in all, and they had guarded the secret zealously. "Say it, then. It's late, and I won't suffer your presence a single moment longer than necessary."

"Yes," he said in a musing tone, "it *is* late and you were shopping most of the day. You must be weary."

He reached down, lifted her ankle, and propped her

heel onto his knee. In a twinkling, he slipped off her black shoe and wrapped his hands around her stockinged foot, his thumbs kneading her sole.

The massage felt heavenly. So heavenly that she almost forgot the impropriety of it. Scandalized, she tugged ineffectually at his firm grip. "Stop that! I never gave you leave to touch me—"

"You always liked for me to rub your feet. Remember how we would dance all night?" With expert skill, he worked a slow path over the bottom of her foot. "Then we'd sit out in the garden and I'd soothe all your aches just like this."

He had soothed other aches, too. He had taken liberties no lady should allow. But she had been young and in love and eager for his caresses.

She was still eager. Her flesh tingled from his deep stroking. The long gown covered her to the ankle, and she was enraptured by the sight of his large hands brushing against her hem. If only he would slip his fingers underneath her skirts. If only he would trace a path up her calf and over her garters, until he reached . . . Her voice breathy, she said, "We haven't been dancing, and you're no longer my beau."

With that, Sophie twisted her foot free and returned it to the floor. But he only lifted her other leg and removed that shoe, as well. "Hold still," he commanded. "I can't give you the proper treatment when you're wriggling."

"There's nothing *proper* about it, Grant. And *I* can't have a serious discussion with my foot in your lap."

His gaze smoldered. "Nor can I. So we may as well speak of something less serious. Your foot, perhaps."

"My foot?"

"You have beautiful feet. They're small and delicate like the rest of you. I especially love the way your toes curl when I rub you right here." Grant gently pressed the pad of her sole, right beneath her toes, making her respond exactly as he'd predicted.

He knew her too well. With each movement of his strong fingers, she could feel herself softening, melting, mellowing. At the same time, a different sort of tension gathered strength deep inside her. It was as if he were steadily redirecting all the energy of her willpower into her loins. He wanted to seduce her . . . and she wanted to be seduced.

Disconcerted, Sophie pulled her foot away, curling her stockinged toes into the soft carpet. "That's enough," she said firmly. "I won't play games with you, Grant. You can't beguile me anymore."

"So I see."

He looked unperturbed, too sure of himself. "No, you don't see," she stated. "You're still angry that I chose Robert over you. But I won't be a salve to your injured pride. If that's why you intruded upon my chamber, you may as well leave this instant."

His eyes narrowed slightly, giving him a calculating look as if he were reflecting on some dark design. Resting his elbows on his knees, he leaned forward on the hassock. "I do want you, Sophie. I won't deny that. But I came here for another reason entirely."

I do want you. He couldn't guess how greedily she drank of his declaration, how parched she had been for a man's attention. "I'm listening," she prompted. "Kindly state your purpose."

"It isn't an easy topic to broach."

"For pity's sake, Grant. Be frank—or be gone."

"Rather, I'll be blunt." His shrewd gaze held hers. "I've heard a disturbing rumor about Robert. That he preferred to bed other men instead of his wife."

Ice encased Sophie. All the simmering desire inside her vanished under the weight of glacial shock. She sat frozen, unable to move lest she shatter into pieces. Dear God, Grant *did* know. How?

Someone had told. Someone had revealed the truth that Robert had been so desperate to hide from the world. But who?

Or was Grant simply making a wild conjecture? Robert had been certain that no one had ever guessed. But perhaps Grant had seen some small sign, and now he was probing for information . . .

Struggling to keep her face blank, she uttered a cool laugh. "Don't be absurd. Since when do you give credence to nasty gossip?"

"I want the truth, Sophie. If you're afraid I'll condemn him for it, please be assured—"

"There's nothing to condemn. Your source is wrong. Completely, utterly *wrong*." Her movements rigid, she rose from the chaise. "There, the matter is cleared up. You may go now."

Springing to his feet, Grant closed his warm fingers around her cold hands. "I can't blame you for concealing it," he said softly. "In fact, I admire you for protecting his good name. It must have been very difficult for you."

The sympathy in his voice almost did her in. Despite his touch, she felt chilled to the core. If only Grant knew.

He could have no inkling of the times she'd wept in her chamber, certain that it was all her fault, that if only she had been more skilled, more beautiful, more loving, she might have been able to stir her husband's desires. Robert had lain with her often during her pregnancy, but only to hold her close, using the excuse that he didn't wish to harm the baby. She had been grateful for his tenderness, for her heart had needed time to heal. But when he hadn't returned to her bed months after she'd given birth, she had gone to him instead. She had needed to feel a man's arms around her, needed to know she was loved and desired. But nothing had gone as she'd hoped . . .

With effort, Sophie forced herself to speak evenly. "You're mistaken. Robert was a fine husband and a wonderful father. I won't allow you to slander him."

Grant shifted his hands to her shoulders. Though he gently kneaded her muscles, his touch felt heavy, relentless. "I've no intention of maligning his memory. I would never betray his secret. Don't forget, he was my friend."

"Was he? Then why did you never write to him?" She struck out coldly in an attempt to keep Grant from probing deeper. "Before you left England, Robert begged your forgiveness. He asked you not to let his marriage ruin your friendship. But you knocked him down with your fists. You stormed out, and he never heard a word from you in all those years."

Grant's jaw tightened. He glanced away a moment, then looked deeply into her eyes. Sincerity radiated from him. "I couldn't write to him," he said, his voice low and gravelly. "Not while he was married to you, Sophie. To the one woman I desired beyond all others."

Grant took a gamble in making that confession. Sophie might use it as ammunition to maneuver him. But he needed to set her off balance, to shake that cool composure of hers. Besides, he could hardly expect her to reveal her secrets if he didn't give away one himself.

She lowered her lashes slightly, shielding her thoughts. He didn't know if she believed him or not. Convincing her would be a pleasure. Her lips were parted slightly, and he craved her kiss. More than that, he craved a long, lusty session in bed with her.

But not yet. Not until he'd pried this one truth out of her.

She twisted free and he let her go—for the moment. Stepping stiffly to the bed, she wrapped her fingers around the post with its blue satin hangings. With her back to him, she looked slender and queenly, her posture rigidly correct. In a voice so low he had to strain to hear, she murmured, "If I tell you about Robert, will you promise to leave me?"

Astonished at the ease of his victory, Grant sucked in a breath. "Agreed." *For now.*

She glanced over her shoulder, her gaze troubled and her face pale. "I'm breaking a vow I made to my husband. I must know that what I say won't go beyond these four walls."

"Agreed again."

Sophie studied him another moment, then nodded. Averting her eyes to the darkened doorway that led to the balcony, she said tonelessly, "All right, then. The rumor you heard is true. Robert had needs . . . that only another man could fulfill. I didn't realize it at first. The first year of our marriage, he gave me no cause to think he led a secret life. He seemed elated to be my husband."

The knot in Grant's chest tightened. He should be wrestling with the confirmation of Robert's propensity, not imagining Sophie locked in a passionate embrace with her husband. Dammit, he couldn't be jealous of a dead man. Leaning against the back of the chaise, he mastered himself. "So he took his conjugal rights. He sired a child."

Sophie laced her fingers and stared down at them. Without a nod or acknowledgment of his comment, she continued, almost as if she were talking to herself. "In the beginning, he came to me quite often. He was thrilled when he found out about my pregnancy. He was loving and tender and . . . and very good to me." As if lost in memories of happier times, she faltered and fell silent.

"And then?" Grant said tersely. "How did you find out?"

"After Lucien's birth, Robert ceased his visits to me. So one night I went to him. But . . . I was unable to stir him to passion. He put me off with an excuse."

"He only wanted to get an heir on you."

Sophie didn't respond to the biting comment, nor did she look at him. "He had been going out sometimes in the evenings. To his club, he said. But I feared . . . that he'd acquired a mistress. He denied it, yet he was evasive, too. So one night I took a hackney cab and followed him to a house near Covent Garden. I waited outside for a time, but then . . . it became too much to bear. The door was unlocked. I went inside and . . . and I saw him . . . I saw *them* . . . clasped in an embrace . . ." A violent shiver convulsed her. Melting against the bedpost, she released a choked sob and buried her face in her hands.

Grant sat thunderstruck. Sophie had witnessed *that*?

Cursing under his breath, he sprang to her side. He pulled her to him, wrapping his arms around her in an instinctive effort to give comfort. He half-expected her to thrust him away, but she was too overcome by her emotions. She huddled against him, clutching blindly at his coat as she wept.

Unlike other women he'd known, Sophie didn't cry with beautifully glistening eyes and gently quivering lips. She bawled with all the gusto of her passionate nature, with great noisy sobs, with tears pouring down her cheeks. Within moments, her nose was red and her eyes swollen, and his collar was damp from the flood.

He fumbled for his handkerchief, hoping that Wren had remembered to tuck one in the inside pocket of his coat. Finding the square of folded linen, Grant dabbed at her wet cheeks before pressing it into her hand. She blew her nose and took several ragged breaths in a woeful struggle to regain control of herself.

He felt helpless in the face of her tears. He had wanted her warm and vulnerable, all of her defenses down. But not like this, not in raw agony.

Murmuring soothing nonsense, he stroked the softness

of her hair. It was done up in curls, thick and silky to the touch. A long time ago, he had enjoyed teasing her by stealing a pin and then ransoming it for a kiss.

His chest ached at the memory. Dammit, why hadn't he coerced Sophie to marry him when he'd had the chance? So what if he hadn't had tuppence to his name? He should have carried her off to Gretna Green and damn the consequences. If she hadn't wed Robert, she wouldn't have suffered the shock of discovering her husband's true nature.

She wouldn't have felt compelled to kill him.

Bloody *hell*. He'd found her motive at last. But he hadn't expected to feel this powerful, protective surge of sympathy for her. Or the furious wish that *he* had been the one to murder Robert.

"I'm sorry," she murmured, her voice muffled by his coat. "I—I've never told that to another soul. Perhaps . . . it was more than you wanted to know."

Grant held her tightly. He ought to gloat that her ambition for a title and wealth had reaped such a bitter harvest. So why the devil could he think only of making her happy again? He tilted her chin up. "*I'm* sorry. I'm sorry that you carried such a burden alone. I'm sorry that Robert treated you ill."

Frowning at Grant, she used his handkerchief to blot the last of her tears. "But he didn't, at least not purposely. He took great pains to shield me from the truth. He was absolutely horrified that I'd suffered such a shock. His concern was for *me,* not for himself. And he did everything in his power to make it up to me—"

"Dammit, Sophie! Don't defend him."

She gripped the lapels of his coat. "I know how you feel, Grant. For a long time, I was appalled and furious, too. I felt betrayed in the worst sort of way. But if you could have seen how tormented Robert was, perhaps you'd understand. He desperately wanted to live a normal life, to have a happy marriage."

"He married you to protect his reputation," Grant said flatly. "He was hiding behind your skirts."

She shook her head emphatically. "He truly believed that he could conquer his weakness. He saw marriage to me as his best hope for that. He was determined to change himself, to overcome what he saw as a shameful blemish upon the family honor. Can you fault him for that? *I* couldn't."

"He was unfaithful to you."

"Yes, but not in the same way as a husband who takes a mistress. Robert had strong urges that I couldn't possibly satisfy. In time, I realized they were a fundamental part of him. He couldn't alter his true nature no matter how hard he tried, no matter how hard *I* tried . . ." Turning her head, Sophie bit her lip.

The haunting sadness on her face tore at Grant. How was he to believe her capable of murder when she looked like *that*? When she sounded so accepting of Robert's foible? Had she killed him in a fit of despair?

Damn. He didn't want to think about that now. He didn't want to forgive Robert, either. Yet Grant felt his anger drain away as he reluctantly viewed the situation from her perspective. Maybe she was right, maybe Robert was to be pitied, not despised. After all, he hadn't been able to change himself, not even with the powerful inducement of having Sophie in his bed.

Grant imagined having Sophie in his own bed. He'd show her exactly what it felt like to be desired by a man. He'd keep her in a state of bliss that would make up for all her years of celibacy and disappointment.

He was keenly aware of her slim, lithe body in his arms. They were melded from chest to hips, and he had an erection the size of a stallion's, but she seemed too absorbed in the past to notice. Grant wanted her to notice, to know she was desired. Sliding his hands down her back, he spread his palms over her rounded bottom and brought her flush against him.

"With me," he said, "you don't even have to try."

Her breath caught. Startlement shone in her eyes as well as the softness of dawning passion. She moved her hips sinuously in an unmistakable invitation. "Oh, Grant . . ."

Longing weakened her voice, and he knew only a heartless bastard would use her defenseless state to his own gratification. Only an unprincipled cad would take advantage of her vulnerability. He was all those things, and he ought to seize the opportunity. But instead he suffered an unfamiliar twinge of conscience.

Cursing himself for a fool, he moved his hands to her shoulders and held her back. "I thought you should know how much I want you," he said huskily. "Before I depart."

As if his words had awakened her from a bone-deep lethargy, she blinked those soft green eyes at him. Then a cool, refined manner settled over her. "Oh. Yes, I appreciate it."

She appreciated what? That he had demonstrated her effect on him? Or that he would go away without pressuring her? Grant didn't want to mislead her into thinking he'd given up, so he stated, "I'm only leaving because I made a promise to you."

She nodded solemnly. "It's important to keep your promises."

Already regretting his idiotic chivalry, he released his hold and stepped back. "I'll see you on the morrow, then."

"I've no plans to go out. I expect I'll be in the library most of the day." Sophie glanced down at the crumpled handkerchief she still clutched. "I'll have my maid wash this for you."

"Keep it." He rather fancied the notion of her sleeping with his token under her pillow. She looked beautiful standing there in her stocking feet by the bed, the firelight casting a soft glow over her womanly form. Her copper-brown hair had been mussed by her spell of weeping, and he wanted to see it cascade in a glorious mass down to her waist. This time, he'd hold the hairpins in ransom for her body . . .

But no, he was leaving. He, the most dishonorable rake in England, was going to behave for once. He wanted Sophie with her strength fully intact, not because she was too fragile to resist him.

He turned, intending to depart by means of the balcony. The prospect of all those thorns made him grimace, unlike earlier when they had posed only a nuisance on his way to a greater goal. He had taken only two steps when Sophie's melodious voice halted him.

"Grant?"

Like a well-trained lapdog, he spun back around. Sophie stood gazing at him with her hands clasped before her and a determined expression on her delicate features. "About tomorrow," she said musingly. "There's something you should know."

"Know?"

Sophie inclined her head in a regal nod. To his complete and perfect amazement, she said, "Tomorrow, if it can be arranged, I should like to begin our affair."

I languish in prison. Each day, the Warden devises new ways to Plague (I say) and Improve (she says) the future Duchess of Mulford (me). If I be lax in posture, I am to wear a cursed Backboard for half the day. If I raise my voice, I am forbidden all conversation. If I gaze out the window, I am given to copy a passage from my book of Sermons about the dangers of Idle Minds.

Would that I had the time for Frivolity and Idleness! My poor head is stuffed with the myriad duties of a Duchess. Worse, I have yet no word from William. My Faithful Mary reports he has gone to attend his Father in Lincolnshire. My sore Heart awaits his return.

—the diaries of Annabelle Chatham Ramsey, 3rd Duchess of Mulford

11

The following morning, on her way into the library, Sophie nearly collided with someone. Absorbed in thought, she hadn't been watching where she was going. She had to jump back to avoid a man who tottered beneath a crate loaded with books.

Elliot poked his unkempt head around the side of the box. He was a study in brown, from the reptilian eyes that glowered in his dry lizard's face to the scraggly locks that hung to the shoulders of his earth-drab coat. "I say, have a care where you're walking."

"Pardon me," Sophie murmured, wondering why he was still here when it was nearly eleven. Then her gaze sharpened. "May I ask what are you doing with those books?"

"Borrowing them, of course. That is, if Your Grace will permit me."

His snide tone irked her. As much from annoyance as curiosity, she motioned for him to set down his burden. "I would like to see what it is you're taking."

Elliot's scowl deepened, making the crow's-feet lines around his eyes more pronounced. He obeyed her request, albeit grudgingly, and with his customary air of injury. "Robert always let me borrow books from the library. Surely you won't rescind that right."

Sophie had no wish to foster enmity, so she gave him a conciliatory smile. "Of course not. But I would like to have a glance. There's a particular volume I've been searching for this past week, and I wouldn't want you to carry it off by mistake."

She crouched down to poke through the collection of old books inside the wooden crate on the floor. Vertot's *Revolutions of Rome*. Plutarch's *Lives*. Bladen's *Caesar*. A number of other tomes were written in Latin or Greek, and she had only a rudimentary notion of the titles. None of them had been penned in a feminine flowing script with curlicues and occasional ink blots.

Dusting off her hands, she straightened up and eyed Elliot. "You wouldn't happen to have come across a journal, would you? It was written by Lady Annabelle, the third duchess."

"What would *I* want with a lady's diary?" Elliot asked, his thin lips parting to reveal pointy white teeth. "I'm a scholar, not a dandy. Fripperies don't interest me, nor do tiresome accounts of society events."

Sophie remembered Helena's plan to find him a wife. "Society is more than parties and balls. It can also provide an opportunity to develop close friendships. Aren't you ever lonely out there at your work site?"

"Lonely?" He sent her a blank stare. "Why should I be?"

She did not know how to answer the question. How did one explain the needs of the heart to a man who preferred the isolated world of his obsession? "Have you ever thought about marrying? Perhaps if you found a lady who shared your interests—"

"Bah. No such female exists." He pointed a leathery finger at her. "All of you women are the same. You stuff your heads full of fashion and gossip and silly romantic nonsense. I've no time for such rubbish. I'm off to Surrey now. Good day!"

Bemused, she watched Elliot heft the crate and totter out of the library. Quite clearly, the dinner party would be an unmitigated disaster if Helena had invited only a crop of buffle-headed debutantes. Elliot would make his usual rude comments and turn himself into a pariah. But the solution was so obvious that Sophie laughed out loud at its simplicity.

She must remember to ask Helena if there were any bluestockings on the guest list. If not, she would invite a few likely candidates. If Elliot could be seated beside a lady as avidly intellectual as himself . . .

Sophie chuckled again, this time at herself. Matchmaking had never been a particular interest of hers. But today she wanted everyone to be as full of silly romantic nonsense as herself.

No, that wasn't quite right. What she felt had nothing to do with silliness or romance. The excited fluttering inside herself was due to sensual anticipation.

Tonight, she and Grant would make love. For the first time in ten years, she would abandon the proper behavior of a duchess. She would know a man's passion, feel his hands on her bosom, his mouth on her bare skin. She in turn would be free to explore his muscled form, to kiss him with utter abandon. He would cover her with his heavy weight, press her down onto the bed, fill her completely . . .

Sophie took a deep breath and released it slowly. Her heart pounded and her legs quivered. She had surprised herself the previous night with her impromptu proposal. Until Grant had unearthed the needs buried beneath the hard ground of her respectability, she had been the model of propriety. She had thought herself sensible, disciplined, and content with her celibacy. Other ladies trapped in such a marriage might have sought relief in discreet affairs. But Sophie had always regarded her vows to Robert as sacred and binding.

Her parents had given her the perfect example of marital happiness. They had wed late in life, and she had been their only child. Not a day had gone by that she hadn't seen the signs of their devotion to each other revealed in kisses and smiles. They had never spent a day apart from each other, and when her mother had succumbed to a lung fever shortly after Lucien's birth, her aging father had passed on only a few months later. Sophie had always suspected that he'd died of a broken heart.

During her first Season, she had dreamed of finding such a love with Grant. But cold reality had crushed that hope. *Damnation! I can't afford a wife, but I'll have to marry you now . . .*

Thank heavens she was no longer that foolish young girl. Grant didn't want anything more from her than a tumble between the sheets. She too craved only a temporary liaison, the chance to experience the fullness of physical pleasure. But as a mature woman, she had the sense not to rush blindly into an intimate relationship. She must keep a level head and hold Grant to certain standards of behavior.

Sophie sat down at the escritoire where she often worked on her compilation of the Ramsey family history. Today, however, she intended to write down her rules for the affair as she'd promised him.

She selected a quill from the top drawer and then opened the silver inkpot. With the pen poised over a sheet of paper, she considered a moment, then wrote, "The trysts shall be confined to your town house. Under no circumstances will you attempt a seduction at Mulford House."

She had been so furious at him last night for climbing the trellis to her bedchamber. It had been an invasion of her private domain, and he had caught her off guard, coaxing her into acknowledging Robert's secret. She had broken her vow . . . and yet she felt only a lightness of spirit.

Twirling the feathery quill, she gazed unseeing at a shelf of books. Confessing the truth had lifted a weight from her. The stormy bout of tears had been cathartic, washing away a shroud of guilt and regret. Throughout, Grant had been remarkably understanding, even tender toward her. Their closeness had unlocked the chains of her reserve, freeing her to admit to her desire for him. She craved an affair—provided that Grant agreed to abide by her guidelines.

Sophie dipped the nib into the inkwell. "Absolute secrecy is required. You will give no indication of my identity to anyone, not even to your servants."

After his initial surprise at her proposal, he had offered to make discreet arrangements for the evening and suggested the pretext of attending a play together. He had been thoughtful and chivalrous, and Sophie was determined not to dwell upon any hidden purpose in him.

If his gallantry was merely an elaborate ploy to win her confidence and exact some sort of carnal revenge, she

welcomed it. They would be using each other for pleasure. Fierce, wild, reckless pleasure. The expectation
made her flushed and restless, impatient for an end to the
hours of waiting.

Nevertheless, she knew she had to protect herself, for
she was taking a far greater risk than Grant. She bent
over the paper again, her pen making a faint scratching
sound. "You must take the utmost care to guard against
consequences."

Lifting her head, Sophie bit her lip. Bearing a child
out of wedlock would be ruinous. Her scandalous behavior would reflect upon Lucien and upon the innocent
baby, as well. After their kiss on the day they'd visited
the Tower, Grant had mentioned that there were ways to
prevent pregnancy. She must ask him how to take those
precautions.

By approaching lovemaking with rationality and fore-
thought, she could enjoy her secret indulgence and have
a memory to savor in the years to come. Without the
sustenence of love, the fire inside her eventually would
burn out.

Her attention returned to the list, and she dipped the
pen into the inkwell again. "The duration of the affair
shall be at my discretion." She paused a moment, then
added a codicil. "At such time as I decide to end the liaison, you will sign the papers renouncing your guardianship of Lucien."

Sophie frowned at that last sentence. It sounded cal-
lous and mercenary, and she certainly didn't mean to im-
ply that she was trading her favors in exchange for
Grant's signature. On the other hand, how could she continue to see him after their passion was spent? The memory of their intimacy would cause an awkwardness
between them. Worse, the longer he lingered in her life,

the greater chance there was that he might guess the truth about Lucien.

Her stomach tensed. That of all things worried her. It wasn't Grant's anger that she feared, though he certainly would be furious that she had lied to him. No, it was the threat of his possible actions that sent her to the verge of panic. What if he decided to acknowledge Lucien as his? What if he resorted to legal process in order to press his claim? What if he took her to court and she was required to testify under oath as to her son's sire?

The thought horrified her. Early in their marriage, Robert had assured her that no one could ever dispute Lucien's position as his heir, not even in the unlikely event that the truth were to be made known. Without question, Lucien *was* Robert's son under English law. Unless a man openly renounced the child born of his wife, that child was legitimate.

Yet Grant had never been one to refuse a challenge. He might be ruthless enough to make his claim anyway, despite the odds against him. He couldn't win his case. But he could cast doubt upon Lucien's heritage. He could make her son the subject of whispers and innuendo.

"Pardon me, Your Grace."

Sophie looked up from the desk to see Phelps standing in the doorway of the library, staring intently. Heat stung her cheeks. Surreptitiously, she moved the list of rules out of sight even though the butler couldn't possibly read it from a distance of several yards. "Yes?"

"There is a man to see you," he said, almost with relish. "I bade him wait downstairs in the kitchen."

Puzzled, Sophie set aside her pen. Clearly, the visitor was no one from society, or Phelps would have ushered him into the drawing room. But she seldom dealt with the tradesmen who came to the back door. "Shouldn't you summon Mrs. Jenks or Lady Helena?"

"Nay, Your Grace. He asked specifically for you."

Resigning herself to the interruption, she slipped the list inside a drawer and rose from the desk. "Who is he? Did he give his name?"

The butler's thin lips twisted. "Hannibal Jones, an officer from Bow Street Station. He insists upon questioning you in regard to . . . a murder."

"I want candles—lots of them," Grant said as he shrugged off his soiled coat. "Make sure they're lit by seven o'clock."

Wren acknowledged the order with a grimace. The small man showed far more interest in examining the gluey stain on the sleeve of Grant's dark blue coat. Bringing it to his nose, he sniffed it. "Codfish an' cream. Ye been lollin' in the gutters at Billingsgate Market?"

"I had an unfortunate encounter with a soup ladle. I'll tell you about it some other time."

Foolishly eager to call on Sophie, Grant plucked a burgundy coat from the back of a chair. He had wasted half the morning tracing a lead from his aunt Phoebe about a wealthy cit who had recently hired a French chef. But the cook wasn't Monsieur Ferrand. When Grant had suggested that the man had changed his name because he'd poisoned a duke, the temperamental chef had yanked the ladle from his pot of soup and had swung it at Grant.

Instead of going straight to Mulford House, Grant had been forced to stop here to switch coats. The delay chafed him, even though he was only going to fetch the list of blasted rules that Sophie had promised him. He had to admit to a certain curiosity. What the devil would she put on that list? Would he be limited as to the ways he could touch her hallowed body? Would he be required to address her as "Your Grace" even in the throes of passion?

Perhaps she intended to snap orders at him as if he were a pet dog.

Like bloody hell.

He accepted Wren's assistance in donning the clean garment. "Have Mrs. Howell change the linens, too. And leave a plate of cheese and fruit on the table by the fire, along with a good bottle of burgundy and two glasses."

"Two," Wren muttered sarcastically. "As if I thought ye were wantin' candles and fresh sheets all fer yerself."

Wren had made a swift recovery from the blow to the head. The wily codger had been a cantankerous patient, abandoning his sickbed two days after being struck by the intruder. Grant had accepted the futility of ordering Wren to rest. Aside from making good on his threat to tie the old man to the bedpost, Grant couldn't stay home all day to stand guard.

He looked into the mirror to adjust his white cravat. "Make sure the draperies are closed. And set a wood fire, not coal."

"Mayhap to please the duchess, ye'd like a bit o' French perfume sprayed in the air. Or an ermine seat fer the chamberpot."

Catching the reflection of the valet's jaundiced blue eyes, Grant shot him a black stare. "I don't recall saying who would be with me tonight."

Wren didn't quail. "She be the only female who's ever tied ye into knots. Ever since ye come back t' London, ye've been wound tighter than Mrs. Howell's hair bun."

Wren was right about that. But tonight Grant would ease the tension that gnawed at his gut. Now that he'd had time to think about it, Sophie's abrupt turnabout made sense. She must have realized that since he knew about Robert, he also knew she had a powerful motive for murder. So she would use her beautiful body to distract him.

Little did she know, she was playing right into his capable hands.

He turned to Wren. "Once you've finished your tasks, you and the Howells are to stay belowstairs. Or take the night off if you like. I shan't be needing your services."

Disapproving, the old man shook his grizzled head. "Ye best have a care. If ye're wrong and the duchess ain't guilty of murder—"

"She is."

"—ye could be ill-usin' the lady just like ye done years ago."

Grant bit back a retort. Sophie had used *him*—but Wren didn't know that part. She had made her opinions clear to Grant bluntly and cruelly, after they'd made love and then again, a fortnight later, when he'd learned of her betrothal and had gone to her in a wild fury.

He seized hold of her shoulders, wanting her with a desperation that made his chest ache. "You can't marry Mulford. What if you're carrying my child?"

Stepping back, Sophie gave him a cool stare. "I'm not, thank God. Our liaison was purely for pleasure, and I wouldn't wish to pay for that mistake."

"A mistake?" To his shame, his voice choked. "My God, Sophie. You said you loved me."

She laughed. "You of all men should know the nonsense spoken by lovers. I wanted only to satisfy my curiosity that night, to see for myself if your reputation was deserved." As if he were a side of beef, she looked him up and down. "A pity you can never make me a duchess."

That memory burned like acid in his gut. She had married Robert by special license the very next day. Grant had left England for Rome, where he had turned to high-stakes thievery as a means to pay his debts. Success had required him to utilize every scrap of cunning and ingenuity that he possessed. There had been little time left to dwell upon the past.

But he had never forgotten Sophie.

Tonight he would have her in his bed again. He would use every trick in his considerable repertoire to give her a carnal experience she would never forget. He would make her so enthralled, so smitten, she would confess the truth about her husband's death.

But he wouldn't question her tonight. Tonight Grant intended to satisfy the cravings that had plagued him for the past ten years.

Tonight was for lust alone.

O, Woe! The most dreadful event has come to pass! It all began when poor Quimper, my dancing master, twisted his foot in the midst of my lesson in the ballroom. Thusly freed for half an hour, I returned early to my chamber in hopes that my Faithful Mary had delivered news from my Dearest Love. Instead, I discovered the Warden searching my desk!

Ere I could gasp in protest, she opened the secret compartment and snatched up the treasured bundle of letters from William. In triumph she bore them away and locked me here in my chamber. I await now in my prison cell to learn what Torture she will devise as my Punishment.

—the diaries of Annabelle Chatham Ramsey, 3rd Duchess of Mulford

12

The first thing Sophie noticed about Hannibal Jones was his towering height. His tousled dark hair nearly brushed the ceiling of the housekeeper's parlor. The Bow Street Runner had craggy features and an unkempt appearance from his rumpled red vest to his dingy greatcoat. His watchful eyes, however, hinted at a sharp mind. In his rawboned hands he held a small notebook and the stub of a pencil.

Seating herself on a straight-backed chair, Sophie could scarcely contain her morbid curiosity. "I'm happy to answer any questions you might have," she said. "However, I know of no one who's been murdered."

Jones remained standing. From his superior height, he

held her gaze with a foreboding intensity. "With all due respect, Your Grace, I believe you may. Early this morning, the magistrate received a letter. It alleged that the previous duke—your husband—didn't die of natural causes. He was poisoned."

The room tilted and swayed. Sophie sat paralyzed, struggling to attach meaning to his words. Despite the warmth of the fire, goose bumps crawled over her skin. "*Robert* . . . ? No, you're mistaken. I—I was *there*."

"Precisely, Your Grace. That is why I wish to question you."

Jones was serious, very serious. Her heart pounded in heavy strokes against her rib cage. She felt dizzy, short of breath. "I don't understand. Who would send such a letter?"

"I'm afraid the tip was anonymous." He paused, his pencil poised over his notepad. "You look rather pale. Shall I call for a glass of sherry?"

Closing her eyes, Sophie shook her head. Her hands were trembling and she doubted she could hold on to a glass. In her mind she fought off nightmarish images from Robert's fatal illness. The pain he had suffered . . . the helplessness she'd felt at watching him waste away . . .

Someone had done that to him? *Deliberately?*

Bile stung the back of her throat. Taking several deep breaths, she slowly opened her eyes again. "This is a mistake," she repeated. "Or a terrible jest. I can't imagine why anyone would . . ." She swallowed hard. "I assure you, Robert died of a digestive ailment. Dr. Atherton will confirm it."

"I've already spoken to the physician, and he admitted the duke's symptoms were consistent with arsenic poisoning."

The revelation caused another earthquake in Sophie. It couldn't be true. *It couldn't be.* She felt stunned by the doctor's statement. "I—I'm flabbergasted. Dr. Atherton never said a word of it to me."

"Apparently he hadn't considered the prospect until now." Jones's bony face settled into lines of disapproval. "At least not until I posed the subject to him in no uncertain terms."

She clung to a thread of desperate hope. "But surely he meant . . . it's only a *possibility*. It doesn't make sense. Robert was kind, gentle, amiable. I can't imagine who might wish to . . . to . . ."

"To murder him?" As if gauging her reaction, Hannibal Jones studied her with narrowed eyes. "There's something else you should know, Your Grace. The letter accused *you* of the deed."

When Grant arrived at Mulford House, he discovered that Sophie already had a visitor. He felt as disappointed as a moon-eyed youth denied the company of his first infatuation. That was ridiculous, considering that he'd come here to get the list of bloody rules outlining the parameters of their affair. He should have let her send it to him by messenger.

Hell, why not admit it? He couldn't wait seven hours to see her again. He wanted to touch her *now,* to kiss her, to tease her, to coax her into a state of high arousal. To make Sophie forget her cold-blooded, businesslike approach to their liaison.

Instead, he stood in the entrance hall with old Phelps. The butler hadn't changed in thirty years. He had the same dismal, downturned mouth and cold gray eyes that Grant remembered from visits here as a child. "Do you know how long she'll be busy?"

"I cannot precisely say." Phelps paused, and a trace of cunning entered his ancient features. "One never knows with a man of his ilk."

Grant frowned. "What man?"

"An officer of the law." The butler squinted his eyes as if in venomous speculation. "He mentioned something about a murder investigation. I assured him Her Grace couldn't possibly assist him, but—"

"Bloody hell!" Jolted out of his complacency, Grant demanded, "Where are they?"

"Downstairs in Mrs. Jenks's parlor—"

Grant shoved past the disapproving butler and headed down the long echoing corridor that led to the rear of the house. Evidently, Bow Street Station had gotten wind that Robert had been poisoned.

A knell of horror echoed in Grant. Had Atherton realized that he'd misdiagnosed Robert's illness? Had the physician suffered an attack of conscience and alerted the magistrate?

No, Atherton was too pompous to admit a mistake. Had someone else seen Sophie poisoning Robert? One of the servants? Someone who had been conscience-stricken and had decided to come forward with the secret?

The thought made Grant ill. Sophie couldn't be hauled off to prison. The notion of her being confined to a dank, rat-infested cell appalled him. He'd intended to conduct the investigation himself. He wanted to punish her in his own way, to bind her to him . . .

At the end of the corridor, he thrust open a door half-hidden in an alcove. He pounded down the winding stone steps, startling a young maid who was toting a hob filled with coal up the stairs.

"Where is the housekeeper's chamber?" he snapped.

The freckle-faced girl shrank back against the wall as if he were a madman. Wordlessly, she pointed to the left.

Grant strode in that direction, bypassing the stout oak door to the wine cellar and then the pantry where an aproned footman stood polishing the silverware. The servant held his head cocked as if he hoped to overhear the conversation taking place across the narrow passageway, behind the door bearing a card lettered with the name Mrs. Jenks. Several other curious servants lingered in the corridor, but they scattered at a scowl from Grant.

He didn't bother knocking. Going straight inside, he shut the door against prying eyes and ears. The cozy, low-ceilinged parlor had dark striped wallpaper and a fire dancing on the hearth. At a glance, he assessed the rangy man who glowered at him from across the room.

Then Grant focused his attention on Sophie, sitting on the straight-backed chair in front of a small writing desk. Her rigid posture conveyed shock.

She sat so still she might have been carved in stone. Her cheeks were a pale marble, her eyes fixed like emeralds, her folded hands a sculpture in her lap. A plain black gown draped her slender form. She looked fragile, exquisite . . . and so stunned he wanted to gather her in his arms and protect her from harm.

He checked the impulse. She was playing a role designed to elicit sympathy, that was all. Dammit, he'd intended to broach the topic of the poisoning himself so that he could assess her immediate reaction. He had wanted to see if he could detect a flash of fear in her eyes, a hint of guilt or a betraying nervousness.

But this stranger had stolen his chance.

"I'm conducting a private interrogation, sir," the officer said with authority. "I must ask you to leave us."

"I must insist upon staying." As Grant strode forward, he had to tilt his head back slightly to meet the officer's eyes. It was a rare occurrence for a man to top Grant by some three or four inches. Assuming a commanding stance with his hands on his hips and his feet planted apart, he said coldly, "I'm Grant Chandler, guardian to young Mulford. Who the devil are you?"

"Hannibal Jones of Bow Street Station." The officer appeared unintimidated, determined to finish his inquisition of Sophie. "I've been authorized by the magistrate to question the duchess in regard to a murder."

Sophie uttered a small sound of distress. She lifted her anguished eyes to Grant. "He says that Robert was poisoned," she murmured. "He thinks that I . . . that *I* murdered him."

The starkness of her expression made Grant's chest tighten. God, could she really feign such shock and disbelief?

What if Wren was right? What if she *was* innocent?

The powerful thought shook Grant. It chilled his blood and made him queasy, but he sternly assured himself that she was acting out of self-preservation. Somehow, he had to get her out of here. If she said anything to incriminate herself . . .

He wheeled on Jones. "This is an outrage. Who told you such a lie?"

"We received an anonymous letter stating that last summer the duchess administered poison to her husband—"

"Anonymous?" Grant released a bark of harsh laughter. Thank God the witness had been too much the coward to sign his—or her—name. "On that flimsy basis, you came here to badger the duchess in her time of mourning. Without a shred of evidence, you would accuse her of this monstrous deed."

Looking somewhat abashed, Jones shuffled his big feet. "The doctor who treated His Grace confirmed that the symptoms were consistent with arsenic poisoning. And the magistrate is obliged to investigate all the allegations that come to his attention. Especially one so serious in nature."

"Even without proof? Or do you plan to exhume the corpse and check for poison?"

Sophie made a strangled sound of distress. Grant hated

bringing up the gruesome prospect, but it was necessary to drive home his point to Jones.

"Certainly not," Jones said, frowning. "No test can prove the presence of arsenic in the body. We can try a case only on a confession from the perpetrator. Or on sufficient circumstantial evidence."

Grant had known that, but he'd wanted to force Jones to admit it aloud. To make him see the futility of his objective.

"Circumstantial evidence," Grant repeated in a scathing tone. "Did it never occur to you that this letter might be a vicious fraud? Her Grace is a beautiful, wealthy, titled woman. There are those who envy her, who might wish to cause her trouble or taint her reputation."

"There is that possibility, I'll trow, but—"

The door opened and Helena hurried into the small parlor. A black spinster's cap crowned her primly styled blond hair, and her birthmark appeared as a splotch of red wine on her ivory cheek. Her wide blue gaze surveyed the three of them, stopping on Sophie. "What on earth is going on here? Phelps said you were being questioned by an officer of the law."

Grant opened his mouth to explain, but Sophie rose to her feet and sent both him and the Runner a quelling glare. She went to Helena, taking her arm and guiding her to a chaise. "I'm afraid Mr. Jones has brought distressing news. You'll want to sit down."

Sophie was the duchess again, Grant noted. It was as if she'd donned a cloak of dignity that masked her thoughts and emotions. Did she have a core of inner strength that enabled her to comfort her sister-in-law? Or did she seek to foster the image of the kind, caring lady who could do harm to no one?

"Phelps mentioned something about a . . . a murder," Helena said with an expression of dread. "Has one of our neighbors . . . ?"

Sophie took hold of Helena's hand, gently rubbing it. "It's Robert," she murmured. "Jones claims that Robert was poisoned."

Helena's jaw dropped. She swayed on the chaise, looking as if she might swoon. Her disbelieving gaze flew from Sophie to the runner, then back, as if to seek proof they were jesting. "Impossible! It must be a . . . a horrid misunderstanding. Who would want to kill my brother?"

"Jones said . . . I would."

Sophie's quiet admission hung like a miasma in the cozy parlor. With a controlled grace, she left her sister-in-law and returned to her straight-backed chair. But when she glanced at Grant, her eyes were troubled green pools.

"*You,* Sophie?" Helena said with open incredulity. She slowly shook her head. "But that is . . . that is nonsense. I refuse even to consider it!"

"My lady," Hannibal Jones said, walking closer to her. "I presume you are the duke's sister. I'll need to question you, too."

Helena's face hardened to a cold, aristocratic mask. She looked up at him as if he were a worm beneath her finely shod foot rather than a man twice her size. Her voice dripping ice, she said, "Do you accuse me of collaborating in this crime?"

Jones ducked his chin, but went on doggedly, "Nay, my lady, I mean no disrespect. I merely need to hear your recollections of the duke's death."

She rose to her feet. "Riffraff! How dare you set foot in this noble house and ask these impertinent questions. I intend to go straight upstairs to write a letter of complaint to the magistrate."

"Both of you ladies should leave," Grant said, seizing the opportunity to eject Sophie from the room. "I'll handle this matter." Somehow, he'd convince the bloodhound to back off the scent.

But Sophie remained seated with her shoulders squared and her posture erect. "No," she said firmly. "I have nothing to hide. I believe we *should* answer his questions."

Jones nodded in satisfaction. "I'll interview each of you alone, then, beginning with you, Your Grace." He looked at Helena. "My lady, if you would step outside? And you too, sir."

As Helena departed in a huff, Grant silently cursed Sophie's recklessness. Didn't she realize the danger in taking the ruse too far? "I'm staying," he said flatly.

"I'm afraid it is the policy of the court to obtain the statement of each witness individually——"

"Mr. Chandler isn't a witness," Sophie said. "He's been out of the country for nearly ten years. He returned only a fortnight ago."

"I see," Jones said, a trifle testily. With a jaundiced eye, he gauged Grant and apparently realized the futility of trying to expel him. "Well, then, Your Grace, you may begin by telling me about the dinner at which your husband became ill."

Grant listened to her testimony while carefully assessing her manner. She spoke quietly, with her chin held high. She answered each question without hesitation, telling Jones every detail about the final two weeks of Robert's life. While describing the pain and suffering he had endured, tears glinted in her eyes and her voice trembled. Never once did she deviate from the image of the grieving widow determined to put her husband's murderer behind bars.

Grant's sense of unease increased. If Sophie was lying, she was an actress worthy of star billing at the Covent Garden Theatre. Again, he wondered. Was it possible that he was mistaken about her? That she was innocent of any wrongdoing?

No, the letter from an anonymous witness proved otherwise. He couldn't let himself be swayed by her pretty face and smooth words. She had deceived him once, and she wouldn't do so again.

But the time had come to broaden the scope of his investigation. In order to avoid stirring Sophie's suspicions, he had to take a hard look at other possible suspects. It was time for him to act a role as brilliant as hers.

16 November 1701

I was summoned this morn to face Mulford, whose grim face showed his displeasure over my purloined letters to William. His scolding made my ears ring. Do I not know (he asked) the dangers of carrying on a Flirtation? Do I not realize the Great Honor he bestows upon me with his Betrothal? Will I bring shame upon him with my Wickedness?

By reply, I said that I am happy to know he can speak more than a dozen words at one time. Mulford was not amused by my saucy manner. He informed me that my Faithful Mary is to be replaced by a maid of his choosing. Tho' I protested mightily, he would not relent.

Cold, arrogant man! I hate him!

—the diaries of Annabelle Chatham Ramsey, 3rd Duchess of Mulford

13

Sophie entered the library with the desperate hope of finding relief from the emotional tempest inside herself. But her sanctuary seemed different somehow—empty, desolate, unwelcoming. Behind her, the latch clicked as Grant shut the door, the sound echoing into the vast silence.

The tall shelves of books, the landscape paintings, the comfortable groupings of chairs and tables all looked the same. She could smell the familiar fragrance of dust and old bindings along with the faint tang of coal smoke from the fireplace. Nothing had changed—except herself.

"Your husband didn't die of natural causes. He was poisoned."

Horror encased her in an icy fog. She gripped the back of a chair to steady herself. During the long ordeal of answering the Runner's questions, she'd struggled to keep her emotions at bay. But now she felt the full force of the blow.

Someone had killed Robert. Gentle, quiet, generous Robert had been the victim of a murderer. It seemed incredible, yet there had been that letter. The letter that named *her* the perpetrator.

Grant appeared beside her, and he pressed something into her palm. Her cold fingers closed automatically around a crystal glass. With his hands cupping hers, he guided it to her lips and tilted the rim.

Fiery liquid washed over her tongue and burned the back of her throat. She gasped and swallowed convulsively, feeling the liquor blaze a path down to her stomach. Coughing, she said, "That . . . that was Robert's brandy. I never drink it."

She tried to give the glass back to Grant, but he refused it. "Finish up," he ordered. "It's medicinal."

"No, it'll only make me dizzy."

"It'll help you feel better," he insisted. "Trust me."

Concern deepened the brown of his eyes. She *did* trust him, Sophie realized. After weeping in his arms the previous night, and then seeing him defend her against the murder allegation today, she had undergone a profound change in her views. She felt an undeniable closeness to him, a connection of their spirits. Perhaps his arms were the refuge she hadn't found within the four walls of this library.

She lifted the glass and took another sip. Warmth spread through her body, tingling into her fingers and toes. The tension in her muscles eased fractionally, and the cloud of panic and disbelief began to dissipate, allowing her to think more clearly.

Grant stood beside her, close enough for her to feel the heat of his body. Close enough for him to catch her if she swooned.

But she wouldn't swoon. She needed to make sense of the charge against her. Taking a shaky breath, she said, "Do *you* believe Robert was deliberately poisoned?"

Grant glanced away, his brow furrowed. When he returned his gaze to her, his strong features had a grim, closed look. "It would seem so, yes. Unless you can think of someone who wants you thrown into prison on a pretext."

Icy fingers prickled her spine. Could someone despise her so much?

A few days ago, she might have identified the culprit as Grant himself. But in her heart she knew he wasn't capable of something so devious and cruel. "If there is such a person, I can't imagine who it would be."

"Do you have any enemies? Anyone you've slighted? Anyone who might bear you ill will?"

"No." Shuddering, she set down the half-empty glass. "Robert and I attended the usual parties each season. But I can think of no one who hated either of us. And since his death, I haven't gone into society at all."

"Take a moment and ponder it," Grant advised. "Consider anyone who might nurse a resentment, however slight. Perhaps even an incident that happened years ago."

The mere thought gave her gooseflesh. Rubbing her arms, Sophie paced the perimeter of the library. The blue and gold patterned carpet muffled her footsteps. She walked slowly past the shelves of books with their fine-tooled leather covers, stepping around the ladder that marked the spot where she'd left off searching for Annabelle's lost diary. But today even the burning desire to know if Annabelle had borne her lover's child seemed trivial to Sophie, outweighed by the need to clear her name.

And to seek justice for Robert.

As she completed her circuit of the room, she stopped in front of Grant. He leaned against the sideboard, and even in her distracted state, she felt the pull of his masculinity. Dressed as the consummate gentleman in a burgundy coat and tan breeches, he nevertheless exuded the sinful attraction of a rogue. It was something in the shrewd set of his mouth and the cynicism in his eyes, as if nothing in the world surprised him anymore.

Would he cancel their plans for the evening? Dear God, she hoped not.

She was appalled by her wicked longing. How could she entertain such thoughts when Robert might have been murdered? It had to be the brandy that made her so weak at the knees.

"I'm afraid I can think of only inconsequential incidents," she said. "Perhaps Lord Harrington resents me for laughing when you rode your horse into his ballroom. Or maybe Lady Dalrymple has never forgiven me for neglecting to invite her to my last dinner party."

Grant gave her a slight smile that didn't reach his eyes. "There are those who must envy your position in society."

"Enough to accuse me of murder?" She shook her head. "I don't believe it. It's absurd."

Grant turned to pour himself a tumbler of brandy from the decanter. "Then we have to assume the letter is based on truth. That Robert really was poisoned." Resuming his stance, he took a sip and regarded her over the rim of his glass. "The next step is to determine who had cause to wish him dead."

Her stomach churned. Had his watchful gaze taken on a sinister aspect? An unwelcome thought struck her. God help her, if he believed . . .

Lifting her chin, Sophie said slowly, "*I* had cause. I knew Robert's secret. Do *you* think I killed my husband?"

As always, Grant's dark eyes were impossible to penetrate. He wore the blank expression of a man who wishes his thoughts to remain hidden. The fire hissed into the silence as if to add its reproachful commentary.

Smiling, he shook his head. "You? Of course not."

Sophie released a breath as the anxiety inside her abated. She didn't know what she would have done if he'd looked away or expressed even the slightest doubt. It was disturbing to realize how much Grant's opinion had come to matter to her.

She focused her mind. "I need to act swiftly," she said, thinking out loud. "If Jones has too much time to dig, he might find out about Robert's secret life."

"My thoughts precisely." Grant strolled around the library, his drink in hand. "But it isn't only *you* who needs to act. As Robert's friend, I have an interest in this, too. And I believe we should first have a look at Elliot."

Her heart lurched. "Because of the Chichester artifacts."

Grant nodded. "I gather that he and Robert had quarreled over them."

"Yes, a few weeks before Robert fell ill." Sophie sank down on a chair and struggled to put Robert's cousin in the guise of murderer. Had Elliot been so angry that he would poison Robert? "They had a great shouting match. Right here in the library. Robert wished to donate the antiquities to the Montagu House Museum, but Elliot wanted them for himself."

"I presume that Robert never got around to deeding them to the museum. The artifacts have remained in your possession."

"They belong to Lucien," she clarified. "They're in a bank vault at present. Even if I wanted to give them away, I couldn't. The trustees are holding the items until Lucien reaches his majority and *he* decides what to do with them."

"I see." Sipping his brandy, Grant paced to the map table and riffled the pages of an atlas. He'd always had a habit of wandering restlessly whenever he was deep in thought, she remembered. "Elliot was present at dinner that night, or so you told the Runner."

"He'd come to borrow some books from our library. He often does." Elliot had had the opportunity, she knew. Had he stolen into the kitchen to add poison to Robert's favorite prune tart? The image made her tremble. "But most of the time, Robert and Elliot got on well. They enjoyed debating historical topics. It's difficult to believe Elliot would turn so malicious."

"What about Helena, then?"

Sophie's eyes widened. For a moment she couldn't speak. "That's preposterous. Why ever would you think *she* would—"

"Murder her own brother?" Grant finished. "Perhaps because they were always like oil and water. Robert was cowed by her, at least when he was a boy. Helena never liked that he grew up and she could no longer tell him what to do."

"I'll agree she can be overbearing, but she loved Robert. It's a far cry from petty quarrels to murder."

Grant took a book from the shelf and tilted it to read the gold lettering on the spine. "There's one event that would have made her furious enough to kill him. If she'd discovered his secret."

"*No.* I never saw any indication that she knew." Leaning forward, Sophie gripped the arms of her chair. "You must understand, Robert was extremely careful, and so was I. We made certain that no one had any cause to think we were other than a happy, loving couple."

For that reason, they had shared a bed from time to time, albeit chastely. At home, he'd often kissed her cheek or showed his affection in other ways, bringing her flowers and jewelry and books. At parties, he spent more time at her side than propriety allowed, as if they were besotted newlyweds.

It hadn't all been a sham, either. Robert had been truly fond of her, and she of him, and if at times she had felt stifled, if she had ached from unfulfilled yearnings, then so be it. She'd owed so much to him. He had taken her in when she was desperate and alone. Without a qualm, he had given his name to her son.

To Grant's son.

Her heart beat faster as she saw Grant watching her. She couldn't regret deceiving him, she wouldn't. He had abhorred the prospect of marriage. *Damnation! I can't afford a wife, but I'll have to marry you now* . . . The memory of his horrified words still cut at her pride. She and Lucien would have been nothing but a burden to Grant. She was glad she had driven him away with cold, harsh lies.

"What do you know of Robert's lovers?" he said suddenly. "Did he ever speak of them to you?"

"There was only the one man, someone Robert had known for a very long time." She shook her head. "But how could *he* have poisoned Robert? He wasn't in this house. He never came here."

"Perhaps he bribed a servant to add the poison."

A spasm of disgust wrenched her. "But why? Why would he?"

"A lovers' quarrel. Or a deep-seated guilt over his desire for a man. I won't know until I question him." As if impatient to act on the suggestion, Grant stalked toward her. "What is his name?"

"Robert never told me. He never wanted me to know anything about his other life. He was extremely strict in that respect."

"But you've been to his lover's house."

Sophie crossed her arms, hugging herself. "I very

much doubt that I could find it again. It was dark, I was distraught. I was following Robert in a hansom cab, so I didn't get a good sense of the direction."

Grant drained his glass and set it down. "There must be some way to track down the man. Was there no reference to him in Robert's effects? A letter or an address?"

"Not to my knowledge." A thought pushed into her mind, something Robert had told her long ago. He had wanted her to have a means to contact him should an emergency arise during his absence . . .

Spurred by the realization, she drew a breath to speak, then thought better of it. There was no point in revealing to anyone else that Grant knew Robert's secret. She must handle the delicate matter herself.

Sophie rose to her feet. "Perhaps you'd like to take a look through Robert's desk," she offered. "Many of the papers have been cleared away, but there may be some left. I'll show you to his study."

She started toward the door, but Grant caught her hand and drew her close. His fingers felt strong, large, and slightly rough, and his thumb stroked over the tender skin of her inner wrist. With that one touch, the atmosphere between them altered, becoming charged with sensual awareness. "Sophie," he murmured. "I trust our plans for this evening haven't changed."

The concentrated look in his eyes ignited a flurry of sparks inside her. In spite of everything, her heart took a wild tumble and her head swam. This time, she couldn't fool herself that it was the effects of the brandy.

Was she wrong to indulge herself on the very day when she had learned the awful truth about Robert's death? Yet in some curious way, she knew Robert would have approved. He had always sought her happiness. She wondered if in arranging the guardianship, he had intended more than simply restoring Lucien to his rightful father. Perhaps he had also wished to bring her first love back into her life.

The thought pulsed in her. She wanted Grant to make love to her right now, right here in the library, on the floor, on the chaise or wherever he wished. She wanted him to sweep away her rationality and inundate her with the pleasures of the flesh.

But that would be madness. Unbridled recklessness belonged to her youth. Hiding her inner turmoil, she gave him a cool nod. "I see no reason to postpone, provided you'll abide by my rules."

His lips quirked as if he found the topic an entertaining diversion. "Have you compiled your list, then?"

"Indeed so. I'll fetch it." He released her hand, and she went over to the desk, retrieving the paper from the drawer and returning to him.

"It's rather short," Grant commented as he took the paper from her. "I was expecting a ten-page legal document at the very least."

Dry amusement softened the austere lines of his face, giving her a heartbreaking reminder of the man she had once loved with all the passion of girlhood. She was older and wiser now. Yet her palms felt damp with nervousness as he began to read aloud in his deep baritone.

" 'The trysts shall be confined to your town house. Under no circumstances will you attempt a seduction at Mulford House.' " One of his eyebrows arched sardonically. "Rather limiting, don't you think? Spontaneity and variety can be very stimulating."

Though a wayward curiosity tempted her, she shook her head. "My son lives under this roof. I'll hear no more on the subject."

With a shrug, Grant turned his gaze back to the list. " 'Absolute secrecy . . . take the utmost care to guard against consequences . . .' " His dark eyes met hers again. "I presume you're referring to conception."

"Yes." It was absurd to feel the heat of a blush. "Bearing a child is simply out of the question. But you said there were methods of prevention."

"The woman usually takes care of the matter." He gave her a piercing stare. "Of course, such knowledge is the province of a courtesan, not a lady."

She held herself with stiff dignity. It was no concern of hers how many women he'd bedded. "I must be protected, Grant. It's imperative."

He looked at her for another full minute. "There's another way," he said finally. "I can withdraw from you before spilling my seed."

Sophie was too relieved to feel flustered by his frank words. Of course. Why had she not thought of that?

Long ago, Grant had not been so careful. How well she recalled the keen joy of being one with him, the rising excitement and the ecstasy that followed. In the aftermath, they had basked in spent passion, their bodies still joined . . .

She curled her fingers around his wrist and gripped hard to impress upon him the seriousness of the subject. "You must promise me to do so. There can be no mistakes."

"We are in agreement on the point," he said curtly. "Now, shall I continue with your list?"

She released her hold and nodded. "Go on."

" 'The duration of the affair shall be at my discretion.' " Grant paused as he reached the final, most important point. " 'At such time as I decide to end the liaison, you will sign the papers renouncing your guardianship.' " Lifting his head, he glared at her. Anger blazed in those black depths, and he snapped his fingers against the sheet. "What the devil is this?"

"It's necessary, Grant. I can't continue to see you once the affair is over. Surely you can understand that."

"It sounds to me like payment for services rendered."

Though her heart tripped, she kept her gaze steady. "That wasn't my intention," she said with outward calm. "You'll have to accept my word on that. And I will not engage in an intimate relationship with you unless you consent to every point on my list."

He fixed her with a cool, calculating stare. The impenetrable mask had slipped over his features again. Sophie lifted her chin and returned his look, although inside she was a roiling mass of anxiety. What if he refused to acquiesce? What if he challenged her or tossed the list into the fire? Could she abandon the affair she desired with all her body and soul?

She didn't know.

"You drive a hard bargain," Grant said slowly. "I've never allowed any woman to dictate terms to me."

Her heart sank. But she kept silent. She had said all she could on the matter. The decision was his now.

After a moment, he folded the paper and tucked it in an inner pocket of his coat. His manner was controlled, though a banked heat burned in his eyes. With lazy deliberation, he reached out and traced her lips with his thumb. "But for you, duchess, I'll make an exception. I accept your terms. Be ready for me at seven."

As Sophie stepped down the short flight of steps and into the wine cellar, the chilly dampness made her shiver. She wrapped the shawl more securely around her shoulders and ventured toward the glow of lamplight at the far end of the room.

A short while ago, after a futile search of Robert's desk, Grant had returned home. He had been polite and formal while bidding her goodbye. Apparently he meant to honor her request for discretion, and she should be glad of that. So why did she have the furtive wish that he had ignored her rules and subjected her to a mad, passionate kiss?

Sophie firmly pushed that folly from her mind. He had agreed to renounce his guardianship, and that was all that mattered. She should be triumphant, for it proved he had no true interest in Lucien's welfare. Yet she felt angry instead and curiously wounded—because Lucien would be terribly disappointed. But no mother could protect her child forever from the harsh realities of life.

She turned her mind to the task at hand. Very soon, she would need to change into an evening gown in accordance with the ruse of attending the theater. She must allow time to say goodnight to her son, too. But first, she had to conduct this one vital errand.

The subterranean chamber with its stone walls kept the air at a consistently cool temperature. Long shelves held huge wooden casks of wine stamped with the names of vineyards in Spain, Italy, Portugal, France. In the past months, the contents of the cellar had gone largely untouched. Robert had loved his wine, and he also had loved giving parties, but she and Helena drank only an occasional glass at dinner.

The layer of sawdust on the floor muffled her footsteps. As she proceeded to the end of a tall rack filled with dark green bottles, she could hear the tapping of metal on metal, the shuffle of movement, the liquid splash of wine into a container. She turned the corner and paused in the shadows beyond the light from the oil lamp.

Phelps stood behind a long wooden table that bore the tools of his trade: a hand drill for boring holes in the casks, a mallet for pounding in corks, a copper funnel for filling bottles. The butler had removed his black coat and wore a long white apron over his shirt and trousers. His head was tilted back as he drank from a glass goblet.

She stepped into the golden lamplight.

His rheumy eyes widened and he set down the goblet, so quickly that red wine splashed like a bloodstain on the tabletop. The sharp scent of it filled the air. Clearing his throat, he snatched up a rag and fussily swabbed at the spillage. "Your Grace! I—I was testing the suitability of the vintage."

So he nipped at the wine, did he? After all these years, she found the discovery of a flaw in Phelps more amusing than alarming. In truth, catching the butler at a disadvantage might aid her cause. Diplomatically, she said, "I presume you're preparing for the dinner party on Thursday."

His shoulders relaxed a fraction. "Indeed. Lady Helena has instructed me to select only the finest wines. But of course I must make certain that my choices haven't gone to vinegar."

"Of course," Sophie said dryly. Pressing the advantage, she set about her purpose. "I'm sure you're aware that Bow Street is investigating the duke's death. Hannibal Jones intends to question the staff."

The butler's ancient face settled into a baleful expression. "Yes, Your Grace. He has requested that I provide him with a list of those on duty during His Grace's illness."

"Has he interviewed you, then?"

"Nay, he is to return on the morrow." Bristling with indignation, Phelps picked up a bottle and began to vigorously polish it. "May I say, I find it most intolerable that such a common, ill-kempt fellow is allowed to poke about the kitchens and interfere with the duties of decent, hardworking servants. I personally have checked the credentials of each member of the staff. Everyone has an exemplary record as befitting a ducal household."

"No one is accusing you of slacking in your duties," Sophie said, although she cast a pointed glance at the wine goblet.

A trace of color touched his cadaverous features. "Pray forgive my verbosity, Your Grace," he said with grudging humility. "But if I might add one more item. I mean to inform Jones of my own supposition on the culprit."

Startled, she took a step closer to the table that separated them. "Who is it? What do you know?"

"Undoubtedly, the criminal is Monsieur Ferrand. May you recall that I advised against hiring him?"

"The chef? What purpose would he have had?"

Phelps gave the bottle another zealous rub. "Why, his very nationality, of course. One can never trust a froggie. It is clear to me that Ferrand poisoned the duke in retaliation for the French loss at Waterloo."

Sophie bit back an inappropriate smile. She doubted Jones would give credence to the wild theory, but she would add the chef to her list of suspects. "I see. Do you know where he went after leaving us?"

"To a common family. Newberry, I believe." Phelps sniffed disdainfully. "Cloth merchants by trade."

"I see. But Jones is certain to ask questions about other people, as well. I want you to cooperate with him to the best of your abilities." Sophie paused, then added softly, "With one exception."

Phelps waited in stony silence, and she wondered if he comprehended her meaning.

Robert had entrusted the old family retainer with the information she sought. Her husband had told her that if ever she faced a crisis in his absence, to tell Phelps, and he would summon Robert. But Sophie had never had occasion to acknowledge that Phelps knew the truth. The delicate matter had remained unspoken, and the necessity of putting it into words mortified her.

She kept her gaze stern and authoritative. "I'm referring to the duke's . . . friend. You are to make no mention of him. Is that understood?"

A look of pained resentment crossed Phelps's face. His mouth worked as if he were about to speak. Then he lowered his eyes and gave a small nod.

"There is something else I require of you," Sophie went on doggedly. "I must know this man's name."

The butler stiffened. "Begging pardon, Your Grace, I swore an oath to the master—"

"My husband is dead. You answer to me now."

Phelps looked so thin-lipped and obstinate, she feared he would refuse. Considering his long years of service to the family, she hesitated to threaten him with dismissal. But if it was necessary . . .

Much to her relief, he gave a creaky bow and his hooded gaze met hers. "As you wish, Your Grace. I will tell you."

19 November 1701

My mornings are spent in Duchess lessons, my afternoons in Scripture readings, in particular those relating to Obedience and Chastity. My pens and ink have been taken away, so I have fashioned a quill from a peacock's feather and made ink from lampblack mixed with vinegar. I keep them hidden with this Journal in a secret place where the Warden will not think to look.

O, woe. My dearest William is gone still to Lincolnshire.

—*the diaries of Annabelle Chatham Ramsey, 3rd Duchess of Mulford*

14

For a woman about to embark upon a passionate affair, Sophie looked entirely too composed.

As he deftly drove the curricle across a busy street, Grant glanced at her. She sat beside him in the open carriage, her gloved hands folded in her lap and her posture prim and ladylike. A dark cloak concealed her curves, its voluminous folds more suited to a nun than a lover. The chilly evening breeze stirred the black veil that hid her face.

Absolute secrecy is required.

Did she think he'd take out an advertisement in the *Morning Post*? Or perhaps announce his conquest of her from the rooftops?

Grant tamped down his annoyance. He knew as well as she that a scandal would put an abrupt end to their liaison. Such an event would hardly suit his purposes. Winning

Sophie's trust required stripping away her defenses and making her a slave to pleasure. She was too clever to be easily caught, but so much the better. He was looking forward to long nights of raw, unbridled rutting.

The duration of the affair shall be at my discretion.

The devil it would. He would decide when and where to terminate their relationship. It would be over when he'd had his fill of her, when he had obtained her confession of murder.

Or perhaps not. Perhaps he'd never have enough. Perhaps he'd use her guilt as leverage to keep her as his permanent mistress . . .

He vanquished the thought. There wasn't a woman in the world who could hold his attention for more than a few weeks. If he had brooded over Sophie for ten years, it was only because he had never purged her from his system. Beginning tonight, he would do the job right.

At such time as I decide to end the liaison, you will sign the papers renouncing your guardianship of Lucien.

That particular dictum infuriated Grant. No matter what she claimed to the contrary, she was manipulating him, trading her body in exchange for ousting him from her life—because she believed he would be a poor influence on her son. The thought rubbed him raw. He might be guilty of any number of sins, but he would never corrupt a child.

Although at first he'd viewed the guardianship merely as a means to an end, he had come to like the boy. Lucien reminded him of Robert as a youth, quiet and serious, but with a streak of the devil in him, too. Growing up in a household of women, Lucien clearly needed a male influence in his life, someone he could emulate, someone to teach him how to be a man.

At the memory of those big, trusting eyes, Grant felt his throat catch. Dammit, he wanted to be worthy of Lucien's hero worship. For once in his misbegotten life, he wanted to do something right.

It would be up to him to take care of Lucien if that damned Runner found proof that Sophie had murdered her husband. Her high rank might protect her from being hanged like a common criminal, but she would go to prison. She would languish in a cold cell for the rest of her days.

Curse it! He had to find the evidence first, that was all there was to it. Once he did, Sophie would be in his power. He would force her to release him from his promise to sign the guardianship papers.

He slowed the carriage as they reached the darkened mews behind his town house. They had already decided to enter through the back in order to avoid attracting any attention from curious neighbors. Deftly making the turn into the narrow alley, he kept a watch out for trouble, though he didn't really expect a thief to be lurking in the shadows. Tonight, Sophie would have no need of the ruffian she'd hired.

The trysts shall be confined to your town house.

He suspected one of her reasons for proposing this affair was to have an opportunity to search his bedchamber for Robert's letter. It would be interesting to see how she contrived to do so. She couldn't know the letter was secured in a deposit box at his bank.

The stable yard lay in darkness, and only a shallow basin of light spilled from the open doorway. As he jumped down from the high seat, a bandy-legged groom hurried out of the stable to hold the horses.

Striding to the other side of the curricle, Grant reached up for Sophie. His hands spanned her slim waist, and he felt a rush of carnal anticipation. Her generous breasts and curvaceous hips were the embodiment of male fantasy. Holding her close, he lowered her to the ground. The contact of their bodies seared him with heat. It did her, too, judging by the quick intake of her breath behind the veil. But she stepped back, as cool and polite as a maiden aunt coming for tea.

Grant placed his palm at the small of her back and urged her through the garden gate. As they walked in the gloom of the trees, her feminine perfume blended with the earthy scent of the air. He breathed deeply to forestall his edgy mood.

The night was young. He had many hours in which to feed the hunger that had gnawed at him for so long. Tonight wouldn't be like the last time, when they'd made love once in wild, unplanned haste before splitting apart in a bitter quarrel. Tonight, no unmanly emotions would impair his judgment. He cared only about seduction. He would make Sophie wholly dependent upon him for pleasure.

Grant smoothed his hand down the back of her fine merino cloak. She felt soft and womanly . . . and tense. Too tense.

Stopping her on the gravel path, he pulled the veil from her face and draped it back over her hat. He glided his fingers over the glossy silk of her cheek. "If you're having second thoughts, I won't allow it."

Her face a pale oval in the gloom, Sophie shook her head. "Actually, I've been thinking about Monsieur Ferrand."

Jolted, Grant withdrew his hand. Was her mind so far from passion? "The chef."

"Yes, I need to speak to him as soon as possible. I never felt right sending him off without a reference. Now that I know Robert's death wasn't due to his neglect, I feel even worse about the matter."

His brain felt slow, stupid. "You want to apologize to him?"

"That, too," she said with a quick nod. "But I'm wondering if Ferrand might have seen something suspicious in the kitchen that day. Perhaps someone who didn't belong there."

Pretending an interest in solving the murder was part of her smokescreen, Grant reminded himself. But dammit, why was she speaking of it now?

He drew her up the short flight of steps to the porch that stretched along the rear of the house. "There's one problem," he said. "Ferrand has vanished."

"Oh, but he hasn't." Pausing beneath the colonnaded portico, she caught Grant's sleeve. "Phelps told me today that Monsieur found a position with a wealthy merchant family by the name of Newberry."

Hallelujah. So he wasn't the insolent fellow who'd attacked Grant with the soup ladle. "I'll track him down and see what he knows. Don't give it another thought."

Opening the back door, he ushered her inside the house. The corridor was quiet except for the faint ticking of a clock in one of the nearby rooms. Candles on pedestals cast a sheen over the pale marble floor, lighting the path to the foyer and the stairway that led up to the bedchambers.

The stairway to heaven.

"*I'll* interview Monsieur Ferrand," Sophie countermanded. "I doubt he'll talk to a stranger. He was extremely offended to suffer the blame. It'll take coaxing to convince him to talk even to me."

"We'll go together if you like." Grant had no intention of letting her buy the silence of a crucial witness. He backed her against the wall, fitting himself into the cradle of her hips and relishing the softness of her breasts against his chest. "Henceforth," he said in husky tone, "we'll do everything together."

She looked charmingly rattled. A flush tinted her

cheeks, and her hands came up against his chest as if to hold him at bay. "Kindly desist for a moment," she said in a breathy tone. "This is important. I didn't wish to bring it up until we were completely alone."

"We've more important things to do when we're alone." He unfastened her cloak and pushed it off her shoulders, letting it slither into a puddle on the floor. Despite her widow's weeds, she cut a damn fine figure. The scoop of her bodice revealed the mounds of her bosom and held the promise of hidden treasures. He could scarcely wait to see her naked with candlelight glowing over her skin.

Sophie bent down to pick up the cloak. "We can't leave a trail of clothing, Grant. The servants—"

"Have the night off. There's no one here but the two of us."

He took the garment again and tossed it toward a chair, where it landed in an unkempt pile. At the same time, he enfolded her in his arms again and feathered his lips over her cheek. She smelled faintly of soap and another essence unique to Sophie, an elixir that brought to mind the warm, secret places of her body.

She firmly grasped his shoulders. "Listen, Grant. There's something else I can't easily forget. It's that letter."

He stared at her. The deathbed letter from Robert? Then he realized she meant the anonymous note sent to Bow Street Station. "What of it?"

"Someone is trying to pin the blame on me. But it occurred to me that I might recognize the handwriting."

Clearly, she wanted to know who had witnessed her vile act and might come forth to testify against her in court. But Grant had had enough of grim reality. He intended to claim her full, undivided attention for the rest of the evening.

"So we'll go to the magistrate tomorrow and have a

look at the note." Bending to her, he brushed his lips over hers once, twice, closed-mouth kisses meant to soothe and distract. "No more murder and mayhem, darling. Tonight, we're two strangers without any past."

"Strangers?"

"Yes, perfect strangers. We've never met before this evening." The pretense was similar to a little amusement they'd enjoyed a long time ago. Back then, it had been more like charades, in which they would imitate the prigs of society and try to guess each other's identity.

With one tug, Grant untied the ribbons beneath her chin and removed her black veiled hat. He tossed it onto her cloak and leaned closer to inhale the fresh, rainwater scent of her hair. She had done it up in a loose, attractive style with soft reddish-brown curls framing the classic beauty of her face.

"We saw each other at a party," he went on, embellishing his tale. "I wanted you from the moment I spied you across the dance floor. Even though we'd never met, I was extremely jealous to see you waltzing with another man."

Sophie ducked her chin and smiled, taking on the persona of a flirt. "But sir, I'm a respectable lady. I'm not in the habit of having affairs."

To his satisfaction, she was weaving her own story into his. Grant peeled off her kid gloves, letting them fall where they might. He turned over her hand and kissed the tender palm. "Then I'm honored you would make an exception for me."

"How could I not?" she murmured in character. "I was smitten when you presented me with that lovely rose."

Sliding his arm around her, he guided her down the candlelit corridor. "The creamy petals reminded me of your skin, my lady."

"The *red* petals conveyed your passion for me," she slyly corrected.

As she stroked the imaginary bloom in her hand, his mouth went dry. "Yes, red. Most definitely red. I must have been blinded by your beauty."

Sophie cast him a smoldering look from beneath her lashes. "A charming compliment, sir. But then, you're an irredeemable scoundrel. I mustn't believe anything you say. Decent women avoid men like you."

"Decent women lead dull lives, my lady. You've a bold spirit, I can see it in your eyes. You enjoy playing with fire."

"I'm strong, too, though. Before tonight, I've never strayed from virtue." She trailed her hand across his chest, and her voice lowered to a silken purr. "But you, sir, have tempted me into sin. When I saw you, I could think only of . . . making love."

All the blood in his head flashed down to his groin. Was she speaking as Sophie—or as a character in the damned game? And why the devil should it matter so long as he enjoyed the results?

"Yes, lovemaking," he agreed hoarsely. "That's why I dispensed with social courtesies. I immediately proposed that we leave the party—"

"*I* asked *you*," she amended. "Let it be known, I'm not afraid of seeking what I want."

They reached the dim-lit foyer, and Sophie stepped up onto the first riser of the staircase, turning to block his path. The added height put them face-to-face, and she cupped his cheeks in her palms and kissed him. It was a light, teasing contact of the lips like the one he'd given her upon entering the house.

But Grant had had enough of their tame little diversion. It was time to raise the ante.

He pulled her close, wrapping her firmly within his embrace. At once, he deepened the kiss, using his mouth to caress her and his tongue to nudge apart her lips. Sophie opened to him, offering sweet mysteries for him to explore. Their tongues met, danced, mated. One taste, and he was intoxicated, the blood pounding in his ears and his senses reeling. One kiss, and he plunged into the quicksand of passion.

It had always been like that with her, this hard driving need to join their bodies. He shaped his hands around her bottom and pressed their loins together, showing her exactly what he wanted. Sophie responded with a moan of feminine desire. Looping her arms around his neck, she threaded her fingers into his hair and kissed him back as if she were starving and he was her bread, her life-giving wine. In the exchange of their breaths, he knew she could find only a sample of the feast that awaited her.

The mad urge to take her right here in the foyer pulsed in him. He could draw up her skirts and sink inside her . . .

But he was no randy youth to expend himself in a few quick thrusts. When Sophie returned to her senses, she would be less than enchanted to find herself sprawled on the cold, marble floor where anyone might observe them through the long windows that flanked the front door.

He needed her well pleased, utterly satisfied, and begging for more.

Drawing back slightly, he studied her. She had every appearance of being halfway to surrender already. Her face was flushed and her lips moist from his kiss. She looked adorable, and he felt an odd pang in his chest that was somehow separate from the needs of the flesh.

It must be the prospect of triumph. The moment he had craved for ten years had arrived at last. He had Sophie in his power again, ready and willing to accept him into her body. And this time, she wouldn't escape him. He would make her trust him completely.

With practiced charm, he skimmed his lips across hers, briefly touching her with his tongue. "There's more pleasure to come, my lady. Much more. Tonight will be a night you'll always remember."

21 November 1701

My new abigail looks rather like a rabbit with a plump middle and a twitching nose that conveys her displeasure. Her name is Adelaide, tho' I have dubbed her Laddie. She has not a tender hand with the brush nor a care for my privacy. At night she lies in guard upon the trundle beside my bed and snores loud enough to wake the inhabitants of the cemetery at St. George's.

Still no word from William. How could there be? Alas, my Faithful Mary has been cast out on the street, and I have no messenger anymore.

—the diaries of Annabelle Chatham Ramsey, 3rd Duchess of Mulford

15

A shiver of unruly desire suffused Sophie. She feared she might collapse into a wretched heap at his feet, not from a weakness of resolve, but from the unsteadiness in her knees. A bone-deep longing for him consumed her. The taste of his kiss lingered on her lips . . . nay, *her* kiss, for hadn't she begun it?

Grant was only playing a game, she reminded herself. He had cast himself in a role akin to his own rakish nature. In the flickering lamplight, he certainly looked like a scoundrel shunned by decent women.

The play of shadows gave his face a dangerous aspect. His dark eyes gleamed and his masculine features had a harsh intensity. The swift, strong beating of his heart played against her breasts. Through the layers of their clothing, she could feel the spike of his manhood pressing to the place that ached for him.

Something hot and wild leaped inside her. With her fingertips, she followed the line of his strong jaw and relished its rough texture. She'd had enough of games; now she wanted the real man. "If I truly *had* met you for the first time tonight," she whispered, "I would have come here with you, Grant. Truly, I would have."

"And I would have moved heaven and earth to ensure you did." A corner of his mouth lifted in a wolfish grin. "We *will* move heaven and earth tonight, Sophie. I promise you that."

A hint of calculation edged his smooth tone. But Sophie no longer cared to speculate on his hidden purposes. She would allow nothing to sully the rise of exhilaration. Curving her lips in a come-hither smile, she murmured, "Shall we proceed to the bedchamber, then? I find myself eager to hold you to your word."

Turning, she grasped her skirts and ascended the polished oak staircase. Aware of him right behind her, she swayed her hips and glanced over her shoulder. He followed at her heels, his gaze focused exactly where she wished, and Sophie wanted to laugh from the sheer joy of his admiration.

Over the years, other men had looked at her, gentlemen who gave only covert glances to the happily married wife of a duke. Some of the bolder ones had flirted with her, hinting at their desire for an assignation, but she had been repelled by the notion of breaking her wedding vows. She detested the infidelities that ran rampant in the upper classes. Despite the daunting reality of her own marriage, she still nurtured the core belief that matrimony was a sacred trust. Sophie had remained celibate because she believed a wife was bound to her husband, for better or for worse.

But now she was no longer a wife. She was free to do as she wished.

On the landing, she stopped for another deep kiss designed to entice Grant. She wanted to tempt him, to tease him, to make him lose control. He groaned deep in his chest, and her body throbbed in response, demanding relief from a swelling desire.

Desire for Grant alone.

She wouldn't fool herself into believing that any other man would do. From the first time he had swaggered toward her, the champion of a carriage race, there had been a special bond between the two of them. Perhaps he was imprinted forever upon her heart and mind and body.

No, not forever. He lacked the constancy to pledge his life to her. So she would savor the temporary pleasure he offered and wring every last bit of joy from it.

Arm in arm, they mounted the last flight of stairs and went down a corridor, where he opened a door and allowed her to precede him. As she entered his bedchamber, a clutch of surprise halted her. He had created a romantic setting . . . all for her.

An extravagance of candles lit the spacious room, filling the air with the faint scent of beeswax intermingled with the tang of a wood fire on the hearth. The golden light bathed the pale blue walls and solid mahogany furniture. Rich velvet hangings in a deeper blue draped the four-poster bed with its inviting nest of plump white pillows. The coverlet had been turned down to reveal pristine linens.

The door shut with a quiet click. Grant's arms enclosed her from behind, and he drew her back against his chest, seating her against his masculine form. His warm breath stirred the hairs along her neck. As she relaxed into him, a curious sense of homecoming enveloped her. It felt so right to be held by this man, to breathe in his scent, to feel secure within his powerful embrace.

"Sophie," he murmured in her ear. "You're mine now."

She melted completely. Pressing her cheek to the hard wall of his chest, she spoke straight from her heart. "I've missed you, Grant. So very much. I don't believe I fully realized it until this moment."

The muscles of his arms flexed, the only sign that her words affected him. Seeking the reassurance of his kiss, she tried to turn in his arms, but he wouldn't allow it. "You've missed physical satisfaction," he corrected. "I intend to give you that tonight in abundance. But first, you'll have to agree to *my* rules."

One of his hands stroked her abdomen, the other traced the curve of her hip. The sensations engendered by his touch scattered her thoughts. "Rules?"

"You had your chance to set guidelines, and now I shall, too." He rubbed his cheek against her hair while his hands continued to work their magic. "My rules concern what goes on in this bedchamber."

Sophie tilted her head up to look back at him. In the glow of the candles, his eyes looked almost black, dangerously sensual. The slow pounding inside her quickened, bathing her body in a flush of warmth. "Tell me," she whispered.

"First, I won't be rushed. I mean to savor you tonight."

He cupped her bosom through the barrier of her gown. Her breasts felt heavy and aching as he weighed them in his palms. His thumbs grazed the peaks, and her body responded as if a score of sparks leaped from his fingertips and seared downward, feeding the fire inside her.

Leaning into him, Sophie encouraged his touch. Their first time together, they had hardly paused to savor. They had been caught up in wild, reckless passion. She wanted that wild recklessness again . . . but she also wanted to treasure every stroke, every kiss, every moment in Grant's arms.

"Yes," she agreed, her voice unsteady. "We'll take our time tonight. What is your next rule?"

"That you allow me to lead the way. You must trust me completely." Tipping up her chin, he studied her as a tiger watches its prey. "Can you do that, Sophie? Can you trust me?"

His voice was deep, compelling, addictive. The look in his eyes held the promise of pleasure . . . and peril. She had grown accustomed to her independence, to making her own choices, and he was asking her to relinquish all control to him. Yet when he gazed at her like that, she wanted to give him whatever he willed. "I trust you."

His mouth twisted with satisfaction. "I'm going to undress you now," he said. "Not all at once, but bit by bit."

He shifted his hands to the back of her gown. With each button he opened, he applied a kiss to the place he exposed. He went down on one knee to finish the task, and the brush of his mouth against her underclothing felt wickedly wonderful. Reaching up, he tugged the gown from her shoulders and let it slide to the floor.

"Turn to me," he said.

Her legs felt shaky as she complied. Grant remained on one knee, his hands clasping her waist. She wore no corset, only a simple linen shift, her shoes, and stockings. The heat of his stare scorched her. Yet she stood with her shoulders back, her breasts thrusting proudly against the fabric. She wouldn't permit herself to feel any shyness. This was Grant, the one man she desired above all others. The man with whom she would share her most intimate pleasures. It was a heady moment to see him kneeling before her, as if in adoration.

Guided by feminine instinct, she lifted her arms and drew the pins from her hair. She shook her head to release the tightly bound curls from their confinement, letting the coppery-brown mass ripple down over her breasts and to her waist. The riveted expression on his face was gratifying.

"My God," he said hoarsely, "you're beautiful. Even more so than you were at eighteen."

Sophie had no more than a moment to bask in his compliment. Then he leaned forward and touched his mouth to the juncture of her thighs, kissing her through the thin material of her shift. The shock of his intimacy depleted her of strength. Quivering, she caught at his broad shoulders for support. He nuzzled her lightly at first, then deeper, probing with his tongue, the dampness penetrating the fabric. He splayed his fingers over her bottom, holding her steady while his mouth continued to work its witchcraft, tasting her, nipping at the soft flesh through the linen.

The act was completely outside the realm of her knowledge. Never had she dreamed a man could be so bold. She told herself to stop him, to move away, to chastise him, yet no words came to her mind and no prudent action impelled her limbs. Instead, she found herself provoked by brazen urges.

She parted her legs. She arched her body. She whimpered his name.

But no sooner had she displayed her surrender than he drew back and placed his hand over her in a possessive gesture. "Slowly," he said, his tone almost grim. "Remember my rule."

Rising to his feet, he caught her against him. Instead of heading to the bed, however, he guided her to a chaise by the hearth. She sat in a daze as he stripped off his coat of blue superfine and tossed it onto a chair. He did the same with his waistcoat and then his cravat, undoing the crisp folds and carelessly dropping the length of white cloth on a nearby table. All the while, he watched her, his eyes dark and hot.

She watched him, too. The linen of his shirt stretched across his broad chest and delineated his sculpted muscles. The opened collar revealed a dusting of fine black hairs and a wedge of tanned skin. Tight buff breeches hugged his long legs and his . . .

She averted her gaze. A fever spread from deep inside of her, rising over her breasts and up to her cheeks. It was ridiculous. She had been married for nearly a decade. But how many other widows were so little acquainted with a man's body?

Grant leaned over her. He tipped up her chin, and to her annoyance, he wore a faint smirk. "There's one last rule, Sophie. You mustn't be afraid. You must look and touch as you please."

"I'm not *afraid*." Sophie had never been able to resist one of his dares. So she gazed straight ahead to the placket of his breeches, where the length of his manhood jutted against the smooth fabric. The sight inflamed her senses. Sweet heaven, he was large.

Glancing up at his face, she placed her hand over him, tracing the telltale bulge with her fingertips and rubbing lightly. His amusement faded into a look of concentrated fervor. Inspired, she leaned forward and kissed him in an echo of the kiss he'd given her.

Grant made a strangled sound through his teeth. He pressed her back against the chaise. "Enough, or this will be over far too quickly."

"Perhaps you should rethink your rules."

"Only if you rethink yours."

He looked stern and implacable, determined to have his way. She would allow him his whim, Sophie decided. Her rules were too important to risk losing in a quarrel. Perhaps more to the point, she felt an intense curiosity to discover the delights he had promised her.

He went down on bended knee again and removed her

dainty black shoes. Sliding his hands beneath her shift, he untied the garter around her thigh and rolled off her silk stocking. He did likewise to the other stocking, taking his time, turning a simple task into a sensual adventure in which he stroked her feet and calves and knees.

Then he seated himself on the chaise and brought her into his lap to straddle him. Stunned, she perched with one leg on either side of him, naked except for her shift, which he tucked up around her waist. Her heart thrummed in rhythm with the pulsebeat in her loins. The texture of his breeches against her softest parts caused a rush of voluptuous yearning through her every nerve ending. "Grant . . . shouldn't we be in bed?"

"We'll make our way there eventually. But first, we'll play."

With one hand at the back of her head, he urged her forward to meet his kiss. His mouth sipped at her with erotic sweetness, drawing all the air from her lungs and leaving her giddy and spineless. All the while, his hands drifted over her bosom, grazing the linen-draped tips and then delving inside to cup her soft flesh. Her breasts felt heavy, tingling with a desire that increased with each brush of his fingers.

She caressed him, too, learning the shape of smooth muscles and hard chest through his shirt. Breathlessly, she said, "I know why you wanted to undress slowly. Because it makes us crave the unveiling."

"And the more you crave, the more powerful your fulfillment." He paused, his gaze penetrating her. "Are you craving me, Sophie? Shall I see?"

His hand delved between her legs. Without bestowing the ultimate caress, he skated his fingertips over and around the center of her passion. His teasing maddened her, yet he appeared in complete control of himself, playing her as he would a fine instrument. With her legs spread wide, she felt utterly vulnerable. It was unnerving . . . it was erotic.

Abashed by her wanton needs, she tucked her face in the crook of his neck. "Yes, Grant . . . *please*."

"Look at me," he commanded. "I won't touch you unless you do."

She craved the gift he withheld too much to refuse. Grasping his upper arms, she lifted her head and gazed into his eyes. She saw in his face both the seductiveness of the dark stranger and the warmth of her beloved.

Her beloved. She told herself that she couldn't feel anything for Grant but lust. He was her chosen bed partner and nothing more. Yet she had missed his companionship, his wit, his exciting approach to life. The inexplicable certainty sprang forth from her depths, whispering that she loved him, that she had never stopped loving him, that she never would stop for as long as she lived. Heaven help her, she was such a fool . . .

Then he touched her, and all thought vanished beneath a wave of intense response. Plying her with light, lazy strokes, he built her desire to a fever pitch. It became impossible for her to sit still. Her hips moved in an effort to find surcease to the mounting passion. Moaning, she encouraged him to go faster, harder.

But he didn't. He ceased his caresses, though leaving his finger within her throbbing folds as if to taunt her.

"This is what I've wanted, Sophie," he said in a low, rough tone. "You, hot and slick with passion. Desperate with need for me."

In the midst of her arousal, she sensed in him a darkness so deep she couldn't fathom it entirely. For him, this wasn't love. Grant wanted to prove that he could still enthrall her. Because she had spurned him all those years ago.

The acute need to heal him rivaled the passion that ruled her body. With shaking hands, she took his face in her hands. "Yes, I'm desperate for you," she confessed. "I can't imagine ever wanting any other man. If this is revenge, then I'll gladly give myself to you."

She kissed a path over his jaw and down to the hollow of his throat, letting her lips convey the sureness of her surrender. The harshness of his breathing filled her ears. Against her breasts, she felt the swift, heavy thrum of his heartbeat. He was struggling to master himself, but Sophie would have none of that.

Grasping her hem, she drew the shift over her head and dropped it to the floor. At the same time, she pressed downward, finding the hard length of his manhood. "Make love to me, Grant. I need you."

His hot gaze dipped to her bare breasts. Uttering a harsh sound, he scooped her up in his arms and carried her to the bed. He placed her on the edge of the mattress and knelt between her legs. The coolness of the linens touched her fevered skin. Then the realization of his purpose overwhelmed her.

He bent his dark head to make love to her with his mouth. She sank back bonelessly, her hands tangling in his hair, giving him wordless encouragement. The world blurred beneath a flood of sensations. Licking, nibbling, kissing, he drove her to the verge of madness. All at once, she felt herself plunging over the edge, falling into a sea of pulsating rapture that swept her far, far away.

Slowly, she returned to an awareness of lying on the master bed in Grant's town house. The light from the many candles cast dancing shadows on the blue canopy. She felt utterly depleted of strength, yet enriched with satisfaction. Perhaps tomorrow she would be shocked at her wantonness, but not now. Now she felt steeped in perfect contentment.

At least, that is, until she rolled onto her side and saw Grant standing beside the bed, watching her while he undressed. The dark intensity of his gaze caused a frisson of excitement over her skin. He had yet to find his release, and she yearned to give it to him, to take him into herself.

He removed his shirt and then unbuttoned his breeches. As he pushed the garment off, he didn't turn away, nor did Sophie.

The emergence of his naked body filled her with awe. A sculpture of her ideal man could not have been more impressive. The curve and play of muscles defined his arms and chest. His waist was narrow, his flanks long and firm. Yet he didn't fit any conventional standard of handsomeness. His skin was too brown from the sun, his features too rugged and angular. The proud jut of his manhood took her breath away.

"You're magnificent," she said. "I didn't truly see you the first time we made love, all those years ago. It was dark in the room and I—"

He placed his finger over her lips. "Don't speak of the past. That's another rule I'm imposing. All that matters is now. You and I in this bed, taking pleasure from each other."

The mattress dipped beneath his weight. Drawing her close, he resumed touching her with his hands and mouth. Her incorrigible body responded with renewed eagerness. He lingered over her breasts, tracking his hands over their contours and lightly squeezing, suckling each one in turn.

As her passion mounted, Sophie explored him, too. He was so different from her, hard where she was soft, rough where she was smooth. She thrilled to his low growls of pleasure, to the hitch in his breathing whenever she touched a sensitive place. He was wrong about one thing, she realized. This wasn't entirely about *taking* pleasure. It was also about *giving* joy to one's partner.

As her fingertips sketched his broad shoulders and traced downward, she found a jagged scar across his upper arm. In the glow of the candles, it looked pink, the sign of a newly healed wound. Circling it gently, she asked, "This scar . . . how did you get it?"

He brushed a kiss over her lips. "A bullet. It's nothing."

Her stomach curdled. She reared back to stare at him in horror. "Someone *shot* you? Grant, what happened?"

His gaze was narrowed, his eyelids half-lowered. "I had a nasty encounter, that's all. Forget about it."

She shuddered to imagine what might have happened if the bullet had struck his chest. He had been in Constantinople recently, he'd said. Yet he had revealed nothing of his purpose there, and so much of his life remained a mystery to her. "Was it a duel?" she persisted. "Or were you attacked by brigands?"

"Never mind. Don't think about anything but this."

Clearly determined to waylay her curiosity, he brushed his fingers between her legs. Let him have his secrets, Sophie dizzily decided. She had her own to keep. Like him, she would concentrate on passion. She craved the ultimate joining, and blast his rules. It was time to make his much-vaunted control go up in smoke.

She caressed his male nipples, kissed the faintly salty skin of his abdomen, stroked her fingers down the length of his erection. He was hot and velvety to the touch, and he groaned her name. *"Sophie."*

"I want you inside me, Grant," she whispered, rubbing him enticingly. "Don't make me wait any longer."

Her plea had immediate results. Turning her onto her back, he surrounded her with his scent and heat. The tips of her breasts nestled in the hairs on his chest, the delicious abrasion flashing sparks down to her core. The weight of him pinned her to the mattress, and the broad point of his manhood sat poised at her entrance.

She ached for his possession. Ached to the verge of pain. "Now," she commanded. *"Hurry."*

He held her gaze as he pushed slowly into her. Ignoring her demand for haste, he scowled as if concentrating on the effort to contain his fervor and draw out the experience. But Sophie had had enough of subtlety and savoring. Arching her hips, she sheathed him fully inside herself.

"Oh, yes," he said in a guttural tone. *"Yes."*

She knew exactly what he meant. At last they were skin to skin, coupled as completely as a man and a woman could be. The reality of his solid body pressing into her, his thick length stretching her, felt so right, so perfect. How had she lived without this?

How had she lived without Grant?

In spite of her clamoring urges, she had a foolish wish that the moment could last forever. But forever was not a word that Grant understood. He was a rogue who scorned love and commitment. In all ways but this one, he was the wrong man for her.

But oh, how he excelled at lovemaking.

Gazing into her eyes, he withdrew to her entrance and then penetrated her again, sinking so deeply that she moaned from an abundance of pleasure. Yet still, his smooth thrusts were too controlled to suit her. She didn't want to think, she wanted only to *feel*.

She undulated her hips urgently, and praise heavens, he didn't resist. He increased the rhythm of their mating, transporting her to a place where coherent thought ceased to exist. This was what she wanted. A wild, vigorous ride that swept her into a tempest of sensations. Grant comprised her entire world, his hands on her bare skin, their mouths kissing, tasting, murmuring. When the storm broke, it did so with shattering intensity, and she cried out in a blinding rush of ecstasy.

Drowning in pleasure, she had a hazy awareness of him stiffening, his muscles tightening. As he wrenched himself back and groaned her name, she felt the warm gush of his seed against her inner thigh. He collapsed over her, his chest heaving and his head sinking to the pillow of her breasts.

Her heartbeat gradually slowed. She felt absolutely drained and incapable of movement. Her eyes closed, she drifted in perfect peace.

The world receded to the distant edge of awareness. She sensed darkness and warmth, a cool wash of air as his weight lifted from her. And a few moments later, the softness of a cloth cleansing her.

Then he lay holding her again, the covers drawn over them. Nestled in the cocoon of his body, she slid into blessed oblivion.

"Grant."

The voice of an angel pulled him from the dark depths of sleep. He opened his eyes and peered groggily at the figure bending over the bed. In the muted light, she had delicate features and fathomless green eyes. Her mouth was soft and rosy . . . from his kisses.

Memory blazed through him. Beneath the covers, he sprang to full arousal.

He delved his fingers under the cascade of her hair and encircled her neck, gently urging her closer. "Sophie," he muttered. "My beautiful lover."

Her lips parted for his kiss. At the last moment, however, she pulled away and stepped back from the bed. "It's well past midnight," she said with a hint of anxiety. "You need to take me home at once."

Midnight?

Disoriented, Grant pushed himself up onto his elbow. For the first time, he noticed that Sophie had donned all her clothes. She crouched down on the carpet to collect her hairpins from the floor, the skirt of her black dress pooled around her.

He glanced around. The bedchamber was dim, the air cool. The fire had burned down to a few glowing embers on the hearth. Some of the candles had gone out and the ones that were left guttered in pools of wax. *Impossible.* He didn't trust his own eyes.

"It can't be that late," he insisted.

Sophie straightened, clutching a handful of hairpins which she placed on a table. The same table that held the untouched bottle of wine and two pristine glasses. And the bowl of hothouse strawberries that he'd intended to feed to her.

She sent him a tender look of regret. "I'm afraid it is," she said, lifting the mass of her hair and twisting it into a knot behind her head. "I hope you don't mind, but I looked through your coat for your pocket watch, just to be certain. And it's already half past midnight. We both fell asleep, and it's lucky I awakened when I did."

Sitting up in bed, Grant thrust his fingers through his hair. He was stunned . . . no, mortified. He must have slept for close to three hours. How the devil had *that* happened?

He'd never fallen asleep with any of his other lovers. The very thought repelled him. Somehow, it was just too . . . trusting. And he knew better than to lower his guard with Sophie.

She had milked him dry, exhausted him with the most explosive climax of his life. Yet that was no excuse. He'd planned for a long evening of rutting. He'd intended to enthrall her, to introduce her to the myriad ways of making love. He'd wanted her dependent on him for pleasure. But although he'd brought her to the zenith twice, they'd done the actual deed only once.

Once!

Then he'd fallen asleep holding her. Like some doddering old pensioner past his prime.

Moodily, he watched her move to a mirror, her hands quick and graceful as she adjusted a few hairpins. He remembered those hands on his body, touching him with almost innocent wonder. *I've missed you, Grant. So very much.*

She had strained the limits of his self-control. She had worshipped him with her eyes and mouth, praised him with her sighs and moans, as if he were the master of the universe descended from the heavens to bestow her with the gift of pleasure.

A love god.

Oh, yes, he'd certainly earned that title. He'd had Sophie in his bed at last, and he'd bloody well *fallen asleep*.

His beleaguered brain latched on to something else she'd said. While he lay oblivious, Sophie had looked through his coat. Had she also conducted a search for Robert's letter? Damn! There was another of his plans shot to hell. He'd hoped to catch her in the act and confirm her guilt.

Her glorious hair confined again in a prim bun, she walked to the end of the bed and frowned at him. She looked every inch the proper duchess. "Do hurry and get dressed," she said. "And I need you to help me with my buttons. I couldn't reach all of them."

"Come here, then." He patted the edge of the mattress. "Sit down and I'll fasten them."

Clearly reluctant to approach him in his naked state, she gave him a suspicious stare. At least the covers hid him from the waist down. If she knew the state of his arousal, she'd retreat to the other side of the chamber. Of course, he could chase her down, but . . .

Blast it, he wanted *her* to come to *him*. He wanted to know that he had at least that much hold on her.

His gaze issued a silent challenge. *Afraid?*

Much to his satisfaction, she walked forward and did as he asked, sitting down with her back to him. He ignored her buttons and wrapped his arms around her slender middle. Nuzzling the back of her neck, he breathed deeply of her essence. "My sweet Sophie," he said coaxingly, "we needn't leave quite yet."

She sat tense and stiff. "That's enough, Grant. We haven't any time to squander."

"We'll make time."

"*No.* The play will have ended an hour ago, and Helena will become suspicious." But that breathy voice encouraged him.

"So we were detained." He touched her breasts, stimulating the peaks in the way he knew she loved. "Viscount Hockridge is having a gathering at his house tonight. He invited me. There's our ready-made excuse."

"I haven't attended parties for the past year." Sophie shivered from his touch, though she aimed a stern glance over her shoulder. "Besides, Lord Hockridge is hardly the sort I would visit under any circumstances."

"We stopped in only for a short while." Grant shifted his attention lower, pressing his fingers deep into the folds of her skirt and locating the hidden cleft of her sex. He made his innuendo clearer by whispering, "We made a fast visit, Sophie. No dallying. Five minutes at the most."

She released a shuddering sigh and turned to face him, placing her hands on his bare shoulders. Her cheeks were flushed with arousal, her breathing already quickened. "Five minutes? What about your rule?"

"It doesn't apply anymore. I only wanted to hold back the first time. I wanted to make it memorable for you."

She smiled, tracing his lower lip with her fingertip. "Fast can be memorable, too, I'm sure."

That smile. It set him on fire, sent the blood from his

brain rushing down to his groin. "Ride me, then. You can set the pace."

"Ride you?"

She was a fascinating mix of worldliness and innocence. Turning, he pushed a few pillows against the headboard and then reached for her. But she was already on the bed, her gown rucked up to her waist and her face intent with the realization of his meaning. He helped her crawl onto his lap with her legs bracketing his. His fingers delved beneath her skirt to find her lush and damp, amazingly ready.

Then again, maybe like him, she'd been in a state of readiness since the moment she'd awakened.

Her manner took on a frantic urgency. She braced herself on her knees and brought herself down, encasing him in tight, moist heat. She moaned with pleasure. Her hips instinctively commenced a wild, rocking rhythm, and their mouths met, tasting, licking, inhaling.

She wasn't the only one in a hurry. He was damn near shaking from the mad rush of passion that swept him toward culmination.

It took less than five minutes. Three, maybe. Then she shattered in his arms, sobbing out his name. Only by sheer luck did he remember to withdraw before his own release pounded through him.

They collapsed together, panting and exhausted. Awash in primal satisfaction, Grant pressed his cheek against her hair, relishing the softness and fire of Sophie. He had only meant to lure her with that promise of a quick one. He hadn't really expected her to climax quite *that* swiftly.

Would she never stop surprising him?

Then she surprised him again by laughing softly. "I suspect," she murmured, rubbing her cheek to his, "that you are going to be a very bad influence on me, Grant."

23 November 1701

> *The Warden continues to torment my every waking moment. Indeed, my Youth is wasted on lectures and sermons. Oh, why can it not be the duty of a Duchess to ride madly through the streets or to sing arias from the rooftops? Why can I not ask the hall boy if he cries for his family at night, or play checkers with the scullery maid anymore? Instead, I am made to do Important Tasks like memorize dull passages of Scripture.*
>
> *Such is the Sad State of my life.*

—*the diaries of Annabelle Chatham Ramsey, 3rd Duchess of Mulford*

16

At nine o'clock the next morning, as Sophie stepped out of the hansom cab and asked the driver to wait, she felt a faltering of the resolve that had carried her to this pleasant neighborhood. A small amount of traffic traveled the residential street near Covent Garden, yet she knew there was little chance of being spotted by anyone of her acquaintance. The *ton* resided in more exclusive areas than this one.

But it wasn't the fear of discovery that made her determination waver.

Sophie studied the tidy, brick house in front of her. The windows gleamed, evidence of diligent servants. The residence looked respectable, almost elegant. Yet she felt the cowardly urge to climb back into the cab and return to Mulford House.

She didn't want to mount the stone steps to the porch. Her mind resisted the idea of lifting the brass knocker on the front door. Her heart quailed at the prospect of facing Robert's lover.

She had seen him only briefly that one time long ago, when she had followed Robert to this very house. Back then, she had feared to find her husband with another woman, and the reality had been so much more shocking. Although she had long since come to terms with the pain of that night, she felt out of her depths.

Did she have the audacity to confront the man who had meant so much to her husband? Could she question him about Robert's murder?

She must.

Sophie headed toward the house. There was no time to tarry. She needed to complete this errand and return before ten when Grant would arrive. Today they were going to Bow Street Station to examine that anonymous letter. After that, they would track down Monsieur Ferrand.

But she had to conduct this one interview herself. The questions she needed to ask of Robert's lover were private. Besides, there was another, more compelling reason for excluding Grant.

Robert's lover undoubtedly knew her secret. Robert surely would have told him that Grant had fathered Lucien.

Sophie didn't want Grant to come in contact with the only other person who knew the truth. It would be flagrant folly to take such a risk. If Grant found out she had concealed his son from him all these years, he would be furious. He might try to assert his claim on Lucien.

The very thought made her shudder. Even if he couldn't possibly win his case in court, he could cast doubt on Lucien's right to the dukedom. He could make an innocent child the center of scandal.

And Grant would never forgive her, either. She would

lose him again. She couldn't bear for that to happen, not after only one evening in his arms.

Their lovemaking had been too wonderful for words. Just as he'd promised her, it had been a night to remember. She had felt bereft when he'd taken her home at last. Her bed had been empty and lonely, her dreams filled with heat and longing. Their time together had not slaked her desire for him. Rather, she ached for him all the more.

Had he experienced the same fevered yearnings in her absence? Did he too wish they could have spent the entire night together? Had he awakened in the darkness with her name on his lips—?

"Sophie!"

Her heart jolted. She froze with her hand gripping the iron railing alongside the steps to the porch. For one disoriented instant, she thought fantasy had conjured that deep voice.

Then she spun around. Her eyes widening, she spied Grant standing near his yellow curricle at the curbstone. As she watched in horror, he tossed the hackney driver a coin that flashed in the sunlight. The man caught it deftly, doffed his cap, and drove away down the street.

Leaving Sophie stranded with Grant.

Excessively handsome in a dark green coat and buff breeches, he stalked up the walkway. He wore no hat, and the breeze tousled his black hair. But it was his expression that riveted her. A grim look tightened his face. Nothing in his cold, suspicious manner suggested the ardent lover of the previous night.

He clamped his gloved fingers around her wrist. "Where the devil are you going?" he asked without preamble. "Who lives here?"

His touch, even in anger, made her heart cavort. Sophie hid her inner turmoil behind an expression of cool hauteur. "Good morning to you, too. And how dare you dismiss my cab."

"You won't be needing it. I'll take you wherever you wish to go."

"Then I wish to return home. At once."

He held fast to her hand. "You came here for a purpose. I'm waiting to hear what it is."

"I'm waiting for you to explain *your*self. You were following me as if I were a . . . a criminal." She couldn't imagine why he would have been anywhere near her house a full hour before he was expected. Had he been outside waiting, watching? But why?

"I intended to visit Lucien. But a block away from Mulford House, I spied an unusual sight. A duchess of the realm standing on a street corner and hailing a cab." His scowl deepened. "Now, answer my question. Or shall I knock on the door and find out for myself?"

His determination frightened Sophie. Her mind scrambled for a credible excuse to forestall him. But what could she possibly say? He had neatly trapped her. And he was too clever not to have surmised the truth, anyway.

"The house belongs to a man named Geoffrey Langston," she said.

"Langston?" Grant repeated with a frown. "I know that name."

"Perhaps you heard Robert mention it." Although no one lurked within earshot, Sophie lowered her voice to a tight murmur. "As I'm sure you can guess, Mr. Langston was Robert's . . . friend."

His expression stony, Grant regarded her. "So you lied to me. You did know his identity."

"No! I spoke the truth yesterday. But then I remembered that Phelps knew. Robert had told him—in case of an emergency."

"And you came here without me. After you agreed that we would conduct this investigation together."

Sophie refused to flinch under the glare of those dark eyes. "I came alone out of respect for my vow to Robert. Langston believes his secret is safe. This is an extremely delicate matter, and I must ask you to leave me to it."

"The devil I will."

His fingers tightening around her wrist, Grant gave her a tug toward the porch. Unwilling to create a scene in full view of any watching neighbors, Sophie accompanied him up the three steps. "You're being arrogant and unreasonable," she hissed. "Robert wouldn't have wanted you here. Do you care so little about his wishes?"

"Do you care so little for your own safety, duchess?" he countered. "Langston could be a dangerous murderer. Unless, of course, you've reason to be absolutely certain that he is not."

Sophie didn't quite understand the mockery in his voice. Did he think she was still lying to him about something? Or was he merely hiding his worry for her behind a gruff façade?

Grant was right about the danger, though. Worry had twisted her insides into a knot. "I intend to be extremely careful," she said. "But please try to understand that I need to interview Mr. Langston myself. He surely won't give up his secrets to you, a total stranger."

"He'll talk. I'll make him." Turning away, Grant rapped hard on the door, using his knuckles rather than the brass knocker.

His aggressive attitude daunted her. How different he was from the lover of the previous night. But could she really blame Grant for his anger? She had deceived him by coming here. She had betrayed his trust.

Yet he could have no inkling as to the extent of her dishonesty. Geoffrey Langston knew, though. If he revealed her secret . . .

The faint sound of footsteps approached from inside the house. Sophie caught hold of Grant's arm. "You mustn't bully him," she said in a commanding whisper. "This interview will require tact and discretion. You must allow me to conduct the questioning."

Grant raised an eyebrow. Then to her great relief, he said, "As you wish, duchess. But only because Langston is more likely to answer you than me."

The door opened, and a short, plump housekeeper regarded them with some surprise. "Might I help you?"

"Forgive us for calling so early," Sophie said. "We're here to see Mr. Langston. Is he at home?"

"I fear the master's on his way out, ma'am."

"Please do hurry and stop him, then." Retrieving a small pasteboard calling card from her reticule, Sophie handed it to the woman. "Tell him that the Duchess of Mulford needs to speak to him on a matter of some urgency."

"Aye, Your Grace." The housekeeper dipped a flustered curtsy, then showed them into a spacious parlor to wait.

Although her insides roiled with apprehension, Sophie seated herself on a chaise and strove for a pose of serene dignity. The décor was elegantly masculine, with tall maroon draperies and gold-striped wallpaper. A pair of stuffed chairs bracketed the unlit hearth with its mantelpiece of carved oak.

She pictured Robert in this room with Geoffrey Langston. They had been close friends as well as lovers. Had they sat here and discussed books? Had they spoken of their innermost dreams? The thought clutched at her heart, yet she felt only sadness for Robert that the strictures of society had forced him to live a life of deceit.

Grant prowled to a glass-fronted cabinet to examine a collection of antique snuff boxes. Half a minute later, he strolled to a shelf of books, tilted his head, and scanned the titles. Then he went to a table and picked up a small ebony box. Opening it, he removed a deck of cards, which he idly riffled with his fingers.

The sound grated on Sophie's nerves. "Do sit down," she said. "I won't have you pacing and poking."

Holding the cards, Grant sank onto the chaise and scowled at her. "Sit down, keep quiet. Any more orders, duchess?"

As he spoke, he expertly shuffled the cards. The sight of those capable hands stirred her inappropriately. She flushed at the memory of him touching her, stroking her, guiding her to ecstasy.

She snatched the deck from him and placed it on a table. "Yes. You will not glower or growl. No matter how angry you are with me, you'll behave with charm and courtesy."

"And how will you reward me?" he said in a caressing undertone. "Perhaps afterward, we'll go to my house. You'll allow me to demonstrate my charm on *you*, Sophie. As I did last night."

His suggestion had an instant effect on Sophie. Her nipples tightened inside her corset. Heat bathed her skin. She grew soft and dewy between her legs. Without even touching her, he inflamed her desires.

And by the smirk on his face, he knew it, too.

This was all a part of his revenge, she realized. Grant enjoyed manipulating her into wanting him ceaselessly. Last evening, she had been too far gone in passion to care about his motives for seducing her. But now, in the light of day, she felt a stab of disillusionment. Stupidly, she'd hoped their closeness had forged a bond between them. How wrong she had been.

"Don't provoke me, Grant. I have enough on my mind today."

He studied her, and she had the uneasy feeling that he'd spotted and catalogued all her vulnerabilities. Except one. There was one he couldn't possibly guess . . .

"You're apprehensive about meeting Langston," he said.

"Yes," she admitted. "I am."

Grant put his hand to her upper back, rubbing between her shoulders. "I would spare you this, if you'd let me. You can wait outside in my carriage. But I suspect you won't."

His offer took her by surprise. How had he so quickly switched from seducer to sympathizer? Her foolish heart fluttered. Was it possible that he cared for her, after all, even just a little?

The approach of footsteps broke the spell. With renewed tension, Sophie turned her gaze to the doorway as a man entered the parlor. She knew him from the one brief glance she'd had of him all those years ago.

Geoffrey Langston.

A slim, handsome man in his early forties, he had receding blond hair and pale blue eyes. His high brow and refined cheekbones marked him as the quintessential gentleman. He was dressed soberly in a charcoal-gray coat over black pantaloons.

Sophie had feared to experience a resurgence of the fury and pain she'd felt the last time she'd seen him. But now only nervous tension disturbed her equilibrium. She had to win this man's confidence. She had to determine whether or not he had poisoned Robert.

Langston appeared wary as he came forward. If he was not the murderer, then he would be wondering what brought her here. And if he were? He would be shocked to learn that his vile act was about to be exposed.

He might very well turn dangerous.

His manner stiffly proper, he bowed to her. "Your Grace. This is most unexpected."

The wild irony of the situation crossed Sophie's mind. There was no social etiquette for greeting the male lover of one's husband.

For the sake of the investigation, she would be charming. Rising, she extended her gloved hand. "Mr. Langston. It's a pleasure to finally meet the man who meant so much to Robert."

As he touched her hand, his gaze flitted to Grant. A faint alarm shone in Langston's eyes. He had to be wondering why she had spoken so openly.

She went on smoothly, "May I introduce you to Grant Chandler? He and Robert grew up together."

Langston shook Grant's proffered hand. "Chandler, yes, I remember the name. Robert spoke highly of you."

"I remember you, too," Grant said. "You were his history professor at Eton. And the housemaster where he lived."

"I was a teaching assistant, not yet a professor." Langston spoke tersely, discouraging further commentary.

The news troubled Sophie. She hadn't known the association went all the way back to Robert's school days. It reflected poorly on Langston that he had used his position to commence an illicit affair with a student.

"May we sit down?" she asked. "That is, if we're not keeping you from an important engagement."

"A visit to the bookseller," he said, waving them to the chaise while he went to a chair across from them. Although his manner was polite, he looked edgy and apprehensive. "It can be postponed, Your Grace."

She sat down, smiling, determined to put him at ease. "Please, call me Sophie. We were both close to Robert, and I'd like to think that makes us more friends than strangers."

A dull flush touched his cheeks, and he slid another careful glance at Grant. Clearly, he feared the exposure of his secret. "That's very kind of you . . . Sophie."

"I do hope we can speak frankly," she murmured. "There's no need to prevaricate, you see. Grant knows the truth about you and Robert."

Langston paled. His elegant fingers curled around the arms of the chair. In a shaken, accusing voice, he said, "My God. You told him?"

She swallowed a twinge of guilt. "Pray forgive me. I assure you, I've never breathed a word to anyone else. I promised Robert—"

"Apparently, your vow meant nothing," Langston said coldly. "But then, it's no wonder you would confide in Chandler. The two of you were very close at one time, were you not?"

Fear gripped her by the throat, cutting off her ability to speak. He *did* know about Lucien, she could see the truth in his frosty gaze. But would he use his knowledge as revenge? Would he tell Grant?

"I forced Sophie to confess," Grant snapped. "Because Robert was murdered. He was poisoned."

Langston stared from Grant to Sophie. The angry resentment on his face gave way to stunned disbelief. "You can't . . . be serious."

Sophie felt a breath of relief. Although Grant's stark statement was hardly the subtle approach she had intended, at least it served as a distraction. She sent him a quelling stare before returning her attention to Langston.

Surely the depth of shock on the man's face could not be feigned. "I'm afraid it *is* the truth," she said gently. "Bow Street Station recently received an anonymous tip, and a Runner questioned me yesterday. Even Dr. Atherton has concurred that Robert's symptoms were consistent with arsenic poisoning."

Geoffrey Langston wilted back in his chair. His hand visibly shook as he ran his fingers through his fair hair. "It can't be. I don't believe it. Who would have harmed him?"

Sophie drew a bracing breath. "The magistrate suspects me of the crime."

"You? But why—" In abject horror, Langston slowly shook his head. "Are you saying the Runners believe you killed him . . . because he and I . . ."

"No," she said quickly. "They don't know about you. And please be assured, I've no intention of telling them. But I *am* afraid if they dig too deeply, they may discover the truth on their own. For that reason, I'm hoping you'll agree to help me by giving honest answers to my questions."

Langston blinked as if awakening from a stupor. "I'll do everything in my power to help. But not because I'm afraid of being unmasked. I'll do it for Robert. To bring his murderer to justice."

For a moment, Langston's eyes revealed the starkness of grief. Sophie was struck by the reason for his sober garb, the dark gray coat and black waistcoat. Like her, he was in mourning, and the realization softened her heart.

Grant leaned forward with his elbows on his knees. "Did Robert ever mention having any enemies?"

"Aside from yourself?" Langston said, his sorrow vanishing behind cool contempt. "No, I can't say that he did."

Grant's expression tightened. He looked about to explode, so Sophie said quickly, "You must have had mutual friends. Could one of them have harbored resentment toward him?"

"You mean, do men of my inclination have some secret society?"

"Don't put words in her mouth," Grant snapped. "Just answer the question."

Sophie touched his arm in warning. "There's no need to be surly. We're having a chat, not an inquisition."

Langston gave her a stiff nod of thanks. "Robert and I were always alone here. And since we seldom saw each other outside of this house, we had no mutual friends."

Robert had been extremely careful, Sophie knew. She had not considered how the need for stealth might have affected his partner. Aware that it was a delicate topic, she kept her voice soft and kind. "Did that weigh upon you?" she ventured. "Being unable to acknowledge your feelings in public?"

His eyes narrowed, Langston regarded her a moment. "If you must know, I was jealous of you, Sophie. By law, he was yours. I could never have had that with him."

The observation took her aback. Was Langston resentful enough to have written that note to the magistrate? On the other hand, if he was a grieving mate answering her call for honesty, then she could give him no less in return. "Robert wasn't really mine, either," she countered. "He was yours both in heart and in body."

"I wouldn't be so certain of that."

"What do you mean?"

Geoffrey Langston rose unsteadily and went to stand by the fireplace. "He and I quarreled a few weeks before his death. You see, Robert . . . was always tormented about our relationship. He never quite accepted it. In his heart, he remained devoted to the ideal of being a good husband to you."

Incipient tears thickened her throat. "He *was* a good husband," she avowed. "I never asked him to change himself."

"Nevertheless, he wanted to change. We exchanged angry words over the matter . . . and we spent nearly a month apart." As if struggling to control his emotions, Langston briefly closed his eyes and pinched the bridge of his nose. "When he summoned me to Mulford House, I hadn't even known he was ill."

"You were *there*?" Grant cut in. "When?"

Langston stoically met his glare. "Three days before he died. He wanted to make amends, you see. So he arranged for me to visit him in the middle of the night while everyone was asleep."

Sophie knew instantly which night he meant. Although she had slept beside Robert during his illness, there had been one time when he had insisted she return to her own chambers. He'd promised to leave the connecting door open . . . but she had awakened in the morning to find it closed. "Phelps was on duty that night," she said. "He let you inside."

Langston nodded. "He's the only servant Robert trusted completely. And may I add, it was the one and only time I was ever allowed to visit Mulford House."

Was it? Or had he stolen into the kitchen on the day Robert had first fallen ill? Could Langston have disguised himself as a tradesman, perhaps? Then, on the night he'd come to the house, he might have administered another dose, for Robert had taken a turn for the worse the next day.

Yet Langston looked more saddened than guilty. And why would he admit to the quarrel? No one but he would know of it.

Sophie could understand the underlying bitterness in his voice. How forsaken he must have felt, to be hidden away like a dirty secret, partaking in Robert's life for only a few stolen hours here and there.

Yet what alternative had there been? Even if Robert hadn't married her, he couldn't have lived openly with another man. He and Langston could never have acknowledged their love for each other before the world. Sodomy was a crime punishable by death.

Heartsick, she rose from the chaise and took his hand. "I am sorry," she murmured. "It was an impossible situation, was it not? For all of us, but perhaps most of all for you."

Raw pain haunted his eyes. He gripped her gloved

hands, but only for a moment. Then he stepped back. "You should rejoice, duchess," he said with a hint of irony. "The quarrel gives me a motive. That's why you've come here, isn't it? To accuse me of murdering Robert."

25 November 1701

O, Joy! William is back from Lincolnshire!

This morn, whilst the Warden was tending to a call of Nature, one of the footmen smuggled my Dear Love's letter into my hands. 'Twas brought to the kitchen by my Ever Faithful Mary, who remains devoted to my service despite having been Cruelly dismissed by the Warden.

Hope now abounds in my Heart. William yearns for me! He dreams of my kisses! He wishes to see me! I have hidden his precious letter in my Book of Sermons so that whenever my spirit grieves I might reread his words.

Yet Woe is me, for how am I to escape my imprisonment? And worse, how can I be so sorely tempted to betray Mulford again?

—the diaries of Annabelle Chatham Ramsey, 3rd Duchess of Mulford

17

An hour later, with Sophie at his side, Grant maneuvered the curricle through the traffic along Park Lane. Stately homes on one side of the street faced the leafy green expanse of Hyde Park on the other. The hour was yet early for the *ton*. The social promenade along Rotten Row took place in mid-afternoon, when carriages, riders, and pedestrians would throng the park.

The current lack of onlookers should make Sophie happy. She had already had to compromise her rule of absolute discretion when Grant had sent away that hackney cab. But dammit, he wouldn't allow her to conduct this investigation herself.

After leaving Langston's house, they had stopped at Bow Street Station to examine the note. That had proven to be an exercise in futility. The writer had disguised his penmanship by printing in block letters like a child. However, one thing was certain. The distinction of the wording and the excellent quality of the paper suggested that it was not the work of a common servant.

He glanced at Sophie to see a frown of concentration on her face. Had she been hoping to identify the witness? To find out who had seen her add poison to Robert's food?

To prod a reaction out of her, he said, "You're thinking about that letter."

She lifted her pensive gaze. "Yes, I've been trying to figure out why the sender waited ten months to make the accusation."

"More to the point, why did this person not come forward when Robert fell ill?" Grant asked.

Pursing her lips in frustration, Sophie shook her head. "Perhaps the witness wasn't *sure* what he saw. Perhaps it's weighed on his conscience all this time."

"And what do you suppose he saw?"

"It might have been something completely innocent. Something as ordinary as seeing me add sugar to Robert's tea. Perhaps he thought it was poison."

A clever explanation. Grant put forward one of his own. "Or maybe the letter is a decoy. Maybe the author is not a witness at all, but the murderer himself."

She sent him a startled look. "How so?"

"If the murderer holds a grudge against you, he'd want you sent to prison. Geoffrey Langston certainly fits the bill."

Her gloved fingers clenched her skirts. "But his grief seemed so genuine. And why would a guilty man hand us the means to prosecute him?"

Sophie looked utterly perplexed. Why didn't she seize the chance to use Langston as a scapegoat?

Was it possible that she was innocent?

The notion bedeviled Grant. Langston had admitted to being jealous of Sophie. He had ample cause to send that anonymous letter. Maybe he had provided the damning evidence as a means of thumbing his nose at them. Maybe he was a madman who believed he'd committed the perfect crime.

I fear I've been poisoned by someone dear to me . . .

Blast Robert for being so cryptic in his letter. If he had come straight out and named Sophie, Grant wouldn't be feeling uneasiness in his gut. He wouldn't be wondering if he'd made a big mistake about her. He wouldn't be worried that she would end up in prison on false charges—

"You should have turned there," Sophie said, glancing over her shoulder. "I need to go home, I told you so. Helena will be wondering what happened to me."

"So send her a note. My aunt will give you paper and pen." He guided the matched grays to a stop in front of an elegant town house built of pale stone. Tall pillars held up the triangular pediment over the porch, and the brass fittings on the door gleamed.

Sophie blinked. "Your aunt Phoebe? But I don't wish to bother her."

"That's not my only reason for stopping here. She's a veritable font of information. I'm hoping she'll be able to tell us where the Newberrys live so that we can find Monsieur Ferrand."

He was about to jump down when Sophie placed her gloved hand on his arm. "Wait, Grant."

That one dainty touch caused a flash of heat that scorched him. His body ached to hold her close. He had the vivid image of abandoning the investigation, heading straight to his town house, and making love to her. She would protest the impropriety, but not for long. An impromptu tryst in the middle of the day would appeal to Sophie's sense of adventure . . .

"Aren't you listening to me?" she asked sharply.

"Apparently not," he admitted with a grin. "However, I was thinking *about* you. I was imagining you naked in my bed."

A charming flush bathed her skin. She dipped her chin and scowled at him, managing to look both demure and austere at the same time. "For shame, Grant. You shouldn't say such things while we're out in public."

"No one can hear our conversation." He lowered his voice to a coaxing murmur. "What excuse will we use tonight? A party? Another play?"

She caught her breath. "A dinner party with one of your friends, I think. And tomorrow night . . . the opera?"

"I detest the opera. But we won't really be going there, hmm? We'll be otherwise engaged."

Her blush deepened to a rosy hue. "Yes. Now, do let's go inside and see your aunt."

Grant wasn't ready to give up his fantasy. "We could postpone the visit. It's only a short distance to my house. We could be in my bed in less than a quarter hour."

Sophie's teeth sank into her lower lip. The concentrated fervor in her green eyes seared him. By God, she was actually considering it. Being no fool, Grant reached for the reins.

Sophie stopped him. "*No*. We've an investigation to conduct. Or do you wish to see me arrested for murder?"

The reminder was like a dash of cold water. She was right. Hannibal Jones was out there somewhere, asking questions, stirring up trouble. If he sniffed out the truth about Robert's sexual secrets, Jones would have the motivation for Sophie to poison her husband.

"Until later, then," Grant said reluctantly. "But before the day is done, we'll take our pleasure of each other."

"Yes."

Her prompt, breathy reply tied him in knots again. Damn, he had to get control of himself. The fashionably skintight breeches left little to the imagination. Forcing his mind to grim images of Sophie confined to a prison cell, he jumped down and secured the horses.

A few moments later, they waited in the drawing room while a footman went to see if Aunt Phoebe would receive them. His aunt, it seemed, was engaged with another visitor. That wasn't surprising, considering her vast network of acquaintances.

Sophie walked to his side. "I started to ask you something outside," she murmured. "What reason will you give your aunt as to why we need to find Monsieur Ferrand?"

Aunt Phoebe already knew why. But Grant trusted in her discretion not to betray that fact to Sophie. "With your permission, I'll tell her the truth," he said. "I'd like to ask her opinion on the matter. Even though she's a lodestone for gossip, she's also very discreet."

Sophie considered a moment, then nodded. "Yes, she might have some ideas that we haven't considered. But you mustn't breathe a word about Robert and Mr. Langston. Not to her or to anyone else."

The irony was, his aunt had been the one to relay the rumor that had led him to confront Sophie. Grant wanted to admire her for safeguarding Robert's secret. Yet another part of him wondered if her purpose was to hide her motive for murder.

The footman returned to lead them to his aunt. Grant offered his arm to Sophie, and they walked down a corridor and entered the morning room. The chamber looked as it had in his youth, a cheerful green and yellow room with tall draperies opened to the bright sunlight. His aunt and her visitor sat conversing on a chaise overlooking a view of the garden.

The sight of her guest jolted Grant to a stop.

Aunt Phoebe smiled. "Good morning, darling. What a pleasant surprise. And you've brought the duchess, I see."

He barely heard her. His attention was focused on her companion. His gut tightened as if he'd been kicked in the stomach. Dammit, he should have anticipated this event. After all, they shared the same aunt.

Randolph, that hypocritical saint, was smiling straight at him.

Sophie knew Lady Phoebe's visitor at once. He was Grant's older brother, Randolph, the Earl of Litton. She had seen him from afar at social functions, but they had never been introduced.

If truth be told, she had avoided meeting him. Although the two men had different coloring, the earl bore a striking resemblance to Grant in the strong bone structure of his face. Sophie had wanted no painful reminders of her first love.

But now, sensing Grant's hostile mood, she felt a keen interest in Randolph. She could see nothing overt in the earl's manner that should elicit the sudden tension in Grant. To be sure, Randolph displayed an inbred arrogance typical of a man of his rank. Yet he also had warm blue eyes and an easy smile. His light brown hair was perfectly groomed, his demeanor nonthreatening.

Solicitous of his aunt, Litton lent her polite assistance as they rose from the chaise and came forward. He clapped his hand on Grant's shoulder. "Good to see you again, old chap. May I beg an introduction to your lovely companion?"

His voice terse, Grant performed the formalities. All the while, the muscles of his arm felt rigid beneath Sophie's fingers. According to rumor, he and his brother didn't share the same father. Grant had been the result of their mother's fling with a footman. Helena had said that the old Earl of Litton had favored his elder son and had shunned Grant.

Clearly, the conflict lingered between the brothers, at least on Grant's part.

"Welcome to my home, duchess," Lady Phoebe said. A tall, slim woman dressed in lavender muslin, she had pale skin, iron-gray hair, and a queenly manner. Sophie had crossed paths with her in society, although they had only a nodding acquaintance.

Lady Phoebe started to dip a curtsy, but Sophie stopped her. "Please, that isn't necessary. And do call me Sophie." She included Grant's brother in her smile. "Both of you."

"How gracious of you, Sophie," Lady Phoebe said with a hint of reserve. Turning, she led them to the chaise. A silver tray on the table held the remains of refreshments, two empty cups and a china plate. "It's good to see you out and about again. Having buried three husbands, I must say I've never much cared for the strictures of mourning."

"I've kept very busy," Sophie said. "But I do hope to be attending more parties soon." At least, that was the ruse she and Grant had concocted. Glancing at him, she experienced a purling of excitement deep inside herself.

But he wasn't looking at her.

Grant remained standing, his elbow propped on the white marble mantel. He moodily watched his brother sit down on a chair. "Why was your carriage not outside?" he asked almost accusingly.

"I walked over from Litton Place." The earl grinned, looking decidedly less imposing. "Jane says I need the exercise. She's forever fussing over me."

"As well she should be," Lady Phoebe said. To Grant,

she added, "We've been worried about your brother. He suffered a heart spasm a few months ago. Did you receive my letter?"

"No, I didn't." An arrested look crossed Grant's face, but only for a moment. Then he gave his brother a stare of cool indifference. "Are you recovered, then? You seem hale enough to me."

"Quite," Randolph said with a casual wave of his hand. "Indeed, it was a trifling matter. But you know women. They do like to fret."

"It most certainly was not trifling," Lady Phoebe countered. "You suffered terrible pains in your chest. The doctors favored complete bed rest, but your wife has the good sense to realize that moderate exertion will aid in your recovery."

"She's a country girl, my Jane. We spent our honeymoon last year tramping all over the Lake District."

"Last year," Sophie repeated. She had known of the wedding, of course, for noble alliances were always a topic of great interest among the members of the *ton*. But a sudden suspicion induced her to ask, "Grant, have you met your new sister-in-law yet?"

He gave a curt shake of his head. "No."

"For shame," Lady Phoebe said chidingly, "considering that you've been back in London for over a fortnight. But the oversight can be rectified." She tapped her fingers on the arm of the chaise. "I shall plan a small dinner party. You will attend, Grant, and so will Randolph and Jane. And you, too, Sophie."

"Oh, but I couldn't intrude on a family dinner," Sophie protested.

"Nonsense," the earl said, smiling at her. "Jane would love to meet you. I'll warn you, though, my wife is expecting our first child, and she's forever soliciting advice from other mothers."

She laughed. "I was the same way during my confinement. I could have written a book with all the information I compiled. I would be happy to answer Lady Litton's questions."

"It's settled, then," Lady Phoebe said with satisfaction. "And there's no reason to tarry, is there? Tomorrow happens to be a rather light day on my social calendar. Would that be convenient for everyone?"

"It certainly is for Jane and me," the earl said. "Considering her delicate condition, we haven't accepted many invitations, so I'm sure we're free."

"Unfortunately, I'm busy," Grant said flatly. "I've made plans to go out."

"But only with me," Sophie countered. Ignoring his scowl, she turned to Lady Phoebe. "We were to attend the opera, but I'd much rather come here."

"Why, thank you," the older woman said, casting a crafty glance at her younger nephew. "I daresay Grant will give up the opera easily enough. Whenever *I* asked him to escort me there, he called it a lot of caterwauling. It's a mark of his high regard for you, Sophie, that he would endure it for the pleasure of your company."

Sophie could only imagine what his aunt would say if she knew the truth. That she and Grant had been planning to spend the evening engaged in illicit lovemaking.

A footman delivered a new tray and whisked away the old one. As Lady Phoebe poured tea for Sophie, Randolph slapped his hands on his knees. "Well, if you'll excuse me, I must be off. There's a debate over the budget in Parliament this afternoon, and I shouldn't miss it."

He went to his aunt and bent down to give her a kiss on the cheek. He bade goodbye to Sophie, then gave a friendly nod to his brother. Grant ignored the gesture, although Sophie noticed that his dark gaze tracked his brother to the door.

The earl's departure seemed to loosen the tension in Grant. He left his stance by the hearth and strolled rest-lessly around the morning room, his hands clasped be-hind his back. "If you don't mind, aunt, I'll come straight to the point of this visit."

"First, fetch me a brandy." Lady Phoebe cast a chal-lenging stare at Sophie. "It's an old habit with Grant and myself. Would you care for one as well?"

Amused, Sophie lifted the dainty cup in her hand. "No, thank you. Tea is more to my liking."

Grant went to a cabinet and poured two glasses. As he returned, he handed one to his aunt and said, "I can un-derstand your waiting until Litton left. He's too stodgy to approve of your indulgence."

"Quite the contrary," Lady Phoebe said. "Marriage has mellowed Randolph. He isn't so starchy anymore, nor full of self-importance. You would see that for yourself if you could overcome your pigheaded determination to dis-like him."

Grant's face tightened. He looked as if he wanted to ut-ter a caustic retort, then he glanced at Sophie and said starkly, "I won't discuss him."

"I'm merely responding to *your* ill-bred remark," his aunt said. "If I may add, I'll expect you to be on your best behavior at the dinner party tomorrow evening."

"He'll be charming," Sophie said firmly. "He knows better than to upset Lady Litton in her delicate condition."

Grant turned the full force of his attention on her. "Is that a threat, duchess?"

His angry gaze held the hint of a sensual challenge that heated Sophie from the inside out. She fought back a blush and returned his stare. "It's an observation. I hope you're man enough to live up to it."

Lady Phoebe chuckled. "Well said, Sophie. And do stop glowering, Grant. Tell me what brings you here."

Pacing, his glass in hand, he gave a concise summary of the anonymous letter, the murder investigation conducted by the Bow Street Runner, and the accusation against Sophie.

Lady Phoebe sipped her brandy and listened intently. Oddly, Sophie could detect no surprise in the older woman. It was as if she had already known . . .

A sick dismay struck her stomach. Had word of the scandal already made the rounds of society? Helena claimed their servants were loyal, but what if one of them had whispered it to another servant outside the house? The juicy tidbit of gossip might then have been related to the master or mistress, who hastened to pass it along to other members of the *ton*.

Did Lady Phoebe believe it? Did she suspect Sophie of poisoning her husband? Troubled, Sophie couldn't tell.

"I can't imagine who would make such an accusation," the older woman said. "Have you any idea who wrote that letter?"

"No," Grant said. "The penmanship was disguised."

Sophie shuddered at the memory of gazing down at the letter on the magistrate's desk. The message had been simple, cruel, compelling.

> *No longer can I bear to hide the truth. The Duke of Mulford did not die of natural causes last summer. He was administered a dose of rat poison. Look to his duchess for your culprit.*

"The wording suggests it was most likely written by someone from the upper class," Sophie said, wrapping her cold fingers around the warm teacup.

Grant's aunt frowned. "Have you questioned Mulford's sister, Lady Helena? Or perhaps his cousin? What is his name?"

"Elliot," Sophie supplied. "He's coming back into town shortly for a dinner party at Mulford House. I'll question him then. As for Helena, she simply refuses to believe it's anything more than a hoax."

"She may be right," Lady Phoebe said crisply. "Bow Street will need a credible witness in order to arrest you, Sophie. Since this person seems unwilling to come forward, there is no real proof."

"Exactly my thoughts," Grant said. "We're hoping the chef who worked at Mulford House might offer a clue as to who added the poison to the duke's food. He's presently employed by the Newberrys. Do you know of such a family?"

Lady Phoebe thoughtfully sipped her brandy. "The name sounds familiar . . ."

"They made their fortune as cloth merchants," Sophie added. "I'm afraid that's all I know."

"Ah, yes, now I remember. A few years ago, a bootlicking little man introduced himself to me at the linen-draper's. He struck up an acquaintance and invited me to attend a party at his house." Lady Phoebe thinned her lips. "I didn't go, of course. I've nothing against having friends outside the *ton,* but not of the toadying sort."

Grant stepped toward her. "Do you recall the address?"

She nodded slowly. "I believe it was . . . Portman Square."

Grant expected a volley of questions. Sophie didn't disappoint him.

As they left his aunt's house, she eyed him with a direct, resolute gaze. "Considering how close we were ten years ago," she said, "it seems odd that I've never before met your brother. Does he not come to town often?"

Leashing his temper, Grant decided that apathy might be better suited to deflect her curiosity. "He's always here for the Season. That's when Parliament is in session."

"There's a strain between the two of you. Yet he seems a pleasant man. Why do you dislike him?"

He could shock her with stories about perfect, wonderful Randolph. "We're too different," Grant said flatly. "I prefer to find my friends among the scamps and rogues of society, rather than the dedicated members of the House of Lords."

"But he's *family*. I never had a brother or sister, but if I did—"

"Leave off, Sophie. I don't need him in my life, and that's that."

For a few blessed moments, she fell silent. The sounds of the city rose around them, horses clopping, wheels rattling on the cobblestones, cab drivers shouting to one another.

Then Sophie touched his forearm, rubbing lightly as if to soothe him. Her green eyes studied him as if she could see straight into his soul. "I've heard the rumor, Grant. About how the old earl treated you ill. Because you were not his true son."

Her words struck like a gunshot blast. Pain exploded inside his chest, shattering in its intensity. *How did she know?*

Robert or Helena, most likely. They had grown up in the same area of Sussex. Even so, that didn't make sense. The scandal had been buried too deeply to stir gossip. Old Lord Litton had had too much pride to allow the neighbors to know he'd been cuckolded. He had told no one but Grant . . .

And Randolph.

Fury flared in Grant, burning away his pain. If the truth had been leaked to Robert or Helena, therein lay the source. It was yet another sin to lay at the immaculate feet of his loving brother.

"I won't discuss my past," he said coldly. "That's final."

"But I only want to help you—"

"I haven't asked for help. We agreed upon a physical relationship. That doesn't give you the right to pry."

Sophie compressed her lips. Although she said no more, he could see the curiosity burning in her. It was only a matter of time before she pestered him again.

Spurred by dark determination, Grant guided the horses in a sharp turn off Park Lane and into the heart of Mayfair. Blast Sophie for meddling! Did she really believe he would spill his darkest secrets to her?

But he had a way of stopping her questions once and for all.

A few minutes later, Sophie blinked in surprise as Grant turned the curricle into the mews behind his house. They were supposed to be on their way to Portman Square. But she had been too caught up in their frustrating conversation about his brother to notice her surroundings.

There could be only one reason for him to bring her here.

To her shame, a rush of desire flooded her body. It set her heart to pounding and blurred her mind to all but the anticipation of making love. She shouldn't want him, not after he had put her so soundly in her place, reducing her to the status of a mistress.

We agreed upon a physical relationship. That doesn't give you the right to pry.

With effort, Sophie dredged up a tattered mantle of cool hauteur. "I won't stop here, Grant. You know I won't."

He flashed her a look that held both heat and frost. "Indeed, duchess? It occurs to me that noon is no time to visit Ferrand. He'll be busy preparing a meal for the household. So you and I will have our luncheon, too."

"Luncheon." That couldn't be all he wanted.

He deftly drew the carriage to a halt in the stable yard. "I haven't eaten since breakfast. I'm hungry."

So was she, but not for food. She craved his touch, the taste of his kiss, the fullness of ecstasy. "You agreed to my rules," Sophie said, willing steadiness into her tone. "You promised me absolute discretion."

"We'll be discreet." All smooth, practiced rake, he gave her a half-smile. "We'll stay downstairs. We won't even go near my bedchamber. You have my word on that."

They didn't require a bed to make love. Grant had something else planned for her, something wicked. She could see it in the determined set of his lips, in the hard glitter of danger that shone in his eyes. She could feel it in the reckless leap of her pulse.

A groom came out of the stables to see to the horses. But Sophie was beyond caring if anyone knew of her presence here. She could think only of the firmness of Grant's hands around her waist as he swung her down from the high perch, and then the brush of his body against hers as they walked through the garden and into the house.

A short, scrawny, balding man came trotting down the long corridor. He fairly staggered under the large white bundle in his arms.

In swift succession, Sophie realized two things. First, she knew him from long ago. Wren was Grant's valet. Second, he carried a burden of bedsheets.

A mortifying heat suffused her from head to toe. Those had to be the linens from Grant's bed. The very bed upon which they had lain together. Nothing could have been better designed to throw her into a panic.

But she had played the duchess for so long that aplomb came naturally to her. "Mr. Wren. It's a pleasure to see you again."

"Yer Grace!" Clearly startled, Wren glanced from her to Grant. "I didn't expect ye 'ere."

"We came for luncheon," Grant said. "Will you ask Mrs. Howell to prepare something for us in the dining room in half an hour? We'll wait in my study."

His hand at the base of Sophie's back, he propelled her down the corridor and into a chamber off the foyer. In a glance, she took in the tall bookshelves, the gleaming mahogany desk, the comfortable chairs that flanked the unlit hearth. Swags of deep green draperies and the partially opened venetian blinds allowed only a small amount of natural light. It was a man's room, smelling faintly of cigars and leather.

Grant closed the door and turned the key. She felt that definitive click echo deep inside of her.

Swinging to face him, Sophie saw the erotic intent in his dark eyes. She shivered from the force of it. She felt a dampness between her legs, a tightening of her nipples against the stiff wall of her corset.

But the encounter with Wren had awakened a measure of her common sense. How could Grant even contemplate an encounter right here? And how could she feel so drawn to the notion? Had she no shame at all?

She ran the tip of her tongue over her dry lips. "You're angry because I asked you about your brother," she said. "That's why you brought me here. You wish to distract me."

"I desire you, Sophie. I don't require any excuse."

His gaze pinning her, Grant shrugged out of his coat and dropped it on a chair. He unbuttoned his waistcoat and took a step toward her.

She retreated. "This wasn't part of our agreement."

"You never specified *when* I could have you. Only that our encounters would happen here at my house."

"But it's the middle of the day. There are servants around."

"Then try not to scream when I make you come."

On that deliberately crude statement, he picked up a pillow from one of the chairs and placed it in her arms. Irked, baffled, and aroused, she looked down at the pillow. The raggedness of her breathing made it difficult to speak. "What—"

"Over here, darling." Sliding his arm around her, he compelled her to the desk. "Lie down," he said, turning her to face the flat expanse.

She fathomed his purpose at once. A dark excitement pulsed in her loins. The harshness of his gaze both thrilled and appalled her. As she watched, he unbuttoned his breeches, releasing his turgid manhood. The sight of him in full arousal robbed her of strength. "Grant," she murmured. "We shouldn't . . ."

"We should," he said. "You'll enjoy it. Trust me, darling."

They were the words of an unprincipled seducer. Yet she responded with melting passion. Her legs unsteady, she did as he commanded, leaning over the desk, the pillow cushioning her cheek and breasts. He lifted her skirts and petticoat, pushing them above her waist. Cool air rushed over her exposed, fevered flesh.

She felt utterly at his mercy. Grant wished to subjugate her, to reduce their lovemaking to raw, animal rutting. She shouldn't want to be taken in so coarse a manner. Yet as his hand skimmed over her backside, she moaned softly and opened her legs wider.

A hazy realization entered her mind. He couldn't *take* her body because she gave it freely to him. She would foil his purpose by wholeheartedly embracing the pleasures of this unbridled mating. Nothing else mattered but satisfying the primal needs inside herself.

"You're not to turn over," he said, his voice cool and

compelling in contrast to her heat. "Our bodies will touch in only one place. Here."

His finger entered her folds. Her entire awareness focused on that one spot. She could hear the wet suction of his caresses, but it didn't embarrass her, only enhanced the surging thrill of passion. She clutched the pillow and moved her hips, striving for surcease from the madness. For timeless moments, he played with her, too slowly to bring her to the pinnacle, until she almost wept with frustration. She bit down hard on her lower lip to keep from begging. Yet only when a whimper escaped did the tip of his manhood probe her entrance. It was as if he'd been waiting for her to invite him inside.

Trembling, Sophie fought the urge to turn, to draw him into her arms. She wanted him to hold her. She wanted to be skin to skin with Grant, to feel well and truly . . . *loved.*

Was this his way of reminding her that she meant nothing to him? That she was merely a female body in which to sate himself?

She wouldn't care, she *didn't* care.

"Now," she whispered. *"Now."* With fierce demand, she swirled her hips and enticed him fully into herself.

Bracing his hands on the desk, he slid into her, stretching her, filling her in glorious possession. The harsh rasp of his breathing told her that for all his pretense of control, he too hovered on the brink of madness. "Sophie," he muttered. "You're mine. Tell me so."

Greedy for the final pleasure, she cast a glance over her shoulder at him. "Yes, I'm yours. As *you* are *mine.*"

Savage with lust, his gaze glittered down at her. He slowly withdrew before plunging deeply into her again. True to his promise, he touched her nowhere else, and his ever-quickening thrusts heightened her awareness of their private parts. Closing her eyes, she lost herself to the frantic ride, straining, seeking, searching for heaven. She was scarcely aware of burying her face in the pillow to muffle her cries. Her muscles convulsed deep within her, convulsed again and then . . . released her into radiant waves of rapture, a pleasure so intense she knew nothing else.

Slowly, she returned to the awareness of lying on the desk, her cheek pressed to the pillow. With his own release, Grant had collapsed over her, and his body surrounded her in blessed heat. How she relished his weight, his nearness, the warmth of his breath on her neck. In the afterglow, she fancied they were one person, one heart, one soul. Surely he too felt a deeper intimacy than the mere physical. How could he not?

Lifting himself, Grant gave her bare backside a light slap. In a well-satisfied voice, he said, "Get up, duchess. Now that we've enjoyed our dessert, I'm hungry for luncheon."

His cold-blooded manner was a blow to Sophie's heart. The pain of it took her breath away. Just as swiftly, anger rose from her shattered emotions. He was a cad to speak so callously when she was completely vulnerable, all her defenses down. Well, she wouldn't let him see how much he'd hurt her.

Rising, she matched his cool indifference. "Yes, do let's hurry. We've a mystery to solve, and we've wasted enough time already."

Mulford kissed me. I am still shaken. Even my pen wobbles.

'Twas my own saucy manner that provoked him. He called this day to check my progress in the Warden's school of Duchess Lessons. Then he bade her leave so that he might speak to me. Have I (he asked) put all Flirtation out of my mind? Will I come to him pure of mind as well as body?

I long for William's kisses, said I. That imprudent admission angered Mulford. He pulled me close, forced his lips upon mine, placed his hand upon my bosom. And I, surely the Greatest Wanton who ever lived, took pleasure in his kiss. O, how could I have been so brazen? Mulford wants only Father's wealth. And I want only William.

—the diaries of Annabelle Chatham Ramsey, 3rd Duchess of Mulford

18

Clara Newberry bore all the hallmarks of the newly affluent. Her plump figure hinted at too much leisure and too much food. Diamonds glinted at her ears and throat. Her brown hair was curled into a style that even Grant recognized as overly elaborate for daytime.

And she fawned over Sophie with all the fervor of a social climber.

As the three of them proceeded along the basement corridor, Mrs. Newberry gushed, "I am certainly your most devoted servant, Your Grace. But are you quite *sure* you wouldn't wish to speak to Cook in the blue drawing room?"

Sophie smiled politely as if she hadn't answered the same question a dozen times already. "I am certain, Mrs. Newberry. Thank you."

She and Grant had agreed beforehand that it would be best to interview Ferrand in his own environs, in the hopes that he might be more forthcoming. Grant had favored slipping in the servants' entrance without troubling the mistress of the house at all. But Sophie had insisted on following correct procedures.

And because she was still annoyed with him, he'd allowed her that concession. She looked every inch the dignified duchess in an elegant black bonnet that covered her beautiful copper-brown hair and a modest pelisse over her mourning gown. No one would ever guess that only a short time ago, she had been moaning and gasping in a wildly improper mating.

"Welcome to our humble kitchen," Mrs. Newberry said with an extravagant wave, the diamonds flashing on her beringed fingers. She stepped aside deferentially to allow Sophie to enter, followed by Grant.

The ostentatious display of wealth in the upper floors of the Newberry house extended down to the kitchen. A plethora of oil lamps lit the cavernous chamber, gleaming over the copper pots that hung from hooks over a massive iron stove. A long, glass-fronted cabinet displayed an enormous set of gold-rimmed dishes. Even the sounds and smells held a certain richness, the clatter of silver cutlery in the scullery and the aroma of baking that wafted from the brick ovens.

Grant spotted Monsieur Ferrand at once. The chef stood at one end of a long oak table, mixing something in a wooden bowl while several kitchen maids sliced vegetables under his watchful eye. Short and husky, he wore a white coat over dark knee breeches, pale stockings, and buckled shoes. His pointy chin jutted at a prideful angle.

As he spied the invaders to his domain, his nostrils flared and his lips thinned in a thoroughly disagreeable look. He set down his bowl with a thump and glared malevolently.

With calm indifference, Sophie addressed their hostess. "We would like to speak to Monsieur Ferrand alone, if you please."

"Alone?" Mrs. Newberry squeaked. "But I thought I—"

"You'd best return upstairs," Grant broke in. "Else you'll make the duchess very unhappy."

Alarm crossed Mrs. Newberry's pudgy face. She dipped a deep curtsy worthy of the Queen's Drawing Room. "Oh, pray do as you will, Your Grace. Of course, you must consider my house as yours." Backing out the door, she added, "Only please do remember your promise not to steal Monsieur away from us."

"Pardonnez-moi?" His fist raised, the chef barreled toward them. "I will not go back to zat house. Bah! Here I stay!"

Sophie afforded him a cool nod. "I would speak to you on another matter entirely. Perhaps in the servants' hall, if you will be so kind as to lead the way."

Ferrand glowered for another moment as if he would refuse. Then, muttering in his native tongue, he snatched up an oil lamp and stalked ahead of them, going into a spacious chamber with a long dining table and a myriad of straight-backed chairs. Grant shut the door, then went to draw out a chair for Sophie.

He caught a whiff of her scent, an essence that brought a rush of erotic memory . . . pressing deeply into her . . . hearing her cries of delight . . . reveling in her explosive climax . . .

In the aftermath, he had no longer been able to resist his need to embrace her. Having demonstrated that he wanted only primitive rutting, he should have felt the triumph of a conqueror. Instead, he'd had the uneasy sense that *she* had conquered *him*.

Ever since then, Sophie had become the unruffled duchess. She had been a witty companion over luncheon, yet he couldn't shake the feeling that her true thoughts were hidden from him. Her reserved manner had made it clear that she too wished to keep their relationship on a purely physical level.

He wouldn't be irked, dammit. It was every man's dream to have a beautiful, responsive mistress who made no demands on him, who offered her body for his exclusive use without asking anything but pleasure in return. Only a cursed fool would want to possess her mind and soul, too.

He was cursed.

Sophie looked across the table at Ferrand. "As I'm sure you can surmise," she said, "I'm here in regard to my husband's death last summer. There has been a disturbing new development." She told him about the letter sent to Bow Street and the ongoing investigation, without mentioning that she herself had been accused of the crime.

Ferrand bristled, his face flushed with anger. "*Sacrebleu!* Now you say zat I feed rat poison to ze duke?"

"No, monsieur, I'm not accusing you—"

"But I am," Grant said. "At least on one count." He strode forward to glare down at the chef. "You despise the duchess for sending you off without a reference. Perhaps *you* wrote that letter to the magistrate. To make her look guilty."

Her green eyes widening, Sophie glanced at him. It was clear she hadn't considered that possibility. But Grant wondered if the chef had noticed her acting suspiciously in the kitchen that day and he hadn't figured out her purpose until much later.

Ferrand stood up, the chair legs scraping on the stone floor. He made a rude gesture at Grant. "*Merde!* You English, you are all mad, all fools. I will not listen."

Grant shoved him back into the chair. "Mind your manners. You *will* answer my questions. Now, did you send that letter?"

"Oh, but he couldn't have done so," Sophie protested. "I'm sure he cannot write English well enough."

"He could have paid someone to write it for him. A street scribe."

"No, no, no!" Ferrand declared. His dark eyes narrowed, he leaned forward as if to confide a secret. "But I will tell you zis. I t'ink I know ze killer."

"Who?" Grant asked.

"Zat butler. Monsieur Phelps." A look of loathing on his face, Ferrand rubbed his palms together. "*Oui*, he is a sly one, zat Phelps. He watch over ze duke's food. When I bake ze prune tart, he steal one. To taste, he say. But now I t'ink he add poison. He is ze murderer of ze duke!"

"Dear heavens," Sophie said faintly. "That is a very interesting theory. We shall certainly consider it."

By her placating tone, Grant could see she believed the proposition about as much as he did. His hands behind his back, he paced the length of the room and then came back to stare at Ferrand. "We intend to look at every person who was in the kitchen that day," he said. "It should be fairly simple to compile a list of servants. But was anyone else present? Any deliverymen? Anyone from abovestairs?"

"Zat woman." His lips curled, Ferrand muttered in French.

"Are you referring to Lady Helena?" Sophie asked.

"Her ladyship, *oui*. She is in my kitchen every day. She order me do zis, order me zat." As he spoke, he made wild gestures with his hands. "She say ze prune tart make His

Grace ill. Bah, I tell her! It is my . . . how do you say . . . *pièce de résistance.*"

"Your specialty," Sophie said. "Yes, my husband was very fond of it."

"So Helena was in the kitchen that day," Grant stated. "Perhaps while you were preparing the evening meal?"

Ferrand's bushy brows clashed together in a frown. "*Alors!* P'raps *she* add ze poison. She murder ze duke, her brother!"

Make up your mind, Grant wanted to snap. But he had to find out if Sophie also had been present. And he needed to do so in a circuitous manner, without alerting her to his suspicions. "What of the duke's cousin, Elliot? He was visiting at the time."

"I see zat one, *oui,*" Ferrand said contemptuously. "Always, he chase ze maid in ze scullery."

"*Elliot?*" Sophie said in abject astonishment. "With a *maid*? But . . . who?"

"Zat silly girl, ze one with ze large . . ." He gestured at his chest.

"Bosom?" Grant said. It should be simple enough to find the scullery maid with the ample breasts. Sophie still looked stunned, so he quickly said, "Is there anyone else you remember? A tradesman? Or someone else who wasn't usually present in the kitchen?"

Ferrand lifted his shoulders in a Gallic shrug. "Many come, many go." Then he frowned at Sophie. "You, duchess. You do not come to ze kitchen much. But you do zat day."

The pronouncement stabbed into Grant. His gaze riveted to Sophie. The glow of the oil lamp fell upon her delicate features framed by the black brim of her bonnet. She tilted her head in puzzlement, and a faint frown touched her expression.

"Did I?" Her face cleared. "Oh, yes, I remember now

That was the day I found the diary in the attic. I went looking for Helena, to tell her about it."

"What diary?" Grant asked.

"Annabelle's." She turned her guileless green eyes toward him. "Remember? You took it from my desk the first day you came to see me."

He stared back at her. That ancient, leather-bound book with its faded, girlish writing had nothing to do with the problem at hand. Or did it? Grant could think only of one fact. Sophie had been in the kitchen that day.

Ferrand had just placed her squarely at the scene of the crime.

The following morning, Sophie paused in the doorway of the nursery. To her surprise, Grant stood beside Lucien, who sat at a small table. Their backs to the door, they didn't notice her. The two chattered away while Grant built a towering structure made entirely of playing cards.

"How much taller will it be?" Lucien asked.

"Quite a bit. I've still half a deck left to go."

The boy bounced excitedly in his seat. "It shall be the largest card castle in the world. People will come from miles around to see it."

"From as far away as Russia and Constantinople, no doubt. Hold still now, scamp, lest you knock it down by accident." Grant carefully added another pasteboard rectangle while Lucien cheered.

Her heart melting, Sophie leaned against the doorjamb. Her throat felt tight with a happiness she oughtn't feel. She should be alarmed to see Grant here, to know that every moment he spent in Lucien's company would make their parting all the more difficult for her son. She should remind herself of the rule she had imposed on Grant, that he would renounce the guardianship once she decided their affair was finished.

The trouble was, she simply couldn't imagine a time when she would grow weary of making love with Grant.

The previous evening, on the pretext of attending a party, they had spent long, blissful hours in his bedchamber. Their time together had been a feast of sensual delights, with Grant introducing her to more ways in which to arouse each other, more ways to satisfy their gnawing hunger. Like him, she was determined to keep their relationship purely physical.

She had succeeded until this moment.

Watching him with Lucien made Sophie ache with a longing of the heart. They were a handsome pair, both in blue coats and buff breeches, almost as if they had deliberately dressed alike. There was Grant with his dark coloring and strong, capable hands, and Lucien with glints of auburn in his brown mop of hair, a diminutive version of his sire. In profile, their faces bore a strong resemblance, although Lucien's had yet to gain the strength of adulthood.

Father and son. What if she had told him about Lucien from the start?

The unbidden thought terrified her. She couldn't allow herself to fall into the trap of imagining how very different her life would have been if she had wed Grant instead of Robert. Grant wasn't the marrying kind. He would have resented her for leg-shackling him. And how could he have supported a family, anyway?

Damnation! I can't afford a wife, but I'll have to marry you now.

He had acquired a comfortable fortune in the intervening ten years. But he had won it at the gaming tables. The dice could have fallen on rocky ground just as easily. Most likely, he would continue his dissolute ways, and he could lose it all again in an unlucky night. Men like him simply didn't make good husbands or fathers—

Sophie stopped the dizzying, dangerous thought. Since when had she begun to think of Grant in terms of marriage?

"Mummy, look. Look at what Mr. Chandler made for me." Lucien had twisted around in his chair to wave at her. "It's a castle."

"So I see," she said.

His bright-eyed happiness filled her with warmth, a feeling that multiplied when Grant turned and smiled at her.

That slow tilt of his mouth characterized his devil-may-care nature. It held the secret knowledge of their affair and the promise of more pleasure to come. And it was entirely inappropriate, given the circumstances.

Firmly closing the lid on all improper thoughts, she started forward, determined to behave as the composed duchess.

Grant glanced at Lucien. "Don't make a move, scamp. Don't even breathe lest our castle come tumbling down."

Then he sauntered forward to meet Sophie. His gaze dipped to her mouth, and she knew he wanted to kiss her. He didn't, yet he managed to fluster her nonetheless by taking her hand in his and gently rubbing the back. "Good morning, duchess. You're looking exceptionally fine today."

"A lavish compliment considering I'm in my customary black."

"Yet you do have a radiant glow today. I wonder why."

His cocky smile implied that he was remembering how they had spent the previous evening. Since the start of their affair, she *had* been aware of an inner luminescence that could only come from enjoying frequent relations with a man. She wouldn't allow herself to think it meant anything deeper. "Flatterer," she said lightly. "You shouldn't—"

The sound of falling pasteboard drew their attention to Lucien.

The lofty structure collapsed into a pile of playing cards that tumbled over the table and onto the floor. Lucien put his hand to his mouth, but a muffled chirp of laughter escaped.

Grant gave a growl of mock anger. He stalked to the boy and caught him up beneath his arms, dangling him in the air. "You did that on purpose, scamp. Admit it now. You couldn't resist poking it with your finger."

"I didn't, I didn't," Lucien chanted, though his gleeful face betrayed him.

"Is that so? I'll have to torture the truth out of you, then."

He engaged Lucien in a mock battle, pinning him to the rug and tickling him without mercy. Giggling, Lucien fought back, punching Grant's chest with his small fists. Groaning as if injured, Grant allowed the boy to escape, and they circled each other, lashing out with pretended blows, Grant catching him now and then to tickle him again.

Sophie found herself laughing with them. The rough-and-tumble game was exactly Grant's style. Robert had never played so boisterously with Lucien.

The disloyal thought troubled her. Robert had been a wonderful father, taking Lucien on walks to the park, reading to him each evening. Yet perhaps Lucien also needed to experience manly camaraderie, to enjoy the fun of a rambunctious wrestling match.

Lucien jumped on Grant and pinned him to the floor. "I win! I win!"

"Beaten by an eight-year-old. I shall never live down this defeat."

"I'm *nine*," Lucien corrected. "I turned nine last month, and Mummy gave me a huge tin of marbles."

Smiling, Grant sat up. "Is that so? Your mother didn't tell me. What *is* your birthdate, by the way?"

The question plunged Sophie into a pit of horror. Time seemed to stand still. Her heart lurched and her palms dampened. Grant wore a faintly quizzical look, the beginnings of curiosity. Dear God, if he put two and two together . . .

Before Lucien could do more than open his mouth to reply, she clapped her hands and walked briskly forward. "That's quite enough play for one morning," she said in a bright, no-nonsense voice. "Lucien, it's time for your studies. You should have begun half an hour ago. I'll summon Miss Oliver while you pick up the cards."

Lucien looked crestfallen. "Must I? Mr. Chandler promised to help me make a toy sailboat." He turned to Grant. "Please tell Mummy. We were going to take it to the park."

"I never said we would do so today," Grant said, ruffling Lucien's mop of hair. "Right now, I've important business to attend to with your mother. We'll make that boat very soon, though, I promise."

In short order, Miss Oliver and Lucien were ensconced in the schoolroom, and Sophie headed downstairs with Grant. She was shaken by the closeness of her escape. "We've quite a lot to do today," she said quickly, on the off chance that he might still ask about Lucien's birthdate. "We should interview some of the servants in the kitchen, in particular the scullery maid—"

"In a moment." Grant stopped her on the second-floor landing. The dull light of a gray, drizzly day filtered through the leaded-glass window, the dimness wrapping them in intimacy. His large hands swallowing hers, Grant gazed directly into her eyes. "I want to speak to you about Lucien."

An iron weight compressed her lungs. Struggling to

draw a breath, she had a keen awareness of his power over her life—and Lucien's life. "We need to be thinking about the investigation. We've already wasted part of the morning."

"It's only half past nine," Grant said. "And I merely wish to say he's a fine boy. You've done well raising him."

The comment eased her alarm somewhat. Knowing that Grant approved pleased her more than it should. "Thank you," she said warily. "But I cannot take all the credit. Robert was an excellent father. Shall we go now?"

When she would have drawn away, Grant held tightly to her hands. "You don't want me talking about your son," he stated. "Because you're counting the minutes until I sign those papers."

A quarrel, *yes*. A quarrel was a distraction to keep Grant from asking too many probing questions. And to keep herself from falling to pieces.

Sophie brought up her chin and coolly met his gaze. "At the risk of repeating myself, it's important that he not become too attached to you. Otherwise, he'll be hurt terribly when you leave."

"He needs a man in his life. What if I said I wanted to commit myself to his care? Would you rescind your rule?"

"You'll tire of the role," she said, denying a flutter of impossible longing. "You aren't a family man, Grant. You're a gambler and a libertine and a skirt-chaser, all the qualities I don't want my son to grow up to emulate."

Grant tightened his mouth, though the darkness of his eyes masked his thoughts. "I happen to like children— much to my surprise, I'll admit. Maybe I wouldn't mind having a few of my own."

Of all the responses he could have made, that was the last one Sophie had expected. A plethora of emotions choked her. Guilt, for having deceived him about Lucien.

Hope, for against all sanity, she ached to believe him. And jealousy, for she didn't want to think of him taking another woman to wife.

"I would advise you not to act upon your whim," she said coldly. "It would be irresponsible to sire children outside of marriage. And you certainly *aren't* the marrying sort."

Anger emanated from him, Sophie could feel it in his tight grip. But she didn't care. It was better to foster an estrangement than to let him guess how foolishly, how recklessly she wished he could be the man she wanted him to be.

With an abrupt tug on her hand, Grant hauled her down the second-floor corridor. She hastened to keep from stumbling. He threw open the first door on the left. It was the Blue Bedchamber, one of a dozen guest rooms. The curtains were drawn, the air dim and faintly musty with disuse. Large white dustcloths shrouded the bed and the other furnishings.

Unbidden, a thrill eddied through Sophie. Her heart pulsed madly, the sensation traveling downward to incite heat between her legs. Unless there was a guest, no one ever ventured in here. She and Grant could make love without being caught . . .

Dear God, what was she *thinking*?

Grant kicked the door shut and pushed her up against the wall. Fury glittered in his eyes as he pressed himself to her. "How is it that you know so much about me, Sophie? Do you believe this"—he rolled his hips against hers—"gives you access to my mind?"

She caught her breath. The heat of him surrounded her, and she wanted nothing more than to melt in his arms. "Release me at once. You're breaking my rule."

"I'm bending it. There's a difference. Now, answer my question."

She had to force her thoughts away from the magnetic pull of his body. Physically, he was the most perfect of men, with hard ridges of muscle in his chest and arms, narrow hips and powerful flanks.

Pressing her palms to his coat, she tilted her head back to study his strong features. "All right, then, I *don't* know your thoughts," she said stiffly. "How can I? You refuse to talk about anything in your past."

"You have your secrets, too. Don't you, sweet Sophie?"

A sharp edge underscored his husky voice, and she quivered from a jab of raw fear. Lucien. He must mean Lucien.

But if Grant suspected the truth, why didn't he say so? Was he trifling with her as a tomcat toys with its prey? Was he waiting for her to confess? She would never do so; she couldn't take the risk of jeopardizing her son's reputation, his position in society.

"Not talking, are you?" Grant said silkily. "Shall we put our mouths to better use, then?"

He brushed his lips against hers, his tongue seeking entry. Sophie hesitated only a moment before opening to him. She needed to distract him, didn't she? And dear God, temptation had never felt so good. Grant kissed with tender expertise, exploring her with sensitivity and skill. The sensations he provoked made her body soften and tingle.

Yet she desperately held herself aloof. She could allow him no more than this one concession. Drawing back, she forced firmness into her voice. "That's enough, Grant."

He moved his head lower, and his warm breath seared her throat. "It's not enough," he murmured, kissing her skin. "I could take you right here, Sophie. We could do it without moving from this spot."

Despite her better judgment, she was transfixed by the notion. "Standing—"

"I'll lift you." He did so effortlessly, clasping her sides as he held her against the wall, his hips pantomiming the act of love. "You can wrap your legs around my waist."

She couldn't without raising her skirts. No, she couldn't because she *mustn't*. Yet a reckless fever swept over her. In a matter of moments, he could be inside her, filling her aching center. There was little risk of discovery here . . .

Even a little risk was too much.

"Absolutely not," she said, appalled at herself. "Put me down, or I shall scream."

He held her in place. A rakish determination tilted one corner of his mouth. "I'd rather hear you cry out with pleasure. Why don't you break your rule? We can enjoy each other right here, right now."

Desire and mortification waged war inside her. How dare he tempt her like this? Her hands on his chest, she gave him a hard shove. To her satisfaction, he lost his grip on her and staggered backward a few paces.

She liked having her feet planted firmly on the floor again. "That's enough, Grant. You're violating our agreement. I won't have you seducing me in this house."

He regarded her through narrowed eyes. "I can't help myself, darling. I'm a skirt-chasing libertine, remember? Seducing women is what I do best."

The hint of irony in his tone caught at Sophie. He was playing the knave on purpose, she realized. Was that why he'd pulled her into this deserted bedchamber? Because he was furious at her for labeling him an unprincipled rogue? Or perhaps even . . . *hurt*?

She studied his moody features through the dimness. It was a novel idea to think Grant might *want* her good opinion. Yet he hid his vulnerability behind a mask of outrageous behavior. Had he learned that habit in childhood?

The thought mollified her anger. Going to him, she caressed the shaven smoothness of his cheek. "You may seduce me tonight, *darling*," she purred. "In the meantime, we have work to do."

Leaving him off balance, she walked to the door and opened it. She sensed his presence right behind her in the moment before he slid his hand down her back to caress the indentation of her waist. His breath stirred the fine hairs at the nape of her neck.

"Sophie . . ." he murmured.

"Sophie?"

The feminine voice echoed in the wide corridor outside the bedchamber. It was shocked, chiding . . . and very familiar.

With a stiffening of alarm, Sophie spied Helena marching straight toward them.

2 December 1701

Three days have passed since last I saw Mulford. 'Tis well he stays away, for I am mortified by my Wanton behavior. He is a Cold and Cruel man who keeps me locked in the prison of my house, guarded in daytime by his aunt, the Warden, and at night by Laddie of the twitching nose and beady eyes. Meanwhile, Mulford is off enjoying his manly freedom.

Our Wedding is set for less than a month from now, on the first day of the New Year. I must not succumb to panic. I must remain steadfast in my Determination to see William.

—*the diaries of Annabelle Chatham Ramsey, 3rd Duchess of Mulford*

19

Lady Helena Ramsey displayed all the outraged censure of an embittered spinster, Grant thought. Beneath the dainty black cap that enveloped her blond hair, the wine-stain birthmark looked stark against the pale white of her skin.

She stopped in front of them, her fists gripped at her sides. "What on earth is going on?" she snapped, glaring from Sophie to Grant. "Why were you two in that bedchamber?"

Wouldn't you like to know? Grant didn't care a farthing for his own reputation. But he wouldn't give the woman cause to reproach Sophie. "Good morning, Helena. You're just the person we were seeking."

"In there?" Her tone dripped with disbelief.

"Of course not," Sophie said calmly. "We were looking for evidence. Elliot sometimes uses that bedchamber."

Helena pursed her lips so tightly they almost disappeared. "Surely you can't suspect Elliot of . . ."

"Of poisoning your brother?" Grant jumped on Sophie's excuse and embellished it. "Elliot wants the Chichester artifacts. Robert refused to give them to him. That might indeed cause him to commit murder."

Helena frowned, glancing up and down the otherwise deserted corridor. "Kindly keep your voice down. I've had a difficult enough time keeping the servants from speculating, what with that Bow Street Runner pestering them with questions."

The reminder of Hannibal Jones made Grant tense. "Then let's discuss the matter in private," he said. "Perhaps in your chambers." Maybe he could pick up a clue there, something to implicate Helena and exonerate Sophie.

He wondered about Robert's elder sister. In their youth, Grant had witnessed the way she had browbeat Robert. She had wanted to control his every move, to make him behave with rigid propriety. If by chance she had discovered the nature of his relationship with Geoffrey Langston, she might have been outraged enough to kill her brother.

And maybe he was grasping at straws in order to convince himself of Sophie's innocence.

Helena regarded him now with disapproval. "It is inappropriate for an unmarried woman to entertain a gentleman in the bedchamber," she said, giving Sophie a significant look. "And there is nothing at all that I wish to discuss with someone who is not a member of this family. I'm not even entirely convinced that Robert was poisoned deliberately."

Sophie took her sister-in-law's arm. "Dear Helena,

don't be cross. We're only trying to find out the truth so we can stop Jones from coming round. Now, you know so much of what goes on in this house. Won't you please discuss the matter with us in the library?" As she spoke, Sophie steered her toward the staircase.

Grant followed in their wake. He didn't mind taking up the rear. It gave him a chance to admire Sophie's trim figure.

Even though he knew every inch of the fine body beneath her drab black gown, the sway of her hips held his rapt attention. Damn, he should have seduced her in the bedchamber when he'd had the opportunity. He should not have felt any scruples. She believed him a cad, anyway, so what did adding one more sin to his list of misdeeds matter?

Yet he hadn't been able to bring himself to do it. Not against her wishes. Oh, she'd have given herself willingly enough. With just one kiss, Sophie had been halfway to surrender. But afterward, she would have loathed him for breaking her damn rule. And his gut resisted the prospect of inspiring her hatred.

That was why he had pulled her into the bedchamber in the first place. Because she had accused him of being a gambler and a libertine. Because she had declared him unfit to be a father.

His own words came back to plague him. *I wouldn't mind having a few of my own.* God, what had possessed him to say *that*?

He liked Lucien more than he'd anticipated. Maybe because the boy had a fresh, bright-eyed view of the world. Or maybe because he reminded Grant that innocence still existed. Whatever the case, Lucien's hero worship somehow made Grant want to *become* a hero.

But it was a tremendous leap from a guardianship to setting up his own nursery. He abhorred the notion of being tied down. Sophie was right, he wasn't a family man. Once he was through with her, he intended to live the high life, to stay out until dawn, to play cards with knaves like Kilminster, Hockridge, and Updike. To enjoy all the women he wanted.

The trouble was, he wanted only Sophie. Two sessions in his bedchamber and another in his study hadn't even begun to sate his passion for her. Despite their physical closeness, she maintained an intriguing air of mystery.

Descending the staircase with her sister-in-law, Sophie behaved as the aloof, regal duchess, always in control, ever capable of handling any crisis. But she hadn't appeared so calm earlier.

When he had asked her about her secrets, she had looked terrified, guilty as sin. He had literally *felt* a tremor run through her. She was hiding something. It had to be her involvement in Robert's death.

Because what the devil else could make her so afraid?

As she and Helena sat down in the library, Sophie aimed a quelling stare at Grant. She tried to convey the silent message that he was to allow her to handle Helena. He met her gaze, his dark eyes as devilish as ever. It was a look that always caused a little lurch deep within her.

Rather than sit with them, he strolled to the window and peered out at the gray weather. She hoped to goodness he would behave.

Returning her attention to Helena, Sophie said, "Phelps made a list of servants for the Runner, didn't he?"

"Yes." Perfectly composed, Helena sat with her hands folded in her lap. "However, I expect it is a futile effort. Obviously, someone sent that letter as a cruel prank. To seek a murderer under this roof is patently absurd."

"We'd all like to think so," Sophie said with feeling. "But we have to prove it to the satisfaction of the magistrate. For that reason, I'd like to speak to all the servants on that list."

"I already have the matter in hand," Helena said crisply. "It's best that *I* interview the staff. I know each and every one of them far better than you do."

Grant turned from the window. "Then did you know that Elliot has been carrying on with the scullery maid?"

Helena started in astonishment. "I beg your pardon?" she said in a freezing tone.

"It's a rumor we heard, that's all," Sophie said, intervening quickly. "I was very surprised to hear it myself. Had you had any suspicion of it?"

"Certainly not, else I'd have put a stop to it at once." Noticeably disconcerted, Helena stared down at her hands. "I'd seen him in the kitchen a time or two, but . . ." Her head came up, her troubled gaze on Sophie. "It must be nonsense. Who told you such gossip?"

"We spoke to Monsieur Ferrand yesterday. He's presently employed by a cloth merchant named Newberry. He mentioned that Elliot was in the kitchen that day."

Helena looked as if she'd swallowed a snail. "Ferrand! He's the one who served tainted food to Robert. I wouldn't trust a word he said!"

"But we no longer know for certain that Robert's death was due to Ferrand's neglect," Sophie gently pointed out. "We may have been wrong to dismiss him. And if we are wrong, then perhaps we *can* trust his word."

"Bah, he is a Frenchman!" Helena said with a sweep of her hand. "I wouldn't be surprised if *he* is the one who put rat poison in Robert's tart. It happened directly after the French defeat at Waterloo, you know!"

That was the same theory Phelps had expounded. Although Sophie found it rather far-fetched, she resolved to ask the other servants if Ferrand had ever expressed antipathy toward the English. She couldn't afford to leave any stone unturned.

For that reason, she tried to put Helena in the guise of a murderess. Robert's sister was a strong, controlling woman, set in her ways. But could she have killed her own brother? Sophie's stomach twisted. Had Helena sent that letter to the magistrate?

Grant strolled to the fireplace and rested his forearm on the pale marble mantel. "Have you had a particular need for rat poison here?"

"Occasionally," Helena admitted. "This is London, after all. But I can assure you, this house is spotless. I would never allow vermin to thrive in the family home."

"No one is disputing your fine supervision of the staff," Sophie said. "I'm sure Grant is merely establishing that poison is readily available in the house. It's kept downstairs in the pantry, is it not?"

"Yes." Helena thoughtfully tipped her head to the side. "You've had need of it, too, Sophie. Remember the damage the rats did in here last year?"

"They ate the binding glue on a few of the books," Sophie told Grant. Her skin crawled as she remembered making that discovery, finding droppings and bits of chewed pages scattered over the carpet. "Luckily the books were fairly new and easily replaced."

His keen dark eyes rested on her. "Where did this happen?" he asked.

She pointed. "On the lowest shelf to the right of the window."

Grant strolled over there and crouched down to inspect the area. "I see someone has caulked a small hole in the molding," he observed. "Did you set out the poison yourself, Sophie?"

"Goodness, no. One of the footmen took care of the matter."

Grant got to his feet and strolled toward the women. "Helena, I don't suppose any of the footmen reported a significant amount of poison missing, did they?"

Helena shook her head. "Not to my knowledge. But . . . it wouldn't take much to sicken a person, would it?"

He shrugged. "I'll ask Jones. By the by, will your cousin be returning to London anytime soon?"

"For his birthday dinner tomorrow." Helena gave Grant an imperious look. "I have known Elliot all my life. I can assure you, *he* is not the culprit."

Seeing the signs of anger in her sister-in-law, Sophie said quickly, "It's only a possibility. And if Elliot was in the kitchen that day, he might have seen something significant." Turning to Grant, she added, "You're invited to the dinner, by the by. That is, if you'd care to attend."

"Thank you, I shall," Grant said in a distracted tone. "In the meantime I'd like to question the scullery maid."

After a tiresome day spent interviewing the servants, Sophie found it a relief to enjoy dinner at Lady Phoebe's house.

Most frustrating of all had been the thwarted interview with the scullery maid, Alice. When Grant had posed the first question about Elliot, the girl had swooned. Clearly, Alice was terrified about losing her position—or she hid some other secret. Sophie intended to find out the truth tomorrow.

In the meantime, she would relax. She would take pleasure in the company. She would forget all her troubles.

Yet she was aware of the tension between Grant and his brother.

Grant focused his attention on the ladies and ignored

Randolph. At least the two men hadn't quarreled. By the dessert course of apricot cake, she had to admit his behavior had been exemplary toward both his aunt and Randolph's wife, Jane, the countess of Litton.

Lady Phoebe had deftly directed the conversation, entertaining them with stories of society scandals during Grant's long absence. "Lord Thurgood traveled to the frontier of America," she said, "and returned with a hat made of a raccoon skin with the tail hanging down the back. He wore the vulgar thing every day in Hyde Park, at least until Lord Barrymore's mastiff got loose and snatched it right off Thurgood's head."

Everyone laughed. "The poor man," Jane said merrily. "He did love that dreadful hat. When he wrestled it away from the dog, there was nothing left but bits of fur."

From Randolph's description of a country girl who enjoyed walking, Sophie had expected Jane to be a sturdy, no-nonsense woman with large feet and a brisk manner. Instead, she was a porcelain doll with dainty features, a mass of curled blond hair, and a sweet disposition. The gentle swelling beneath her pale blue gown showed the advanced state of her pregnancy. She sat beside her husband, and from time to time, they touched hands or shared a loving glance.

Now, however, Randolph eyed his younger brother. "I find myself most curious about *your* travels, Grant. Aunt Phoebe mentioned that you went as far afield as Constantinople and Russia. What were you doing all those years?"

Grant drank from his wine glass, then said casually, "Stealing jewels, of course."

Silence descended over the table. The earl looked thunderstruck; Jane appeared equally startled with her silver fork poised over her plate. Grant's unsmiling face held a hint of savagery that belied his gentlemanly garb. For one dizzying moment, Sophie wondered if he was telling the truth.

Lady Phoebe glowered imperiously. "Don't prevaricate, nephew. Tell us some genuine stories. It's time you did."

Grant flashed a winning smile at his aunt. "Forgive me for teasing. Perhaps you'd like to hear about the sultan's palace I visited in Smyrna."

"Goodness, yes. How did you come to know a sultan?"

"It was an unexpected encounter. He was quite amazed to meet an Englishman, I must add."

Mockery glinted in his eyes, Sophie noticed. It suggested there was more to this story than he'd admitted. "How long were you a guest in the palace?" she asked.

He turned his dark gaze on her. "Oh, it was merely a short visit. But I did have the chance to view the throne room, the inner gardens, even the sultan's private apartments."

"How romantic," Jane said, her blue eyes bright with interest. "Was it decorated in the fashion of the *Arabian Nights*? Was the furniture made entirely of gold? Were there slaves waiting upon the sultan?"

Grant smiled. Apparently his animosity didn't extend to Randolph's wife. "The furniture was indeed inlaid with gold," he said. "The palace has some two hundred rooms, including a cloistered harem for the sultan's many wives. It is guarded by eunuchs."

"Eunuchs?" Sophie questioned.

He gave her a bland look. "Men who have been . . . altered. The sultan cannot have virile men guarding his women, can he?"

"Here now," Randolph protested. "This is not a suitable topic for the ladies."

"It is most fascinating, dearest," Jane said firmly. Despite her fragile appearance, she seemed determined not to be intimidated by either man. "It must have been an interesting experience to speak with a foreign ruler, to see how different his life is from ours."

"Don't think too highly of the sultan," Grant said. "His wealth is derived from the sale of opium. He controls vast fields of poppies in the hills and mountains to the north. He's a despot who rules with an iron fist."

Randolph frowned. "He doesn't sound like a decent sort of chap at all. What was the nature of your visit?"

"A business transaction," Grant said coolly.

The two men regarded each other. Grant's expression taunted his brother, but Randolph said no more. From his troubled stare, he must be thinking the same thoughts as Sophie. That Grant had been involved in something shady, either gambling or making an illegal deal of some sort.

Randolph seemed to have risen above the need for sibling rivalry, Sophie reflected. What had happened in childhood to make Grant so resentful? Had Randolph bullied him? Or was Grant simply jealous of the favored elder brother? Had he transferred his resentment of the old earl to the new one?

Lady Phoebe stood up at the head of the table. "We ladies shall leave the gentlemen to their brandy. We'll retire to the drawing room."

The announcement took Sophie by surprise. Wasn't Lady Phoebe worried that the two men would come to blows? Who would mediate their quarrels? But politeness prevented her from protesting, so she rose to join Jane and Lady Phoebe.

As they proceeded out the door, she took one last glance at Grant. In deference to the ladies, he and Randolph had arisen from their chairs. Both men radiated a stiff discomfiture. But Grant appeared downright grim.

With his jaw set and his eyes narrowed, he looked menacing enough to kill his own brother.

. . .

"Brandy?" Randoph asked, fetching a decanter and two glasses from the sideboard. His voice was hearty, his manner obliging.

Grant detested that sham geniality. Despite feeling restless and trapped, he resumed his seat and leaned back in cool nonchalance. "Leave off the performance. There's no one to witness it."

Randolph sat down at the head of the table, poured two measures, and pushed one glass toward Grant. "It isn't an act," he said calmly. "I asked Aunt Phoebe to leave us. I wanted the chance to speak to you alone."

"We've nothing to talk about." *Everything was said years ago.*

"Yes we do. Or rather I do." Randolph took a drink, then pinned Grant with those razor blue eyes. "I . . . wish to apologize."

"Apologize?"

Randolph nodded. "In our younger days, I behaved abominably toward you. I said things that should never have been spoken—or even thought. It was wrong of me. I would trade a considerable amount of my fortune for the chance to erase those words."

A tribe of emotions ambushed Grant. Shock, pain, re-sistance . . . and hope, dammit. He crushed his stupidity. He was furious, that was all. Because his brother believed a mere statement of reparation could gloss over years of insults.

"So you think you can sweep the past under the rug?" A sour taste in his throat, Grant thrust his glass away. The amber liquid sloshed over the side and stained the white tablecloth. "It can't be done."

Randolph gazed steadily at him. "You've every right to be angry. It's no excuse, but . . . I was influenced by our father."

"Your father. Not mine."

"By law, he *was* your father, Grant. You're the second son of the fourth Earl of Litton, and nothing will ever change that."

No longer able to sit still, Grant shoved back his chair and sprang to his feet. "Then I curse my father. I renounced both of you long ago. You may go to the devil with him."

Randolph compressed his lips. "It's foolish to carry grudges. You could no more help the circumstances of your birth than I could. We are born into a life, and we must make the best of it."

"That's what I've done," Grant said, pacing the length of the dining room. "I've chosen my own life. So leave me to it."

But Randolph went on, undaunted. "There's something I must ask of you. It's something very important, given the somewhat precarious state of my health."

Grant stopped prowling. The seriousness on his brother's face unsettled him against his will. "Precarious?"

"Yes," Randolph said in a steely tone. "I've a chronic weakness of the heart. The doctors say I could suffer another seizure at any time—five minutes from now or five years. It's in the hands of God."

"Then you certainly don't need me."

His brother didn't crack a smile. "I do need you, Grant. You see, I've named you as trustee of my estate in the event of my death."

Grant stood unmoving. Randolph would charge him with his entire fortune? He, the black sheep of the family? *Why?* "The devil you say—" he bit out.

"I also need your promise," his brother added soberly. "It is on a matter of far greater importance to me than wealth. I must know that if I should die, you'll watch out for Jane and the baby."

. . .

"What do you suppose they're saying?" Sophie fretted.

She sat beside Randolph's wife on the chaise. Opposite them, Lady Phoebe poured three steaming cups of tea. The ormolu clock on the mantelpiece ticked monotonously. More than ten minutes had passed since they had left the men in the dining chamber.

"I expect," Jane said, accepting a cup from Lady Phoebe, "that Randolph is telling Grant about his heart condition. He wouldn't speak about it in my presence. He believes I don't realize the seriousness of it."

Sophie instantly forgot her own troubles. "I knew that he'd suffered a chest spasm last year, but I thought he was fine now."

"Yes, he is, for the moment, thank God," Jane said softly. "But I suspected he wasn't telling me everything, so I took the precaution of finding out for myself, with Aunt Phoebe's help."

"Men believe we ladies are too delicate to bear unpleasant truths," Lady Phoebe said. "Fiddle-faddle, I say. Men may fight the wars, but women bear the children and manage the households. We require no coddling."

Stirring cream into her tea, Sophie understood too well. Robert had been like that, and at times she had felt stifled by his zealous effort to protect her.

Lady Phoebe went on, "With Jane's permission, I spoke to the physician myself. I secured a full report."

Jane smiled fondly at the older woman. "I am quite jealous of your abilities. Everyone always tells you whatever you wish to know."

"It took long years of practice," Lady Phoebe said with a sage smile. "One must know when to coax and when to bully and when simply to listen."

"What did you find out?" Sophie asked.

Her pale features turned grim. "That my nephew is

likely to suffer another attack, and that next time it may
be fatal."

The shock of that reverberated inside Sophie. How
dreadful for Jane, newly wed and so very happy with their
first child on the way. "Is there nothing that can be done?"

"I believe so," Jane averred. "There was a man with a
similar condition who resided in the village near my father's home in Devon. He scorned the doctor's diagnosis
to remain an invalid. He walked briskly every morning,
and ate only fish and vegetables each day for dinner. He
lived to be ninety years old. So that is the regimen I am
requiring of my Randolph." Her somber expression softened as her mouth curved in a sweet smile. "At times, he
grumbles, but he will do as I say."

The marriage was clearly a love match, and Sophie
found herself envying their happiness. Despite the
tragedy hanging over their heads, they were devoted, af-
fectionate, and tender, all the qualities she longed to share
with Grant. If only he would open his heart to her.

And to his brother.

She glanced worriedly at the empty doorway of the
drawing room. "I hope Grant isn't upsetting your husband."

"It takes quite a lot to anger Randolph these days,"
Lady Phoebe said. "Since marrying Jane, he isn't the arrogant, toplofty man he used to be."

Sophie saw the opportunity to satisfy her curiosity.
"Please don't think me presumptuous, but I've heard
about Grant's parentage. That his mother had an affair."

"A shocking business," Lady Phoebe said with a grimace. "A countess carrying on with a footman. But far
worse was the way my brother Bertram treated her child.
Grant found no love at all in that house. I brought him
here as often as I could manage it."

Sophie's heart clenched. "Did he and Randolph know
the truth as children?"

"Yes, Bertram told him once in a fury, in Randolph's presence. After that, the brothers fought constantly. Grant was a hothead, and Randolph always knew precisely what to say to set him off. A whispered taunt, and Grant would fly at him with fists swinging. And because he started the brawl, the blame always fell upon his shoulders. My brother believed his eldest son was a saint and Grant a devil."

"A child often behaves according to the expectations placed upon him," Sophie mused. "If the earl told him he was unworthy of the family name, it is little wonder he grew up thinking himself a devil."

"Randolph is not a saint," Jane said firmly. "Like Grant, he is a very stubborn man. But since the onset of his illness, he has changed for the better. He very much regrets his past behavior. If he has any sense at all, he will apologize to Grant."

"If Grant has any sense," Sophie said, "he will accept the apology. But he was also in the wrong for losing his temper so easily."

Lady Phoebe peered keenly at her. "You seem very interested in my nephew, Sophie. I must say, he appears to be still enamored of you."

Sophie felt the rise of a blush. Did Lady Phoebe guess the truth? That she and Grant were having an affair? Did Jane know? But it was only a temporary liaison, and from the look of interest on both women's faces, she knew they were hoping for marriage.

That would never happen. No matter how much she might wish for it.

Sophie made light of the matter. "We're merely old friends," she said. To Jane, she added, "Grant is the guardian of my nine-year-old son."

Thankfully, Jane didn't press the issue. "Then you are

an experienced mother. Might I ask your advice on a matter of importance?"

"Certainly."

"Must I banish my baby to the nursery as convention dictates?" Jane stroked the mound of her belly. "Or might I keep the little one in my bedchamber as I would vastly prefer?"

"I kept Lucien in a cradle beside my bed for the first few months," Sophie said. "It makes the nighttime feedings much easier."

"Oh, I'm so glad to hear you say so. It seems much more practical to me. I shouldn't like to give my baby to a wet nurse."

They discussed the various methods of quieting a fussy infant and when to introduce solid foods. At a lull in the conversation, the suspense was too much for Sophie, and she said, "Mightn't we go see what's keeping the men?"

Chuckling, Lady Phoebe set aside her teacup. "They've had over half an hour together, and I've heard no furniture crashing or furious shouting. However, we shall go see at once if they are hale and hearty."

6 December 1701

O, Joy! St. Nicholas has given me a fine gift on his Feast Day. As I sat in the family pew at St. Paul's, guarded by Mother on one side and the Warden on the other, I glimpsed at the rear of the crowded cathedral the dear features of my True Love! At once, I contrived a coughing fit and escaped out to the narthax. Alas, I had but a moment to gaze into those deep blue eyes. William slipped into my hand a note begging me to meet him at his rooms.

My heart aches with longing. I must find a way to evade the Warden's watchful eyes. I must!

—*the diaries of Annabelle Chatham Ramsey, 3ʳᵈ Duchess of Mulford*

20

Upon entering his bedchamber, Grant told himself to take Sophie straight to bed. He told himself to stop thinking and concentrate only on primitive instincts. But his clamoring mind refused to settle.

He jerked off his cravat and discarded his coat and waistcoat. Sophie slipped out of her pelisse and shoes, then curled up on the chaise with her stockinged feet tucked beneath her gown. She graced him with a sensual smile and held out her hand. "Come," she murmured, "sit with me."

It was an invitation to make love. Yet to his chagrin, he wanted to talk to her first; he craved it more than bedsport. "In a moment."

Grant snatched up the poker and stirred the fire. He

stalked around the bedchamber and lit several more candles. He kicked off his shoes and tossed them in the dressing room.

All the while, Sophie gazed steadily at him. Desire warmed those green eyes, along with something indefinable. Something that made him long to rest his head on her breasts. And not for the purpose of lovemaking.

To spill his guts.

God! He had climbed the stone walls of fortresses, stolen into palaces in the dead of night, been chased by sword-wielding guards and ferocious dogs. Yet nothing scared him more than revealing the turmoil inside himself.

For once, Grant wished she would harangue him with questions. He wished he hadn't made it so damned clear that he wanted only a physical relationship with her.

He couldn't trust her, he reminded himself. The charge of murder hung over Sophie's head. Rather than acquit her, he kept finding circumstantial evidence that supported her guilt. Although she seldom visited the kitchen, she had been there on the day of the poisoning. She knew the rat poison was kept in the pantry. She'd stayed close to Robert during the two long weeks of his final illness.

But none of that mattered now. Grant desperately wanted to talk to her. To unload the millstone that had been placed around his neck by Randolph.

He gripped the bedpost. "You want to know what my brother said," he accused. "You're curious."

"I would like to understand you," Sophie said with a trace of tartness. "To know what you're thinking and feeling. But I won't pry."

His chest tight, he blew out a breath. Blast it, why was he hesitating? Because he feared her ill opinion? He didn't give a damn what anyone thought of him.

Forcing out the words, he said, "Randolph's heart con-

dition is more serious than I thought. He could suffer another attack at any time. He could die."

Sophie nodded without surprise. "Jane told me as
much. She's worried about him, too."

"I'm not *worried*," he exploded. Driven by the force of
his emotions, Grant paced around the room. "At least not
in the sense you mean. It's just that . . . he's assigned me
as sole trustee of his estate. He wanted my promise that in
the event of his death I would watch over Jane and his
child."

Sophie arched an eyebrow. "Did you promise?"

"Of course. What other choice did I have?"

"Your other choice was *no*. But you agreed, and I'm
glad. Brothers should turn to each other in times of need."

He stomped straight to her and gave her an intimidat-
ing glower. "Don't spout such idealistic nonsense. Besides, he and I are *half* brothers. My mother rutted with
the footman, remember?"

Sophie compressed her lips. "You've missed my point.
Whether you like it or not, there is a bond of blood between you and Randolph. He recognizes that, and you
should, too."

"No, *you've* missed the point. He's a bloody fool to put
his entire estate into my hands. I might gamble it all away,
lose everything except the entailment. His widow and
child could be left penniless."

"He trusts you, Grant. He knows you're not a thief."

Yes I am. The confession almost slipped from his
mouth. But he'd have to be an imbecile to give her ammunition to use against him. He had admitted it once already
at the dinner table. Because he'd wanted to shock his
saintly brother.

His saintly, ailing brother.

Grinding his teeth, Grant spun away from her and paced
to the window. He parted the curtain to peer out at a night

as black as his soul. "Randolph has every reason in the world *not* to trust me. We hated each other as children. I left Kendall Park when I was fifteen and saw him only when I was unlucky enough to run into him in society. Before I was twenty-five, I'd gambled away a considerable legacy from my grandmother. I'm a rake, a scoundrel, and a lazy ne'er-do-well."

Sophie laughed. "You certainly aren't lazy. You've worked hard all your life to earn your bad reputation."

He scowled over his shoulder at her. "What is that supposed to mean?"

Her expression sobered, and she watched him with earnest concern. "I can't pretend to know much about your upbringing, Grant. But I believe . . . your father wrongfully cast the blame for your mother's mistake upon you, an innocent child. He withheld his love and treated you with disdain. And perhaps . . . you strove to become exactly what he believed of you."

Her words flayed him raw. *Was* that the case? If he couldn't be the best son, he would strive to be the worst? Hoarsely, he said, "You know nothing."

"You're right, I shouldn't speculate." Sophie patted the cushion beside her. "Sit with me now. Tell me a little about Kendall Park. That's where you grew up, is it not?"

He found himself walking to the chaise, settling on the edge, resting his elbows on his knees and avoiding her gaze. His palms felt sweaty at the notion of revealing his past. But he could feel her warm presence, smell her feminine scent. He found her nearness both arousing and . . . comforting.

He closed his eyes and pictured his childhood home, a rambling mansion with stone walls covered in ivy. A wave of nostalgia caught him unawares, and the words spilled out of him in a rush. "The house sits atop a knoll overlooking thickets of wood and farmland. I had five

hundred acres in which to roam whenever I could escape
the schoolroom. There's a river that runs through the
property, and Rand and I used to fish there when we were
young." Caught up in the memory, he instinctively used
his brother's nickname. "One spring day, I hooked the
king of all trout. I was younger than Lucien, seven perhaps, and the tug of the fish pulled me straight into the
water." Grant had gasped for breath as the icy depths
closed around him, flailed in panic as the rushing waters
swept him downstream.

"What happened?" she asked.

"Rand jumped in and hauled me back to shore. I was
cold and wet and shivering. And still hanging on to that
damned rod. He tried to make me return to the house, but
I was bound and determined to land that fish."

"Did you?"

He gave a brusque nod. "But in the meantime, Rand
had run to fetch the earl. He came striding down the em-
bankment, and I was so bloody proud of that trout flop-
ping on the ground. It was bigger than any fish I'd ever
seen. I couldn't wait to show it to him. I still considered
him to be my father, you see, and I had the foolish hope
of winning his praise. But he kicked that trout straight
back into the river. And he thrashed me for ruining my
clothes."

Sophie made a sound of distress. "How dreadful," she
said. "But is it possible he was frightened for your safety?
That perhaps he wanted to teach you a lesson?"

Grant snorted. "He taught me a lot of lessons, then.
Litton used every excuse to beat me. He kept a birch
switch in his study expressly for that purpose."

In his mind, Grant could see that whip leaning against
the corner behind his father's desk. He vividly remembered having to bend over, then hearing the peculiar
whistling sound of the switch coming down to strike his

backside. It wasn't the pain he'd hated so much; that had been easily endured. It was the humiliation of the position, the sense of helplessness.

An uneasy realization made his stomach curdle. He forced himself to speak it aloud. "I did the same thing to you, Sophie. Yesterday, in my study, I wanted to humble you. To impose my will and make you do as I wished. Maybe I'm more like the earl than I thought."

Her fingers pressed into his arm. "No!" she said fiercely. "You're not like him in the least. And it was *not* the same thing. We are both consenting adults. That makes all the difference in the world."

"I wanted to debase you," he snapped. "To show you that our relationship is merely physical. I treated you no better than a whore."

"Yes, you are at fault for that. You've been very determined to prove I mean nothing to you." Her rebukeful stare made him ashamed, then she went on briskly, "Nevertheless, what we shared was no punishment. We both took pleasure in the act. It was an erotic adventure."

He should be glad she was letting him off the hook so easily. Yet he wanted to shake some sense into her, to make her rail at him for being cruel and unfeeling.

An ironic humor twisted his mouth. When had Sophie ever behaved as she ought? And she was right to say they both had enjoyed that coupling. "This is your prime opportunity to scold me," he said. "So hurl your recriminations, Sophie. Tell me I'm a beast. Make me grovel."

"You're not a beast. You had an unfortunate upbringing, through no fault of your own." She moved her hand to his upper back, lightly stroking him through the linen of his shirt. "Did the earl ever thrash Randolph?"

Grant stiffened at the memory. "No, never," he said curtly. "Randolph was the golden boy, the heir who could do no wrong. He received high marks on his schoolwork, while I was in a hurry and made too many ink blots. He was always perfectly dressed, never muddy from crawling through the underbrush like me, never having torn clothing from climbing a tree, never dirty with ash from venturing down the chimney."

"You didn't," Sophie said with a trace of laughter. "Why on earth would you go down the chimney?"

A reluctant grin tugged at his lips. "I saw the climbing boy do it, to clean out the soot. It looked like great fun. In truth, I entertained the notion of running away from home and earning my bread in that manner. At least until I got stuck, and a groom had to toss me a rope and haul me out."

"My goodness. I'm beginning to truly appreciate Lucien's quiet nature."

"You should be glad he doesn't have an older brother around to tell him he's a worthless bastard." His gut twisted into a knot. He clamped his mouth shut. Why the devil had he admitted *that*?

Sophie's hand went still, a warm spot in the middle of his back. "Randolph really did so?"

A deep-seated resentment festered in Grant. Maybe if he told her the whole truth, she'd understand why he despised his brother, why it was impossible for them ever to be friends. "Yes, he did, at every opportunity. Our father—*his* father—took great care not to let the world know he'd been cuckolded. But at home, when it was just the three of us, he made no secret of my parentage. Randolph learned at Litton's knee that I wasn't a true Chandler, that I didn't belong in the family. And he never let me forget it."

Sophie looked aghast. "You struck back with your fists, I imagine."

"I bloodied his nose often enough. Then Litton would thrash *me*. But I didn't care so long as I had the chance to knock Randolph down in the dust. He's two years older than me, so I couldn't always manage it at first. But I learned a few dirty tricks from watching boys fight on the street. And I was disreputable enough to use them."

Instead of criticizing him for being dishonorable, as Grant expected, Sophie said something else entirely. "What a cruel, embittered man your father must have been, to have done that to you both."

"Both?" Grant sat up straight and glared at her. "Litton despised only *me*. Randolph had everything, privilege, pure blood, the love of his father."

"Your brother was also taught to hate," she countered. "What sort of legacy is that? Randolph was emulating his father's behavior. He didn't know any other way."

"So you would excuse him," he said coldly.

Sophie gave an impatient shake of her head. "No, I'm merely trying to see the situation from his perspective. Only think of how Lucien copies your actions. If you showed him a bad example, he would imitate it, too. Would he be to blame? Or would it be your fault?"

Grant resisted acknowledging the truth in her statement. "It isn't the same," he snapped. "Lucien is only nine. Even as an adult, Randolph continued to belittle me."

"I agree, that was wrong of him." She gripped his hand as if to convey the urgency of her words. "Yet he's finally realized his mistake. He wishes to make amends, Grant. He wants to start over, to be a true brother to you."

That unwelcome glut of emotions constricted his throat again, anger, resentment, and . . . hope. Pulling his hand away, he slammed his fist down on the back of the chaise. "Blast it, Sophie. You can't erase the deeds of a lifetime with a few words of remorse."

She was silent a moment, her eyes troubled but resolute. "You're right, it's impossible to change the past. But you do have the power to determine your future. You

can accept the olive branch from him and gain a family—
or continue on your same course of needing no one but
yourself. It's certainly safer that way."

He almost choked. Was she calling him a coward?
"You have no idea what you're saying. You never lived
through the hell of my childhood."

She tilted her head, her brows drawn together in a
frown. "Did the two of you fight *all* the time? There must
have been some good memories."

Impossible. Against his will, however, he recalled
Rand showing him how to fly a kite, Rand helping him
build a tree house in the woods, Rand sharing the pocket
money that Litton had given him . . .

"Think about the happy times," Sophie urged, as if she
could read his mind. "Let the rest go. It's a burden you
needn't carry anymore. And remember, he saved your life
when you fell into the river. That was an act of love, not
hatred."

"Maybe he wanted to keep me alive so he'd have
someone to torment." But even Grant knew he was being
absurd.

He felt as if he were foundering in those raging waters
again. He couldn't believe he had admitted so much to Sophie. They were experiences he had never shared with anyone else. Yet he felt lighter somehow. As if bringing those
memories out into the light had made them less oppressive.

Sophie watched him anxiously. "You must give your
brother a chance," she said. "He may not be around much
longer. Won't you at least treat him with civility?"

An automatic refusal sat on the tip of his tongue. He
didn't want to contemplate his brother's illness. All his
life, Grant had rushed into danger without a care for his
own mortality. He had never understood how most men
could prefer the dullness of home and hearth. But now he
could comprehend Randolph's concerns. He could imag-

ine the cold fear of knowing he might die at any moment, that he would leave his wife and child unprotected. If he had a family, if Sophie and Lucien were his, he would move heaven and earth to ensure their safety . . .

"I've no wish to exacerbate his condition," he forced out. "I'll do my best not to quarrel with him. Whether or not he and I can ever be friends, though, remains to be seen." Loath to admit to any unmanly emotions, Grant made light of the situation. "But it's becoming devilishly tiresome, the way everyone keeps appointing me guardian of their offspring."

Smiling, she slid her hand down his forearm to link her fingers with his. "Perhaps they see the good in you. You hide it well, but it's there."

Grant held tightly to her fingers. Absurd, how happy her statement made him. He couldn't remember ever feeling so full, so elated, as if he'd conquered the world. He told himself that her opinion didn't matter, that he needn't rely upon anyone but himself. Yet he felt as if she had given him a rare gift, one that filled a breach within him and made him complete.

Was this love?

The notion both exhilarated and terrified him. Surely he wasn't so half-witted as to fall in love with Sophie. Again.

He brought her hand to his lips. She smelled faintly of roses. "Fancy that, you calling me good," he drawled. "Only this morning, I was a skirt-chasing libertine."

"You may chase all you like," Sophie said tartly. "So long as it is only *my* skirt you're after."

Leaning forward, she kissed him, the tip of her tongue tasting him with amorous intent. The sensual feast of her soft mouth filled him with fire. He too was ready to abandon their serious conversation for the needs of the flesh. Tonight, he would make up for that episode in his study.

He would love her slowly, touch her all over, relish every moment of their coupling.

Slowly, they divested each other of clothing, kissing and caressing all the while. Sitting up, she slipped her leg over him in preparation to ride him right there on the chaise. But Grant caught her in his arms and carried her to the bed.

He felt a strong compulsion to cover Sophie with his body, to feel her beneath him, to mate with her in that most basic of all positions. Not because he wished to dominate. Because he wanted to experience the act in its simplest, most elemental form.

Laying her down on the cool linens, he set himself to the pleasurable task of enhancing her arousal. He ran his fingers over the tight peaks of her breasts, traced the curve of her hips, caressed the smoothness of her thighs. And he played with the soft, hidden folds between her legs until she writhed and moaned to the verge of release. Only then did he mount her.

Sliding into her, he struggled to master himself. She was tight . . . hot . . . velvety. The overload of sensations tested the boundaries of his self-control. He lowered himself so they were pressed together as close as humanly possible, skin to skin, chest to breasts, her legs surrounding his. Their union felt more perfect than any other in the realm of his experience.

He pressed small, sipping kisses over her face. "Sweet Sophie. You're everything to me. I wish this moment could last forever."

God, what was he saying? He couldn't have forever, especially not with her. He was only opening himself up to pain and disillusionment. But when she moved her hips and whispered his name, he lost the ability to analyze the raw emotions inside him. He wanted only to savor her, to make her savor him in return.

He withdrew, then pushed gradually into her again, as deeply as he could go. The lazy rhythm of his thrusts made her quiver and moan. Sophie touched him all the while, stroking his chest, his arms, his jaw. They kissed with open mouths that shared the very breath in their lungs.

Her green eyes held tenderness and mystery, and she reached up to trace his cheekbone with the tip of her finger. "Grant," she murmured. "My beloved."

A tidal wave of longing swept away his restraint. He forgot his resolution to keep the pace slow and steady, to prolong the act. Her soft words of love pushed him over the edge into madness, and he lost himself to the wild ride for fulfillment. They were one in the delirium of desire, their bodies striving, seeking, straining for the ultimate reward. He felt the tensing of her body, heard her gasps of delight as she neared the pinnacle. In the instant she convulsed with a keening cry, he came with her, emptying himself into her in one final exhilarating plunge.

Long moments later, in the extraordinary peace of the aftermath, he returned to awareness. It was then that Grant realized his mistake.

He was still sheathed inside her. He had forgotten to withdraw.

11 December 1701

The final fitting of my Bridal gown took place today in my bed-chamber. As I was made to promenade before the Warden and My Mother, I spied my reflection in the pier glass. 'Twas a startling sight, that elegant lady with her pale blue satin embroidered in gold, and tiers of lace on the quarter sleeves. I daresay I looked as Haughty and Cold as Mulford himself. O, Woe! I am doomed to be a Duchess.

Can it be only five days since I saw my Dear William? It seems a thousand years since then.

—the diaries of Annabelle Chatham Ramsey, 3rd Duchess of Mulford

21

Warm and replete from Grant's lovemaking, Sophie resisted the return of reality. Her breasts absorbed the strong beating of his heart. His intense dark eyes held hers, and she saw on his rugged features an echo of her own shock. Deep within her lay his thickness, somewhat diminished now, yet firmly seated in her womb. Heaven help her, he had spilled his seed in her. An odd elation caught her unawares.

Then panic surfaced from the confusing swirl of emotions inside her.

His weight felt suddenly suffocating. Planting her hands against the wall of his chest, she gave a hard shove, but he didn't budge. "Sophie," he murmured, his tone conciliatory.

"Please . . . let me go."

He must have heard the tremor in her voice, for he lifted himself from her at once. Sitting up, she felt the telltale trickle of his seed between her legs. Grant had not taken any precautions. They had been foolish, careless. And this time, if there were consequences, she didn't have Robert to rescue her.

This time, her reputation reflected not only on herself but also on Lucien. To bear a child out of wedlock was unthinkable. She couldn't let herself believe the possibility was minimal, either. Ten years ago, it had taken only one time for her to conceive.

Shaking, she buried her face in her hands. "Dear God," she whispered. "Oh, dear God."

The mattress shifted under Grant's weight, and she sensed his warmth beside her. "I broke your rule," he said in a low tone. "I'm sorry. It was unintentional."

Her head shot up. "*Sorry?* I cannot bear a child. Do you have any notion how people would react? I'd be shunned. And because he is my son, *Lucien* would be shunned."

Grant ran his fingers through his tousled black hair. "It was only one time. Surely the odds are against it."

"The odds," she repeated disbelievingly. "This isn't a game of dice, Grant. We're speaking of a *baby*."

Too distraught to sit, she scrambled off the bed and collected her clothing. She wanted nothing more than to collapse on the floor and sob. Dear heaven, she could be facing an unwed pregnancy. Again. What would she do? Where would she go?

Would Grant offer her marriage? If he did, she mustn't let herself be tempted to accept him. Not until she could think clearly. Not until she knew he loved her.

Sweet Sophie. You're everything to me. I wish this moment could last forever.

Despite her predicament, she yearned for him. Had he

really meant that? Or had he merely spoken those tender words in the heat of passion?

Linen rustled as he rose from the bed. "If I could change what happened, I would," he muttered. "I want you to know that."

Sophie looked at him in the wavering light of the candles. His chiseled features held a sincere remorse that wrapped around her heart. Striving for coolness, she said, "There's no point in dwelling on the matter. What's done is done. And . . . it was lovely."

She uttered those last three words without conscious intent. For better or worse, she loved Grant. It seemed only right to accept his seed into her body. Deep down, she craved to feel his baby kicking inside her womb again. A part of her fervently *hoped* it would happen.

Had she taken complete leave of her senses?

With shaky hands, she drew on her shift. The past two nights, she had stayed much later, but it would be perilous to linger now. Already, she was tempted to abandon caution and give herself to him again.

As she perched on the chaise to don her silk stockings, Grant hunkered down in front of her. The firelight shone on the naked splendor of his chest. The scar from a bullet wound on his upper arm served as a reminder of the mysteries he had yet to reveal. In spite of her fright, she longed to know everything about him, to deepen their connection. Yet therein lay danger.

By unburdening himself of the past, he had brought them closer together. But true intimacy had exacted its price. It had made them reckless.

He picked up one of her garters and tied the strip of black ribbon around her thigh. Very casually, as if he were discussing the weather, he said, "If you find yourself with child, you must tell me at once. I'll marry you, Sophie. I can afford a wife now. Perhaps not in the luxury to which you're accustomed, but you'll be comfortable enough."

Sophie sat frozen, unable to speak for the riot of conflicting emotions inside her. She wanted to rejoice, to blurt out her love for him. And she also wanted to weep, for his words were a knell from the past.

Damnation! I can't afford a wife, but I'll have to marry you now.

As he reached down to pick up the other garter, Sophie forced herself to face the galling truth. Grant had no real desire to wed. He hadn't offered out of love or even friendship. He would marry her out of necessity. Only if circumstances forced him to do so.

Only if he had no other choice.

She hid her pain behind the mask of the calm, composed duchess. "Well," she said lightly, "we'll have to pray it doesn't come to that."

His intent gaze studied her. "Yes."

Rising gracefully, Sophie picked up her gown from the floor and stepped into it. As she adjusted the bodice and sleeves, the only sounds were the rustling of fabric and the hissing of the fire. Grant didn't speak, nor did she. Undoubtedly, he was grateful that she wasn't still scolding him. But she had no wish to reveal her pain by making a spectacle of herself.

After a moment, Grant drew on his breeches. Then he came from behind and fastened her buttons as he always did. "When was the last time you had your courses?" he asked.

It was ridiculous to blush. After sharing such intimacies with him, she shouldn't feel shy about discussing her menses. She schooled her mind to practicalities. "Nearly a month ago. We should know within a few days. In the meantime . . . it mustn't happen again."

"It won't. I'll be more careful next time."

"There won't be a next time." Although her heart was breaking, she made the only possible choice. For Lucien's sake. And for her own. "I'm ending our affair, Grant."

His hands stilled on the last button. Then he spun her around to face him and gripped hard to her shoulders. His features were taut, his dark brows lowered in a frown. "Because of one mistake? My God, Sophie! I told you it wouldn't happen again."

It took every ounce of her willpower to step back. She couldn't maintain her resolve while he was touching her. Unwilling to look at the bare expanse of his chest, she studiously kept her gaze above his neck. "It's too great a risk. Tonight proved that. I won't be forced into marriage."

Scowling, he combed his fingers through his hair again. "I see," he said coldly. "God forbid you should ever have to marry me. You'd have to relinquish your status as duchess."

"This has nothing to do with status. When—if—I marry again, it will be for love alone. Not because I feel compelled by circumstances."

"Sentiment be damned," he snapped. "If you're with child, you're marrying me. My baby won't be born a bastard. Nor will I ever allow any other man to raise my son or daughter."

As he wheeled around to collect the rest of his clothing, Sophie stood unmoving. Her heart beat in slow, heavy strokes. His voice had been harsh, decisive, uncompromising.

Dear God, she'd had no idea he felt so strongly about fatherhood. Or perhaps she'd seen the signs but ignored them. She had believed him to be a conscienceless rake who shunned all responsibilities. She had convinced herself that he wouldn't want to be a father to Lucien.

How wrong she had been.

Now that she knew a little of Grant's past, Sophie could see he was not the hard-hearted rogue he showed the world. He knew firsthand the horror of being raised by a man who was not his true sire. Although his experience had been a tragic anomaly, it had shaped him nonetheless. It had made him determined to protect his own child.

I happen to like children ... maybe I wouldn't mind having a few of my own.

When he'd said that earlier in the day, Sophie had believed him to be voicing a whim. Like the rest of the world, she'd been ready to think the worst of him. But Grant had spoken from his heart. He had revealed something intensely personal—and she had scoffed at him.

He took a candle and vanished into his dressing room, no doubt to tie his cravat in front of the mirror. Listening to his faint movements, she stepped into her shoes. Her movements stiff and mechanical, she tidied her hair and put on her bonnet, looping the ribbons beneath her chin.

Grant deserved to know the truth about Lucien. But how could she find the words to tell him? He would be horrified. How could she bear his rage, his censure, his pain at having been cheated out of the first nine years of his son's life?

And he would insist upon marriage. She knew that fact beyond a shadow of a doubt. Grant would never settle for anything less.

The notion of being his wife appealed to her enormously. It would be heaven to belong to him forever—and hell to know that he might never forgive her for lying to him.

Grant emerged from the dressing room, the consummate gentleman in his tailored gray coat and buff breeches. He helped Sophie don her pelisse, then politely offered his arm. His aloof manner made her heart ache.

Only minutes ago, they had made love with wild, impassioned fervor on the tumbled bed.

He was angry that she'd ended the affair. Only imagine how much more furious he would be when she told him the truth.

As they walked out of the bedchamber, he spoke tersely. "I intend to break another of your rules."

"Pardon?"

In the dimness of the passageway, his gaze bored into her. "I won't sign the guardianship papers. Robert entrusted me with the care of his son, and I fully intend to honor his wishes."

"I—"

"Don't argue the point, duchess. I'm already aware that I'm a cad for breaking my word. But I refuse to abandon Lucien. Despite what you believe to the contrary, I won't disappoint him. Is that clear?"

Sophie's stomach clenched with misery. Tears clogged her throat and stung her eyes. "Yes," she murmured.

As they started down the stairs, she lowered her gaze. His arm felt firm and steady beneath her fingers. Oh Lord, how badly she had misjudged Grant. Even without knowing that Lucien was his son, he cared for the boy. Truly, sincerely *cared*.

She was ashamed at how she had doubted Grant and belittled him at every turn. How many other rogues would have bothered to show kindness to a small child? How many would have played tin soldiers with him or taken him on a drive to the park?

The tapping of their footsteps sounded lonely in the staircase hall. She glanced up to see him staring grimly down at the foyer. Her palms felt like ice. This was her opportunity to confess. She had to do so without delay, else the weight of the secret would smother her.

Sophie drew a deep breath. Her voice quiet with remorse, she said, "Grant, there's something I must—"

He thrust his hand over her mouth. He stopped her halfway down the stairs.

Startled, she realized several things in quick succession. Grant wasn't looking at her. His full attention was focused down toward the ground floor.

A glimmer of candlelight shone in the shadowed foyer. The glow emanated from the room to the left of the doorway. The study.

The room had been dark when they'd arrived an hour ago.

He bent his mouth to her ear. "There's an intruder," he muttered. "Go back upstairs."

She pried his hand from her mouth. "Surely it's Wren," she whispered. "Or the housekeeper."

Grant shook his head. "They've strict orders to stay belowstairs at night. Now *move*."

His hand at her waist, he gave her a little push back up toward the first floor. She obeyed slowly while glancing over her shoulder.

In stealthy silence, Grant proceeded down the stairs. He was a dark shadow in the gloom. She had not known he could move so quietly, like a panther on the prowl. His furtiveness sent a chill through her.

He truly believed a burglar had broken into his house.

Someone had done so a week ago, she recalled uneasily. Grant had mentioned that the man had knocked Wren unconscious. Was it the same intruder? Why had he returned?

Reaching the upper-floor landing, Sophie grasped hard to the smooth oak of the balustrade. Her heart thumped with fright. What if the robber had a gun?

Grant had no weapon. He could be shot. He could *die*.

She had to help him.

Glancing around, she spied a small porcelain vase on a table against the wall. It wasn't much, but it would do.

She heard Grant's harsh muffled voice, then a man's guttural reply. The noise of a furious scuffle exploded from the study. Sophie didn't hesitate. Clutching the vase, she sped down the stairs and into the study.

The room lay in shambles as if the burglar had been searching for valuables. The contents of the desk drawers had been strewn everywhere. Books from the shelves were heaped on the floor. Even the paintings on the walls hung askew.

In the middle of the rug, Grant grappled with a husky, dark-skinned man. The intruder wore shabby brown clothing and, oddly, a white turban on his head. A foreigner. Even as Sophie formed that impression, Grant landed a hard punch to the man's jaw. He staggered backward into a chair and lost his balance. The fall knocked off his turban, revealing a completely bald skull.

Lying in the shadows, the man reached beneath his belt. Metal glinted in his hand. *A knife.*

She gasped. And instantly regretted distracting Grant.

His attention flicked to her. At that precise moment, his adversary lunged up from the floor. His arm flashed out, the blade arcing toward Grant's chest.

This time, Sophie screamed. She gripped the vase high in preparation to strike. But before she could take more than a few steps toward them, the intruder wrestled Grant to the desk and lodged his arm against Grant's throat. He positioned the tip of the dagger just below Grant's eye. He pressed delicately, making a slight depression in the skin without drawing blood.

Sophie froze. She didn't dare hit the man now. One slip of the knife and Grant would be blinded in one eye.

Unmoving, Grant glared balefully up at his captor.

"You're wasting your time," he ground out. "The letter isn't here."

"Letter?" the intruder scoffed in a gravelly foreign accent. "I am Bahir, servant to the sultan Hadji. You steal his stone."

Sophie slowly lowered the vase. The sultan? A *stone*?

Over dinner at his aunt's house, Grant had described his visit to a palace in Smyrna. Sophie had had the impression there was more to the story than he'd revealed. She also remembered that cryptic answer he'd given to his brother's question.

What were you doing all these years?

Stealing jewels, of course.

"Sophie." His voice grating, Grant spoke without moving his gaze from the foreigner. "Leave here. At once."

"She stay," Bahir countered. "She not want her lover to die."

Ice encased Sophie. She was terrified to make a sound. Without hesitation, this man would kill Grant.

She buried her horror beneath a veneer of haughty disdain. Without moving from her position a few feet away, she forced strength into her voice. "Release him," she said coldly. "Whatever it is you want, he cannot give it to you if he is dead."

Watching Grant closely, Bahir chuckled. "A brave one, your Sophie. She is a lioness in the bed, yes?"

Grant uttered a fierce growl. His fists clenched at his sides, he moved slightly, and the point of the knife pierced his flesh. A tiny bead of blood adhered to his bottom eyelashes. "Your quarrel is with me. Leave her out of this."

Bahir shoved his arm harder against Grant's throat. "*I* give the orders, by Allah. You return the Devil's Eye. Or lose your own eye."

The click of a cocking gun came from the doorway. "Let 'im go, lest ye've a mind to see yer Allah tonight."

With a burst of relief, Sophie spied Wren standing in the shadows. The small, wizened old man pointed a long-barreled pistol at the intruder.

Bahir made the mistake of glancing over his shoulder. Grant took instant advantage. He seized the arm holding the knife and shoved it away from his face. At the same time, he thrust the heel of his other hand against Bahir's chin. The two men struggled against the desk, and somehow Bahir managed to keep his arm pressed against Grant's windpipe.

Muttering, Wren hesitated to fire. Sophie knew he feared to hit Grant by mistake. She surged forward, raised the vase, and brought it down hard against the back of Bahir's head. Shards of porcelain rained to the rug.

Bahir stiffened. Then he toppled to the floor and lay still.

Grant didn't look at all grateful. He scowled at Sophie, then knelt on one knee to examine Bahir. Wren trotted to the window and yanked off the tasseled gold cord that held back the curtain. He brought it to Grant, who tied Bahir's wrists behind his back.

Grant stood up. He and Wren shared a wordless communication. Then the valet stood guard over the prisoner. And Grant strode to Sophie.

He looked grim, remote, furious. Determined not to be intimidated, she glared back at him. But the tiny smear of blood beneath his eye drained her of strength. Her legs wobbled perilously. The thought of what might have happened made her teeth chatter.

"Grant," she murmured. She reached up to brush her fingertip over the mark. "Oh, *Grant*."

Frowning, he turned his head to evade her ministrations. Grasping her arm, he steered her to the door. "You should have gone upstairs as I told you," he snapped. "I'm taking you home."

She balked, glancing back at the unconscious Bahir. "No! First you should summon the watchman to take that man to jail."

"I'll see to the matter later."

Grant led her out into the gloomy foyer and down the corridor toward the back of the house. Here, a few candles in sconces lit the way, casting a soft glow over the fine furnishings and the pale marble floor. The place looked so ordinary, so *real*.

The fog of shock lifted from Sophie's beleaguered brain. Her mind assembled all the scattered pieces of the puzzle into a cohesive whole. Grant's cryptic remarks. His gunshot scar. His unwillingness to speak about the past ten years. His acquisition of wealth, which he claimed to have won at the gaming tables.

He had lied to her. In the most vile manner.

Near the back door, Sophie pulled out of his grip and swung to face him. Though she knew every inch of his face, he suddenly looked like a dark, frightening stranger. "You have no intention of handing Bahir over to the law," she said slowly. "You dare not. He'll tell the magistrate about the jewels you stole from the sultan."

Grant remained silent for a moment. In the candlelight, his hard features held a calculating look. As if he were debating how much to tell her. "One jewel," he clarified. "A large, rare ruby once owned by Cleopatra. It's called the Devil's Eye."

His admission gripped her by the throat. "You're a thief," she whispered. "You weren't just taunting your brother at dinner. You were speaking the *truth*."

"That was a slip. I never meant for anyone to find out." He stepped toward her, taking her hand, rubbing it soothingly. "Sophie, I've put that life behind me. I've no intention of ever stealing anything again. Please believe that. I took only from those who had gained their wealth by foul means. The sultan profits from the ruination of others through the sale of opium."

Grant was justifying his actions. As if he believed she would shrug away his crimes as mere schoolboy pranks. She was appalled, insulted . . . and *hurt*. Terribly hurt that just when she had begun to think more highly of him, her hero had turned out to have feet of clay.

She wrested her hand free. In her most imperious tone, she commanded, "You will give the ruby back to Bahir."

"I don't have it. I sold it in Rome to an agent of the Russian tsar."

"Then you'll give him the money to purchase it back."

"It's too late. The tsar commissioned me to steal the Devil's Eye. He's coveted the stone for a long time. He won't relinquish it, not for any price."

Dread invaded Sophie. She trembled from the force of it. "If you don't return the jewel," she said, willing steadiness into her voice, "Bahir will put out your eye. He might *kill* you."

"Never mind Bahir. I'll handle him."

Grant tried to prod her toward the door, but she resisted. Sickness stung her throat. "*Handle* him? Do you mean . . . *murder*?"

"No, of course not. I'll put him on a ship back to Turkey. He won't return."

He met her gaze directly, without any hint of subterfuge on his sternly handsome face. A powerful yearning swept through her. She wanted to bury herself in his arms and forgive him his foibles. To regain her fledgling trust in him. But how could she ever trust him again?

She stepped back, putting distance between them. "I don't believe you. I *can't* believe you."

Grant reached out as if to touch her, then thrust his fingers through his hair instead. "I'm not a murderer. You know me better than that."

Sophie shook her head. "I only thought I knew you."

Dear God, she couldn't tell him the truth about Lucien now. She couldn't allow her son to associate with a jewel thief. Then another dismal thought reverberated inside her. She now had the perfect means to oust Grant from her life once and for all.

She had to do it, for Lucien's sake.

Imbuing her voice with a wintry chill, she went on, "You are no longer welcome at Mulford House. Henceforth, you will stay away from me. And from my son. Or I shall see you punished for your crimes."

13 December 1701

Yestereve was the most Marvelous, Wondrous night! At long last I have seen William, and with no one the wiser. Here is a Faithful Accounting of my escape. The Warden took ill after dinner with a belly-ache (caused by bilious thoughts, no doubt). She commanded Laddie's services, and several other retainers as well, and in all the Commotion, I was forgotten.

My impetuous Heart knew no bounds. Quick as a wink, I donned my cloak and slipped out into the frosty night. With nary a care for Robbers or Brigands, I hastened through the darkened streets to the rooming house wherein lives my True Love.

—the diaries of Annabelle Chatham Ramsey, 3rd Duchess of Mulford

22

"Ye should've let me slit 'is throat," Wren declared. "The brigand'll be back, ye mark me words."

The gray light of morning stung Grant's eyes. Heading into the dressing room, he went straight to the washstand and splashed cold water on his face. He had the very devil of a headache. After taking Sophie home the previous night, he had transported Bahir to the docks, found a ship set to sail at dawn for Constantinople, and paid a hefty sum to the captain to keep the Turk imprisoned in the hold until the ship reached its destination.

Then Grant had returned home to drink himself into oblivion.

"I won't commit murder," he said gruffly. His face dripping, he groped for a towel. "I haven't yet sunk that low."

Sophie thought he had. Her eyes had been cold with distrust. And maybe she was right. During the fight in the study, he'd been furious enough to beat Bahir to a bloody pulp. But it was one thing to kill a man in self-defense, and quite another to execute a bound-and-gagged prisoner.

"Huh," snorted Wren, slapping a length of linen into his hand. "*I*'d've done the deed. I'd've paid him back fer brainin' me."

The throbbing in Grant's temples intensified. It was galling how wrong he'd been about the reason his chamber had been ransacked. Sophie hadn't hired a thug to search for Robert's letter. It had been Bahir looking for the Devil's Eye. Bahir had also been lurking in the mews that one night and had stolen Grant's horse.

Now, Grant was plagued by the certainty that he'd misjudged Sophie. That she had *not* poisoned Robert. That he had focused his investigation so closely on her that he'd lost all perspective. He intended to give serious thought to her innocence—as soon as his head ceased its infernal pounding.

"Piece o' filth like that don't deserve to live," Wren grumbled.

Grant felt like a piece of filth himself. Even in his cups he had not been able to forget the shock and disgust on Sophie's face when she had learned of his thievery. She had regarded him as if he were some low form of life that had crawled out from underneath a rock.

You are no longer welcome at Mulford House. Henceforth, you will stay away from me. And from my son. Or I shall see you punished for your crimes.

His throat felt unnaturally thick. He threw aside the

towel and stomped to the clothes press, where he snatched up a shirt at random.

"This 'ere one's fresh from the laundry." The valet held out a crisp white shirt. "Ironed it meself whilst ye was sleepin' away 'alf the day. Cleaned up yer study, too, afore Mrs. Howell could howl." He chuckled at his own jest.

Utterly without humor, Grant took the garment. "What time *is* it?"

" 'Tis near noon already."

"Good God. Why didn't you say so?"

Wren regarded him sagely. "I'd best order ye a pot o' strong coffee an' a spot o' breakfast."

The valet trotted out of the dressing room before Grant could say the mere thought of eggs and bacon made his stomach lurch.

He donned the shirt and then performed his ablutions, shaving with frothy soap and wincing from the scrape of the razor on his overly sensitive hearing. He'd planned to continue his interrogation of the servants at Mulford House today. He especially wanted to interview that scullery maid, the one who had swooned when he'd asked about Elliot swiving her. If she knew something to implicate Robert's cousin—

Nicking his jaw, Grant cursed. He pressed a corner of the towel to the raw spot. Sophie didn't want him in her house. No doubt she'd given Phelps orders to bar the door if Grant dared to set foot on the property. Of course, he could always bully his way inside. Or use the servants' entrance in the rear.

But Sophie would find out, and he deemed it best not to antagonize her. She held the upper hand now. She had the power to ruin him in the eyes of his aunt and his brother . . .

Wren returned from his errand. As if their conversation hadn't been interrupted, he said, "The duchess weren't too 'appy to find out ye was a thief, eh? She raked ye o'er the coals, I'll wager. Will she turn ye in, d'ye think?"

"It would serve no purpose," Grant snapped, donning a tan waistcoat and fastening the buttons. "My crimes were done overseas. The local law won't bother investigating something that happened so far beyond the reach of their jurisdiction."

But if she were angry enough, she might use her status to persuade the magistrate to lock Grant in jail for a time. The gossip would flash through the *ton*. Aunt Phoebe would be devastated.

"Seems t' me, a duchess could command the ear of the prime minister or mebbe the Prince Regent. She might get ye banished from England." On that ominous statement, Wren paused. "O' course, yer brother is an earl. Nobody'd believe ye t' be a jewel thief. All ye 'as t' do is deny it all."

Therein lay the problem. If Grant were brought in for questioning, he would confess to stealing the Devil's Eye. To do otherwise meant branding Sophie a liar.

Turning up his collar, he savagely thrust a cravat around his neck. He could never gainsay the word of a lady. It was one of the rules of gentlemanly behavior drummed into him by a long-ago governess. And his sense of honor wouldn't allow him to lie under oath, either. Wouldn't Sophie find *that* amusingly ironic?

Wren stood watching, his arms crossed. "O' course, mebbe ye'll be lucky. Mebbe the duchess will only tell yer aunt."

Lucky? Aunt Phoebe would regard him with bitter disappointment. He could endure a thrashing more easily than he could her censure. Although she'd stood by him during his years of dissipation, this time he had committed criminal acts. She might well cut all ties with him.

And Randolph would find out. His straitlaced brother would be horrified. He'd remove Grant's name as trustee. Like Sophie, Rand wouldn't allow a common thief to guide the care and education of his heir. He wouldn't want Grant associating with either Jane or himself. He would banish Grant from his life once and for all.

The thought was remarkably depressing.

"Lemme do that afore ye choke yerself," Wren admonished. "Sit down now. An' don't give me no guff about it."

A glance in the mirror confirmed to Grant that he was making a botch of the neckcloth. "Be quick about it, then. I haven't all day."

"Emptied that decanter in the study last night, did ye? Don't bite *my* 'ead off for yer own mistakes."

Grant glared. Then he swallowed his bruised pride and muttered an apology. "Sorry. But why the devil did I ever turn to thievery?"

Deftly tying the strip of starched linen, Wren chuckled. "Ye needed the funds. An' ye needed somethin' to take yer mind off the duchess."

The second reason had been the primary one, Grant knew. After Sophie had spurned him, he'd gone to Rome, where he had conceived his new career one night after watching a con artist fleece a pitifully drunken old count in a high-stakes game of dice. Over the course of the next month, Grant had shadowed the crook, learned his daily routines, and discovered he had a demanding mistress. Upon observing the man purchasing a costly suite of emeralds, Grant had slipped into her apartments that night and stolen the gems while the two made clamorous love in the next room.

The thrill of success had indeed proved a distraction from brooding about Sophie. He had gone on to pursue bigger game, petty despots and disreputable businessmen. Over the years, he had developed a reputation as a master thief in the underworld of the Continent. He had convinced himself that he was justified in robbing the unscrupulous. And he had reveled in the glamour, too, of being admired by men for his daring and sought after by women to share their beds.

Until last night, when he'd come face-to-face with the consequences of his actions. And with his own mortality. For the first time in his misbegotten life, he cared whether he lived or died.

Because he loved Sophie. The certainty of it burned in his heart.

It had been in that moment of icy fear, with the tip of a knife pressed to his eye, that he had known the truth. All of his desperate thoughts had involved Sophie. The horror she'd feel at witnessing his blinding. The terror that he'd never see her again. The dread that even if he survived the assault, she'd never be able to look at him without remembering his sins.

Wren finished fussing with the cravat. "Mebbe ye should visit the duchess. Butter 'er up. Buy 'er some jewelry or such."

A gift purchased with his ill-gotten gains. Grant could imagine how well *that* would go over. But Wren was only trying to be helpful. "Right," he muttered.

He snatched his burgundy coat from the valet, slung it over his shoulder, and tramped out of his chambers, heading to the staircase. A diamond necklace wouldn't get him back into Sophie's good graces. He'd need a miracle for that.

By his own stupidity, he'd ruined his chance to win her heart. Sophie would never marry him now. Not even if she was carrying his child.

Like a well-aimed punch to the gut, the thought laid him low. Nothing would please him more than to have a family with her. To raise their children with all the love

and warmth he had never known in his youth. To have Sophie at his side, in his arms, forever.

He'd picked a hell of a time to turn domestic.

At the top of the stairs, he glowered down at the foyer.
Mrs. Howell stood by the open front door. The gangly
form of Hannibal Jones loomed on the front porch.

For a moment, Grant considered ducking out of sight.
He was in no humor to be grilled by the Bow Street Runner. But maybe the man hadn't come in regard to Robert's
murder.

Maybe Sophie had told Jones that Grant was a thief.

The pain in his head descended to his chest. Dammit,
he wouldn't hide like a frightened schoolboy. If she desired his punishment, let her have it.

He continued down to the entryway, where the plump
housekeeper bobbed a curtsy. "Mr. Jones has come to
call. Shall I show him into yer study?"

"I'll see him in the breakfast room."

As the tall Bow Street Runner stepped inside the
house, Grant gave him a terse nod. The study door was
closed, and he didn't know how thoroughly Wren had tidied the mess. It was best not to reveal that he'd bound
and gagged a foreign national and dumped him onto a
ship bound for the Turkish coast.

"Oh, sir," Mrs. Howell said as he started down the passage. "The postman brung this for ye."

She handed him a folded paper sealed with a wafer.
For one heart-twisting instant, he thought Sophie had
written to say she'd forgiven him. But he didn't recognize
the penmanship. He tucked the note into the inner pocket
of his coat. It was likely an invitation. His aunt would
have spread the news of his return. *God*. She was about to
have the inglorious prestige of being kin to a common
thief.

He led the Bow Street Runner down the corridor and

into a pleasant chamber with a view of the garden. The overcast skies cast a gloomy pall over the pale green walls and white mantelpiece. To his intense frustration, the long mahogany table held no silver coffeepot.

He waved Jones toward a chair. "Have a seat if you like."

"I prefer to stand, sir."

"Suit yourself."

Hiding his tension, Grant walked to the window and glanced out at the sodden garden. A misty rain dripped from the trees and puddled on the gravel walkways. He wondered if this was to be his last moment of freedom before Jones hauled him off to jail.

Turning, he braced his shoulder against the window frame. "State your business," he drawled. "I haven't all day."

Jones observed him closely. He held a tattered notebook in one rawboned hand and the stub of a pencil in the other. As if he could scarcely wait to record Grant's full confession. "I've uncovered a fascinating tidbit of information," the officer said. "It involves you, Mr. Chandler."

"I'm a fascinating fellow, or so the ladies tell me. Which of my many exploits has caught the attention of your sharp ears?"

"Not an exploit, but a fact, sir. A rather inexplicable one, I might add." The Runner paused as if for dramatic effect. "Well before the magistrate received that anonymous letter, you knew the duke had been poisoned."

Grant froze. So this meeting wasn't about his thievery, after all. He didn't know whether to rejoice or to curse.

Clasping his hands behind his back, he strolled to the fireplace. "I presume Dr. Atherton told you."

"I had occasion yesterday to ask the physician a few additional questions. He mentioned you'd been to see him last week, that you told him His Grace had died from ingesting arsenic." Jones took a step closer. "I am very interested to know how you came by your knowledge."

Grant shrugged. "It was merely a hunch."

"A hunch, sir? He said you were quite insistent on the matter."

Grant stared straight into the Runner's suspicious eyes. "Dr. Atherton misconstrued my firmness of manner. It is my nature to be decisive. That is the way one must deal with underlings."

Jones didn't appear intimidated. "Dr. Atherton also revealed that you'd received a letter from the duke on his deathbed. That the duke claimed he'd been poisoned."

Grant's blood ran cold. But he reminded himself the letter was safe in a deposit box at the bank. Jones would never find it. "A mere ploy," he said, affecting an offhand manner. "I'd hoped Atherton might be more forthcoming if he thought the duke had written to me."

The officer looked deeply skeptical. Like a bulldog after a bone, he said, "Then perhaps you have reasons of your own to suspect the duchess. You know her character quite well, I believe."

Fear and fury waged war in Grant. "I beg your pardon?"

"You do have superior knowledge of Her Grace." With a small, triumphant smile, Jones concluded, "You see, Mr. Chandler, I have found out about the two of you."

Kneeling beside a wooden crate in the library, Sophie rummaged through the load of books that Elliot had returned a short while ago. The box contained a collection of history texts, most of them dealing with ancient Rome and Greece. She didn't really expect to find the missing second volume of Annabelle's diary, but she methodically unloaded the crate, anyway.

Sophie desperately needed the distraction of work. After a night spent tossing and turning, she had drifted into an uneasy slumber just before dawn. Then she'd overslept until nearly noon when her maid had brought word of Elliot's arrival. Sophie had dressed quickly with the intention of interviewing him about Robert's death.

By the time she'd come downstairs, however, Elliot and Helena had gone out to the shops. Apparently, Helena intended to coerce him into purchasing suitable attire for the birthday dinner tonight. Frustrated and out of sorts, Sophie had sent Phelps on an errand and now she awaited his return.

She drew a small, dusty volume out of the crate. Absently brushing it off with her handkerchief, she attempted to decipher the faded gold lettering of the title. An old book of sermons. One part of her mind idly wondered why Elliot had borrowed it, while another part traveled the same well-worn path as it had since the previous night.

Grant was a burglar. He broke into people's homes and stole their valuables. He had acquired his fortune through criminal means. He claimed to have robbed only the unethical of their ill-gotten gains.

As if that would excuse his actions.

Despite her disgust, however, Sophie found herself intensely curious about his misdeeds. How had Grant managed to sneak into the sultan's palace and make off with the Devil's Eye? Perhaps somehow he had acquired the floor plans for the palace and found a secret passageway. But surely a stone of such great value would have been kept locked in a stout safe. How had he opened it? Was that scar on his arm the result of being shot by one of the sultan's guards? Had he worked alone? Or with an accomplice? Wren might have helped, but he was getting up in years . . .

Sophie realized she was still staring down at the book of sermons. Her heart thumped with an appalling excitement. For heaven's sake, what was she thinking? Grant was an unsavory villain. She shouldn't be pondering his exploits as if he were the dashing hero in a tale of derring-do.

His nefarious deeds had brought danger to his very doorstep. For as long as she lived, she would never forget the horror of seeing that knife point resting a fraction of an inch from Grant's eye. The memory had given her nightmares. What if Bahir returned? What if next time, he succeeded in killing Grant?

She felt sick with worry. Although she disapproved of Grant's deeds, she didn't want him to *die*. In truth, if she were honest with herself, she still loved him. Only because . . . because he was Lucien's father.

And if that reckless bedding yesterday evening resulted in another child? Would she tell Grant this time? Would she allow him back in her life . . . as her husband?

Before she could settle on any answers, the butler's voice rang out. "Your Grace, I have brought the girl," Phelps said.

In the doorway, the old retainer stood at stiff attention. Behind him, a stout young maid hovered nervously in the corridor.

Sophie replaced the book in the crate and stood up, dusting off her hands. "Ah, Alice. Do come in."

The girl took a single step and halted. The voluminous white cap on her head framed broad, plain features and worried hazel eyes. Her overly abundant bosom strained at the bodice of her apron.

"Obey the duchess," Phelps barked. "And be quick about it, for you're needed back in the kitchen!"

Alice scuttled forward, her fingers clutching at the gray serge of her gown. Phelps glared down his nose as if expecting her to steal one of the books from a nearby shelf. The sour set of his mouth conveyed his objection to allowing such a menial servant into this upper sanctum.

His supercilious bullying irked Sophie. The man was growing more insufferable in his dotage. Perhaps it was time to speak to Helena about his pension. "That will be all, Phelps."

"If I may say, Your Grace, her services are needed belowstairs—"

"I am well aware of the dinner party tonight," she stated coldly. "And by the by, remove Mr. Chandler's name from the guest list. He is unable to attend. Now do close the door on your way out."

The butler flashed the scullery maid another veiled glance, then made a creaky bow and left the room, shutting the door behind him.

Sophie took a deep breath to ease her anger. Alice was a shy, apprehensive soul overly awed by her social betters. She looked as if she might bolt at the slightest provocation. "Come," Sophie invited gently, "sit down for a moment."

The girl's eyes widened. "Sit? M-me?"

"Yes, you'll be more comfortable over here." Tempering the unorthodox invitation with a warm smile, Sophie directed her to a chair by the hearth. Alice perched on the very edge. She gazed down at the rug, glancing up now and then like a fearful puppy, eager to please yet wary of a beating.

Sophie sat down opposite her. "I am concerned for your health, Alice. How are you feeling today?"

"W-well, Yer Grace."

She didn't look well. A few freckles stood out against the paleness of her skin. Dark, half-moon rings underscored her eyes. The whiteness around her mouth hinted at queasiness.

Sophie thought it best to get straight to the heart of Alice's troubles. To do otherwise would only prolong the girl's wretched suspense. "How far along are you, my dear?"

Alice jumped. "M-m'lady?"

"You're carrying a child, are you not? That is why you fainted yesterday. You are in the family way." Sophie was only voicing a guess. But the maid's reaction proved the suspicion correct.

Alice's chin quivered. Her chapped red hands twisted in her skirts. All at once, tears overflowed her eyes and dripped down her cheeks. "D-don't sack me, Yer Grace. I can do me job, I promise ye. Ye mustn't toss me out into the streets." Whimpering, she buried her face in her apron.

"I intend nothing of the sort." Disregarding social strictures, Sophie went to the girl, sitting beside her and patting her broad back. "Forgive me, but I must ask you some blunt questions. Who is the father of your baby?"

The apron muffled her voice. "I—I daren't say . . ."

"Is it Mr. Elliot Ramsey?"

Alice wept louder, giving Sophie her answer.

"Look at me," she commanded softly. As the girl complied, Sophie asked, "Did Mr. Ramsey force you to lie with him?"

"F-force?" Her face blotchy with tears, Alice gave her a woeful look. "Nay, 'e were a gennleman."

A gentleman. Elliot had chosen his victim well. Had he been present, Sophie would have cheerfully broken a vase over his head. "Have you told Mr. Ramsey of your condition?"

Alice shuddered. "I—I couldn't."

"Have you lain with any other men in the past few months?" Sophie felt compelled to ask the question. "Tell me the truth now. Could someone else have sired this child?"

"Oh nay, Yer Grace! Me mam raised me a good girl."

Sophie believed her. Alice had the guileless features of a country milkmaid. Blast Elliot for taking advantage of a defenseless servant!

Marriage was unthinkable. Which left Alice in the lurch. Once her loss of virtue became known, no decent household would hire her.

Sophie's heart went out to the girl. Pregnancy should be a time of joyful anticipation, not worry and dread. Yet how well she could understand the terror of facing an unknown future, of knowing the tiny new life inside herself was dependent upon her alone. Even now, she might be in the same situation. Again . . .

But she had wealth and privilege. She could go to the ducal estate to await the birth. She would face gossip and censure, but at least she and her child wouldn't starve.

Ashamed of her own selfishness, Sophie said, "Have you made plans for when your condition becomes apparent? And for when the baby arrives? Is it possible for you to return home to your parents?"

"Nay, ma'am. Me dad, 'e would take a stick to me fer bein' a sinner." Alice slipped her hand over her midsection. "I'd be afeared fer me babe."

That settled it. Sophie would speak to Elliot the moment he returned. "You must set your mind at ease, Alice. I'll see to it that you and your baby are cared for. You have my solemn vow on the matter."

A spark of hope brightened Alice's eyes. She dropped to her knees and reverently kissed the hem of Sophie's gown. "Oh, Yer Grace," she sobbed. "Bless ye. Bless ye."

The homage embarrassed Sophie. Quickly, she urged

the girl to resume her seat. "There *is* a certain price for my aid. I expect your help on a matter of importance."

Alice regarded her with worshipful attention. "Oh, aye, ma'am! I'll do anything fer ye!"

"Then you must tell me everything you recall about the day the duke fell ill last summer."

13 December 1701 (cont'd)

With much Surprise and Pleasure did William receive me. O, how handsome he looked in fine brocaded garb. He was about to depart to meet friends (he said), but gladly did he abandon his plans for the Night. The next few hours passed with the sweet, swift beauty of a Dream. We spoke of everything—and nothing. We kissed and caressed and—I dare say no more, for 'twas a Joy that even in memory makes me flushed with happiness.

Most marvelous of all, he has received a small inheritance and at last can afford to take a Wife. Thusly, we planned our elopement.

—the diaries of Annabelle Chatham Ramsey, 3rd Duchess of Mulford

23

Night had fallen by the time Grant returned from a futile trip to Surrey.

Thoroughly disgruntled, he leaped down from the curricle, left the horses to the care of a groom, and stalked through the darkened garden behind his town house. He had spent the entire drive back to London cursing himself for his stupidity.

Of course, Elliot had not been at his work site. Elliot had come to town. For the bloody dinner party that had slipped Grant's mind completely.

Grant had forgotten because his thoughts had been focused on Sophie. For too long, he had ignored his gut instinct that she was incapable of murder. But talking to her about his brother had opened Grant's eyes. How had he ever thought Sophie a cold, grasping villainess? She was too true and honest in her emotions to have poisoned anyone.

And he had lost her. Through his own stupid fault.

On the long drive to the Roman ruins, he'd had plenty of time to think. He had reexamined all the evidence from the angle that Sophie was *not* the murderer.

She had married Robert for wealth and status. Yet now Grant knew she'd also felt a true affection for Robert.

Robert's predilection gave her a motive for murder. But she had treated Geoffrey Langston with respect rather than heap the blame on a likely suspect.

Someone had accused her of the murder in that anonymous letter. But the real killer must be seeking a scapegoat—or held a vendetta against both her and Robert. Langston and Elliot were likely candidates.

Sophie knew the location of the rat poison. So had several dozen other people in the household, including Helena and probably Elliot.

Sophie had been in the kitchen on the day Robert had fallen ill. So had Helena and Elliot.

Initially, Grant had believed Sophie guilty because Robert hadn't confided his suspicions to her. But apparently Robert had been extremely protective of Sophie. Had he also feared to endanger Sophie by telling her the truth? Because the killer might then go after her?

Grant reached the back door of the house. The night was cold and damp, and despite his greatcoat he felt chilled to the bone. He'd been a bloody fool, that much was certain. He'd been blind to any argument that pointed the finger of suspicion away from Sophie. He'd been ready to blame her because he'd *wanted* to believe the worst of her.

Even after ten years, he'd needed a sop to ease his

bruised pride. Because deep down, her rejection of him still hurt.

He couldn't fault her anymore for choosing a title and security over him. It wasn't as if he'd been some damned matrimonial prize. He was even less of one now.

Opening the door, he walked into the house. The soft candlelight in the corridor reminded him of the past three nights when he had brought Sophie here. He had been bent on seduction for the sake of revenge. He'd wanted to make her utterly dependent upon him for pleasure. And to purge himself of his obsession for her once and for all.

Trudging up the staircase, Grant tried to ignore the hollow ache in his chest. He was determined to make amends by trusting in Sophie's innocence. He would believe in her completely on faith. Without proof.

But Hannibal Jones was equally determined to implicate her.

Grant had come within an inch of thrashing the Bow Street Runner. For one awful moment, when Jones had hinted that Sophie and Grant were having an affair, he had been furious enough to murder the officer for spying on them. In the nick of time, Grant had realized Jones was referring to their long-ago courtship.

Jones believed that Grant was withholding the evidence from the law. That he was protecting her from prosecution.

The officer's persistence worried Grant. Surely the man couldn't amass enough circumstantial evidence to secure a warrant. Sophie was a duchess, and the magistrate would demand iron-clad proof rather than risk making an embarrassing mistake. So Jones would keep digging. He would ignore all other possibilities. Just as Grant had done.

Meanwhile, the real murderer was on the loose. Judging by that anonymous note, he—or she—harbored ill will toward Sophie.

For that reason, Grant resolved to attend the dinner party—against her wishes. He would mingle with the guests and watch both Elliot and Helena. Short of making a scene, Sophie didn't dare eject him.

And if she branded him a thief in front of all those people?

She wouldn't. She had too much dignity to behave so crassly in public. She cared too much for her reputation.

But what if she did?

He strode into his bedchamber. The candles were lit here, too, as if Wren had been expecting Grant to charm Sophie back into his bed. Savagely, he tore off his coat and hurled it onto the chaise. As he did so, a pale rectangle fell out of the inner pocket.

He reached down to pick up the letter that Mrs. Howell had handed him earlier. An invitation, he'd assumed. He'd been busy with Hannibal Jones at the time.

Grant made a move to toss it into the fire. But the penmanship caught his attention. There was something peculiar about it, the letters straight up and down, almost as if the writer had disguised his handwriting. And the spidery strokes somehow reminded him of that note received by the magistrate at Bow Street Station.

Frowning, Grant broke the seal and unfolded the paper. The message was brief. Yet he had to read it twice before the meaning sank its claws into him.

The Duchess of Mulford has lied to you and to the world. The young duke has no blood ties to the Ramsey family. He is your son.

* * *

"A clever transformation, don't you agree?" Helena murmured.

Sophie followed the direction of her gaze to Elliot. Some fifty guests chatted in the Grand Saloon at Mulford House. Footmen in blue livery circulated with silver trays of champagne glasses. Across the ornate room, Elliot stood amid a cluster of giggly debutantes.

For once, Robert's cousin appeared neat and presentable. His thinning brown hair had been trimmed and combed. He wore a tailored green frock coat over sleek-fitting pantaloons. At his throat, a crisp white cravat complemented his sun-darkened skin. He looked every inch a gentleman . . . a disgruntled, ill-at-ease gentleman.

Was he also a murderer? Sophie couldn't answer the question. Alice had been unable to provide any clue to implicate him.

"You have indeed wrought a miracle," Sophie said tactfully. "How did you manage it in so short a time?"

Helena's mouth curved in a crafty smile. Despite the wine stain birthmark on her cheek, she looked beautiful tonight, her blond hair a perfect foil for the elegant black gown. "It was simple. I hinted that one of those Roman relics might make an appropriate wedding gift to him."

Her audacity shocked Sophie. "The Chichester artifacts belong to *Lucien*. You can't give them away."

"For heaven's sake, I've no intention of doing so," Helena said, looking somewhat irritated. "It is merely a means to prod Elliot in the direction of the altar. I thought you were in favor of him settling down with a suitable bride."

Sophie had gone along with the plans for this birthday dinner. She had seen no harm in presenting Elliot with an opportunity to find a wife. She had even added a few bluestockings to the guest list, and one of them stood talking earnestly to him, a tall, thin, severe lady in an ill-fitting brown dress.

But Sophie's tacit support of the matchmaking venture had vanished when she'd found out about Alice. At present, Sophie was too disenchanted with his behavior to foist him on any unsuspecting lady.

Upon his return from the shopping excursion with Helena, Sophie had taken him aside and delivered a severe lecture about his duty to the scullery maid. He'd tried to deny his impending fatherhood. He'd grumbled and quarreled, but she had coerced him into a promise to provide for Alice and the baby. Ever since then, he had been pouting like a small boy who'd been chastised for sneaking a sweet.

Helena, however, didn't know the truth. And Sophie had no intention of telling her just yet.

"Ah, Miss Morton is sitting all alone," Helena said, peering toward a rather thickset girl dressed in pink frills. "I must introduce her to Elliot." For a moment her keen blue gaze returned to Sophie and scanned the deep plum silk of her new gown. "By the by, you look lovely tonight. A pity your Mr. Chandler is unable to join us."

As Helena sallied forth into the crowd, Sophie told herself to feel relieved, not irked. She had expected criticism for abandoning full mourning, rather than a compliment. Yet she bristled at Helena's acerbic tone in regard to Grant. Unaware of the true reason for his absence, her sister-in-law was pleased that he had declined to attend.

Well, so was Sophie. She had no wish to see him again. Not ever. That clutch of pain in her heart was only a temporary aberration.

She was *glad* she'd discovered his true nature before telling him about Lucien. Before she'd done something so foolish as to give Grant a reason to marry her. She wouldn't allow herself even to think she might be pregnant again.

Determined to forget him, she accepted a glass of champagne from the tray of a passing footman. Then she strolled through the crowd and played the role of gracious hostess. Thankfully, no one appeared to have heard so much as a whisper of gossip about the murder investigation. As Helena had said, the servants were too loyal to the family to spread rumors.

As Sophie greeted friends and exchanged pleasantries, the buzz of voices and the festive atmosphere struck a chord inside her, and she felt something dormant stir to life within herself. How she'd missed society during her time of mourning. An evening of pleasant company was the best possible way for her to forget her troubles.

And to forget how she'd spent the past few evenings. To forget about making mad, passionate love with Grant.

The ache inside her intensified. Her mind only kept drifting to him because . . . because she'd half-expected him to show up at this dinner party in defiance of her ultimatum. He'd wanted to interview Elliot, and surely Grant wouldn't abandon his goal to find the murderer.

He wouldn't so easily give up on *her*. Or would he?

Two late arrivals appeared in the doorway, and Sophie felt a lifting of her spirits. She hurried forward as Caroline and her husband strolled into the chamber. The older woman greeted her with a warm hug redolent with perfume and affection. "My dear Sophie. That is one of the new gowns we chose, is it not? Of course it is, and the color suits you so wonderfully."

Sophie desperately craved the balm of friendship. "Caro! I'm delighted you're back."

"I'm delighted to be here," Caroline said, her sparkling blue eyes lighting her otherwise plain features. "My carriage broke an axle on the way back from Wimbledon, and my maid and I had to wait a *very* long time on the roadside. Then when I finally arrived home—frightfully late, I might add—James was still at Parliament." She flashed a mock glare at her husband. "After an absence of nearly a week, one would expect one's spouse to be waiting with open arms."

The Earl of Belgrove kissed her gloved hand. A reserved, distinguished man with a thatch of graying black hair, he had a stern countenance—except when he gazed upon his wife. "An important vote was at stake, my love. However, I *will* make it up to you."

Husband and wife shared an intensely private smile. They were a handsome couple, the earl so tall and dignified in sober dark blue, and Caroline plump and sprightly in yellow silk. Watching them, Sophie felt a wistful pang in her breast. They had been happily married for more than twenty-five years. How she had hoped to find such companionship and love with Grant . . .

"I shall hold you to your promise, darling," Caroline said to him. "However, for now you must run along and allow Sophie and me to catch up on our gossip."

"As you wish," the earl said meekly. Bowing to the ladies, he strolled toward a group of gentlemen who were deep in discussion.

"I don't mean to separate the two of you—" Sophie began.

"Oh, it's quite all right," Caroline said airily, linking arms with her. "James would vastly prefer to be debating politics. He would only cast a damper upon our conversation. Shall we take a turn around the room?"

As they strolled the perimeter of the saloon, Sophie bit her lip to keep from spilling out her troubles. A party was no place to discuss murder—or heartache. "Tell me, how was your visit with the dowager?"

Caroline wrinkled her nose. "Quiet and dull, of course. The poor old dear kept dozing off during conversations, and it was rather embarrassing to find myself talking to no one. On the bright side, I did embroider an entire set of pillow covers while I was there." She cast a significant glance at Sophie. "I do hope *your* life has been more exciting this past week."

If only Caro knew. "Far *too* exciting, I fear," Sophie murmured, keeping her voice low so that no one else could overhear. "Will you visit in the morning? I've a number of events to relate to you."

"Dear me, that sounds intriguing. Can you not give me a hint at least? Would these events involve a certain dashing, dark-haired gentleman?"

Sophie strove to keep her expression neutral, her tone light. "Yes, Grant had some involvement. But lest you raise your hopes, he won't be courting me. I assure you, I've no interest in him at all."

"Oh? It's quite obvious that he's interested in *you*."

"Perhaps he was at first. But matters have changed."

"Indeed?" Frowning slightly, Caroline glanced at her, then surveyed the milling guests. "I wouldn't think so, judging by the way he looks at you."

It hurt to speak of him. Why did Caroline, usually attuned to nuances, persist in the subject? Sophie would have to make herself clearer. "We did become quite . . . *close* this past week. However, our association is finished. I won't be seeing him again, not ever."

"Hmm. I can't imagine how you'll avoid it."

"Pardon?"

Caroline glanced away again before returning her highly curious gaze to Sophie. "Brace yourself, my dear. It appears you have an uninvited guest. Unless my eyesight fails me, Mr. Chandler is coming straight this way."

Sophie's heart stopped almost dead. Then it started up again, drumming against her ribs.

Turning, she spied Grant making his way through the clusters of noble guests, pausing now and then to greet someone with a nod or a few polite words. Despite his risqué reputation, he was the brother of the Earl of Litton; people remembered him even though he had been away from society for so long. The ladies in particular whispered among themselves, and a hum of interest swept the gathering as mothers recognized the presence of another matrimonial prospect.

Sophie felt a flare of hot possessiveness. She wanted to announce in no uncertain terms that this tall, rakishly handsome man was already claimed—by her.

Nothing could be more impossible. Or more imprudent.

But her senses sprang to life regardless of logic. Grant was *here*. He had come, after all. He meant to win his way back into her good graces.

She wouldn't let him. No, she wouldn't. And yet—

From halfway across the chamber, his dark gaze seared her. He bowed to a lady. He spoke to a group of gentlemen. But all the while, his attention remained fixed on Sophie.

With hard, chilling intensity.

The foolish hope faltered inside her. With a painful twist in her stomach, she realized he was angry. Where was the seductive, charming man she had known in his bedchamber?

Of course, she had never really known him. He had hidden the secret source of his wealth. He was a jewel thief, and he associated with rough, unsavory characters. The faint red mark beneath his eye showed where Bahir had held the knife. Grant was a dangerous man, a man who had no place in her life—or Lucien's. Against her express wishes, he had the gall to stroll into her house and invade her dinner party.

With a steely arrogance, he continued his approach. As if *she* were the one in the wrong.

Sophie lifted her chin and narrowed her eyes. She could be cold and angry, too. She had every right—

"It seems a storm is about to break," Caroline murmured. "Here comes Helena, too."

Robert's sister sailed through the crowd, reaching them at the same moment as Grant. His manners impeccable, he bowed to the women. "Lady Belgrove. Your Grace. Lady Helena. It's a pleasure to enjoy the company of three such lovely ladies."

"Mr. Chandler," Helena said coolly. "This is most unexpected. Sophie told me you wouldn't be attending our little party."

Grant's eyes flicked to Sophie. The look was hooded, impenetrable. "A misunderstanding."

"On your part," Sophie snapped. Aware of Caroline's and Helena's scrutiny, she compressed her lips. She was never so rude in company. What was it about him that brought out the worst in her?

And the best. Dear heaven, the way he could make her *feel* . . .

"I'm sorry if my presence is an imposition," Grant said, appearing anything but regretful. He stepped toward Sophie, and she felt a shock of awareness as his fingers closed around her bare arm. "Perhaps, duchess, you and I should discuss the matter in private."

15 December 1701
17 Days until the Grand Wedding

Much to my woe, my Mother is happily counting down the days until my Grand Wedding to Mulford. Today I spent the day in the company of her and the Warden, so that we might arrange the seating for over two hundred guests. How the task made my Head ache! I wanted to shout, I will not be a Duchess! I will be William's wife and live in his cozy lodgings and never invite more than ten friends to dinner.

But I dared not reveal my Secret Plans. The elopement shall take place on the day after Christmas. I can scarce bear the dreadful suspense.

—the diaries of Annabelle Chatham Ramsey, 3rd Duchess of Mulford

24

Sophie had no wish to be alone with Grant. "There's nothing to discuss," she said. "Since you're here, the footman will set another place."

"Nevertheless, I'd like a word with you," he said, drawing her forward. "If you ladies will excuse us."

Sophie had one last glimpse of Helena's disapproving expression and Caroline's keen interest. Then Grant steered her on an inexorable path to the doorway. A number of guests eyed them curiously, but he didn't seem to care if he caused gossip. Within moments, they were walking down the opulent corridor, their footsteps echoing on the white marble.

The candlelight flickered over his rigid features. He

stared straight ahead as if he couldn't bear to look at her. Alarm quivered along her nerves.

Grant wasn't merely angry. He was *furious*. It showed in the tautness of his mouth and the pressure of his fingers around her arm.

Intuition told her his mood had nothing to do with the murder investigation. Or with the fact that she'd banished him from her life. That left only—

No. No, she wouldn't let herself revisit *that* fear. Too many times already, she had worked herself into a state of panic, only to discover her mistake. He didn't know about Lucien. He *couldn't*.

Pulling her into a deserted sitting room, Grant released her arm and turned to shut the door. A branch of candles sat on a table, softly glowing over the mahogany wood, the crimson upholstery, the gold-tasseled draperies. A fire crackled on the hearth; every room on this floor had been readied in case any guests chose to wander during the course of the evening.

Without his touch, Sophie felt cold. She rubbed her arms and wondered if she ought to sit down. No, better to stand. She didn't want him looming over her, putting her at a disadvantage. At least not until she understood the source of his black mood.

Grant stepped toward her. His jaw was tight, his expression icily blank. There was something terrifying about that look. Something that made her insides clench with dread . . . and regret. Only yesterday, he had held her with such loving tenderness.

He reached into his pocket and drew out a paper, which he thrust into her hand. Then he prowled the small chamber as if he couldn't stand still, not even for an instant.

She stared down at the folded note. His name and address were neatly penned on the outside in an unfamiliar hand. What was it? Why had he offered no explanation?

And why did she have the most awful apprehension in the pit of her stomach?

Slowly, she opened the letter, the paper rustling and her fingers trembling. She wanted to read the message . . . and she didn't. Morbid curiosity won out. Immediately, she wished it hadn't.

> *The Duchess of Mulford has lied to you and to the world. The young duke has no blood ties to the Ramsey family. He is your son.*

The words swam before Sophie's eyes. She felt sick with panic. It couldn't be . . . *no.* She wanted to run out of the room, to burrow beneath the covers of her bed, to awaken in the morning and find out this had all been a nightmare.

Like a gunshot, Grant's voice broke the silence. "Well, duchess? Nothing to say for yourself?"

Her neck felt stiff as she raised her head. He paced toward her, stopping directly in front of her. His image was blurred as if viewed through a block of ice. "I . . ."

"Go on," he snapped. "Let's hear your excuse. You've had ten years to think of an excellent one."

Her chest felt too tight to draw a breath. When she tried to swallow, a ball of cotton blocked her throat. Wild denials raced through her head. But in the end, she whispered, "It's true. Lucien is . . . your son."

Something glinted in Grant's eyes, something fearful. It was almost as if he'd *wanted* her to deny it. He stared at her, his chest rising and falling as if he too found it difficult to breathe. For one hideous moment she feared he would strike her.

He pivoted away, ran his fingers through his hair, and then turned back to her. "Damn you, Sophie! Why didn't you *tell* me?"

It was a question she'd answered satisfactorily many times in her thoughts. She had convinced herself that she'd had no other choice. But now her mind went blank. Looking at Grant, she couldn't think of a single valid reason.

She could only wish it were possible to turn back the clock. Because pain lurked behind the rage in his dark gaze. *Anguish.* She had hurt him terribly. "I—I'm so sorry . . ."

"Sorry." He shook his head slowly. "Sophie, I asked you straight-out if you were with child. And you lied to me. You turned down my offer of marriage. You went after Robert and his title instead. Without even consulting me, you let another man raise *my son.*"

Put so starkly, her deed sounded heartless. Unforgivably cruel. "Please try to understand," she whispered. "I was young . . . frightened. And . . . and I *did* start to tell you . . . yesterday, on the stairs."

"Yesterday?" He made a humorless, skeptical sound. "That's ten years too late."

Crumpling the note in her hand, Sophie took a step toward him. "You didn't *want* to marry me, Grant. You *didn't.* You said . . ." Her voice wobbled, but she went on, "You said you couldn't afford a wife, but you'd *have* to marry me. Those were your exact words. You felt *forced.*"

He gave her that blank, frigid, disbelieving stare. "You're right, I was in debt. But you should have trusted me to provide for you. I would have secured the money to support you and Lucien."

"How? By stealing it?" She was shocked the moment the words left her mouth. It was unfair of her to assume he'd have turned to thievery if he'd stayed in London.

His face had gone ashen with anger. "Yes, I've been a jewel thief," he said bitterly. "But at least I've never stolen a child."

Sophie could say nothing to that. Oh, God. He was right. How he must loathe her. She wanted to cover her face and weep.

"Perhaps you deceived Robert, too," Grant said after a moment. "Perhaps when he realized the truth—that his heir was not of his blood—you poisoned him. Because you wanted your son to inherit."

The awful accusation struck from out of nowhere. Numb with horror, she gaped at him. "You can't really think—"

"That you'd rid yourself of an inconvenient husband? It certainly makes sense." He strode away, then turned to regard her coldly. "Your son becomes the duke. And you have a title and an enormous fortune at your disposal. I wonder what Hannibal Jones would say to that."

A chill slid through her veins. Grant was serious. He wore that flinty mask again, the dead-eyed look of a stranger. The iciness of it made her teeth chatter. "You're *wrong*. Robert knew the truth from the start. We never consummated the marriage. Never."

He said nothing for a moment. "So you lied about that, too." His contemptuous gaze flicked up and down her. "Or perhaps you're lying now."

"Grant, *listen*. I went to him as soon as I realized . . . I told him what had happened . . . and he offered to marry me. He was . . . a dear friend."

"A pity he isn't here to corroborate your story."

Sophie felt helpless in the face of Grant's accusations. She'd branded herself a liar in his mind. There was nothing she could say in her defense that he would believe. Yet she lifted her hands beseechingly. "You know me better than that. How can you even think me capable of . . . of murder?"

"I'll tell you how. On his deathbed, Robert wrote to

me. He said that someone very close to him had given him poison. My immediate thought was that *you* had done so."

Sophie's mind twisted in bewilderment. She needed time to think, to sort through the tangle of revelations. But Grant stood grimly waiting for her response. "You received a letter? From *Robert*? He *knew*—?"

"Yes." His voice was clipped, harsh, unemotional. "He begged me to return to London. Of course, by the time I received the letter, it was too late. But I came here, anyway. For the express purpose of investigating you, Sophie."

Everything in her resisted his words. But memories came flooding back. His probing queries about her marriage. His interest in the use of rat poison in the library. The calculating way he had stared at her.

Before her weak legs could collapse, Sophie groped for a chair and sank into it. All that time, he had believed her a murderess. While he had seduced her, he had also been seeking proof of her crime. He had thought her guilty even before . . .

She looked up sharply. "Did *you* write that letter to Bow Street? Because you wanted the Runners to help in finding evidence against me?"

Grant scowled. "Good God, no. I never wanted the law involved. I've been on the hop ever since, trying to keep them off your scent."

"But . . . why?" Anger stirred in the midst of her shock. How dare he pretend to help her. Stiffening her spine, she matched his coldness. "I should think it would suit your purpose to see me arrested."

"There are other forms of punishment."

The implicit threat resonated in her loins. A deep, dark pulse of desire made her breasts tighten and her skin prickle with heat. She was appalled at the involuntary response. What did he mean? That he would *force* her to be his mistress? But she had been that without any coercion.

Veering away from the dangerous topic of intimacy, Sophie said, "Apparently, someone is as eager as you are to discredit me. So who *did* write that letter? And this one?" She held up the crumpled note.

"I don't know." He took the letter from her, folded it, and replaced it in the inner pocket of his coat. "But I intend to find out."

She scrambled to think who might have guessed Lucien's true sire. Helena? Elliot? Had one of them seen Lucien and Grant together and realized the truth? Or perhaps Geoffrey Langston?

And . . . oh, dear God. Did that person intend to discredit Lucien?

Controlling her fear, she rose to her feet. "You may investigate me as you please. I have nothing to hide. But I meant what I said last night. I don't want you anywhere near me or my son."

Grant's face tightened with forbidding determination. "He's *my* son, Sophie. You've denied me the chance to be his father. I'll be damned if I'll walk away from him now."

"And what if Bahir returns? Or some other ruffian from your past?" The thought made her feel ill, and she shook her head emphatically. "Lucien could be in danger if he associates with you. I won't allow that. I *can't*."

"I don't know how the hell Bahir tracked me down, but trust me, there will be no others. I always worked in absolute secrecy."

"Apparently, you weren't as skillful as you like to believe," Sophie snapped. She fought the urge to relent. Surely even the slightest risk was too great. "And what if you find yourself short of money again? Will you return to thievery? Will there be other ruffians in your future to hold a knife to your eye or a pistol to your head?"

He made an impatient slash of his hand. "For God's sake. I told you last night I was done with that."

She had to be firm. She mustn't let herself weaken. What if Lucien had been there last night to witness that horror? "I'm sorry, Grant. I have no choice. I must protect Lucien."

The cold steel of his gaze bored into her. "You *should* be sorry," he said in a deceptively quiet tone. "You've had him for nine years. It's my turn now."

A quagmire of emotions sucked at her balance. Guilt, for she had denied Grant his son. Wretchedness, for she knew that he loved Lucien. And most of all, fear. "You can't take him away from me. The case would be thrown out of court."

"I've no intention of taking legal action. Unlike you, I believe a child belongs with both his parents." Grant walked closer, stopping only a few inches away. "Resign yourself, duchess. You and I are going be married."

Throughout dinner, Grant was intensely aware of Sophie. She sat at the head of the table, chatting with the guests on either side of her as if nothing had happened. As if he hadn't just torn apart her life. She never once even looked at him.

He was seated midway down the enormously long, linen-draped table, too far away to hear her conversation. So he talked horses with the old gentleman on his right. Or rather, Lord Somebody-or-Another talked, rambling on about bloodlines and paddocks and saddles while Grant nodded sagely now and then. But it gave him an excuse to covertly watch Sophie.

In the candlelight, her skin had the translucent glow of

a pearl. The upsweep of coppery brown hair enhanced the delicate beauty of her face and throat. The low cut of her bodice drew his gaze to her rounded breasts.

She was *his*. His alone. No other man had ever touched her. In spite of his fury, he felt a powerful possessiveness. He wanted to make love to her.

No. He wanted to punish her. She had duped him in a way that brought the bitterness of gall to his throat. Of all the sins he'd attributed to her, separating him from his child was the worst. And there she sat, smiling at the be-jeweled matron beside her, listening with polite attention. Her cool, composed manner gave away nothing of the turmoil she must be feeling.

She had to be dazed from the exposure of her secret. He had caught her completely off guard. Her shock had been great—but not so great as his.

Lucien was his son. *His son.*

Grant had trouble adjusting his mind to the concept. That charming scamp was *his*. The knowledge expanded his chest with a sweet, painful intensity. It made his eyes smart and his throat thicken. He tried to imagine Lucien as an infant, all tiny fists and trusting eyes. As a toddler taking his first steps. As an excited little boy opening his birthday presents.

But Grant's mind came up blank. For him, those memories didn't exist. Sophie had stolen them. And all because she'd been affronted by the manner of his marriage proposal.

You didn't want to marry me . . . you said you couldn't afford a wife, but you'd have to marry me. Those were your exact words . . .

He called up the memory. Lying in bed with her in the blissful aftermath. Feeling a sickening jolt of awareness that he'd taken Sophie's virginity. Despite his dissolute reputation, he'd known better than to prey upon innocent young ladies. He'd known—yet his rationality had been lost to the explosive madness of desire. He had never felt that intensity of passion with any other woman.

So maybe he *had* been too blunt. Maybe he'd momentarily forgotten that women liked soft words and romantic gestures. But he'd been bowled over by the enormity of his actions. He'd been worried about his ability to support a wife. Surely Sophie should have realized the necessity of *that*.

"You're ignoring me, Mr. Chandler," Lady Belgrove chided. "You should have better manners."

Pulled back to the present, Grant turned to his dinner partner on the left. Sophie's friend Caroline was a middle-aged woman with brilliant blue eyes that missed nothing. The knowing smile on her matronly features plainly said that she knew his attention had been focused on Sophie.

He had no doubt that Lady Belgrove had finagled the seating arrangement. She was very curious about his relationship with Sophie. Through the first few courses of dinner, she had asked him veiled questions about his plans for the future. She reminded him of Aunt Phoebe, with benevolent eyes and a steely disposition. "Forgive me," he said smoothly. "I was discussing a sale at Tattersall's with Lord . . ."

"Carrington," she murmured in amusement. "My, you *are* distracted tonight. And Sophie as well. She looked quite pale when the two of you returned to the party."

Grant took a drink from his wine glass. He had deftly sidestepped Lady Belgrove's comments and questions, but hell, maybe that was the wrong approach. Spreading the word could only help his cause. "As a matter of fact," he said in a low, confiding voice, "she *was* overwrought. A woman often is when a man proposes marriage."

Lady Belgrove had been eating chocolate cream from a

little white dish, but now her spoon clattered onto her plate. Delight animated her face. "Truly?" She glanced at Sophie and her smile faltered. "Oh, dear. She didn't refuse you, did she?"

Hardly. "She accepted, of course. But we're keeping the engagement quiet for now."

"You may trust in my discretion. I suppose you'll want to wait until she's out of mourning."

The buzz of conversation and the clink of dishes masked their words from the other guests. But Grant kept his voice down, anyway. "Actually, we intend to marry very soon by special license. I can't bear to be apart from Sophie. I lost her once, and I won't lose her again."

Although Lady Belgrove smiled, she didn't look entirely fooled by his romantic declaration. Clearly, she was sharp enough to sense undercurrents. "You are a very lucky man, Mr. Chandler. Sophie is a kind, loving, wonderful person. I trust you'll devote yourself to her."

He would take his pleasure of Sophie. But devotion? His chest hurt from the wound of being cheated out of half of Lucien's childhood. Those lost years were irretrievable.

Grant flashed Lady Belgrove his most confident smile. "Set your mind at ease on the matter. I intend to take excellent care of her."

"And Lucien," Lady Belgrove said, watching him earnestly. "Forgive me for being blunt, but he is an important consideration. Some men wouldn't care to raise another man's son."

Grant's hand froze around his wine glass. God, if only she knew how her kind, loving, wonderful Sophie had deceived him . . .

"I already regard Lucien as my own son," he said with unflinching sincerity. "Remember, Robert handpicked me to be his guardian."

Lady Belgrove studied him a moment, then gave a nod

of satisfaction. Her eyes sparkling again, she raised her wine glass and said, "Yes, you're quite right. I wish the three of you all the happiness in the world."

Happiness. He could no longer imagine it. Suppressing a craven wish to gaze at Sophie, he deftly turned the topic to Lady Belgrove's family, and she launched enthusiastically into stories about her three sons, the older two grown and married, and the youngest away at school. Grant enjoyed her company, yet a part of his mind dwelled on his own thoughts.

He understood now why Robert had appointed him Lucien's guardian. Robert had known the truth. Sophie had not been lying about that, as Grant had accused. Grant had lashed out in fury, wanting to hurt her as she had hurt him. And he had needed to coerce her into marrying him.

How can you even think me capable of murder?

He didn't. Despite her deception, he believed she *was* innocent. The murderer had written those two letters, the first accusing her of poisoning Robert, and the second one revealing the truth about Lucien. Was it Geoffrey Langston? Or someone in this household, someone who knew Sophie well? Lady Helena . . . or Elliot?

Both sat too far away for Grant to engage in conversation. As the evening wore on interminably, he quelled his impatience. After dinner, instead of the gentlemen and the ladies separating, the entire group proceeded into the drawing room, where several of the young ladies took turns displaying their varying skills on the pianoforte.

Grant waited for a chance to catch Elliot alone. But a gaggle of giggling debutantes, maneuvered by the ever-vigilant Helena, constantly surrounded him. It was obvious from Elliot's fidgeting and stifled yawns that the company bored him. Finally, as the hour grew late and the guests began to depart, Grant made his way toward Robert's cousin.

A footman appeared in the doorway of the drawing room and spoke to Sophie. She cast a distressed, wide-eyed glance at Grant. Then she murmured something to Helena and hastened out into the corridor.

That glimpse of worry on Sophie's face pulled him like a magnet. He veered away from Elliot and caught up to her at the staircase, wrapping his fingers around her slender arm. As Sophie looked up, a keen sense of possessiveness gripped him anew. She would be his wife. *At last.*

"Where are you going?" he asked.

"Lucien has taken ill. Miss Oliver sent for me."

The news jarred him. "I'll accompany you."

"It's only a stomach upset. You needn't trouble yourself."

Anger flashed through Grant. Was she trying to keep him from his son? "It's no trouble, duchess. Let's go."

Sophie gave him a wary, eloquent look, then nodded. Side by side, they went up the stairs to the nursery. "This way," she said, leading him down a corridor and into a dim, spacious chamber lit by a candle on the bedside table and the fire on the hearth. In the gloom, he could see the shadowed shape of a hobbyhorse, the dark lumps of furniture, a shelf of books. In the broad expanse of the four-poster, Lucien looked very small beneath the covers. He appeared to be asleep.

Miss Oliver jumped up from a straight-backed chair beside the bed. A white nightcap perched on her head and a high-necked dressing gown covered her sturdy form. With agitation rather than her usual briskness, she rushed to Sophie. "Your Grace," she murmured, "I am sorry to pull you away from your party. But I thought perhaps you would wish to be here."

Sophie patted the woman's hand. "You were absolutely right to summon me." Glancing at the bed, she whispered, "How is he?"

"He only just dropped off to sleep. The poor dear awakened half an hour ago, moaning and crying. He retched several times, I'm afraid. He seems a little better now, and I wasn't certain if you'd wish me to send for Dr. Atherton."

"We'll see."

Sophie hurried to one side of the bed, while Grant went to the other. Lucien lay on his side, facing Grant, his cheek nestled on the pillow and his eyes closed. Beneath the covers, his knees were drawn up and his small form curled into a ball as if his stomach pained him. Grant felt a twist in his own gut—and a sense of helplessness. He could stitch a knife wound and set a broken arm, but he had absolutely no idea what to do for an ailing child.

Sophie gently placed her hand on Lucien's brow. "No fever," she whispered over her shoulder to Miss Oliver. "That's good."

Grant gazed down at that small shadowed form as if seeing Lucien for the first time. The soft, childish features. The thatch of brown hair. The little hand that gripped the coverlet. Awe washed through Grant, along with a powerful concern. Did all parents feel so anxious over every childhood sickness?

Sophie held Lucien's wrist. "His pulse is rapid," she murmured.

"What does that mean?" Grant asked, straining to keep his voice calm.

She looked somberly at him, as if she'd forgotten his presence. "It's only an observation. Perhaps he ate something that disagreed with him." Sophie shifted her attention to the governess. "What did he have for supper?"

"Nothing unusual," Miss Oliver said. "One of his favorite meals, in fact. Toasted cheese and a cup of milk."

By odd happenstance, Grant spied a crystal goblet on the bedside table where he stood. The deep shadows had almost hidden it from view. He picked it up, noticing that it was over half full. "This glass?" he asked.

Miss Oliver tilted her head, a look of puzzlement on her face. "Why, no. He used his pewter cup, as he always does."

"You've never seen this before?" Grant said. "You're certain of that?"

"Absolutely, sir," she stated. "His Grace takes his meals either in the schoolroom or down in the kitchen. He's allowed to bring only water in here."

Grant looked across the bed at Sophie. As if transfixed, she stared at him, and a silent communication leaped between them. The dawning terror in her eyes spread to Grant, infecting him with a powerful, staggering suspicion.

Poison.

Impossible.

It must be.

Every pore in his body went icy with sweat. For one frozen moment he couldn't move or speak. The goblet in his hand felt cold and deadly. If he'd had the slightest lingering doubt about Sophie, the horror on her face settled the matter once and for all. She would never, ever harm their son.

But *someone* wanted Lucien dead.

Involuntarily, Grant lifted the goblet and sniffed it. It smelled like . . . milk. Common, ordinary milk. But he knew from his study of poisons that arsenic had no odor. The chill of the liquid would mask any slight taste.

Leashing panic, he set down the goblet and snapped his gaze to the governess, who watched him in baffled alarm. "Who came into this room this evening?"

"Only myself, sir." Miss Oliver put a quavering hand to her maidenly bosom. "The footmen and maids were busy with the party. And I must say, I don't remember seeing the glass when I put the young master to bed."

"She's right," Sophie said in an unsteady voice. "It wasn't there when I kissed Lucien good night. That goblet is our fine crystal, and I would have noticed it."

"Were you in your chamber all evening?" he asked Miss Oliver.

"Yes, I read for a time before I fell asleep, perhaps around ten o'clock."

The hour was well after midnight. The killer had had ample time to leave the goblet. Thank God, Lucien hadn't drunk all of the milk.

Feverishly, Grant thought back to the party. Elliot had left the dinner table once, presumably to answer a call of nature. Helena had also vanished for a short time. And the goblet was from the set used at dinner . . .

"I vow, I heard nothing." The governess looked stricken as she glanced down at Lucien. "If I've done something wrong, I'll never forgive myself."

Grant would never forgive himself. "Send a footman for Dr. Atherton. And if Lady Belgrove is still here, ask her to come upstairs. If she's left already, have someone fetch her from home."

"Certainly, sir. At once."

As Miss Oliver hurried out of the room, Sophie frowned at him across the bed. "Caroline?"

He paced the murky bedchamber. "Lucien cannot remain in this house a moment longer," he said, keeping his voice low. "He'll be safer next door. Miss Oliver can stay with him."

"Dear . . . heaven . . ." The image of despair, Sophie sank down on the edge of the bed. "Who would do this? *Who?*"

There were two possibilities, Grant thought grimly.

Proper Helena, who might have guessed that Lucien was
Grant's son and not the true heir. Or Elliot, who would do
anything to get his hands on the Chichester artifacts.

Grant burned to throttle both of them. Hardly aware of
what he was doing, he paced to Sophie. Their eyes met,
and again he had that uncanny sense of communication,
as if they were one mind, one body.

He didn't know who moved first, but suddenly she was
in his arms, clinging as fiercely to him as he did to her.
She buried her face in his cravat and a sob escaped her. "It
wasn't me, Grant. I swear it."

Mortified, he remembered his accusations. "I know. I
believe you." Oh, God. She felt so perfect in his embrace.
He breathed in the scent of her hair, felt the comforting
softness of her body. "Lucien will be fine. I doubt he
drank enough to cause him real harm."

"Oh, I pray you're right," she said fervently. "I hope—"

Lucien gave a small moan. As one, they let go of each
other and spun toward the bed.

His dark lashes fluttering, the boy opened his eyes. A
groggy smile lit his wan features. "Mr. Chandler. I was
wishing and wishing you'd visit me."

Grant's chest clenched. *I love you. I'll keep you safe.* "I
was downstairs at the party. With your mother."

Bending down, Sophie brushed a lock of hair from Lucien's brow. "How are you feeling, dearest?"

"My stomach was hurting. But I feel better now."

She hugged him tightly, her eyes soft and shiny with
tears. "I'm so glad to hear that."

Grant sat down on the bed. "I need to ask you something, scamp. Did you happen to see who left this glass of
milk here?"

Lucien blinked at the bedside table. "I dunno . . . I had
a dream . . . someone tapped on my shoulder. Then I
woke up and saw it there."

Grant exchanged a glance with Sophie. Her eyes mirrored the shock and horror inside him. The killer must have deliberately awakened Lucien.

Sophie showed the boy a reassuring smile. "Would you like to go on a little adventure? To spend the night at Lady Belgrove's house? You've always admired Philip's room."

Lucien looked uncertain. "C-can Mr. Chandler go, too?"

"Oh, dearest, that may not be possible—"

"I'll carry you over there," Grant broke in. "Then I have something to do for a little bit, but I'll return if you like. I'll sleep on a pallet in your chamber, how's that?"

Lucien looked as if he'd been given the moon. "Truly?"

"Truly." Grant ruffled the boy's unruly mop of hair. Aware of Sophie watching, he added gruffly, "I'll be there for you. Always."

25

"I don't believe it," Helena said flatly. "All children take ill from time to time."

In the gloomy environs of the library, Sophie studied her sister-in-law's face for any sign of guilt, but could see only an annoyed skepticism. The guests were gone, Lucien was safely ensconced next door at Caroline's house, and Grant had herded Helena and Elliot in here without a heed for their protests.

Grant stood with his arm resting on the mantelpiece, the cousins sat side by side on the chaise, with Sophie on a chair opposite them. Helena still looked fresh and unruffled in her elegant black frock, while Elliot had changed into a shabby green dressing gown. His big toe poked out of the hole in one of his brown stockings.

"I agree, this *is* nonsense," Elliot concurred grumpily.

"I'm returning to Surrey early in the morning, and I'm weary—"

"You're going nowhere," Grant cut in. "You will remain in this house until I determine who put that glass of poisoned milk beside Lucien's bed."

In the shadows cast by the dying fire, he looked harsh and sinister—and Sophie was desperately gratified to have him on her side. She felt weak with the lingering horror of Lucien's illness. He was so small. If he had drained that goblet, he might have died like Robert . . .

"You can't force me to stay," Elliot snapped. "My workers will dig where they oughtn't. I've already lost a day because of this ridiculous party."

"Now, now," Helena said soothingly. "You were a huge success with the ladies. If you remain in town for a few more days, I can invite a few of your favorites for tea. Whom did you like best? Lady Camilla? Or was it Miss Poole?"

Elliot regarded her as if she'd grown another head. "You can tell all of them to stuff it, that's what. Fluffy little twits wouldn't know a spade from a pickaxe."

"My dear cousin, only consider that the right woman could enrich your life and offer you companionship at the end of your workday. You're forty years old and it's past time you took a wife."

He glowered at her another moment before springing to his feet. "Then so I shall. I'll marry Alice!"

Startled out of her morbid thoughts, Sophie blinked in surprise. She knew of only one Alice. Helena did too, for she looked thunderstruck, her mouth working soundlessly and her fingers clutching at her skirt.

"Are you referring to Alice . . . the scullery maid?" Sophie asked.

"I most certainly am," Elliot averred. "The gal's used

to a simple life. She's no silly flirt who babbles on about ribbons and lace and other twaddle. *She* won't mind living in a little hut near the ruins."

Grant shifted his feet impatiently. "Your marriage plans are hardly the issue here. I want to know which one of you two went up to Lucien's chamber tonight—"

Helena let out a belated shriek. *"The scullery maid?"*

Elliot rounded on her. His lizardlike face wore a gloating look, almost as if he relished upsetting her. "Yes, indeed. She and I are eminently well suited. Don't know why I didn't consider it before now. Alice doesn't chatter my ears off. She doesn't care about fripperies. And she'll be well occupied when the baby arrives—"

"Baby?" Grant asked.

"Baby!" Helena exclaimed.

"Elliot is going to be a father before the year is out," Sophie explained. "That's why Alice fainted when we interviewed her." She directed that last remark at Grant, then returned her attention to Elliot. She tried to picture him sitting contentedly by his fireside with plain, placid Alice knitting a baby blanket. It was an odd fancy, but . . . "Elliot, are you certain that marriage to you is what *she* wants?"

Elliot looked nonplussed by the question, his usual arrogance faltering. "I, er . . ."

Helena uttered a garbled gasp. "What *she* wants? Of course the grasping little upstart will seize the opportunity. Why, she very likely put the scandalous notion in his head!"

"Mind your tongue," Elliot ordered. "You're speaking of my future wife. And your future cousin-in-law."

Against Helena's pale skin, the birthmark on her cheek stood out like a blotch of blood. She surged to her feet and fixed Elliot with an imperious glare. "You cannot nake so improper a marriage. You'll ruin this family. I won't be made a laughingstock."

"You haven't any choice," Elliot retorted. "Perhaps tomorrow I'll go down on bended knee right there in the kitchen—"

"Oh!" Helena cried out. "I refuse to listen to this abomination a moment longer. I'm going upstairs. You should, too, Elliot. Perhaps a good night's sleep will cure you of this folly!"

Helena pushed past her cousin and marched toward the door.

"Wait!" Grant snapped. "We aren't through here."

Without missing a stride, she said over her shoulder, "*I* am through, Mr. Chandler. With the entire lot of you!" She vanished out the door.

"And good riddance," Elliot said, rubbing his hands together. "That should take the biddy down a peg or two. Don't need *her* to find me a wife."

Not wanting to be the only one left sitting, Sophie stood up, too. "You mustn't marry Alice just to spite Helena. I won't permit you to ill-treat the girl any more than you've already done."

"I'm doing right by her," Elliot objected. "I'm making her respectable. That's more than a girl like her can expect."

He spoke the truth, but Sophie wasn't satisfied. "She is not to be your personal slave, Elliot. I want your promise that you will afford her all the honor due the wife of a gentleman."

He sullenly tugged at his cravat. "I'm marrying her, aren't I?"

"Promise me," she repeated firmly.

"Oh, blast it, all right. What d'you think I intend to do to the girl? Lock her in chains and whip her?"

"You might poison her," Grant cut in. "Just as you did Lucien and Robert."

Elliot's lip curled in a sneer. "For the last time, I know nothing of any poisoning. I refuse to stay awake all night and listen to these melodramatic accusations."

Grant stepped forward to block his path. "I'll find the proof, then. In the meantime, if you set one foot outside this house, I'll make you regret it."

Muttering under his breath, Elliot stepped around him and trudged out of the library, leaving Sophie alone with Grant.

"Blast it all!" Grant stalked to the door and slammed it shut, the sound echoing through the gloom. "He was too damn anxious to get out of here. He must be lying. He has to be."

Sophie no longer knew what to think. As much as she wanted the culprit caught, she could understand Elliot's annoyance with Grant. She herself still smarted from the blow of being accused of murdering Robert. "Perhaps someone saw him or Helena going up to the nursery. Or filling a goblet with milk in the pantry. We can ask the servants in the morning."

"Alice," Grant said, pointing at Sophie. "That's who we need to question. Elliot could have persuaded her to take that glass of milk up to the nursery. Was she employed here at the time of Robert's death?"

The thought unsettled Sophie. "Yes, but . . . she seems an honest person. There must be some other explanation."

"We're running out of possibilities." He prowled through the shadows, wending his way around tables and chairs. "Although I intend to have another talk with Geoffrey Langston."

She stepped toward Grant. "Why? Doesn't what happened tonight exonerate him? What reason could *he* have to harm Lucien?"

"He's Robert's heir."

"But I'm *sure* he knew . . . he *must* have known that Robert didn't sire Lucien."

Grant turned to face her. In the flickering glow of a branch of candles, he regarded her with a bleak stare. "Lucien now bears Robert's title. He's the Duke of Mulford, just as Robert was."

A horrified understanding devastated her. Langston had been angry at Robert for ending their relationship. What if he had transferred his resentment to Lucien?

She lifted a cold, trembling hand to her mouth. The crushing weight of fear and guilt squeezed her breast. Although rationality told her otherwise, she felt responsible nonetheless. "Then you're saying . . . if I hadn't married Robert, Lucien would not be in danger."

"Don't put words in my mouth," Grant said roughly. "I know you would never harm our son."

Our son. The words lingered in the silent air of the library.

Sophie felt perilously close to tears. How he must resent her for keeping Lucien all to herself. Impossible as it was, she longed for Grant's forgiveness. If only he would reach out to her. If only they could find solace in each other, as they had for a moment upstairs. But the chasm between them seemed wider and deeper than ever.

He was a thief, she reminded herself. He had come to London for the express purpose of proving her guilty of murder. But his sins paled in comparison to hers. *At least I've never stolen a child.*

As if he could no longer tolerate the sight of her, Grant turned away and picked up a book from the crate Elliot had returned that morning. "There's no point in further speculation," Grant said over his shoulder. "You might as well go on to bed."

Come with me. She couldn't ask him that. And not just

because of his promise to Lucien. "You're going to Caroline's, then?"

"Yes. You and I can talk again in the morning."

As he riffled the pages of the book, a piece of paper fluttered to the floor. Unthinkingly, Sophie bent down to pick it up. So did Grant.

Their hands brushed, and the contact sent a flash of awareness up her arm and over her skin. They crouched there, staring at each other, and the cool indifference in his gaze magnified her wretchedness. The tears were stinging the back of her throat now, threatening to fall.

She would not weep. She didn't want him to think she was trying to coerce his sympathy.

He drew back his hand, letting her take the folded paper. Unable to bear his scrutiny, she looked down at the old-fashioned vellum. It was coarse and yellowed with age. In faded ink, a name was written across the front.

Annabelle.

Sophie blinked. Then blinked again. Could it be—

No. Impossible.

But a rising excitement pushed her troubles aside. Very carefully, she unfolded the old parchment, and a musty odor wafted to her. The light was too dim for her to make out the spidery handwriting.

"We'd better go," Grant said. He stood up and held out his hand to her.

She accepted his assistance with alacrity, springing to her feet and taking the parchment over to a table to examine it by the illumination of a candle. The handwriting was cramped and small, designed to fit the most possible words on the page. Age had rendered the ink almost illegible. But it was a man's penmanship, and at the very bottom, a signature—

"Are you staying here, then?" Grant asked.

Her heart thumping, she glanced up at him. "This letter . . . it's from William to Annabelle."

"Who?"

"Annabelle was the third duchess, the one who wrote a diary over a century ago. Remember? You found it in my desk that day, when you'd just returned to London." He had been looking for proof of her guilt, Sophie realized belatedly. But that didn't matter now, not when she held an actual letter from Annabelle's lover. "Before she was married, she had a lover named William. She said she'd hidden one of his letters in a book of sermons. That book." Shaken, Sophie pointed to the dusty old volume Grant held.

He frowned at it, then set it down on the table. "Right. That's very interesting."

He didn't sound interested in the least. But *she* was. "Her diary never mentions his last name, and I've always wondered . . ." Sophie returned her attention to the faded signature.

As she deciphered the last name, a flash of shock held her immobile. Her thoughts scattered. And her mind gathered all the bits and pieces into a unified whole. *"Oh . . . dear . . . God."*

"Is something wrong?"

Slowly, she lifted her gaze to Grant. Disbelief swirled inside her. But it had to be true. *It had to be.*

"I think . . . Oh, Grant . . . I believe I know who poisoned Lucien."

25 December 1701
8 Days until the Grand Wedding

My Parents presented me this day with a special gift. 'Twas a baby's fine christening gown embroidered by my own Mother with my initials intertwined with Mulford's. 'Tis for my first-born son, their grandson, who will be a duke.

They looked so proud and joyful, I wanted to weep. I wanted to say that tomorrow I elope with my Dear William. But their gift has caused me to see the Selfishness of my ways. No longer can I think only of my own Happiness. No longer can I behave as a child. My family must come first. Thusly, I am resolved to marry Mulford.

—the diaries of Annabelle Chatham Ramsey, 3rd Duchess of Mulford

26

As Grant and Sophie walked through the darkened corridors, he had the peculiar sense that they were the only two people in existence. Gloom shrouded the formal rooms on either side of them. The only sounds were the echo of their footsteps and the bong of a clock marking the hour of two.

The candle in his hand cast wavering shadows over the tunnel-like passageway. In the pale illumination, Sophie looked quietly resolute—and too beautiful for words. His earlier fury at her had subsided to a dull ache. A more immediate urgency gripped him.

Finding the murderer.

Although she had explained her conjecture, his mind

still reeled with doubt. Perhaps because the solution literally had fallen into their hands. Or perhaps because he
couldn't believe how far off the mark they'd been.

"This theory of yours had better be right," he muttered. "Frankly, I find it hard to imagine a murder could
be based on an incident that happened over a century
ago."

"It's a matter of bloodlines," Sophie whispered. "And I
know I'm right. I can *feel* it."

All Grant felt was anxiety at allowing her to walk into
a potentially explosive situation. "You should let me handle this business."

She gave him a cool glare. "My husband was murdered and my son poisoned. Unless you're prepared to tie
me up, don't bother arguing."

He liked the "tying up" part. He'd like to tie Sophie to
her bed and spend the rest of the night making love to her.

But he also shared her hunger for justice.

As they made their way down a winding stone staircase, he focused his thoughts on the task ahead. For Sophie's sake, it was best to catch their quarry asleep. Too
groggy to put up a fight.

They entered the subterranean chill of the basement
corridor. The tomblike silence reminded Grant of a sar-
cophagus. Quietly, he motioned her into the darkened
kitchen. "In here."

"What are you doing?"

"Finding a weapon."

He opened several drawers before discovering a selec-
tion of knives in various sizes. Bypassing the larger spec-
imens, he chose one with a four-inch blade, sharp enough
to maim, yet small enough to keep hidden in the palm of
his hand.

Sophie watched in obvious aversion. "Do you really
think you'll need that?" she whispered.

"It's always best to be prepared."

"I see you're proficient with knives."

Judging by her frown, she was remembering his felonious past. But her secret had been far worse than his. Her secret had brought them down here tonight, for if she was right, it was tightly interwoven with the past.

As they left the kitchen, Grant asked in a hushed tone, "Which door?"

"The last one on the right."

"I don't suppose I could persuade you to wait here."

"Absolutely not."

Although he had expected the answer, it frustrated him nonetheless. "You'll stay behind me, at least."

"Only if you allow me to conduct the interview."

A compromise. Her safety in exchange for interrogation rights. He didn't like it, but . . . "Agreed, duchess."

As they proceeded down the corridor, he felt tense and alert. The knife in his hand hadn't alleviated the sense of impending doom. He'd learned to trust his instincts, and something told him to take especial care.

Or maybe it was Sophie's presence that unsettled him. He was used to working alone, without having to worry about protecting a woman.

Upon reaching the door, he tested the knob. It was unlocked, and the door swung open without any creaking of hinges.

Holding the candle, he led the way inside. The feeble light penetrated the darkness, revealing a small antechamber with furnishings of surprising luxury. An elegant writing desk. A gold-striped chaise. A polished oak fireplace, where coals still glowed faintly in a bed of ashes.

He headed through another doorway, the plush carpet cushioning his footfalls. This shadowy chamber was somewhat larger than the first one. It was dominated by a large four-poster.

Thick velvet hangings enclosed a bower of complete darkness. Even with the candle held high, he couldn't see into that blackness. Aware of Sophie right behind him, he silently made his way to the bed.

It was empty. The linens were pristine, the pillows plumped, the coverlet untouched.

What the hell—

The back of Grant's neck prickled. He had the icy sense of being watched. Spinning around, he spied the figure in the shadows.

Sophie drew an audible breath. She too had seen the butler.

Phelps sat in a thronelike chair in the corner of the bedchamber. He blinked his rheumy eyes as if he'd been dozing. In his black suit and starched collar, his polished shoes shining in the light of the candle, he looked like a malevolent old king.

For a few ticks of the clock on the bedside table, the old retainer stared at them without expression. Then he made a creaky move to rise.

"Stop," Grant ordered. "Stay right where you are."

Phelps thinned his lips. "I cannot sit in the presence of the duchess."

"I command you to do so," Sophie said coldly. "You will not stir until I give you permission."

Phelps slowly resumed his seat. "Why have you come here?"

"I believe you know," she said with an underlying sharpness. "But first, we will speak of your past. Your family has served the dukes of Mulford for over a century. Beginning with a man named William Phelps."

Phelps lifted his chin warily. "He was my great-grandfather."

"He was also a gentleman of limited means. He courted Annabelle, the third duchess, before her marriage."

The butler's clawlike fingers convulsively gripped the arms of the chair. "You cannot know . . . His last name is not mentioned in her diary."

"How the devil do *you* know that?" Grant broke in. "Were you snooping in the duchess's desk?"

Phelps glowered. "Quite the contrary. *I* placed the diary in the attic for Her Grace to find."

"Ah," Sophie said, as if it all made sense to her. "So Annabelle gave it to William for safekeeping."

"The diary has been passed down from father to son," Phelps said proudly. "Since you were researching the Ramsey history, Your Grace, you needed to know the importance of my family to the dukes of Mulford."

"But . . ." Sophie tilted her head in obvious confusion. "As you said, William's last name doesn't appear in the diary."

"Regardless, his presence must be noted and remembered. It is a point of honor."

"Honor be damned," Grant interjected. "You haven't any—"

Waving him to silence, Sophie took a step forward. "Do you have the second diary?" she asked Phelps. "The one I've been searching for all these months? Does it prove Annabelle's first son was really William's child?"

The butler's cadaverous chest rose and fell as if he wrestled with powerful emotions. He looked from her to Grant, then back again. And he inclined his head in a haughty nod. "Indeed. For more than a century, the dukes of Mulford have had Phelps blood running through their veins."

The astonishing fact sank into Grant. His hand felt clammy around the handle of the knife. *My God.* No wonder Phelps had tried to kill Lucien.

Lucien represented the end of the Phelps legacy.

Sophie drew a shaky breath, as if she too struggled to

absorb the truth of her conjecture. "So, all these years the men of your family have served the dukes of Mulford. They have striven to protect them because they are . . . cousins. And yet you poisoned Robert."

Bitter resentment glinted in Phelps's eyes. "He was a disgrace to the family honor, carrying on with that Langston fellow. Whenever they quarreled, His Grace would come to me. He would sit in the cellar, drink wine, and weep like an infant."

"Someone dear to me . . ."

A chill swept Grant. He should have realized that Robert had desperately needed a confidant. Robert had carried an enormous weight of guilt, and he would never have unburdened himself to Sophie or Helena.

"Robert trusted you," Sophie accused Phelps. Her voice trembled and her hands were clenched at her sides. "You were always there while he was growing up. He put his faith in you, and in return, you took his life."

"He would not sire children." The butler's mouth twisted as if he'd tasted something sour. "For many years, I was fooled. I thought if he'd sired one child, he could do so again. Until one night last summer, he drank too much wine and confessed that his heir was not of his loins."

In the candlelight, Sophie looked pale and intent. "Then you've known about Lucien for months. Why did you wait . . . until tonight?"

Phelps shifted his spiteful eyes to Grant. "Mr. Chandler needed to learn the truth about the boy first. So that he too could suffer when I punished you for your deceit."

Fury flashed through Grant, burning away his shock. Phelps had preyed upon a defenseless young boy. And he had written that letter to the magistrate. He had brought the law down on Sophie, so that she would be imprisoned—and possibly put to death—for a crime she hadn't committed.

Grant's fingers tightened around the knife. He wanted nothing more than to plunge it into the old man's heart— if indeed he had one.

"Damn you!" he growled. "You left that goblet of poisoned milk by Lucien's bedside. That's why you're still dressed. Because you needed to collect the glass and dispose of it."

Phelps regarded him with disdainful arrogance. As if he himself were the duke. "You have no proof. The child merely suffered a stomach upset."

The man actually believed he could win. He was blindly self-righteous. Or stark, raving mad. "And what about Robert?" Grant demanded. "How do you intend to weasel out of *that* murder?"

"I will testify that I saw Her Grace add poison to her husband's food."

"I'll see you in hell first."

Infuriated, Grant started forward, but Sophie clamped hard to his arm. "Wait. I want the second volume of the diary. Where is it, Phelps?"

The butler compressed his thin lips. But for an instant, his gaze flicked to a cabinet against the wall.

"Over there," Grant told Sophie, nodding at the piece.

As if he'd been poked by a pin, Phelps stiffened. "The diary is mine. You cannot show it to anyone. I vowed to my father to guard the family secret, as he vowed to *his* father."

"Then you'll sign a full confession," she said coolly. "If you'll admit to murdering Robert, I'll keep William and Annabelle's secret safe. Like you, I've no wish to heap scandal upon the honored title of Mulford."

She marched to the bedside table, found another candle, and touched the wick to the taper that Grant held. Then she opened the top drawer of the cabinet and rummaged inside.

Grant had to admire her mettle. She had struck out cleverly at Phelps, threatening the one thing he held dear—the noble family he had served all his life. In the butler's twisted reasoning, he would sooner kill both Robert and Lucien than openly contest the succession.

A bleak panic contorted the butler's aging face. His knobby fingers clenched compulsively at his knees. "Master Elliot must inherit. He must marry well and sire a son to preserve the family bloodline."

Sophie turned her head sharply. "Helena wants Elliot to marry, too. Did she plan this with you?"

"She doesn't know your disreputable secret. Rather, *I* suggested that Elliot's birthday would be the perfect opportunity to secure a noble bride for him."

"Your ploy worked," Grant said. "But not as you intended. Elliot is marrying Alice."

Phelps looked as if he'd been gut-shot. His jaw dropped, his eyes widened, his face paled to a cadaverous whiteness. "Impossible."

"It's the truth," Sophie stated. "She's in the family way, and he intends to do right by her."

A frightful fury descended over Phelps's gaunt features. His nostrils flared, giving him the aspect of a beast scenting its prey. He surged from the chair, his action surprisingly swift for so ancient a man.

"Trollop!" In his hand glinted something metallic. A pistol.

Time slowed to a crawl. Grant rushed to shield Sophie, but his movements felt sluggish. He should have seen that gun. If she was hurt . . . or killed . . .

He reached her, pushed her behind him. "Stay down," he hissed.

For once, she had the sense to obey. Keeping his gaze trained on Phelps, he heard her retreat into the darkness.

But instead of lunging after Sophie, the butler dashed for the door.

Alice. He was going after *Alice*.

Grant took a running leap and brought down his quarry. The two of them landed on the carpet with a jarring jolt. Beneath him, Phelps lay on his side, all bony limbs and ancient flesh.

Grant caught the hand with the pistol and pinned it to the floor. He pressed his knife to that scrawny throat. "Lie still!"

In utter disregard, Phelps bucked with manic vigor, as if madness fueled his decaying muscles. He exuded the raw, feral odor of desperation. Legs kicking, body twisting, arms writhing, he managed to inch toward the outer door. It was like wrestling with a living corpse.

Applying hard pressure to the spindly wrist, Grant forced the clawlike fingers to open. The pistol dropped, and he thrust it away. The gun skittered across the carpet and into the shadows.

Grant held the knife against the butler's windpipe. He could picture the blade slicing through the jugular vein, spurting blood. A life for a life.

But he couldn't do it. He couldn't kill a demented old man.

The butler's struggles gradually grew feebler. His breath sawed in and out with guttural gasps. Yet Grant didn't slacken his grip. "Get me something to tie him up," he snapped over his shoulder.

"You needn't shout."

Sophie was already standing over him, holding a cord from the bed hangings. While he held Phelps pinioned, she secured his wrists and ankles.

The butler remained defiant in spirit, if not in body. "You daren't turn me in," he said hoarsely. "I shall expose the young duke as a fraud!"

"Then it will be your word against mine," Sophie said.

Although she spoke coldly, when she gazed at Grant, her eyes revealed anguish and uncertainty.

That look struck deeply into his chest. She knew, as he did, that the matter depended on his word, too. If Phelps revealed that truth, Grant might have to swear under oath that he had not sired Lucien.

Or he could claim the boy. He could let the world know that Lucien was *his* son.

Trudging up the darkened staircase, Sophie held the candle in one hand and Annabelle's diary in the other. She would read it soon, but not tonight. Tonight, weariness dragged down her spirits. She should be thrilled that the murderer had been caught. But she felt only . . . numb. The tumultuous events of the evening played over and over in her mind.

Phelps. Who would have thought the old butler hid such an explosive secret? She had never realized the extent to which Robert had confided in him. But it made sense. Phelps had, after all, been with the family all of Robert's life. And Phelps was only other person in the house who had known about Geoffrey Langston.

Now, Phelps sat bound in the wine cellar, the stout door locked and guarded by two footmen. In the morning, she and Grant would take him to Bow Street Station for arraignment. If he refused to confess, she would use the second diary to prove his motivation.

And then Phelps would have his revenge. He would tell the world about Lucien.

Would Grant corroborate the story?

She felt cold and shivery. Grant loved Lucien. Surely he wouldn't foster gossip and innuendo that might hurt their son.

It wasn't that Lucien would lose his rank. The law

clearly stated that unless a man denounced his wife's first-born son at birth, that boy remained his legitimate heir.

But people would wonder why Robert had been unable to sire a son of his own. They might even discover his secret. And they would gossip about Sophie, too. They would say she had tricked Robert. She only cared because eventually, someday, the rumors would reach Lucien's ears.

Had Annabelle suffered the same worries about her son?

Gripping the precious diary, Sophie headed into her bedchamber. The room was dim, lit by a low-burning oil lamp on the bedside table. If her eyelids weren't drooping, she would curl up in bed and read the diary. She would find out Annabelle's hopes and dreams—

Sophie halted in the middle of the rug. She couldn't say precisely what had made her stop. But a shiver crawled down her spine. Her mouth went dry. Her muscles stiffened.

Slowly, she turned around. No one peered from the shadows.

She forced herself to relax. Her nervousness must be an aftereffect of that encounter downstairs, of seeing Phelps in the gloom, watching them. But she wouldn't let that experience make her frightened of the dark.

Walking briskly across the chamber, she placed the diary on a table. Then she carried the candle into the dressing room. Everything looked perfectly in order. There was the clothes press that held her undergarments. The tall, mahogany wardrobe filled with gowns. The mirrored table where she sat to do her hair.

Yet she wished she hadn't sent her maid to bed—only because of all those hooks and buttons to undo.

Then it happened. As Sophie set down the candle, a dark reflection in the mirror caught her eye. A moving shadow. *Behind her.*

Fear throttled her throat. A scream fought for release. Instinctively, she raised her arms to ward off danger.

Too late.

The blow reverberated through her skull. Her legs buckled, and she staggered sideways. She clutched at the table. But her fingers had lost all strength. Unable to stop herself, she slid down, down, down into blackness.

2 January 1702
My Second Day as a Duchess

I hereby commence a new diary and a new Life. And with new Life inside me, as well. The secret knowledge fills me with Shame . . . and Joy. I am to bear William's child. I did not realize that Truth until the very eve of my Wedding, and then 'twas too late to call off my Nuptials. How could I have brought Infamy down upon my Dear Parents?

O, woe, I have deceived Mulford, too. When he came to my bed last night, I contrived to leave a spot of blood on the sheets. 'Tis a Grievous Sin to dupe my Husband, I know. Yet I would sell my very soul to protect my child, William's child. The secret will be mine—and William's—forever.

—*the diaries of Annabelle Chatham Ramsey, 3rd Duchess of Mulford*

27

Grant raced the curricle through the crowded city streets. Pedestrians scuttled out of his path. Other vehicles quickly maneuvered to the side. He narrowly missed hitting a pieman trundling his cart across the cobblestones. Curses and shouts followed in Grant's wake.

Terror drove him to recklessness. His heart pounded. His hands felt slippery around the reins. He gripped hard, frustrated by the mid-morning traffic. Would he reach Sophie in time?

Or was he already too late?

A short while ago, he had brought Lucien back to Mulford House. The boy had rebounded from his illness with amazing resilience. They had been chattering silly nonsense, and Grant had been feeling lighthearted, relaxed for the first time in months. Years, in fact. Of course, Phelps still had to be put behind bars, statements had to be made, Sophie's name cleared. But Grant had looked forward to their marriage. He wanted to be Lucien's father, to have Sophie for his wife. He had allowed himself to hope they might eventually forgive each other for all the lies and deceptions.

Then he had gone down to check on Phelps. Only to discover—

Damn! Grant swerved hard to the right as a cat streaked across the street, chased by a mangy dog. His morbid thoughts leaped just as swiftly.

He'd dashed upstairs to tell Sophie the grim news. But she wasn't there. An upstairs maid had handed him a note. And his world had shattered into pieces.

Sophie had been kidnapped. She was being held for ransom.

By that rat's ass, Bahir.

Somehow, the sultan's minion had escaped his shipboard prison. He must have entered Mulford House sometime during the dinner party. And he had lain in wait for Sophie.

Icy fear spurred Grant. He clenched his teeth to contain a rush of panic. If Sophie came to harm, it would be his fault.

His fault.

He guided the smartly trotting horses around a turn. He could smell the docks now, a pungent, fishy, seaweedy odor. At least it told him he was heading in the right direction. Somewhere in the rabbit warren of these moldering buildings, Bahir held Sophie prisoner. He had demanded the sum Grant had received for the Devil's Eye.

Grant would gladly give up his entire fortune to keep Sophie safe. But he hadn't wasted precious time stopping at his bank. It would take him too long to secure that much gold. Gut instinct told him to *hurry*. Now if only he could locate that blasted address—

Someone stepped out of a doorway. He pulled to a hard stop to avoid running her down. The slattern struck a pose, sagging tits thrust out and hands on her skinny hips. "'Ey, guv'nor, wot's yer 'urry?"

He dug in his pocket for a gold guinea. "The Black Owl Tavern—where is it?"

Greedy blue eyes widened in a face that hadn't seen a washbasin in years. Abandoning the lewd posture, she pointed ahead. "Turn right at 'Arry's grog shop an' 'tis o'er another lane."

He flipped her the coin. She snatched it out of the air and stepped nimbly back. Slapping the reins, he urged the horses onward, picking up speed down the alley. At the cross street, he edged past a dray carrying a load of ale barrels, earning an oath from the burly driver.

Grant paid no heed. He followed the whore's directions, which proved blessedly accurate. Up ahead, a faded sign creaked in the breeze, the peeling paint depicting a black owl.

The note had instructed him to leave the money in a rubbish bin behind the tavern. Then he was to go into the tavern and wait for Sophie.

Like bloody hell.

Leaving the curricle parked half a block away, guarded by a well-paid street urchin, Grant surveyed the narrow street with its dilapidated buildings. He doubted Bahir would hold Sophie in one of the tiny rooms above the tavern. There, he'd be a sitting duck.

But behind the tavern loomed a huge, ramshackle, half-burned warehouse. Though the roof was gone, the brick walls remained standing, the windows cracked and soot-blackened.

Grimly, he headed around the block to seek the best way inside.

Sophie sat on a half-broken chair in the deserted warehouse and watched Bahir crack a walnut with his yellowed teeth. Her head throbbed, her eyes felt gritty, and her skin had goose bumps from cold and fear. But at least she wasn't trussed up like a Christmas goose. Only her wrists were tied in her lap.

Bahir clearly disdained all women as weak, feeble creatures. He seemed to have forgotten that she'd smashed a vase over his head in Grant's study two nights ago. Or maybe he simply discounted that feat as an aberration.

She'd allowed him the illusion. At present, it was her only weapon.

Bahir had the real weapons. A knife with a wicked, shiny blade. And a long-barreled pistol stuck in the waistband of his breeches.

The husky Turk stood several yards away, leaning against the brick wall. He used the tip of his knife to pry out the meat of the walnut. Empty shells littered the floor. He popped the morsel into his mouth, chewing noisily. All the while, he peered across the open expanse of the warehouse.

Bahir had chosen their hiding place well. The alcove had once been an office, though the door was long gone and the roof open to the gray skies. A charred, musty smell lingered from a long-ago fire. The crumbling inner wall concealed them while allowing Bahir to survey the entire area.

From here, he could see the rear of the tavern through a soot-streaked window at the far end of the building. He was watching for Grant.

The cold air penetrated her thin gown, numbing her to the bone. But it was fear that made her shiver. She knew in her heart that Grant wouldn't simply drop the money and leave.

He would find her. He would risk his life . . .

She had to be ready. She had to convince the Turk to untie her hands.

In a cowed, servile tone, she said, "Please, sir, I—I fear your efforts are for naught."

Bahir directed a scowl at her. He had a broad, flat, dark face, a sneering mouth. "Be silent."

"B-but Mr. Chandler is a scoundrel. He won't bring you any money."

Bahir snatched another walnut from a sack on a small table. "You are his woman. He will come."

"We—we've quarreled." It wasn't difficult to make her voice wobble. She had only to remember the fury on Grant's face when he'd found out about Lucien. Besides, her teeth were chattering from the cold. "He c-cares nothing for me anymore."

"Do not lie. I watch. I see him kiss you."

Her skin crawled. She wanted to leap up, to claw the smirk off his face. But she cultivated the role of a weakling. "He's c-cast me out. He might not even read that note. If—if he thinks it's from me, he'll toss it into the fire."

Bahir narrowed his dark eyes skeptically. Tilting his turbaned head, he cracked the walnut with his teeth. The sound grated on her nerves. Then he used the knife to dig out the inside of the shell.

Chomping on the nut, he divided his attention between her and the door. "We wait for Chandler."

"But . . . there's no need to wait. I'm far wealthier than he is. Perhaps if—if I might be allowed to write a note to *my* banker—"

"No!" A cold, cruel fury twisted Bahir's face. "Chandler steal the Devil's Eye. *He* will pay."

His anger daunted her. She had no wish to antagonize him. Very carefully, she murmured, "P-please let me finish. I can give you twice the gold that he can. You'll have enough for yourself as well as for the sultan."

Bahir gave a harsh laugh. "I not give gold to Sultan Hadji."

Confused, she frowned. "That *is* why you came to England . . . isn't it? Because the sultan sent you?"

"Sultan Hadji not want gold. He want my head." Bahir made a savage sawing motion at his throat. "I was leader of guards, but no more. By Allah, I kill Chandler! I send *his* head to the sultan."

Even as she reeled in horror, Bahir made a lightning-fast move. He hurled the knife in a blur of steel. It thunked into the charred wood of the doorway. Directly above her.

Sophie flinched. A gasp choked her, and her blood ran icy cold. A few inches lower, and . . . oh, dear heaven, she didn't want to consider what might have happened.

Bahir chuckled again, clearly enjoying her fear. Anger drove away her shock. His aim *had* been accurate. Bahir hadn't intended to hurt her; he'd only wanted to frighten her. He wouldn't harm her because she was his bargaining chip.

His means of luring Grant here. To murder him.

Bahir strutted toward her, obviously intending to fetch his knife. She couldn't wait. She must seize this chance.

Bracing her numbed feet on the floor, Sophie gathered her strength. He was not a tall man, though broad and muscular, a formidable opponent. She didn't stand a prayer of getting the knife out of the wood. His big hands would snap her in two before her fingers could touch the haft. But if she could startle him, grab his pistol—

Then *she* was startled. By a movement behind Bahir. By the glimpse of someone scrambling silently onto the half-crumbled wall of the alcove.

Grant.

Joy and fear jolted her in equal measures. Her heart knocked against her ribs. She lowered her eyes lest she inadvertently alert Bahir.

But as she stared down at her tied hands, Sophie saw the image of Grant. Half-hidden in the shadows, he wore only a shirt and breeches, even his feet were bare. In his teeth, he carried a knife. He looked dark, dangerous—and very, very dear to her.

His presence warmed all the cold places inside her. But . . . oh, merciful heaven. If Bahir were to see him . . .

Grant was more frightened than he'd ever been in all his years as a thief. The knife still quivered in the doorframe above Sophie's head. Bahir was walking toward her. Grant knew with absolute certainty that the Turk wouldn't hesitate to use her as a shield. Or to slit her throat.

Grant had only a few seconds to get into a favorable position. He didn't dare throw his own knife; Bahir would seize the pistol from his waistband and shoot. And if he jumped too soon, Bahir would have too much warning.

Then the bastard would grab Sophie.

She raised her head again. Grant tried to flash a silent communication to her. *Run to safety. Let me handle him.*

But she kept her gaze trained on Bahir. In a breathy, girlish, silly tone, she said, "Oh! Oh, my goodness, sir. You—you are very good at throwing your knife. And with such amazing accuracy! Why, it must have taken you years to master such a fine skill. I am certain you must win every contest you enter!"

Her babbling masked any small sound Grant made, and he blessed Sophie for that. In the midst of his fear for her, he was damned proud, too. She would never swoon in fright, not his Sophie. Though she must be scared witless, she hadn't panicked. Because of her, he had a chance . . .

A yard away from her, Bahir raised his beefy brown hand. "Silence, woman!"

Before the Turk could slap her, Sophie lunged up from the chair. She rushed straight at him. In that split second of surprise, she sent the big man staggering a few steps. And—wonderful, idiotic woman—she clutched Bahir's pistol in her bound hands.

Grant leaped. Sophie scrambled out of the way as he and Bahir went crashing to the floor. Grant drove his knife where he could, into the soft flesh of Bahir's waist. There was no opportunity to aim well. He felt the blade glance off the man's hipbone.

The Turk howled and fought back. His fist met the underside of Grant's jaw. The jarring blow made Grant's teeth clash, and he tasted blood. With inhuman fury, Bahir thrust Grant onto his back, scattering walnut shells. His thick arm lodged against Grant's throat, cutting off his air.

Black spots swam before his eyes. The relentless pressure drained the strength from his limbs. Holding Grant down with the crushing weight of his body, Bahir went for the knife. It was still embedded in his flesh.

But Grant got to it first. He heaved off Bahir, yanked out the knife, scrambled to his feet. As he gulped in a searing breath, he saw from the corner of his eye that Sophie hovered nearby. "Run," he yelled. "Get out."

He didn't see if she obeyed. Growling like an enraged

bear, Bahir sprang up, using his head like a battering ram. One of Grant's ribs cracked. Pain lanced his chest, but he ignored it. Drawing back his arm, he plunged the knife blade into Bahir's belly.

Bahir stood in a crouch, swaying, his dark eyes wide with surprise. Blood blossomed on his dingy white shirt. His hands clutched his abdomen as if he couldn't quite believe he'd been mortally injured.

He tottered sideways, stumbled on a walnut shell, and sagged against the doorframe. Grant started toward Sophie, his only thought to shield her from the sight. She held the pistol trained on Bahir. As if she'd been waiting for a chance to shoot.

The little fool hadn't run. She had stayed to defend him.

Bahir uttered an inhuman bellow. Even as Grant realized his mistake, even as the Turk wrested his knife from the doorframe and came at him, a shot rang out.

A puff of smoke issued from the pistol in Sophie's hands. Bahir clutched at his chest. Blood seeped in an ever-widening circle from a small hole, dead center. Like a mighty oak, he crashed to the floor and lay still.

Sophie stood unmoving. Savage triumph lit her beautiful face.

Grant felt a surge of love—and fury. He marched to her side, pried the spent pistol out of her tense fingers, threw it aside. The danger she'd faced because of him made him wild. "What the devil were you thinking, to stay here? He could have killed you."

She blinked at him. The fierce look faded and her eyes filled with tenderness. Very gently, she caressed his lips with her fingertip. "Oh, my darling. You're bleeding. Are you badly hurt?"

"Never mind me." He tilted his head away from her soft touch. "You should have run. I *told* you to run."

Her lips pursed, she drew herself up. "And leave you to die? Never."

"You rushed at him, too." His voice thundered, but Grant couldn't stop the image of her lying on the floor instead of Bahir. "You grabbed his pistol!"

"And a very good thing, indeed!" she snapped. "You'd be dead if it weren't for me."

Grant held tightly to her shoulders. "*You'd* be dead if Bahir had gotten his hands around your pretty throat."

"Pardon me," she mocked. "I suppose you'd rather I behaved like a meek little woman."

"Yes! No, blast you! I love you just the way you are!" Grant paused, realizing what he'd finally admitted aloud. The words he'd never spoken to any other person. A deluge of unmanly emotion swept away his anger.

Her expression softened. "You love me?"

"I do," he said without hesitation. "I'm mad about you, Sophie. *I love you.*" Though his ribs hurt and his mouth stung, Grant slid his arm around her slender waist, drew her out of the alcove and away from the dead man. His bare heel stepped on a walnut shell, but he ignored the jab. He deserved far worse than that for endangering her.

He guided her to a patch of light that streamed through the open roof of the warehouse. Like a portent of hope, the sun had broken through the gray clouds and illuminated her warm green eyes. He ought to let her go. But he held her close, heedless of his bruises. His voice rough with feeling, he said, "You should have let me protect you. For once, you should have trusted me to take care of you."

"Oh, Grant. I *do* trust you." She brushed her fingers over his face. "I stayed because I love you, too. I couldn't let Bahir kill you."

I love you, too. How long he'd waited to hear those words. They were a ray of sunshine in the darkness of his soul. "I'm a thief—I *was* a thief. If not for me, you wouldn't have been kidnapped by that bastard. You should despise me."

"We've both made mistakes. I should have told you about Lucien. I was young and foolish and desperate." She glanced away, her expression troubled. "And if it hadn't been for *me,* Phelps wouldn't have killed Robert."

The reminder jolted Grant. He placed his hands on her shoulders, gently soothing her. "Sophie, I must tell you. Phelps is dead."

Her eyes widened. *"What?"*

"When I went down to the wine cellar this morning, I found him. He'd taken his own life." She didn't need to know all the gruesome details. They'd both had enough of blood and mayhem to last a lifetime.

"Dear God," she said faintly.

She leaned into him, and he held her tightly, allowing her to adjust to the shock. The sounds of the dock came from a distance, men shouting, a ship whistle blowing. Oh, God, she felt so good in his arms. He brushed his lips over the silk of her hair, wanting her desperately, needing to express all the powerful emotions clamoring in him for release.

Then somehow their mouths were joined, and they were kissing with deep feeling, a kiss as much of tenderness as passion, as much of forgiveness as desire. Touching and caressing, they reveled in the mutual joy of being alive, being together again, the rift between them mended at last.

After a time, Grant lifted his head. "We were both foolish, darling. Me, because I was too afraid to admit how much you meant to me. If I'd told you ten years ago that I loved you, things might have turned out differently."

Sophie drew back to stare at him. "You loved me . . . even then?"

"Yes, and I will until the day I die." Though his injuries throbbed without mercy, he fitted their bodies together again. "Which, thanks to you, wasn't today."

"Oh, Grant." She used a corner of his cravat to dab at the blood on his chin. Then she took hold of his arm and drew him toward the door of the warehouse. "We must get you straight home. Where did you leave your shoes and coat? In your carriage?"

"Wait." Bringing her to a stop, he knelt down, right there on the dirt floor. "Sophie, will you do me the great honor of marrying me?"

A small frown drew her brows together. Her teeth sank into her lower lip. "I thought we'd already decided we must. For Lucien's sake." She paused, then added a trifle anxiously, "Will you tell anyone about him?"

He gripped her hands. "Of course not. The bloodline doesn't matter to me. It will always be our secret."

She sighed in relief. "Just as it was with Annabelle and William."

Feeling a lurch of wariness, Grant gazed up at her. Twice, he'd gotten this all wrong. Twice, he'd arrogantly announced that they *had* to marry. What if she refused him?

"Yet they never married," he said quietly. "I want to be Lucien's father. And I want to be your husband. But the choice is yours, my darling. Will you make me the happiest man alive? Will you be my wife?"

Her lips tilted in a radiant smile that made her face glow. Sinking to her knees, she gave him that saucy look he loved so much. The one that banished all his pains, the one that caused a deeper, more primitive ache.

"Yes, I'll marry you," she murmured, "but only if you agree to one rule."

"Shall I fetch you the moon? It's yours for the asking."

"Oh, I desire something far more exciting than that." Her eyes warm with promise, Sophie trailed her fingers down his chest. "I desire you in my bed, Grant. Every night for the rest of our lives."

Coming in February 2006...

Countess Confidential

by *New York Times* bestselling author

Barbara Dawson Smith

Dear Reader,

This is the story of how I, a penniless upstart, became a countess.

I never set out to be the heroine in a romantic tale of derring-do. As a spinster of five-and-twenty, I was much too practical to imagine myself tracking a dangerous criminal or falling prey to ardent nonsense. Nor did I ever envision myself entering the gilded ballrooms of society where indolent aristocrats nibbled cake and traded gossip. But that was before my father was wrongfully imprisoned as a jewel thief.

Determined to uncover the true criminal, I posed as an impoverished widow and secured a post in the grand household of a noble family—the very family that had cruelly cast out my mother many years ago. Of course, they knew not who I was. To them, I was merely a servant, an invisible hireling. And little did I know, my daring plan would throw me into the path of Simon Croft, the almighty Earl of Rockford.

Arrogant, charming, and too handsome for his own good, he might have walked straight off a pedestal in a museum. I had no use for such a rogue, yet from the moment of our first meeting, he tempted my unruly heart. And soon, he threatened my schemes as well, for Simon had secrets of his own....

—Claire, the Countess of Rockford

"Barbara Dawson Smith is always excellent."
—Cathy Maxwell, author of *Temptation of a Proper Governess*

ISBN: 0-312-93239-1

Visit www.barbaradawsonsmith.com

AVAILABLE FROM ST. MARTIN'S PAPERBACKS

CC 08/05

Join top authors for the ultimate cruise experience. Spend 7 days in the Mexican Riviera aboard the luxurious Carnival Pride℠. Start in Los Angeles/Long Beach, CA and visit Puerto Vallarta, Mazatlan and Cabo San Lucas. Enjoy all this with a ship full of authors and book lovers on the **"Authors at Sea Cruise"** April 2 - 9, 2006.

Mail in this coupon with proof of purchase* to receive $250 per person off the regular **"Authors at Sea Cruise"** price. One coupon per person required to receive $250 discount. For complete details call **1-877-ADV-NTGE** or visit **www.AuthorsAtSea.com**

PRICES STARTING AT **$749** PER PERSON WITH COUPON!

*proof of purchase is original sales receipt with this book purchased circled.
**plus applicable taxes, fees and gratuities

Carnival
The Most Popular Cruise Line in the World.

GET $250 OFF

Name (Please Print)

Address _____ Apt. No. _____

City _____ State _____ Zip _____

E-Mail Address

See Following Page For Terms & Conditions.

For booking form and complete information go to www.AuthorsAtSea.com or call 1-877-ADV-NTGE

Carnival Pride℠
April 2 - 9, 2006.

7 Day Exotic Mexican Riviera Itinerary

DAY	PORT	ARRIVE	DEPART
Sun	Los Angeles/Long Beach, CA		4:00 P.M.
Mon	"Book Lover's" Day at Sea		
Tue	"Book Lover's" Day at Sea		
Wed	Puerto Vallarta, Mexico	8:00 A.M.	10:00 P.M.
Thu	Mazatlan, Mexico	9:00 A.M.	6:00 P.M.
Fri	Cabo San Lucas, Mexico	7:00 A.M.	4:00 P.M.
Sat	"Book Lover's" Day at Sea		
Sun	Los Angeles/Long Beach, CA	9:00 A.M.	

ports of call subject to weather conditions

TERMS AND CONDITIONS

PAYMENT SCHEDULE:
50% due upon booking
Full and final payment due by February 10, 2006

Acceptable forms of payment are Visa, MasterCard, American Express, Discover and checks. The cardholder must be one of the passengers traveling. A fee of $25 will apply for all returned checks. Check payments must be made payable to **Advantage International, LLC and sent to: Advantage International, LLC, 195 North Harbor Drive, Suite 4206, Chicago, IL 60601**

CHANGE/CANCELLATION:
Notice of change/cancellation must be made in writing to Advantage International, LLC.

Change:
Changes in cabin category may be requested and can result in increased rate and penalties. A name change is permitted 60 days or more prior to departure and will incur a penalty of $50 per name change. Deviation from the group schedule and package is a cancellation.

Cancellation:

181 days or more prior to departure	$250 per person
121 - 180 days prior to departure	50% of the package price
120 - 61 days prior to departure	75% of the package price
60 days or less prior to departure	100% of the package price (nonrefundable)

US and Canadian citizens are required to present a valid passport or the original birth certificate and state issued photo ID (drivers license). All other nationalities must contact the consulate of the various ports that are visited for verification of documentation.

We strongly recommend trip cancellation insurance!

For complete details call 1-877-ADV-NTGE or visit www.AuthorsAtSea.com

---

This coupon does not constitute an offer from St. Martin's Press LLC

For booking form and complete information
go to www.AuthorsAtSea.com or call 1-877-ADV-NTGE

Complete coupon and booking form and mail both to:
**Advantage International, LLC,
195 North Harbor Drive, Suite 4206, Chicago, IL 60601**